After the Mass he found her on the steps outside, with the canonesse and several other novitiates from the convent, in conversation with the French curé and a Catholic Vietnamese family. When she saw him she left the group and approached him.

'Monsieur Ryan.'

'I have to see you again,' he said.

The canonesse had turned away from her conversation with the priest and was watching them.

'This is so easy for you. Not so easy for me.'

'Easy? Falling in love with a nun is easy?'

Her eyes went wide. She looked around at the canonesse, and then back at Ryan. 'Do not say it if you do not mean it.'

'I mean it.'

She bit her lip, hesitating, then she seemed to make up her mind. 'Tomorrow. In the Botanical Gardens. Ten o'clock.'

She walked away.

He knew the rest of the novices were watching, their eyes lidded with disapproval. Bugger them all. He'd had enough of nuns to last him a lifetime.

Except for this one.

*Also by the same author*
*and available from Coronet*

Venom
Deathwatch
Harem
Fury
Opium
Triad

*About the Author*

Colin Falconer was born in London in 1953. He is a journalist and has written for many national magazines and newspapers. He has travelled widely in Europe and South-East Asia and now lives in Western Australia. He is the author of six acclaimed thrillers, *Venom*, *Deathwatch*, *Harem*, *Fury*, *Opium* and *Triad*, all of which are available in paperback from Coronet.

# Dangerous

Colin Falconer

CORONET BOOKS
Hodder & Stoughton

First published in Great Britain in 1996
by Hodder and Stoughton
A division of Hodder Headline PLC

Coronet paperback edition 1996



10 9 8 7 6 5 4 3 2



British Library C.I.P.

Falconer, Colin, 1953–
Dangerous
1. English fiction – 20th century
I. Title
823.9'14[F]

ISBN 0 340 62446 9

Printed and bound in Great Britain by
Cox & Wyman Ltd, Reading, Berkshire

Hodder and Stoughton
A division of Hodder Headline PLC
338 Euston Road
London NW1 3BH

*this one's to friendship*
*to Arnie*
*and to the Orsom Forsom: Bakes, The Duck, Pelican and Thommo.*
*from the Orthor.*

# ACKNOWLEDGEMENTS:

*I would like to express my gratitude to Australian photographer Tony Ashby, who has spent much of the last ten years in places other people would prefer not to go; places such as Beirut and Belfast, Croatia and Sarajevo and returned with stunning images obtained at great personal risk. I thank him for the time he has taken to describe his own perspectives and experiences. I hope one day he will get the wider recognition his courage and work so richly deserves.*

*I have also drawn extensively on the personal records of many other war correspondents for insights into the nature of the job and the characters and motivations of the men and women who do it.*

*However, this is a work of fiction, and it is not to be inferred in any way that any of the characters portrayed in this book bear any relation in their actions or personalities to any of the fraternity of foreign correspondents and combat photographers, living or dead.*

*I would also like to thank, as always, my editor George Lucas in London, who is a source of endless encouragement and commitment, and Tim Curnow in Sydney, who I value not only as my agent but as my friend.*

*And my wife, Helen, who endures the moods and is, has always been, my inspiration and my good friend.*

*Jajce, Bosnia-Hercegovina*

*October 1992*

'Right about then I knew we were going to die.

'I wasn't frightened. I suppose I had been in too much pain, for too long. There was just this cold dread of more suffering, deep in my guts, and I just wanted to groan aloud with frustration. We had come through so much and here it was, after all this time, death coming out of the mist. No way round it this time.

'There were four of them and they all wore brimless olive wool caps, and they had the trademark long hair and beards of the Chetniks. They were all carrying Kalashnikovs and Bowie knives in their belts and one of them had an RPG strapped to his back. The air was so cold and still you could hear them flick off the safety mechanisms on their rifles with their thumbs, even from a hundred metres away.

'I remember just thinking about that goldfish in its little plastic bag. Strange how the mind works. I felt as sorry for that stupid fish as I did for the rest of us.

'I remember someone waving a white flag in the air and shouting something in Serbo-Croat. But I knew it wasn't going to help us. I could see Ryan's face above me. It was the first time I'd ever really seen him afraid. Not in the way other people show fear, of course. He looked perfectly calm. But there was no excitement in his eyes. I never remember seeing Ryan without that dreamy, almost . . . well, horny look on his face when there was danger. He always seemed to enjoy these situations. But then I suppose he was only ever worried about himself before.

'Ryan shouted something, I don't know what it was. Then I just remember the brown leaves blurred against a dark sky, and the pain in my hip. I tried to scream but I couldn't get my breath, and we were bouncing down the slope and every time the wheels bounced it was like an electric charge shooting through my body. I tried to jump clear but I just couldn't move.

'And then I felt myself falling. When I hit the ground the pain was unbelievable. I didn't know what to do. There was this terrible white light behind my eyes and my whole body went rigid. I couldn't breathe. It seemed like I lay like that for hours but it might not have been more than a minute, I guess. When the spasm passed I didn't care about dying any more. I just wanted to get away from the pain and lie there in the cold mush of leaves and sleep.

'I could hear the Chetniks calling to each other on the track, the crunch of boots on the frozen mud. It seemed like they were just a few yards away. And then I heard the gunfire, and someone screaming. I remember trying to shout something. An obscenity, I suppose.

'And that's all I remember. I suppose I must have passed out. I didn't find out what had really happened until much later.'

*Seventh Regiment Armoury, Park Avenue, New York*

*30 April 1995*

'You're not doing the story justice,' Dave Crosby said. 'It's like skimming through a novel and just reading the last page.'

'The lady here was just asking me about Ryan,' Webb said. 'I was trying to answer her question. I'm sure she doesn't want to hear the whole sordid story.'

'I'm a journalist,' Wendy Doyle said. 'Sordid stories are the only ones I'm interested in.'

Crosby caught the eye of one of the black-jacketed waiters moving among the tables and signalled for another Scotch. 'I wish he could have been here tonight.'

'I don't know why you've got such long faces,' Doyle said, in her harsh Belfast brogue. 'If anyone should miss him, it's me. I was the only one here who slept with him.'

Webb picked at the tablecloth. 'Actually, there's something I think I have to tell you all.'

It was enough to break the tension. There were awkward smiles around the table. Too many ghosts at this banquet tonight, the twentieth anniversary reunion for former Vietnam war correspondents. Sixty-eight empty chairs, one for each of their number who had not come back from that stricken, hot little land. There were name-cards on the linen, gold calligraphy, a roll-call of honour: Flynn, Burrows, Cantwell, Fall and the rest.

Twenty years to the day since tank number 843 had ploughed through the gates of the Doc Lap Palace. Now they were all gathered together one last time in the mock-Tudor drill hall of the old British fort, uniformed Marines guarding the doors, a stiff but somehow appropriate setting for their night of memories and self-congratulation. The silver and crystal glittered under the huge chandeliers, the vast hall hung with red, white and blue bunting. Old Glory hung above the podium. Anyone who hadn't been there would be forgiven for thinking our side won, Webb thought.

Their numbers were drawn not only from the United States, but from Britain, France, Germany, Australia, Japan; all those who received an accreditation from MACV had been extended an invitation. The old guard were greyer now, thicker at the waist, most in suits; only a few rebellious souls, like Crosby, had showed up for the night in their old camous. They had dined on poached salmon and chicken and listened to the speeches made about them with a mixture of derision and a sad pride.

Now the talking was done and the three of them were huddled around the spill of bottles and glasses on their table, indulging for this one night old regrets and dusty triumphs, like the ageing members of a champion football team at the clubhouse bar. There was Webb, the only Britisher in the group, tall, greying, the soft-spoken rebel in his khaki shirt and jeans; Crosby, playing to the hilt his legendary status as the oldest combat photographer still working, a greying ponytail hanging over his camous, his tanned skull polished smooth, as he would have it, by years of close shaves; and Lee Cochrane, the youngest of the vets from the House of Horrors, now a hotshot bureau news chief for one of the networks, looking more like a corporate lawyer in his double-breasted suit and button-down, his only concession to the past the VVA pin in his lapel.

Wendy Doyle had still been at kindergarten when they were chasing medevacs. She had been one of the guest speakers at that night's dinner, an inspired choice, it seemed to Webb. She had followed Crosby on to the podium and had spoken about the role of war correspondents in 1995, and of how the Vietnam generation had been the first and last journalists allowed to cover a war freely, to chase the battlelines wherever they went; they were indeed a select and endangered group. Doyle herself had won acclaim for her reports from Somalia and Bosnia, and her words had made them all feel part of a continuum, a little less like relics from a futile past.

'Where's this famous bottle of Bushmills?' Doyle asked Webb.

Webb reached under the table and retrieved a brown paper bag. He took out the bottle and held it up. 'Ryan gave it to me before he left for Bosnia. I've been saving it for an appropriate occasion.'

'It's probably tea,' Cochrane said. 'Ryan never shouted a round of drinks in his life.'

'Check the seal,' Crosby said. 'It could be cold urine.'

'Three-year-old cold urine at that,' Cochrane said.

Webb called over the drinks waiter and asked for five whisky glasses. He cracked the seal and sniffed carefully at the contents. 'Smells all right,' he said.

'What's that pasted on the back?' Crosby asked him.

'It's something Ryan wrote,' Webb said. He handed the bottle to Crosby who read it, shook his head and passed it without comment to Cochrane. 'Jesus,' he said.

The waiter arrived with the glasses and Webb poured two fingers in each. They raised their glasses but then waited for Doyle to drink first.

'She swallowed it,' Cochrane said, 'so it can't be too bad.'

'For cold urine,' she said, 'it's quite smooth.'

'Like him,' Crosby said. 'What was that Oscar Wilde story? *The Picture of Dorian Gray*. Somewhere out there, there's an oil painting of the bastard. He's bald, wrinkled, with a beer gut and smoker's cough.'

'So back to the story,' Doyle said.

'And this time,' Crosby said, 'start at the beginning.'

Webb shook his head. 'The beginning,' he said. 'The beginning was the first time I ever saw him nearly get himself killed. And that was three minutes after I first met him, right outside the apartment in Saigon.'

# I

## Saigon, December 1969

'I have made arrangements for the correspondents to take the field . . . and I have suggested to them that they should wear a white uniform to indicate the purity of their character.'

– attributed during the American Civil War
to Union General Irvin McDowell

# 1

The gagging stench of gasoline, the gamy smells of rotting fruit and Southern noodles; camouflaged warplanes, rockets slung under their wings, shirtless technicians crawling over the cockpits; a banshee scream as a droop-nosed F-4 Phantom roared from the runway. Heat like a physical blow, taking the breath away.

Just the day before he had been in Surrey, grey and cold.

O'Leary was at the terminal to meet him. Webb had known O'Leary from school. While he struggled through a cadetship at a minor Surrey newspaper, O'Leary had taken up a scholarship at Oxford and then a job at Reuters in the City. It was hearing that O'Leary had been posted to the Saigon bureau that gave Webb the idea to take this gamble, the biggest of his life. He had written to him, asking for help, and to his astonishment – and terror – O'Leary had written back, telling him that if he could find his own way to Saigon, he might be able to help him find lodgings and work.

They drove into the city in a babyshit-yellow Mini Moke, past decaying French villas with green shutters, sandbagged army posts, billboards of oriental girls drinking Coca-Cola, canals as flat and black as bitumen, banana palms. The streets were a buzzing, screeching, choking tangle of Hondas, bicycles and old Dodges with immense tail fins, tiny Renault taxi cabs held together with pieces of wire. Gangs of siclo drivers gathered on the street corners; war veterans with twisted stumps of limbs scuttled along the pavements like crabs among the reeking piles of garbage.

As he looked out of the window he took stock of his life. At twenty-two years old he had spent almost his entire life savings on a one-way air ticket to Saigon. He now had no tangible means of support, no job, nowhere to live and fifty-four pounds to last him perhaps the rest of his life. He knew almost nothing about Vietnam except it was the scene for one of the longest-running front-page stories in history.

'I envy you,' O'Leary said.

'Me?'

'Treasure the moment.'

Webb shook his head. 'Why?'

'Because right now you understand more about Vietnam than you ever will again.'

Among themselves it was known as the Hashish Hilton.

It was an ancient French villa, whitewash peeling from the walls in flakes, with green shutters and a red-tiled roof. It was two minutes' walk from the US Embassy, a five-minute siclo ride from downtown. The front door opened on to the street, a riot of two-stroke motorcycles and belching army trucks, and an alley at the side was lined with noodle shops and small children playing in open sewers.

'I've organised for you to stay here,' O'Leary said. 'A spare room came up last week.'

'That's lucky,' Webb had said.

'For you, maybe. Not for the guy who had the room. He was a stringer for the *Post* and the *New York Times*.'

'Was?'

'Two bullets in the chest. They've evacuated him back to the States. Hope you have better luck than he did.'

'Over there!'

'Where?'

'There!'

'Where?'

'Corpsman!'

'Where?'

'There!'

'Where?'

As they walked in, the litany stopped and the occupants of the room broke into hysterical giggles. O'Leary looked at Webb and shrugged.

A lunatic asylum, Webb thought.

He was assailed by the sickly sweet scent of dope. A Jimi Hendrix riff on the stereo: 'All Along the Watchtower'. On the walls were posters of Lenny Bruce, Hendrix, a *Playboy* centrefold with the blackened face of a dead Vietnamese woman superimposed on her shoulders. In the corner a low table with a bronze Buddha and lighted incense. A flare chute had been draped from the ceiling. A monkey was masturbating on the bookcase, next to a spent artillery casing that had been upturned for use as an ashtray.

Two men were sitting on cane chairs by the window, passing a small bamboo opium pipe between them. A third man was crawling along the black and white tiled floor, as if it were vertical, using the black tiles as handholds.

'Welcome to the Hashish Hilton.'

One of the smokers held out a large brown hand flecked with golden hairs. He had thinning sandy hair and a long, downturned moustache. 'Dave Crosby, from the AP,' he said. 'Glad to know ya. This is Mike Prescott from UPI. The young fella attempting to climb the floor by the more difficult eastern approach is Lee Cochrane. *LA Times*.' He pointed to the monkey. 'The guy on the bookcase thrashin' the stoat is a reporter with NBC. Wouldn't worry about shaking *his* hand, though.'

'Hugh Webb.'

'Who you with, Hugh?'

Webb shrugged, in an effort to express a lifetime's gamble. 'Freelance,' he said.

'Hell, why not. It's a war anyone can join in. Welcome to sunny Saigon.'

O'Leary pulled up two wicker chairs and they sat down. Crosby passed Webb the pipe. 'Have some wacky tobacky.' When Webb hesitated, he said: 'Better get used to it, kid. You won't survive the Nam without it.'

As Webb drew cautiously on the pipe, Prescott said: 'This toke is in memory of Billy Joe Zane, photographer, formerly of Charleston, Carolina, late of the Hashish Hilton, Saigon. May God and *Life* magazine bless him and his sucking chest wound.'

'Amen,' Crosby said.

'You realise you are now in a war zone, Hugh?' Prescott said.

Crosby aped astonishment. 'A war zone? Is *that* why people keep shooting at me?'

'You didn't know?' Prescott said, playing along.

'Well, I'll be dipped in shit. I thought they just didn't like me. I guess that makes me feel a lot better about myself. Thank you, Prescott.'

Webb stared at them, beyond words. But these guys are my heroes, he was thinking. I've seen Prescott's combat photographs in the British newspapers, read Crosby's byline on reports from Hill 875 and Khe Sanh and Con Thien. I've only been off the plane half an hour and here they are sitting in the room with me.

And they're idiots.

Lee Cochrane had frozen to the floor, was screaming that he couldn't get down. The monkey had finished masturbating, leaving an unfortunate residue in the ashtray.

I can't stay here, Webb thought, panicked.

'Rent is fifty thousand piasters a month split six ways,' Crosby was saying.

'Six?' Webb said.

'There is one other member of our band you have still to meet. One Sean Ryan. A subject from one of your colonies.'

'Three things to remember about Ryan,' Prescott said. 'One, if you want to live, don't go in the field with him. He's got a death wish. Two, if he makes a bet with you, take it. The guy gambles on insane shit, and always loses. Three, if you get yourself a girlfriend, don't take her anywhere near Sean. When women get around him, they just goo up and melt like ice-cream on a hot tank.'

'There's only about one woman in Saigon I bet Ryan couldn't roll,' Crosby said, 'and there she goes.'

They all looked out of the window at the same time. A siclo trundled past, steering a hazardous path among the motorcycles and military trucks. They all saw the young nun in the shaded front seat.

And right at that moment Sean Ryan walked in.

'What woman?' he said.

Webb looked up, and for a moment he thought he recognised the man in the doorway. Ronnie Ryan, Sean's father, had been part legend, part joke; the hero of countless bad Hollywood pictures, the pirate hero in tights and sword who always got the girl. The boy from the bush who made it so good he forgot to come back.

Ryan was a youthful version of his father, with shoulder-length jet-black hair, a drooping black moustache, and a perfect set of powder-white teeth. His eyes were a piercing ice blue. His shirt was open to the third button, and there were hippy love beads nestled in the thick mat of hair on his chest.

But there was nothing soft about Sean Ryan. He was a big man, over six feet tall, his stature not diminished by his execrable choice of clothes: an orange and green Hawaiian shirt, and lilac pants.

He came to the window moments before the siclo disappeared behind an olive ARVN truck belching black diesel. 'Top sort,' he said.

'If you can score with her,' Prescott said, 'I'll give you three hundred bucks.'

'But she's a nun,' Ryan said.

'Right. I only bet that much on surefire certainties.'

Ryan hesitated. 'A hundred bucks I get to kiss her.'

'I have to see it,' Prescott said.

'You're on,' Ryan said, and ran straight back out of the door, leaping over Cochrane, who was still prone on the floor, shouting for someone to come and rescue him.

Crosby winked at Webb. 'How about a little bet on the side? Ten bucks he makes it.'

A wall of traffic, ancient blue and white Peugeot taxis and whining two-stroke Honda motorcycles turning the air a sulphurous grey. Ryan signalled to a siclo driver in the heart of this chaos who nonchalantly turned in front of the wheels of an ARVN jeep to ensure he got his fare.

Ryan heard laughter from the balcony above him. 'Follow that siclo!' Prescott shouted.

'Ignore them,' Ryan said, jumping into the cracked leather seat. 'Just pedal.' He pointed to the road. '*Di, di mau!*'

The siclo driver, whose name was Dinh, stood on the pedals and pulled back into the traffic. Ryan heard a screech of brakes, someone punching a car horn. He flinched but kept his eyes on the road ahead of them. No plan suggested itself. On what pretext could he persuade the girl to return to the Hashish Hilton with him? Perhaps tell her someone had left a baby on their doorstep? Could she come with him? Perhaps she might know of an orphanage where the child would be well cared for? She would be suspicious, of course, but he knew what Catholics were like; she would not refuse. When they got back to the villa, a quick wave to ensure Prescott was watching, a peck on her unsuspecting cheek, then inside to collect his money. Another glorious episode in the legend of Sean Ryan.

First he had to catch up with her.

He caught a glimpse of a white habit as a siclo turned at the traffic lights on Hai Ba Trung. In front of them trucks and taxis were snarled for a hundred metres.

Ryan turned around in his seat. '*Di mau!*' he repeated, and Dinh bobbed his head, grinning from under his pith helmet, not understanding. Another crazy American.

They were stalled in the traffic. The left side of the boulevard was clear, the oncoming traffic stopped by the upraised hand of a traffic cop.

Ryan jumped out. 'Get in the front!' he shouted. He pulled Dinh off his seat and pushed him towards the passenger seat. 'I'll drive. Get in!'

Dinh giggled, astonished and embarrassed by this reversal of the natural order of things. How was it ever possible to understand what an American would do next? He hoped he would still get his fare and said so. In response, the American pushed a handful of notes at him and climbed on the bicycle seat. Dinh sat down in the cab to count his money.

Ryan stood on the pedals, pulled on to the other side of the boulevard and raced towards the intersection. He was aware of Vietnamese and Americans stopping on the sidewalk, staring.

A solid wall of traffic was heading towards him, a motorised stampede kicking up a cloud of exhaust fumes.

Holy Christ.

Dinh was screaming in the front seat.

'Hold on!' Ryan shouted.

Ten yards to the intersection.

They were on collision course with a green ARVN truck. Ryan pedalled hard, willing the machine to go faster.

They weren't going to make it.

The siclo did not have handlebars; a chrome-plated bar behind the passenger cab controlled the steering. Ryan heaved it to the left as hard as he could. The machine mounted the kerb and bounced. Dinh decided it was time to bail out. As he jumped, Ryan lost control completely and the siclo skidded into a plane tree.

Ryan found himself lying on his back, staring at the sky.

A crowd had gathered. Amahs in their black tunics; other siclo drivers, sinewy brown legs in oversized shorts, Coca-Cola hats; some crewcut American servicemen also looked on, amused. Dinh was shouting at Ryan in Vietnamese and pointing at his machine, which now lay on its side on the footpath, one wheel buckled, the footrest mangled. Two White Mice – Vietnamese military police – were on their way over.

'Look what this big stupid monkey has done to my siclo!' Dinh shouted at the crowd. 'This is my rice bowl, my livelihood!'

Ryan got to his feet. He was bleeding. Not for the first time in this flaming country, he thought. He reached into his shirt pocket, pulled out a roll of banknotes.

'Why did you let the *khi dot* – the big monkey – drive your siclo?' one of the crowd asked Dinh. 'It's your fault.'

Ryan interrupted the babble of Vietnamese and offered Dinh a handful of banknotes. 'Here, take this. Is this enough? Can you get it fixed?'

Dinh took the proffered fistful of piasters. More than enough. But still he held the money in front of Ryan's face and pretended to cry.

Ryan pushed some more paper money into his shirt.

'There's enough there for a new television,' someone said.

'See if the big monkey will give you the rest of his money,' an old amah said.

Ryan looked around at the crowd, who were pressing in around him, everyone screaming now, the Vietnamese police watching, their thumbs tucked into their belts. 'Bugger it, take the lot,' he said, and he threw the rest of his money at Dinh and walked away.

Women. Sometimes they were more trouble than they were worth.

'No wonder they can't beat the Viet Cong,' Dinh said to the crowd. 'They can't even drive a siclo!'

Crosby looked up. 'Jesus. What happened to you?'

'You're bleeding,' Prescott said.

Ryan stepped over Cochrane and examined his reflection in the little shaving mirror beside the bed. A piece of skin the size of a large postage stamp was missing on his forehead, and his face was streaked with dried blood. He looked down at his clothes. His Hawaiian shirt had a third, interesting hue. His Rolex Oyster Perpetual had a crack across the face and his left arm was streaked with abrasions.

'Who hit you?' O'Leary said.

'Her husband came home,' Ryan said. He turned round, noticed Webb for the first time, and patted him on the shoulder. 'Sean Ryan,' he said.

'Hugh Webb.'

'You must be the freshmeat. Welcome to Saigon, mate. Land of wars, whores and PX stores.'

Webb watched a fresh trickle of blood make its way down his cheek. 'Are you all right?' he said.

'I'll be okay. But let this be a lesson to you, mate. Never mess around with a bride of Christ.'

# 2

The Mini Moke belonged to Crosby. It still had five bullet holes in the coachwork from the battle of Saigon two years before. Ryan commandeered it whenever Crosby was in-country, an arrangement that Crosby went along with on the understanding that he had use of Ryan's air-conditioned top-floor room whenever Ryan was out of town.

Ryan turned off the Tran Hung Dao into the cluttered back streets of Cholon. The air was spiced with the warm, corrupt smell of Asia, a mixture of ripe fruit, incense, sewage and diesel. He braked to avoid a duck, squawking and fluttering, that was being pursued by an old woman. A knot of high-school girls in white silk *ao dai* saw him and broke into a fit of giggling.

He manoeuvred the Moke down a narrow alleyway, stopped outside a high wall topped with razor wire. He lifted two large cardboard boxes from the back seat and went to a rotting mahogany door set in the wall. He hammered three times with his fist.

The young woman who opened the door was a Eurasian, dressed simply in a white habit. She wore brown leather sandals; a rosary hung from her belt, and a silver crucifix hung between her breasts. Her long, black hair framed an oval face of exquisite beauty, high cheekbones and soft brown eyes, a breathtaking melding of East and West.

Ryan stared. It was the nun from the siclo, he was sure of it.

'*Oui, monsieur?*' she said softly, in French.

This was not in the script. His heart was banging in his chest. Where was Soeur Marie, the old Vietnamese who usually attended the door? Ryan said, 'I brought some presents for the children.'

She stood back from the door. '*Entrez*. You must . . . pardon. My English is not so good.'

'Better than my French, I reckon,' he said.

He followed her across the small courtyard, unable to avert his eyes from the gentle sway of her body beneath the *ao dai*. A statue of the Virgin watched disapprovingly from an alcove in the orphanage wall. From a shuttered loggia window he heard a piano playing 'Good King Wenceslas', children's voices singing in lilting Asian accent.

*Where va snow lay roun' abou', dee' and cris' and even . . .*

She led him through the foyer into a sitting room. It was dark inside, and cooler, and smelled of must. A broken fan laboured overhead. The walls were stucco, the floor tiled with terracotta, heavily stained with mildew.

He placed the two boxes on a low mahogany table.

'Please,' she said, and indicated two threadbare armchairs. He sat down. She remained standing.

'The name's Sean.'

'I know. The . . . canonesse told me about you. I am Soeur Odile.'

There was an awkward silence. Arcane aromas of incense on her clothes, mint on her breath. He realised she was waiting for him to open the boxes. Ryan took the Swiss army knife from his belt and quickly cut through the string. Odile reached in: Carnation milk, Colgate toothpaste, some tinned fruit, a single packet of Park Lane filtered cigarettes.

'For the canonesse,' he explained.

She looked shocked.

'We all have our vices. As the bishop said to the . . .' His voice trailed off.

Soeur Odile did not appear to have heard him. She returned the cigarettes to the cardboard box and tore open the second container.

'Medicines in there. Stole them from the hospital at Long Binh.'

'You stole?'

'Borrowed.'

'It is a sin to steal.'

'Depends which way you look at it. The Americans have got plenty and these kids don't have much of anything.'

She picked up a tin of pears. 'You steal this also?'

'No, that's bought and paid for at the PX.'

She looked at him seriously. 'Soeur Marie told me how much you do . . . for the children here. She says you come . . . every month. You are very kind.'

Ryan stood up, embarrassed, uncomfortable. It was like having an angel telling him he was good. It was just a trick of the light. 'Better shoot through, I suppose.' To hell with Prescott and his three hundred dollars. Even Sean Ryan couldn't seduce a nun.

'You would like to take tea?'

He shrugged. 'Yeah, all right. That'd be good.'

She smiled at him for the first time. In another place, from another kind of woman, he would have interpreted it differently.

'Wait here . . . please.'

He sat down again, and she left the room. Ryan looked around. A pale lizard, the colour of alabaster, watched him from the wall, then darted for cover into an alcove, behind another statue of the Virgin. Ryan felt uncomfortable. It evoked too many memories of his local church in Brisbane. He had been an altar boy then. He and a friend, Choko, had got drunk on the holy wine and the priest had thrown them out. He had never been back, there or to any other church, since.

Now he felt like the statue was watching him. He could imagine he saw her lips move. 'What are you doing in here, Ryan?'

'Just having a cup of tea, Mother,' he murmured.

'If you think you're going to seduce one of my nuns, you can just forget it right now.'

'I wouldn't know where to start.'

'*Pardon, monsieur?*'

He looked up. She was standing there holding a tray with two china teacups and a silver teapot. 'Just singing to myself,' he said. 'A hymn.'

She smiled, set the tray down on the table and knelt to prepare the tea. She poured some of the light amber liquid into a cup, added a slice of lemon and handed it to him.

'Thanks.'

She poured tea for herself and sat in the room's only other armchair. A silverfish darted for cover between the cushions. 'You are American?' she asked him.

'Christ, no. Australian.'

'Australia,' she repeated slowly, as if it were the name of an exotic fruit. 'You are a journalist?'

'Photographer.'

There was a silence.

'Your English is very good,' he said.

'Thank you. They teach me at the convent school.'

'Your father was . . .'

'A French soldier. He is killed at Dien Bien Phu.'

'You have family . . . in Saigon?'

'My family are from Dalat. I have not seen them for a very long time. My mother, you understand . . . she breaks the rules. You know?'

'The French soldier,' Ryan said.

She nodded.

'Where is your mother?'

'She is dead. A rocket.'

Ryan sipped his tea. He decided he did not want to know whether the rocket was North Vietnamese or American. The conversation had an intimacy that he had not expected.

'What happens to you?' she said, pointing at the thick pad of gauze on his forehead and the grazes on his arm, now painted with mercurochrome. 'You are hurt . . . taking your photographs?'

'Sort of,' he lied. It had been a long time since he had felt nervous with a woman. Not since he was fourteen. But then this wasn't a woman, this was a nun. He had been schooled by nuns as a kid; a litany of rosaries and raps across the knuckles with a ruler. But none of the nuns he remembered had ever looked like this. If they had, perhaps he'd still go to church. Perhaps.

'Why did you become a nun?'

She looked away. 'This is not a proper question.'

'It's just that . . . well . . . don't you miss . . . I mean, you're a very beautiful young woman.'

Soeur Odile put her teacup on the table. It rattled in its saucer. She folded her hands on her lap to hide their shaking.

Ryan felt the blessed Virgin staring at him. Her expression was not pleasant.

'I do not think also that this is . . . proper. You should not say things like this to me.'

'I'm sorry. I couldn't help myself.'

She put a hand to the crucifix at her breast, an involuntary movement, he guessed. She murmured something that Ryan was unable to hear under her breath, in French. A prayer perhaps. Deliver us from evil.

'I'd better go,' he said. He put his teacup on the table and stood up. Soeur Odile sat quite still, staring at her hands. 'Next time send the old wrinkled one to open the door for me,' he said. 'Then I can't get into any trouble.'

He hesitated, his hand reaching for the door. He wished for a moment for his camera, to capture the image: the innocent beauty of her, lips slightly parted, European features framed by almond eyes and long jet-black hair; the diaphanous shimmer of white, a chevron of light through the window, dust drifting, the glint of silver on the crucifix, the stern image of the Madonna in her alcove. Impregnate the image with the scent of must and patchouli and he might somehow possess the moment, possess her.

But he could not possess either, and so he said goodbye, shut the door, and the moment was gone.

# 3

'If you're going to get hit, don't get hit in the gut,' Ryan was telling Webb. 'I've seen guys with belly wounds and it's not pretty.'

'Second to belly wounds is chest wounds,' Cochrane said. 'Chest wounds suck.'

They all smiled at that. Except Webb.

'Remember,' Crosby said, 'you can never live as long as one day in Vietnam. A hundred years isn't as long as one night in the boonies.'

The thrill of real fear that Webb had woken to that morning had now settled like cold lead in his stomach. The important thing, he told himself, was that the others did not see the fear. But fear has its own particular smell, and these men knew it well.

Cochrane was the first to remark on it. 'You don't have to do this,' he said. 'That's the difference between any of us and a grunt. We can go home any time we want. They have to stay. But we've got a choice. We can always tell ourselves – if I get through today, tomorrow I can pack up and go home.'

'What it comes down to in the end is being scared is better than being bored,' Ryan said. 'The worst thing is that it becomes addictive. Fear, I mean. After a while you can't leave it alone. Like smoking cigarettes. You know it's no good for you but once you're hooked you can't seem to stop.'

It was six thirty in the morning and they were eating breakfast – croissants, *café au lait* – at the Shelf, as residents referred to the terrace of the Continental Hotel in downtown Saigon. The Shelf was the place in which to see and be seen. It overlooked the main square, the former opera house – now the National Assembly – and the War Memorial, a grotesque cement statue that some cynics suggested showed an American soldier pushing a South Vietnamese into battle. The terrace was separated from the footpath and the phalanx of bicycles and mopeds in the square by long cement flower boxes that were perennially littered with cigarette butts.

There were four of them at the table: Webb, Ryan, Cochrane and Crosby, all dressed in green combat fatigues, their flak jackets and steel helmets under their seats. There was good reason for their conformity; as combat photographers their lives depended on them blending into the scenery. If they looked different from the soldiers they went in-country with, they risked being targeted by the VC – or shot at by the Americans themselves.

Ryan had told Webb that they often went on assignments together, as insurance – if something went wrong, you might need a buddy to ensure you got back again. Today he was going out on a patrol into War Zone D with a unit from the 173rd Airborne. He had invited Webb along 'for the ride'. It was to be Webb's first time in the boonies.

Webb now had his press accreditation from the US Military Assistance Command Vietnam – or MacVee, as it was known. All that was required to get one was two letters from organisations testifying that they were prepared to buy his despatches. Webb had one from the Surrey newspaper where he had worked his cadetship, and Crosby had arranged another from AP – he said the agency would give virtually anyone a letter, along with a camera, film and a light meter, and a promise of fifteen dollars for any photograph they could use. Vietnam was a war anyone could join in.

Ryan had taken him under his wing, helped him buy his 'Saigon jacket' from the Indian tailors on Tu Do. It had a white label with his name, and *Bao Chi* – journalist – sewn to the left breast. It was the fashion to have the name of your affiliated newspaper or magazine underneath. Ryan told him that this was sometimes the root of unintended humour, depending on who you worked for; one correspondent had amused the Marines at Khe Sanh when he arrived with *Alan Williams, Queen* taped to his utilities.

Ryan also helped Webb put together his field kit, and showed him how to paint the chrome on his M-3 Leica camera with green army paint so that the metal would not reflect the sunlight and create a tempting target for snipers. He introduced him to the press briefings held by the Americans at the Rex Theatre at five o'clock each afternoon, the Five O'clock Follies as they were known, the Jive at Five. He also gave him a primer on the language of the military's press information officers: 'An "enemy base camp in an inhabited area" – that's a village. "Enemy troop concentration." That's two or more VC suspects in a rice paddy. You'll pick it up.'

Within a few days Webb was given almost complete and unbridled access to the war. Transport around the battlefields and field rations while he was there were free, courtesy of the US Army, and if he was willing to gamble his legs or his life he could be famous, if not rich, overnight. Vietnam was a fast track up the ladder, if you could stay alive.

On this morning Webb found himself thinking more fondly of Surrey than he ever had, but he had gone too far to pull out now.

Cochrane finished his *café au lait*. 'Do you want your roll?' he asked Webb.

Webb shook his head. 'I'm not that hungry.'

Cochrane snatched the croissant and started to butter it. 'First we check the word on the street, make sure there's nothing in the air we want to miss. Like another Tet or an army coup, something like that. Then we get a taxi out to Tan Son Nhut. Me and Dave are heading down the Delta – there's been some action at Can Tho. From there we'll leave you in the capable hands of Deathwish here.'

'Deathwish?' Webb said.

Ryan shrugged. 'Everyone has to have a nickname.'

Crosby grinned and pointed to the MacVee ID tag around Webb's neck. 'Guard that well, boy,' he said. 'It's your passport to hell.'

## War Zone 'D'

Webb was embarrassed about his boots.

They were brand new, and as he looked at the other occupants of the Huey, he noted how everyone else's boots were caked with dirt and dried red mud. He felt like an interloper, a fraud and a spectator. Dead weight. He felt ashamed of his notebooks and his camera now, a gawker at a car smash.

A giddy vision of dark green past the door gunner's shoulder. Webb felt his legs shaking and could do nothing to stop it. He was aware of the rank stink of his own sweat.

The chopper went into a combat dive, a gut-sucking spiral towards the ground. He heard the crew chief's gravel voice close to his ear. 'You feel something furry in the back of your throat, boy, you swallow real hard, man. It's your ass.'

* * *

It was one of the anachronisms of that particular war that you could eat freshly baked croissants for breakfast and two hours later find yourself in the middle of the jungle, surrounded by punji traps and bouncing mines.

The Huey left them at a staging post for a company of the 173rd Airborne. As it lifted back into the air it kicked up squalls of gritty ochre dust that stung the eyes and nose and clung to the throat like cement dust.

Webb felt the stares and looked around. A knot of black Marines read their tags, their eyes sullen with resentment. Ryan was grinning back at them.

'Well, bull-sheet. Co-respondents. We in for some good shit today. These motherfuckers like their meat raw.'

'Hey, hand-job,' one of them called to Webb, pointing to the patch on the breast pocket of his jacket. 'What's a *Bao Chi*?'

'It's gook for motherfucker,' his partner said.

Ryan did not seem disturbed by their welcome. He took out a packet of Marlboro and offered them around.

'Motherfuckers,' one of the soldiers said. 'You come slumming, man?'

'Don't you want people back home to know what you're going through here?' Ryan asked him.

'Some white boy in Cape Cod going to give a hot damn that I'm gittin' my ass shot off here?'

One of them accepted a smoke. 'These guys don't have to be here, cocksuck,' he said to his friend.

'You shittin' me? They ask to come here?'

'They here because they asked to be here.'

'Wish I could get me some of that. I'd go right home again. Day before I get here, man.'

'That's a rog.'

Webb found himself staring at their helmets. In other armies he had seen in photographs and old war footage the helmet was just another part of a soldier's uniform and added to his anonymity. In this one it was used to express each man's individuality. Red packets of Winston and silver cigarette lighters and plastic bottles of rifle cleaning fluid were tucked inside hatbands and scrawled graffiti identified the four black soldiers as *Born to Kill*, *Love Child*, *High on War* and *Why Me*?

Ryan had taken the lens off his camera. He wanted to take a photograph of the group. Webb thought Born to Kill and Love Child looked as if they would rather stitch a line across Ryan's chest with their M-16s.

'You make good bread with these pictures?' Love Child asked him.

'Let it be, shitkick,' High on War told him. 'Somebody got to tell the people back in the world the shit that is going down over here.'

Ryan raised his camera and fired off three quick frames; the four black Marines on the sandbags, their M-16s across their chest, one of them with *Black Power* scrawled in stencil across his flak jacket, High on War with the Ace of Spades tucked into his helmet band, Love Child cradling his M-16 as if it were a baseball bat.

Webb looked into their faces and did not see the gratitude or admiration he had hoped for, only the dumb brutality of the mob. He turned away as another Huey dropped on to the LZ and two corpsmen loaded the body of a soldier who had died earlier that morning. A fleeting image of a body bag, a pair of jungle boots, a cloud of green iridescent flies.

'Hey, freshmeat,' one of the soldiers shouted, 'they going to be mailin' you home to Mamma in a glad bag too.'

Ryan clapped him on the shoulder and steered him away. 'They don't mean anything by it,' he said. 'They're just scared.'

Webb nodded and said nothing. It was going to be a long day's haul.

They set off, single file, into what the Americans called 'Indian country', foot-slogging all morning through rice paddies and fields, the flat landscape broken only occasionally by bamboo thickets or the simple hooches of the farmers. Wooden guard towers rose over the fields.

What am I doing here? Webb asked himself. I'm twenty-two years old. I have a couple of years' experience as a cadet photographer with a provincial newspaper, and now I'm alongside some of the best combat journalists in the business, pretending I'm one of them. I'm going to make a fool of myself, and I could get crippled or killed doing it . . .

The point of the column entered the jungleline. The sun was directly overhead now, squeezing the juice out of them. The only sounds were the faint jangle of webbing and the slop of water in the precious belt canteens.

There was a shout from the treeline, and the soldiers in front of Webb crouched, ready to drop. They waited there, in the sun, for what seemed like hours; Webb felt his thigh muscles starting to cramp. Sweat ran into his eyes.

Ryan shouldered past him, heading for the front of the line in a low, crouching run. What the hell, Webb thought, and followed.

There were three officers gathered around the tunnel opening, an ARVN Ranger with them. They were discussing options. Finally one of the lieutenants produced a hand grenade, removed the pin, and threw it down the hole. There was a muffled explosion and a cloud of choking dust.

They dragged three Viet Cong bodies from the tunnel. So this was their dreaded enemy, Webb thought. They looked like rag dolls, an untidy tangle of limbs in dusty and sweat-stained black pyjamas. Other grunts had gathered around, and Webb heard a flashbulb pop. They're taking pictures for their souvenir albums, he thought with disgust. And then he remembered that was what he was here to do; take photographs. Half a dozen soldiers had magically produced Instamatics from their packs, but Webb, the two precious Leicas slung around his neck, held back.

He looked around and saw Ryan. He wasn't taking photographs either; he seemed to be waiting for something. Webb followed the direction of Ryan's eyes; one of the Viet Cong was still breathing.

The captain had noticed now, and he called for the corpsman, but the Vietnamese Ranger shook his head and knelt down next to the injured Viet Cong.

The wounded man was little more than a teenager, perhaps fifteen or sixteen years old. His black pyjamas had been shredded by grenade fragments, and there were gaping wounds in his stomach. The Ranger took out his knife and very deliberately pushed it into one of the holes and twisted the blade.

'Jesus Christ,' one of the soldiers said, and turned away. A lieutenant stepped forward to intervene but the captain grabbed him by the shoulder and shook his head.

Webb wanted to vomit. The boy – suddenly Webb could not think of him as an enemy – was kicking feebly and screaming.

The Ranger was shouting questions at him, probing deeper into the wound. Webb noticed the blood on the boy's ears. It was all pointless anyway. The concussion of the grenade had probably deafened him.

I have to stop this, Webb thought.

'Captain,' he said.

The officer looked up at him, his face grey. He hesitated. Then he saw Ryan moving in with his camera and that seemed to make up his mind. 'That's enough,' he said.

'But he's VC!' the Ranger protested.

'We'll call in a dust-off,' the captain said.

The Ranger's features twisted in disgust. He spat in the boy's face and wiped the knife blade on his pyjamas before replacing it in its sheath. But instead of backing off he took his revolver from its holster and held it against the boy's head. He removed the safety. 'We just kill him now.'

The captain looked back at Ryan, who had moved to within ten feet. 'Let it be. That's an order.'

Ryan lowered his camera. The boy was still writhing on the ground, clutching at his stomach.

'Get the corpsman here,' the captain said, and walked away.

The night was so black Webb had to touch his eyelids with his own fingertips to satisfy himself that they were really open. Ryan lay beside him, his helmet over his eyes, his lucky green towel carefully arranged over his face to leave just enough room to breathe. His camouflaged utility was rolled down and his hands were tucked under his arms to protect them from the hordes of mosquitoes that had descended on them after sunset.

'What do you think happened to that kid?' Webb whispered.

'I don't know,' Ryan said. His voice was muffled by the helmet and towel.

'You think he's dead?'

'Probably.'

Webb listened to the maddening whine of mosquitoes inches from his face.

'I know what you're thinking,' Ryan said. 'But the war's not going to stop because a couple of blokes with cameras get turned off.'

'I didn't do anything. Ryan. I just watched.'

'Didn't you take any snaps?'

*Snaps*. 'I couldn't.'

'Good-oh. That means I've got an exclusive.'

A long silence.

'That was terrible,' Webb murmured.

'It's a bloody war. What did you think it was going to be like?'

A good question, Webb thought. What did I think it was going to be like? A *Boy's Own* adventure? He supposed he hadn't expected to witness such brutality, first hand, hadn't expected to feel sorry for the enemy. 'I should have done something.'

'We did do something. We stopped that prick shooting him this afternoon. So they'll take him to Long Binh, and if he lives the Vietnamese will get hold of him and *they'll* torture him. And then they'll shoot him.'

'I suppose . . . at least we didn't just stand there.'

He heard Ryan sit up. 'Got news for you, sport. This war is not about your conscience. What happened out there today was no concern of mine or yours. We were just here doing a job. There is absolutely no situation where we should stop working because it's what we show the rest of the world that's going to stir people up to stop this bloody madness.'

Webb heard him shuffle around, settling himself under the towel and helmet once more.

'I couldn't take any photographs because I threw up,' Webb said.

'Well, it's good you didn't eat your bun for breakfast, then,' Ryan said. 'Now go to sleep. We've got another long hike through the boonies tomorrow.'

# 4

An alien and primitive world, gongs banging somewhere in the jungle, the smell of shit and incense, a green and fecund landscape inhabited only by women, children and old men. They walked on through the morning, the heat crushing them. Already Webb had almost emptied one canteen of water. Finally they stopped to rest in a rice paddy, squatting down with their backs against the knee-high embankment of an irrigation channel.

One of the Marines, a long, raw nineteen-year-old from Kentucky, grinned at Webb as he fumbled with his cameras. 'Except for them dead gooks I guess you ain't had much to snap at,' he said. Webb looked up at him. The tag on his fatigues read *McCague*.

Webb shook his head.

'Can't say I'd mind a contact right now, just for a chance to lie down for a while.'

'We're sitting ducks out here.'

'Shoot, we sitting ducks wherever we are. That's the whole point, mister. Only way we ever get to find them gooks is when they ambush us.' McCague sucked some water from his canteen. 'Want to get yourself a picture?'

'Sure,' Webb said, without thinking.

'You send me a copy?'

'What have you got in mind?' Webb answered, more warily now.

'I was figuring to put a few rounds into that treeline over there. Be just like the real thing. Who's gonna know, right?'

Webb thought about it. He had missed two golden opportunities for film the previous day and now it looked as if he might go home empty-handed. The fact was he needed something to sell.

McCague did not wait for his decision. He had already checked the safety on his M-16 and was on one knee, aiming at his imaginary enemy on the other side of the paddy. The rest of his rifle squad were watching him, laughing.

'You crazy motherfucker, McCague,' one of them said.

If McCague had been home in Kentucky he would be spinning the wheels of his hotrod in the main street, Webb decided. Now someone's let him loose with an Armalite in the boonies, and life's still a big joke.

'Ready there, mister?' McCague said.

Webb fumbled for his Leica, adjusting the lens. Without waiting for a reply, McCague fired a rapid burst into the treeline two hundred metres away.

Almost at once there was a sound like angry bees in the air around them. McCague sat down suddenly, staring in dull surprise at the three small holes in the front of his utilities.

'Jesus, shit, someone's busting caps at us!'

'Christ, man, get down!'

'Corpsman up!'

McCague was lying on his back now, his spine arched, his chest heaving, trying to suck in air. His mouth was gaping open like a beached fish.

Webb felt paralysed with shock and disbelief.

Something hit him hard in the side and he fell. He tried to look up, to see what was happening. He heard Ryan's voice close to his ear. 'Keep your head down, you silly bugger.'

'Where are they?' someone else shouted.

'There!'

'Where?'

'There!'

'Corpsman up, goddamn it!'

'Where are they?'

'There!'

'Where, for Christ's sake, where?'

Webb listened to the bedlam around him. Now he understood what it was that Crosby and Prescott had been laughing at that first afternoon in the Hashish Hilton. Perhaps if he ever made it back to Saigon he would share the joke.

The corpsman had reached McCague, was crouched over him, blowing air into his lungs. McCague was making gurgling noises, like a kid blowing bubbles in his bath. The medic pulled a scalpel from his kit and ripped open McCague's shirt. There was a spurt of blood as he made two incisions in the boy's neck, then he pushed a black tube into the trachea. McCague had stopped moving. The corpsman blew into the tube, watching for the rise and fall of the boy's chest, feeling for the pulse at his neck.

There was another shout from along the line, and another.

'I'm hit.'

'Medic up, medic up!'

The corpsman grimaced; frustration, despair. He crawled away, elbows and knees, leaving McCague staring at the blue sky, the black tube flopping from the wound in his neck. Webb found himself following McCague's stare, as if there were really something up there.

Just blue sky, alive with death, pulsing with it. Webb hugged the earth, sucked it, embraced it. His camera was gone, dropped somewhere in the dirt. He looked around for Ryan. He had gone too.

Madness. If I live through this I'm getting out of Saigon, out of Vietnam and I'm never coming back.

The Dakota dived low, with a sound like a foghorn. These things piss blood, Crosby had told him, and now he knew what he meant. It had three mounted machine guns, each with six barrels, firing eighteen thousand rounds a minute, every fifth round a tracer, a solid stream of red, death the colour of carmine. How could anything live through that?

It was followed in by a Phantom, its fuselage camouflaged in green and grey. Steel-ribbed cans rolled and tumbled down the sky, exploding in orange rolling fireballs that broiled into choking black clouds. Webb opened his mouth in a silent scream, the concussion like hot needles in his ears.

As the jets roared for home, the soldiers rose slowly to their feet from behind the embankment. The firefight was over. The forest crackled and burned, the choking black smoke from the napalm drifted over a distant village.

Webb scrambled in the dirt, found his camera. He looked at his watch. The whole thing had lasted less than twenty minutes. He would have guessed three to four hours. A trick of the mind.

And he hadn't taken a single frame.

*And I wanted to be a combat photographer.*

The platoon sergeant was staring at him. 'You hit, man?'

Webb looked down at his utility. There was a smear of blood on the sleeve. He let the sergeant strip off his flak jacket. Fresh blood had soaked into his shirt under his armpit. 'Christ,' Webb said.

'You ain't hit, man,' the sergeant said. 'Someone just bled on you.' He pushed the flak jacket back over Webb's shoulders and walked away.

McCague was still lying on his back, staring at the sky. The rest of his platoon moved around him, their eyes pointedly turned away.

In the distance he heard the chop-chop of the medevac Hueys.

He walked up the line, looking for Ryan. He found him with his back against the embankment, smoking a cigarette. There was a blood-soaked wound dressing on his left shoulder.

'You're hit,' Webb said.

'My bloody oath. Look, I know this is your first war, and you want a good view of it, but if someone shoots at you, it's better to lie down and get out of the way.'

'What happened?'

'Felt something thump me in the shoulder after I grabbed you. Medic gave me some mother morphine. Getting a nice buzz right now.' He fumbled for his cameras with his right hand. 'Make sure you get these to Crosby. He'll ship them out for me.'

'You still shot film?'

'That's my job.'

Webb felt even more ashamed of his own miserable performance. 'I found this,' he mumbled.

'My lucky towel. See what happens when I drop the bloody thing?'

Two Hueys appeared through the haze of a purple smoke flare, each with a red cross painted on the nose. Webb turned away from the stinging dust storm as they settled in the dirt, then helped two corpsmen carry Ryan to the first chopper. He climbed in beside him.

'Got a smoke, Spider?' Ryan asked him.

Webb pulled out his cigarettes, but his hands were shaking so hard he could not light one. Ryan grabbed the lighter from him and lit one himself. Webb sat back on his haunches with his back against the fuselage, unable to stop the shaking. He balled his hands into fists, in an attempt to make his body obey his will, afraid that others would see.

They loaded McCague. He lay there, on his back, staring at the roof of the Huey with that same querulous expression in his blue eyes. Finally the crew chief grabbed a green poncho and covered him with it, leaving just the muddy jungle boots protruding.

'It was my fault,' Webb said aloud.

Ryan's eyes blinked open, and he frowned up at him, not comprehending, lost to the morphine.

'My fault,' Webb repeated. He fumbled for his camera, and guiltily, like a secret pornographer, he kicked back the poncho and took the photograph: the shaved blond head, staring eyes, the black tube still flopping from his throat. Magically his hands stopped shaking while he took the shot.

He wondered if McCague would still like a copy, wherever he was now.

# 5

## Bien Hoa Air Base

The Huey dropped into a deep landing spiral, billowing oily black smoke. 'Hold on to your assholes, ladies and gentlemen,' the crew chief shouted. The machine bounced as it hit the LZ.

Webb saw a knot of nurses, technicians and doctors racing towards the landing pad from the hospital, dragging gurneys between them.

The pilot immediately shut down the engines. Flames were licking back along the fuel lines towards the tanks. 'Get everyone out and get clear,' he screamed at the crew chief. He had many nightmares about dying. Sucking away slowly with ninety per cent petrol burns was one of the worst.

A chaos of panicked shouts and black smoke. Webb helped one of the doctors load Ryan on to a gurney, and together they dragged it back across the runway, towards the hospital buildings.

'She's going to blow!' he heard someone shout.

He stopped, looked back. The crew chief was beside him, still in the heavy crash helmet, his fatigues soaked with sweat. Webb read his name, Jensen, stencilled on his left breast.

'Oh, Christ!' Jensen said.

'What is it?' one of the nurses shouted.

'Where's the head wound?'

Webb was close enough to see Jensen's eyes. He knew what he was thinking. *I'm not going back.*

The Huey was enveloped in clouds of black smoke, but for one moment the smoke cleared and they all saw him, lying on a stretcher besides McCague, unconscious, his head swathed in bloody bandages. 'Oh, sweet suffering Christ,' the pilot said. 'There's one still in there.' He looked around at Jensen. 'Why the fuck is there one still in there?'

'It's going to blow,' Jensen said.

Webb could see flames billowing around the tank. No one moved.

'We can't leave him,' one of the nurses said.

'Half his skull's blown away,' Jensen said. 'He's going to die anyway.'

For Christ's sake blow, Webb found himself thinking. Before any of us have to make the decision. For pity's sake, blow!

'We have to get him,' the nurse said.

'He's a dead man anyway,' Jensen repeated.

The nurse started to run back to the Huey. No one else moved.

Webb had heard what happened when you got burned. It was one of the Vietnam horror stories everyone whispered to the new guys, like a litany, along with the legends of bad belly wounds. With burns you didn't die straight away, even when it was bad. It was the bacterial infection that killed you, a blue-green slime called pseudomonas that smelled so bad even the doctors and nurses couldn't change the dressings without gagging. It was very painful, and very slow. Even if you lived, the scars were so bad you wished you'd died.

But there she was, the little blonde nurse, running back there.

Webb found himself running too.

'That's fucking insane!' someone shouted.

Webb ran, sobbing with fear, dry sobs that racked his chest as he ran. He couldn't see the nurse, and for one shocking moment, he thought perhaps she had changed her mind and he was running in there alone. Then he saw her, as the veil of smoke parted, at the door, pulling at the wounded man's fatigues. He was too heavy, and she couldn't lift him clear.

The fire was inches from the fuel tank, just inches.

They had a few seconds.

They couldn't possibly make it.

Webb grabbed the man's flak jacket, dragged him to the door, and the nurse helped him hoist the man on to his shoulder. He was a big man and Webb felt his knees buckle under the weight.

'Run!' he screamed at her.

She could have gone ahead then, she had done all she could, but she stayed with him as he staggered away from the Huey. Every yard an eternity, waiting for the shock, the blast, the heat, the pain. Another yard, another.

The curtain of smoke parted for him. He saw the knot of doctors and nurses and flight crew gathered around the gurneys a hundred metres away, urging him on.

Another few yards. His knees wanting to collapse under him.

'Keep going!' the nurse screamed at him.

'Get away! Run!'

'Keep going!'

The Huey exploded with a hollow *boom*, and Webb found himself face down on the tarmac, the wounded man's weight crushing his chest. Suddenly there were people around him, pulling him to his feet, ushering him away. The injured soldier was lifted on to a gurney and hurried towards the emergency room.

He put his hand to his face. Thick blood leaking from his nose where he had hit the concrete. He looked up. Just him and the crew chief left.

Jensen stared at him, his face twisted with reproach. Without a word he turned and walked away, and Webb was left alone, listening to the Huey burn.

He was sitting on the step outside the ER when she came out.

She was five foot three inches, perhaps ninety pounds dripping wet, Webb decided. She had a pugnacious look about her, the face of a tomboy, the look of a tree climber and a bubblegummer who had grown up before she was ready. Her blonde hair was pushed up at the back and fixed with pins, but loose strands of it fell over her face. She had her fists in the pockets of her fatigues.

She did not seem surprised to see him. 'Coffee?' she said.

He nodded.

The Huey had burned itself out. A bulldozer was shovelling away the charred remains. 'That was the bravest thing I ever saw,' Webb said.

'Well, you too,' she said.

'No. If you hadn't started running back, I wouldn't have done it. You shamed me into it.'

'You were the only one who ran with me. Jesus.' She folded her arms across her chest, as if she were cold. 'I can't believe I did it either.'

'How is he?'

'The head wound? He died. Just like the man said.'

They walked the rest of the way to the canteen in silence. They got their coffees and sat down at a table. Webb held out his hand. 'Hugh Webb.'

'Mickey. Mickey van Himst.'

'Van Himst. Good Irish name.'

She smiled. 'My father's Dutch and my mother's French Canadian. My real name's Dominique Michelle. But my friends have always called me Mickey, right from when I was a kid.'

'I've never met an American Dutch French Canadian before. What kind of passport do you have?'

She smiled again. 'Senegalese. Actually I'm from San Diego. And what are you? Love the accent.'

'British.'

She looked at the two cameras on the table in front of him. 'Tourist, huh?'

'They promised me five days and six nights in a warm climate. I'll have to speak to my travel agent when I get home.'

Mickey smiled, then put her head on her arm.

'You okay?'

'Hell, no. I thought I was going to die out there. I could do with a drink.'

He reached across the table and touched her hand. To his surprise, she took it and squeezed, hard, her face still buried in her arms. 'How long have you been in Vietnam?' he asked her.

'All my life. Six months. What about you?'

'This is my fourth day.'

Her head jerked up. 'You're not going to last the distance doing things like that.'

Webb thought about the last twenty-four hours. He needed to talk to someone, but now he had the opportunity he didn't know how to put it into words. Most people go through their lives knowing – or thinking they know – who they are. They tell themselves that they are brave, and decent, and honest; or, at least, that if it is asked of them, they can be all these things. In the last few hours Webb had had all these pretensions stripped away. He was no longer sure who he was. By his own estimation he had been alternately a coward, a fool and a hero. He had indirectly caused the death of one man, and saved the life – albeit temporarily – of another. Inside he was a boiling sea of emotion, its force deferred, while he tried to fathom the best way to channel it. A calm surface, bubbling underneath with things molten and angry.

'What are you thinking about?' she said.

'To be honest – I'm trying to figure out what sort of man I am.'

She crumpled the polystyrene cup in her fist. 'Yeah, the coffee in this place does that to you.' Her eyes were clouded, too. He noticed the slight tremor in her fingers.

He remembered guiltily that he had forgotten to ask about Ryan. 'How's Ryan . . . the shoulder wound?'

'T&T – that means through and through. He'll be okay. He'll have a little less meat on his shoulder than he started out with. Modern high-velocity bullets are like that character in Shakespeare. They always get their pound of flesh.' She suddenly realised she was still holding his hand and shoved it away from her as if it were a live snake. 'What am I doing? Holding hands with guys in the canteen. You'll get me a reputation as a romantic.'

Their eyes locked. She had the largest, saddest grey eyes he had ever seen. Then he realised what he was looking at; the thousand-yard stare, the look he had heard about in soldiers who had seen too much.

'I hope they give you a medal for what you did today.'

'Hey, you too. The Correspondent's Cross and bar.'

'I'll just take the bar, as long as it's well stocked.'

The smile disappeared as quickly as it had come. 'Oh God, I thought I was going to burn to death.'

'How could you do it?'

'How could you?'

'Guilt. Shame.'

'Well. Same here, I guess.'

'You haven't got anything to be ashamed of.'

'Don't count on it. But I'm not going to tell a reporter, right?' She stopped, her head cocked slightly. Now Webb heard it too, the familiar chop-chop of Hueys parking on the apron near the hospital. 'Incoming. I got to go to work.'

'Can I see you again?'

She stopped halfway to her feet. 'God, you English are so polite. Sure. You know where I live. Just don't come in on a gurney, or I'll pretend I never saw you before. It's kind of easier that way. For both of us.'

And she ran off towards the sounds of the choppers.

# 6

The AP offices were on the rue Pasteur, a stone's throw from the Gia Long palace, in the ground-floor room of a three-storey apartment building. A din of teleprinters, photographers rushing in and out of the darkrooms, the clatter of typewriters. On one wall someone had taped some black and white photographs, the ones they couldn't use; a navy SEAL with a necklace of human ears, a Marine hooch with a human skull on the tentpost, two American soldiers staring at a severed human head as it floated down a river. Someone had scrawled in a speech bubble on the photograph: 'He was with the AP – but he missed a big story.'

Webb wondered how anyone might find that sort of thing funny.

Crosby came out the bureau chief's office looking grim. Webb sat on the edge of his desk and toyed with the ancient Remington typewriter, avoiding his eyes.

'Sean got a front page on all the major dailies with those shots of the Ranger and the captured Viet Cong,' he said. There was accusation in his voice.

'Yeah, I saw them.'

'You were with Sean. Where're the pictures?'

'I didn't take any.'

'Why not?'

'I was throwing up in the grass.'

Crosby shook his head and slumped into the chair. 'I'd say forget it and go back home, except for these.'

He threw the black and white prints on the desk, five photographs, the total result of two days in War Zone D with the 173rd. Webb didn't even remember taking them, a fast series, one after the other: McCague on one knee, firing into the treeline; McCague dropping the M-16, a look of utter astonishment on his face; in the third frame he was slipping down the embankment, hands limp at his side; the fourth captured the expression of the two Marines closest to him, their faces essays in horror, as he lay gasping on the ground. The last was of McCague in the medevac, full frame, the black rubber tubing hanging from the incision in his trachea.

'These are sexy,' Crosby said.

'Sexy?'

'They're good, very, very good. Of course I don't think anyone can run with this last one. It's a little too graphic for the newspapers, I think.'

Webb blinked. Well, all I did was help a man to die. If that's good, then I suppose I did my job. But how can a picture of a man caught in his death throes be good? How exactly do I measure my new competence?

'I'm glad you like them, Croz.'

Crosby heard the irony in Webb's voice but did not remark on it. 'If you can keep your lunch down, maybe you've got a future.'

A future. In the firefight in the rice paddy he had promised himself he would never go out again. He had made his pact with the divine, as he guessed many men would have done in the same situation; get me out of this, and I'll never bother You again. Instead he found himself flirting with the insane idea of going back. Just once more. Not out of any love for the job, just to prove to himself that he could do it. To find out what sort of man he was. So he would know.

Crosby was still staring at the pictures on the desk. 'The more I look at these . . . everyone else is turned the other way when this guy started firing.' He looked up at Webb. 'How did *you* know what was going to happen?'

Webb shrugged his shoulders. 'Instinct,' he said.

Jimi Hendrix's version of 'The Star Spangled Banner' wailed from the record player. Ryan sat in the chair by the window, his left shoulder heavily strapped, the arm splinted across his chest. In his right hand was a small bamboo pipe, in which he had mixed a concoction of tobacco and marijuana, soaked in opium.

For the pain.

The Hashish Hilton was deserted. Webb and Crosby were at the AP office, Prescott was in the Delta, Cochrane had flown up to Da Nang alone.

He stared at the traffic in the street below, the daily bedlam of taxis, motorised siclos, military trucks and jeeps, the sound muted by the windows. The air conditioner rattled away in the corner, fighting the steamy January heat.

'Holy hell,' Ryan muttered.

A siclo pulled up to the kerb below. A young woman, in a white silk *ao dai* with a mandarin collar, got out. She took a parcel from the seat, and looked up. He imagined she could see him at the window, watching her. Then she disappeared from view.

Soeur Odile.

There was a tentative knock on the door. Ryan took Jimi Hendrix off the record player, found a Bach fugue. He threw open the windows to disperse the dope fumes. He opened the door.

She looked embarrassed, couldn't meet his eyes. The small cardboard box was held in front of her. 'Monsieur Ryan. I was . . . we were all concerned for you when we hear you are hurt.'

'Soeur Odile. Please. Come in.'

She hesitated, then stepped across the threshold. He took the box from her with his good arm. 'What have you got in here?'

'You always bring us so much. I think perhaps now you are hurt . . . we can do something for you.'

The box had been tied with string. As he hunted for his Swiss army knife, Soeur Odile looked around the room. 'You have an air conditioner but . . . the window is open. You always have it this way?'

'They reckon it's better for you.'

'What a cute little monkey . . . oh!'

'Nixon, stop that! Dirty little bastard! Excuse me, Sister.' Ryan chased Nixon off the bookcase. He scuttled away shrieking, and continued with his favourite game under the bed.

'Nixon?'

'We call him that because he's a little w . . . well, because he's always . . . he has bad habits.'

Soeur Odile flushed the colour of bronze. Ryan returned his attention to the box. 'You're the last person I expected to see here. Except maybe for Westmoreland. Good of you to look in.'

'Your arm is very bad?'

'Hurts like a bastard . . . sorry, it's a little painful. But it's still attached, that's the main thing, right?' He couldn't open the box, not one-handed. He threw the knife on the table. 'Can I get you a cup of tea?'

'No, I cannot stay.' She picked up the knife and carefully cut through the string. Ryan looked inside. A Bible, and a small statue of the Virgin. 'From the canonesse,' she explained.

Ryan picked up the leather-bound Bible in one hand. 'Well, give me something to read, I suppose. Has it got a happy ending?'

The flicker of a smile? Perhaps he imagined it. 'I think perhaps it is a useless gift. You are not a Christian, I can tell.'

'Now that's where you're wrong. I'm one of your lot.'

'You are Catholic?'

'My oath. There's a lot of Micks where I come from.'

'Micks?'

'Roman Catholics.'

'Where do you come from, Monsieur Ryan?'

'Sit down and I'll tell you.'

Another moment's hesitation. Ryan felt his pulse racing. A nun. A bloody nun!

She perched on the very edge of one of the wicker chairs, looking as if she were ready to break for the door at any moment. He sat in the other chair, and they weighed each other carefully like combatants in a chess match.

'It's all right,' Ryan said finally. 'I don't bite.'

'I think perhaps this is not . . . proper.'

'Spending time with sinners is an occupational hazard, isn't it?'

'Are you a sinner, Monsieur Ryan?'

'We all are, aren't we? It's just a matter of degree. Isn't that right?' When she didn't answer, he said: 'My old man was one of the biggest sinners of the lot. You might have heard of him. Ronald Ryan.'

Her face glowed with unexpected enthusiasm. 'Yes. I see one of his pictures, I think. He is a pirate. He is very brave.'

'I don't know if he was brave or not. All I know is when I was born he took the soft option and shot through. But that was before he went to America and became famous. Maybe he got a bit braver later on.'

'I see.'

For a moment the expression on her face irritated him. 'What do you see?'

'That you have not . . . forgiven him.'

Forgiven him? Ryan thought. The idea had never occurred to him. Ronnie Ryan was just a fact of his life, like the mole on his right knee. 'I only met him three times. He died when I was thirteen, at the height of his notoriety. I don't think I missed much.'

'You are a lot like him.'

'Yeah, everyone reckons I look like him. I can't help that.'

There was a heavy silence. Soeur Odile had her hands folded neatly in her lap, like white gloves, her spine poker-straight, as if she were being interviewed for a secretarial position at a bank. But there was an unsettling contradiction to her attitude, in her eyes; they had locked on to his, searching his face with a candour he found unsettling. Why is she here? he wondered. At the instruction of the canonesse, or on a whim of her own? 'So – you are a Catholic?' she asked him.

'Not a very good one.'

'You go to Mass?'

'Haven't been to Mass since I was thirteen. I got thrown out.'

'But who will throw you out of a church?'

'The priest. He had no option, I suppose. Me and my mate drank all the altar wine.'

'Why?'

'We wanted to get drunk.'

She stared at him as if this were quite incomprehensible to her. Possibly it was.

'We got our own back, though. It was only a small church and they couldn't afford a proper bell. So they had a record player and an amplifier hooked up to the bell tower. The priest had this LP with bells playing and he used to put that on every Sunday morning. We waited until Christmas Eve and we broke into the church and put on an Elvis Presley forty-five and turned the volume up full blast. Three o'clock Christmas Eve and the whole population of Miller's Creek were in their front gardens, scratching their heads listening to "You Ain't Nothin' but a Hound Dog" coming from the sky.'

He wondered why he had told her that particular story. Had he been trying to shock her? She was staring at him with an expression of utter astonishment. Then, unexpectedly, she smiled. She put her hand over her mouth to disguise it.

'Well, that's better. I don't think I've seen you smile before.'

She looked embarrassed. 'I'm sorry. This is not a funny story.'

'Well, I laughed at the time.'

'You must be very ashamed now.'

'Not a bit of it. If I could have taken a picture of it, I'd have it hanging on my wall.'

'Instead of these pictures?' She looked around, at the black and white glossies that had been tacked to the wall, GIs in jungle fatigues, pictures of the dead and the living, victors and vanquished juxtaposed.

'I'm not ashamed of them. It's what I do.'

'Why do you like to take pictures about wars?' she asked him.

'I don't really know. I've always had a fascination for it, I suppose. I was born the day they dropped the big one on Hiroshima. Perhaps it's in my blood. My mother always used to say I was a war baby, as if it was something special. But I don't know why I do it. I guess I've never wanted to do much of anything else.'

'It is worth all the risk?' she asked him, looking at the heavily bandaged shoulder.

'This? You can't help bad luck. But I guess it's like anything. The more you do a job, the more you learn about it, the less risk there is. I only got this because the bloke I was with was new, and didn't know how to duck.'

'You do not mind if you are killed for a photograph?'

'If I get killed, it won't be for a photograph. It will be for the truth.' A beat. 'Christ, that sounds pompous.' He realised what he'd said. 'Pardon my language.'

She ignored the blasphemy. 'The truth, Monsieur Ryan?'

'All I meant was, if there's no one here snapping away with a camera, how will anyone outside Vietnam know what a shitty little war this is? Pardon my French again.'

She did not seem disturbed by this mild obscenity either. Instead she asked him: 'You think photography can stop this war?'

'Yeah. Yeah, I do.'

'I will pray you are right.'

Ryan felt embarrassed at having revealed this part of himself to her. 'Yeah, well, I suppose it won't happen overnight. Look, I've answered your question. Will you answer one of mine?'

'You wish to know why I am a nun?'

'I don't want to harp on it. You said it wasn't a proper question. But I never ask proper questions. That's why I'm a journo.'

A beat; and then she said: 'You must understand, monsieur. I am not Vietnamese, I am not French. It makes life . . . difficult.'

'So, you're saying . . . it's like a . . . sanctuary?'

'Perhaps. Yes. But also, I have great faith.'

'What came first? The faith – or the sanctuary?'

She studied her hands, one thumb stroking the other as if it were a small, wounded bird. 'My mother wished it.'

'Religious, was she?'

'How long do you live here in Vietnam, Monsieur Ryan?'

'Three years.'

'Then you will know that here we have a very conservative, very formal, society. A woman has her place, you understand? No Vietnamese man will marry me, because I am not Vietnamese. He looks at me, he sees a foreigner. A Westerner looks at me, he sees a "gook". Yes? So my choice is the Church or the Tu Do. My mother prefers I go to a convent. Me also, I think.'

Ryan leaned forward. 'When I look at you, I don't see a "gook". I see a very lovely young woman.'

She stood up, abruptly, as if he had slapped her face. 'I must go now.'

'Sorry. That was the wrong thing to say, right? I seem to be making a habit of it. Please. Sit down.'

'No, really. I must go.'

'You don't have to do what you don't want to do.'

She looked up at him as if he had tried to persuade her the world was flat. 'Perhaps not in your country, Monsieur Ryan. But in Vietnam we do.'

'It doesn't matter whether it's Vietnam or Australia, everyone has a choice.'

'I do not have a choice.'

'Yeah, that's what they told me. My older brother went to work as a roustabout on a station and they told me I'd have to do the same thing. There wasn't any choice. I wasn't good for anything else. When I said I wanted to be a magazine photographer and travel all over the world they all laughed at me. But I figured, if my old man could get away and be a big star, then I could too, in my own way. I figured you don't have to be what other people tell you you have to be. You have to listen to your own heart. You've only got one life.'

'It is different for me.'

'No, it's not. If you want something different from the life you've got, you should go for it. That's all there is to it.'

She looked up at him and for a moment their faces were very

close. She had that look on her face, that look he had seen countless times before on the faces of other women just before he kissed them for the first time. He knew if she was any other woman he would not have hesitated. There was something going on here, something there were no words for. Some people called it chemistry, when suddenly everything meshed, like bringing together two torn halves of a picture.

Her eyes were wide and her lips were a little apart. He leaned towards her; the cross between her breasts glinted dully in the yellow light. He pulled back. Now he would never know what she would have done.

She turned away. 'I must go.'

'You're lovely,' he whispered.

She looked stricken, as if what he had said were the worst thing in the world, the most terrible thing anyone had ever said to her. Perhaps, in the situation, it was. 'I hope you are well soon.' She held out her hand. He noticed she was trembling. He took her hand, held it until she pulled away.

'Goodbye, Sister. Thanks for coming.'

She hesitated in the doorway. She seemed to be making up her mind. 'Monsieur Ryan,' she said, at last. 'There is something you should perhaps know.'

'Yes, Sister?'

'I am not a nun. Not yet. I do not yet take my final vows.'

'You're a novice?'

'Yes. A novice.' She gave him a look that could have meant anything, and then she was gone. He heard her footfall on the concrete stairwell.

He stared at the open door, wondering.

The Cercle Sportif was on Hong Thap Tu Street, a handsome French villa whose gardens served the recreational needs of the American and European community. Westmoreland used to play tennis there. From the verandahs it was possible to watch men play boules under the tamarind trees, while their wives, their bodies glistening with Ambre Solaire and Monoï, sunbathed by the swimming pool.

Ryan signalled the waiter for two more gin and tonics. 'Christ, the Frogs know how to host a war,' he said.

Webb shifted nervously in his wicker chair. He hoped this was on Ryan's tab. He was almost broke. 'I shouldn't be here,' he said.

'Well, you are. Relax. Enjoy yourself.'

The waiter arrived with their drinks and set them on the table. Webb crossed his legs, pulled at a piece of wicker on the arm of his chair, uncrossed his legs.

'Christ, you're like a cat with a cracker up its arse.'

Webb shrugged.

Ryan took a long swallow of gin and smiled appreciatively. He fished out the piece of lemon and ate it whole. 'You can always go back home, Spider.'

'I don't have the money for the ticket. Even if I did, I wouldn't go.'

'Why not?'

'There's nothing to go back to.'

'So what's the problem?'

The clunk of the heavy silver boules, a woman's laughter from the swimming pool, the silky splash of water. Impossible to imagine that a few kilometres away men were screaming in a world of steel and death. Webb shrugged again.

'You thought it was going to be fun.'

Webb lowered his voice. 'I was scared.'

Ryan leaned towards him. 'I remember the first time I got caught in a firefight. Scared shitless. Told myself if I got out of it, I was never going to put myself in a situation like that again. But it's like falling off a horse. You got to force yourself to get back in the saddle.'

'I don't think I can do it.'

'It sounds like you don't have a choice.' He leaned back, and studied Webb with frank, cold blue eyes, as if he were seeing him for the first time. 'You're a desperate little bastard. You'll do anything to break out of the mould. Won't you?'

Webb looked away, over the lawns.

'You know how I know? Because you're like me.'

'I don't have your guts.'

'That's not what I heard. There was this nurse at Bien Hoa. She was telling me how you ran back to the medevac when it caught fire and pulled out some lieutenant with a head wound. Now I couldn't have done that. Not unless there was a picture in it.' He finished his drink, massaged his injured shoulder. 'It's not a question of balls. Your trouble is, you want to be a journo and you want to be squeaky clean. You don't want the grunts looking at you working over dead bodies and blokes with their legs off and muttering under their breath about how you're a bloody parasite. But they're happy enough to have you up there with them when they're in a contact. If they die they feel like at least it's not for some anonymous shitfight no one will ever see or hear about. Understand?'

Webb was not sure he did understand but some of it made sense, at least.

'With what we do you get to like the sick feeling in your gut, the adrenalin rush and all of it. Before you know where you are you're addicted.'

Webb shook his head. 'I promised myself I'd never go back out there.'

'It's up to you. Depends how hungry you are. You can always go home. I'll lend you the cash, if that's the problem.' He grinned. 'Just how hungry are you, Spider?'

The next day Ryan arrived at the orphanage with two cartons containing medicines, soap and tinned food. The ancient wooden gate was opened by Soeur Marie, the old French nun. A few days later he went back, and the old nun was there once more.

He asked for Soeur Odile and was told she was at her prayers.

He had spent a week's retainer on food and medicine and he was getting nowhere. He would have to try another way.

# 7

The morning after his conversation with Ryan at the Cercle Sportif, Webb hitched a ride on a Huey and went out with a Marine patrol in the Delta. The company made one light contact and Webb found, to his surprise, that this time he felt quite calm, almost serene, and was even able to run off several frames of the action. Afterwards the shakes came back, but not as bad as the first time. When he got back to Saigon later that afternoon he developed his film in the AP darkroom, and found that none of it was usable. But as he walked back down the rue Pasteur, he felt a curious sense of accomplishment. Ryan was right. It was like falling off a horse. You just had to get back in the saddle.

He settled into the new routine of his life, slogging through bone-sore days filled with adrenalin, sweat and ochre dirt, building up a personal library of stark film and sweat-crinkled notebooks crammed with unreadable notes and impressions, the nights sleepless, wide-eyed and trembling as the last firefight was replayed in the darkness. Surfing through the weeks on a cocktail of pills and smoke, bennies to wake you up, Seconal to help you sleep, opium to let you unwind.

He hitched choppers to the Delta, slogging through paddy fields and leech-infested streams with the 25th, or rose before dawn for the scheduled early morning flight to Danang. Then overnight at the Press Centre, with its unmade single beds, dirty sheets, beer cans and cigarette butts littering the floor, then out to Dong Ha next morning and a Marines supply chopper to one of the field units.

He jumped into Hueys like taxis, riding out to Quan Tri and Pleiku and the firebases in the Highlands, living with Special Forces and First Air Cavalry companies through long nights of mortar and rocket bombardment, then flying back with the wounded next morning to Qui Non or Danang, covered in blood and mud, to be served T-bones and ice-cream in a spotless mess, laying a starched white linen napkin over his soiled fatigues.

Later he might wash off the dust and sweat at China Beach, where the white soldiers splashed in the surf and the black conscripts hung out in the beach café eating greasy burgers and playing Motown on the jukebox. They said it was always safe to swim at China Beach because the Viet Cong liked to use the beach too.

The war began to take on a surreal quality for him. A sideshow event. A theme park with real blood.

Through the long black nights in the Highlands, huddled in a bunker, with mortars and rockets hissing in, waiting for the NVA sappers to come through the wire, he thought about Mickey van Himst. He even wrote to her, twice, but she never wrote back, and he guessed she was too busy or too exhausted. If he had stayed in Saigon he could have seen her every few days. But he wasn't in Vietnam to make love to nurses, he was here to work, to carve out a career from nothing.

He discovered something else in those first few weeks, something Ryan called the haunting beauty of war. He could find it in an olive-drab Huey in a rice field, a water buffalo bellowing in confusion at the interloper; in the face of a Montagnard woman carrying a pannier of vegetables, a long-legged black Marine staring back at her, a transistor radio held to his ear, an M-16 cradled on his knees; a hand lolling over the side of a stretcher; the face of a battle-haunted crew chief, the words *Burn Baby Burn* scrawled on his helmet.

It was a morbid and possibly unhealthy fascination. Whatever it was, one day he got back to the AP offices in Saigon and happened to glance at the photograph of the severed heads floating down the Mekong and the crude speech bubble scrawled on it in biro. And he caught himself grinning.

Crosby was grinning too when he came out of the office. 'These are great,' he said. He spread the black and whites on his desk. They were still sticky wet from the developing fluid. 'You've got a flair for this.'

Webb wondered whether he should feel proud. The images of the war stared back at him from the desk; a Marine firing a hooch with a Zippo lighter, towering over the Vietnamese woman who looked on in her black pyjamas, her face a portrait in anguish, two children screaming in panic around her legs; another Marine, head bowed, his helmet at his feet, his dead buddy lying a few feet away, a poncho thrown over his body so that only the oversized jungle boots protruded; a small girl, half her face disfigured from napalm, staring up at a huge black Marine sergeant in complete bewilderment.

'I have to be modest. Nixon deserves all the credit here,' Webb said.

'We can't use these,' Crosby said. He pushed two prints to the side; a row of decapitated VC heads, lined on a wall, cigarettes stuck in their mouths; a LURP with a necklace of ears. Their owner called them love beads.

'This one I love,' Crosby said, pushing one of the glossies across the desk, as if Webb hadn't seen it before.

It was the PFC from Ohio, a long, spindly farm boy with a mop of fair hair and huge ears. His buddies in the platoon had nicknamed him Flapper. He was sitting on the embankment in a rice paddy, his M-16 resting against his knees, his hands clasped as if in prayer. He was staring directly at the camera, his expression both wild and vacant.

'The thousand-yard stare,' Crosby said. 'You've got it right there.'

'Yeah,' Webb said. 'I got it right there.'

His name, ironically, was Judge. Webb had been in Quang Ngai province with a company from the Americal division. They had been patrolling a freefire zone, an area designated as hostile. The platoon Webb was with had lost five men that day to booby traps. One had fallen in a punji pit, and had been eviscerated on a wooden stake that had been sharpened to a point and smeared with excreta; another had picked up a booby-trapped teapot in one of the hooches and had lost both his hands; a third, the platoon clown, had seen a wooden plough abandoned in a paddy field and had been unable to resist the temptation of jumping behind it. As soon as he moved one of the handles it had released the pin on a grenade and he had been killed. Two Marines with him had sustained serious shrapnel wounds.

The platoon commander had retaliated by ordering his men to torch the village, killing all the animals they found – water buffalo, chickens, pigs. The mood among the men was dangerous.

* * *

It was late afternoon and the sun was swollen and the colour of copper. A Marine called Tonelli pointed to an old man leading a water buffalo across the rice paddy five hundred metres away. 'How come everyone in this damn country looks like Ho Chi fuckin' Minh?' he said.

'Maybe it is Ho Chi fuckin' Minh,' a black corporal said. He had *Death Is Nature's Way of Telling You to Fuck Off* scrawled on his helmet.

Tonelli unslung his M-16. 'Bet you five bucks I can drop the fuckin' water buffalo.'

'You couldn't hit jack shit from here, Tonelli.'

'Watch me, motherfucker.'

He fired a short burst, three rounds, as he had been trained to do. The buffalo dropped on to its knees. They could hear the farmer shouting in rage and despair as he tried to pull the wounded beast back to its feet.

'What do you think he's saying, Flapper?'

'I think he just called you a dick-grabbing, spaghetti-eating Mafioso, Tonelli.'

'Maybe I should teach him a lesson. Reckon I could just about zap that gook from here.' He fired another short burst and the others laughed. 'Missed the little motherfucker.'

'I told you, Tonelli. You couldn't hit your own dick with a howitzer.'

There was shouting from the front of the line. 'It's that fucking Lieutenant Bradley,' Tonelli said. 'What's his problem? We got a contact here.'

The black sergeant fired at the old Vietnamese. 'Shee-it,' he said. 'Missed the no-good motherfucker.'

'Lucky son of a bitch, ain't he?'

'No wonder you guys never hit any VC,' Judge said, laughing. 'You always aim too high.'

He was still laughing when he put the M-16 to his shoulder and pulled the trigger. Even from that distance they saw the man's conical straw hat disintegrate. His head seemed to explode and the almost decapitated body slid down the body of the dying water buffalo.

When Webb looked around Judge wasn't laughing any more.

The lieutenant bawled him out and threatened to put him on a charge. But they all knew it would never happen. More and more officers were getting fragged – having grenades tossed their way when they weren't looking – and Bradley was not going to risk becoming another victim over some dead gook peasant. Chalk him up to the VC body count and let the matter end there.

When they stopped to rest an hour later, Judge came looking for Webb. 'It was just a joke, right?' he said, looking for absolution from an outsider. 'I never meant to hit him or anything. We was just fooling around.'

'Sure,' Webb said. 'You were just fooling around.'

When Webb had joined Baker Company on that patrol, Judge had been nineteen. When Webb left them, three days later, he looked about thirty-five.

By then Tonelli had kicked a mine and was being choppered back to Long Binh. Webb had jumped on the same medevac. Just before it lifted off, Judge had grabbed his arm. 'I didn't mean to do it,' he said to Webb. 'I didn't mean to do it.'

'Had this guy just been in a firefight?' Crosby asked him.

Webb put the black and white back on the desk, his mind jolted back to the present. 'I guess you could say that,' he said.

## Bien Hoa

She was having supper in the mess hall, at a long table, with several other nurses and doctors from the ER. She looked up and saw him, and her expression changed from weariness to surprise. She stood up and came over. Webb was aware of heads turning in their direction.

'Hello,' he said.

'Hello yourself. You look exhausted. Where have you been?'

'Up at Quang Ngai with the Americal.'

'Yeah?'

'I only got back this afternoon.'

'Get some snaps for the family album?'

'Something like that.'

'You came straight out here?'

'Kind of.'

She seemed impressed with that. 'You eaten?'

'Not yet.'

'Better join us over at the mess.'

'Just some coffee, maybe.'

She made the introductions, and one of the surgeons made desultory conversation until she returned with the coffee, and then his attention returned to the shop talk of the others; a discussion about a surgical procedure that should have worked but didn't.

'How's your friend?' Mickey asked him.

'He's fine. He's got more scars than an old tomcat.'

'He was lucky. T&Ts – through and through gunshot wounds – almost count as minor wounds in here. Most of the guys we see . . .' She stopped herself. He guessed she didn't want to bore him – and herself – with more talk about the hospital. 'What brings you out this way?'

'You.'

She smiled, and somehow contrived to look like a little girl again. She had one of the most mobile faces he had ever seen; one minute she could look fifteen, the next fifty. She pushed an errant lock of hair out of her face and put her chin on her hand. 'Well, you know,' she said. 'One burning helicopter and I'm anybody's.' The smile fell away as abruptly as it had appeared. 'That wasn't fair. I'm bagged. I guess it's the heat. Plus I've been changing dressings on pseudomonas all afternoon. You ever seen guys with eighty and ninety per cent burns to . . . sorry. I don't think I'm in very good shape right now.'

'You look good to me.'

'That's sweet, but it's not true.' She finished her coffee. She was right, he thought. She looks exhausted, not just physically, but mentally and emotionally. She had the same look in her eyes he had seen in Private Judge's.

'A few of us are having drinks in the lieutenant's hooch. Want to come over?'

'Sure, why not?' he said.

The lieutenant was the hospital's neurosurgeon, halfway through his tour. The party was to celebrate the fact that he was over the Hump – halfway through his twelve-month service in Vietnam. His hooch was equipped with a record player and a refrigerator; Webb and Mickey arrived to Simon and Garfunkel's 'Mrs Robinson'. The doctors and techs and nurses were all drinking but none of them seemed drunk. There was shop talk, medical jargon Webb didn't understand, complaints about the 'lifers' and the army regulations. A few people were talking about the first things they were going to do when they got home.

Mickey drifted away among the crowd. For a while Webb thought he had been dumped. He stayed for a while, talking to an ER tech from Georgia who wanted to tell him about the trout fishing in the Alleghenies. Webb was about to leave when Mickey magically reappeared at his side. 'Let's go back to my room,' she whispered.

Mickey shared a hooch with five other nurses, and her room was not much bigger than a store cupboard. There was room for a bed and a small wardrobe with hanging space, little else.

She flopped down on the bed and Webb shut the door. The only light in the room filtered through a small window that opened on to the compound. 'I'm drunk, Hugh,' she said. She put up both her hands, like a child, to indicate that she wanted him to take off her T-shirt. Afterwards she lay back on the bed and slid out of her fatigue pants. She lay on her back, in her underwear.

She held out her arms. 'You want to sleep with me?'

Webb looked at her. He guessed that in a few moments she would be asleep. 'I'm not big on necrophilia,' he said.

'Oh boy, dead people. If it's corpses you want, I can really help you out there.'

Her arms flopped back to her sides. Webb lay beside her on the narrow cot, and put his arms around her. She snuggled her face into his chest. He felt wetness on his T-shirt. She was crying. 'It's okay,' he said.

'No, it's not okay. It's never going to be okay.'

He didn't know what to say or do and so he just held her.

After a while he no longer felt the trembling in her shoulders and he knew she had stopped crying. He thought she was asleep. But then she whispered, 'I'm all right now.'

He felt her fingers stroking his cheek.

'We had a mas-cal this morning,' she said. 'Two a.m. You wake up and you get out of bed, you're still mostly asleep, and you find yourself looking at an eighteen-year-old kid, a virgin, doesn't even shave yet, and he's had his penis blown away by a bouncing mine. On the next gurney you got a guy who tells you his wife has just had a baby. And you lift up the dressings and you know he's never going to see that baby because something just blew up in his face and he's going to be blind. And he's not going to be able to throw that kid a ball either because the same booby trap that took his eyes took his hands as well.'

Webb held her tighter.

'Then, right in the middle of this good shit, we have to wheel an NVA chest wound into theatre. And the guy with no eyes and no hands is still waiting in the corridor and we've got this fucking NVA colonel in there. Because that's triage procedure, because the NVA is not stable and protocol says he's next to go. But Nurse Mickey van Himst puts on her latex gloves and spits on them. If he gets an infection and dies, well, fuck him. See, I wanted him to die. I wanted to push him right off that gurney and leave him there to choke on his own blood. Only now I'm ashamed, because now the war owns me too, it's made me hate like everyone else. It's made me so I don't know who or what the hell I am any more.'

Webb stared into the darkness and thought about the teenage Viet Cong he had made no move to help when the Ranger was torturing him, about PFC McCague, killed posing for a photograph that eventually earned him sixty dollars from AP.

'We all do things we're ashamed of,' he said. 'It doesn't mean we're bad people.'

'Yes it does,' she said. She curled into him like a child, and he held her. After a while her breathing became deep and even and he realised she was asleep.

Some time during the night he heard the hum of rotors, and then someone running down the corridor outside, hammering on the doors. 'Let's go, Mickey. Mas-cal. We're on!'

By the time he had dragged himself from his own pit of sleep she was already out of bed, fumbling in the darkness for her clothes. He raised himself on his elbows and peered into the dark, but by then the door was yawning open and she was gone. He saw the other nurses running out of the hooch.

At dawn the helicopters were still coming, landing one after the other on the pad outside the hospital. Webb got dressed and drove back to Saigon. By ten o'clock that morning he was back in the Delta with the 25th.

# 8

The cathedral was on the Tu Do, across the road from the post office, a monstrosity in red brick. Ryan had not been inside a cathedral – or any church – for over ten years. He sat at the back during the service, and neglected the opportunity to take confession. He did not think the priest had all day to sit there and listen to his litany of sins, and besides, it would be a hypocrisy. In the circumstances.

He watched her at the brass communion rail, her hands joined in prayer, eyes closed. Ryan, also on his knees, could not take his eyes from her. Perhaps he alone of the congregation did not, at that moment, have his mind on the Eternal.

Candles threw dancing shadows on the walls.

What am I to do?

Odile had asked the question many times, but the Divine had so far withheld judgment; at least the sign she had been seeking was not evident to her yet. She had asked to be free of her burden. She had asked for some clear signal that if she chose this other way her soul would not be for ever stained by her own carnality. She wanted to live as simply as other women. In the darkness of the cathedral she looked for grace.

If only it could ever be that simple. She looked up at Christ's tortured body on the Cross and asked for strength. She raised her face to the Madonna and begged for purity. She stared into the candles on the altar and prayed for faith. But it was not there.

For the first time she questioned her own future. Just a few weeks ago, before she had met Ryan, her choices in life had been clear. She knew her place in the world and she had accepted it, if not with joy then with resignation. But what had been clear had been muddied. He confused her. He had raised for her the question: why can I not live like other women?

She wished he had not brought her this hope. He had offered

her the faintest promise of personal happiness over a life of value and belonging. It had to be an illusion conjured by the Devil. She would push him away for as long as she had the strength.

After she had accepted Communion, Odile rose from the altar steps and walked, head bowed, back to the pews. For a moment she raised her eyes and she saw him, in the shadows at the back of the church, and her eyes widened in recognition and surprise, and then she knelt down beside her fellow nuns, her back towards him, and lowered her head once more in prayer.

After the Mass he found her on the steps outside, with the canonesse and several other novitiates from the convent, in conversation with the French curé and a Catholic Vietnamese family. When she saw him she left the group and approached him.

'Monsieur Ryan.'

'I have to see you again,' he said.

The canonesse had turned away from her conversation with the priest and was watching them.

'This is so easy for you. Not so easy for me.'

'Easy? Falling in love with a nun is easy?'

Her eyes went wide. She looked around at the canonesse, and then back at Ryan. 'Do not say it if you do not mean it.'

'I mean it.'

She bit her lip, hesitating, then she seemed to make up her mind. 'Tomorrow. In the Botanical Gardens. Ten o'clock.'

She walked away.

He knew the rest of the novices were watching, their eyes lidded with disapproval. Bugger them all. He'd had enough of nuns to last him a lifetime.

Except for this one.

# 9

The caretaker at the Hashish Hilton was a Vietnamese called Duc, who had almost inevitably been rechristened Donald by the tenants. Donald acted as their intermediary with the Tonkinese landlady, and organised their food and their laundry, cronying the work out between members of his immediate family, who all lived in one of the downstairs rooms. For a little extra he procured opium or girls.

When Ryan got back to his apartment he found Cochrane lying on his bed, smoking opium. Donald's uncle lay on the floor, on some raffia matting, lighting pipes for Cochrane and for Prescott, who sat in Ryan's chair by the window. Mick Jagger was wailing his way through 'Paint It Black'. Webb sat at the foot of the bed, smoking a large opium-laced cigarette. The air conditioner had broken again and the air was thick with pungent opium smoke.

'Sean,' Webb said.

'Spider,' Ryan said. It was an Australian tradition, Ryan had explained to him. All whites were called Chalkie, anyone with ginger hair was called Blue, and anybody called Webb was Spider.

'How's the arm?'

'Still bloody sore. You got back from Quang Ngai in one piece?'

'Brought you this,' Webb said. He held up two bottles of Courvoisier. 'From the PX at Danang. A small token of my esteem. That bullet in your shoulder had my name on it.'

'Then it's a bloody good job you've got a short name, mate.' Ryan took the proffered bottles. 'Been hearing great things about you. Croz reckons you're David Bailey in jungle greens.' He unscrewed the Courvoisier and fetched two beer glasses. He splashed some brandy in each. 'Health.'

'Long life.'

'Christ, no. If I thought I was going to have a long life I'd have to start eating properly and taking care of myself. Jesus, will you look at those two reprobates?'

Cochrane was asleep. Prescott was staring dreamily out of the window, smiling.

Ryan sat down on the end of the bed, resting the Courvoisier on one knee. Dust drifted on the yellow light that slanted through the blinds. Heat, shirts sticky with sweat, the muted honking of Saigon traffic. 'So. You've been here six weeks. Have you figured out a reasonable political solution for the Vietnam question?'

'Not yet.'

'That's good, because I've been here three years and I'm stuffed if I know what's going on.'

'I don't think the Americans can win.'

'Shit, everyone knows that, from Nixon down. Just as well. I don't think they should win.'

'I don't know about that.' Webb swallowed some brandy. 'I don't like what the Americans are doing here. But I think I'd like the communists a lot less.'

'That's what you think, is it?'

'Yes, that's what I think.'

Ryan savoured the brandy, rolling it around his tongue. 'Think about it, Spider. We're supposed to be saving these people from communism. Which people? Most of the population live out in the boonies, they grow some rice, the family car is a water buffalo. Democracy, communism, it's all the same to them. The only thing they know for sure they don't like is napalm. Is it really going to make bugger all difference to them who runs the country?'

'Then why is everyone in Saigon so scared of the communists?'

'Because the Americans have filled their heads with shit.'

Webb shook his head. 'I don't know. I think the Americans are here for the right reasons. They're just going about it the wrong way.'

'Know what this American colonel said to me the other day? He had the perfect solution for Vietnam, he reckoned. First, you go round the whole country, get everyone you're absolutely certain is on your side and you put them on a boat. You sail that boat into the China Sea. Then you nuke the whole country, north and south. And then . . .' Ryan drained his brandy and poured another. '. . . then you sink the boat. For Christ's sake, how are you going to win hearts and minds with that attitude? And don't tell me he's Robinson Crusoe. Ninety per cent of the Yanks, from the generals down, think the same way.'

'Does it matter what they think if they get the right result?'

'What's the right result?'

Webb shrugged his shoulders, knowing Ryan's argument was more persuasive. 'If you have any better ideas I'm sure Abrams would love to hear them. Trying to find the Viet Cong is like trying to find a needle in the proverbial haystack.'

'Know how the Americans find a needle in a haystack? They napalm the haystack and anything that's left is going to be a needle.'

Webb didn't have an answer for him. He had come to Vietnam to make a name for himself as a journalist and a photographer, but every day he was becoming more scared and more confused by the moral dilemmas that were thrown in his face. What had seemed like a simple war between his own country's traditional allies and the communists, a word he had equated with villainy from childhood, had been filtered through his own experience into a conflict far more complex, more tragic, more disturbing. But if the Viet Cong were fighting for the right to govern their own country after all, it did not necessarily mean that the young Americans he had seen fight and suffer and die in the jungles and rice paddies were wrong, too. To say so in his despatches would seem like a betrayal of their courage. They had not asked to be here.

Ryan finished his brandy. Webb held out the bottle and poured three fingers into his glass. The combination of opium and brandy was making him feel light-headed. 'You ever think of getting out of Vietnam?' he said.

Ryan shook his head. 'Not me. It's not much of a war,' he said, 'but right now it's the only one I've got.'

The noise of the Saigon traffic was muted here, and almost drowned by the chirrup of crickets. A few old amahs squatted on their haunches on the grass and sparrows argued and fluttered in the bushes.

Ryan wandered around the gardens for almost half an hour before he found her, sitting alone on a wooden bench in the shade of a giant tamarind tree. She was wearing a white silk *ao dai* with a mandarin collar, her hands clutched tightly at her knees. She looked as fragile as porcelain.

He sat down beside her. She did not look up.

He wanted desperately to touch her, to tell her it was all right. 'Odile,' he said.

He had not called her 'sister', as she was accustomed. 'Monsieur Ryan,' she said, carefully.

'I thought you might not come.'

'Of course I must come. I promise you.'

It was sticky hot. His shoulder itched under the heavy swathe of bandages. 'I can't stop thinking about you, Odile. Night and day. I even dream about you.' He turned and looked at her. 'Bad dreams.'

'It is a sin. You must ask for absolution.'

'From you?'

'From your priest. Your confessor.'

'I don't have a confessor.'

She would not meet his eyes. But she knew what this was about, Ryan thought. If she did not want me to tell her I loved her, she would not have come here today.

'You make my life impossible,' she whispered.

'Like you're making mine.'

'I do not do anything to you.'

'You drive me crazy. Isn't that enough?'

She stood up. 'If you do not stop, I will go.'

'Okay,' he said. 'Okay. I'm sorry.'

She sat down again, slowly. 'If you do not confess your thoughts, you will be damned.'

'Damned if I do, damned if I don't,' Ryan said. He grabbed her hand. She tried to pull away.

'Listen, I haven't met many women that I've really admired. Not just for their looks, for what they are.'

'It is impossible for us. I come here today to tell you this.'

'Is this what you want? Do you really want to shut yourself away for the rest of your life knowing there was a bloke who was crazy about you, who loved you with a passion, who would have married you and given you children? I've never known a woman like you, never. I want you, Odile. I want you more than I've ever wanted anything. I won't let you walk away from me. I won't lose you. I won't.'

She was breathing very fast. He noticed the fluttery rise and fall of her breast beneath the *ao dai*. I mean what I say, Ryan assured himself. Right now, I mean it.

He reached up with his good arm and stroked her hair. 'You've got the most beautiful eyes I've ever seen,' hc said, and his voice was gentler now, almost dreamy. 'It's like looking into the ocean.'

She moved away from him on the bench. 'I must have time to think,' she said.

She stood up abruptly and walked away, slim and straight, a nun in white silk, leaving the ghosts of patchouli and incense. The most exotic creature he had ever seen.

God forgive me, he thought.

Odile walked quickly, blindly, her head aching. She realised she was breathing too fast, tried to fight her body's instincts to run, to cry. She had come here today to end this, to return to the safety of a life ordered by duty, by virtue. But it was as if she had been in a dark room all her life and now her jailer had left open a door, just a little, enough to let in a shaft of light. Impossible not to approach that door, to want to see beyond.

If only her faith were a little stronger. But she knew in her heart that the convent was not a home, but a haven, and that all that frightened her now was her own fear.

'What are you thinking about?' Mickey asked him.

'Nothing,' Webb said, forcing the face of Private Judge from his mind.

'We have an agreement, remember?'

He did remember. He would not talk about his work, and she would not talk about hers. But some of the sharper memories had a way of forcing themselves unbidden into his consciousness, and lately it was happening more and more often.

Mickey finished her beer and Webb signalled the waiter for another. They were in the Royale, a seedy, once glorious old hotel in a side street between the Tu Do and the Nguyen Hue, the Street of Flowers. Outside, the street boiled in the noonday sun.

'My Mister Nice Guy,' she said.

'How do you mean?'

'Last time you were up at Bien Hoa I was rolling drunk. You could have done what you wanted.'

'How do you know I didn't?'

'No cold, sticky mess in the middle of the night. It's where women first learn their job in life is to clean up after men.'

He grinned. 'You were upset. It didn't seem right.'

'Please, don't say stuff like that. Before I know it, I'll end up liking you.'

'I went to an English grammar school. We were taught to be polite.'

'I've seen a movie about an English school. Did you wear black cloaks and roast little boys over hot fires every day?'

'No, that's only in public schools. They're called public schools because they're private. I went to a grammar school. That's different. You only get to roast young boys on special occasions. Christmas, Easter.'

'It sounds quaint.'

'Yes, I suppose it was. The beatings were a drag, though. The sodomy was the best part.'

She laughed. 'I never met an Englishman before. A pity. I watched a lot of movies back home with Englishmen in them and I always loved the accent.'

'What actors in particular?'

'Sean Connery. Nach. And Michael Caine.'

'Sean Connery isn't really English. He's Scots. Michael Caine's a Cockney.'

'What's a Cockney?'

'It's someone born around the East End of London.'

'You don't talk like either of them. Where are you from?'

'A place called Kingston-upon-Thames. It's just outside London.'

'What's it like?'

'Well, nothing like Saigon.'

She grinned. 'Does it have thatched cottages and a haunted church and a duke and everything?'

He shook his head. 'I grew up in a semi-detached bungalow in a street where all the houses looked the same. My father worked in an insurance office in London and we went to Brighton for our holidays. You have no idea.'

'If this place is better, then it must have been a real bummer.'

Their lunch arrived. A sallow-faced Vietnamese in a white jacket brought a tray with two plates under silver covers. He set them in front of them and removed the covers with a flourish; two small water buffalo steaks and two spherical mounds of mashed potato.

'I've been safe all my life,' he said. 'It was killing me.'

It struck her as a curious thing to say. Mickey had been safe all her life, too, and she saw nothing wrong with it. It was the death and the suffering at the ER in Bien Hoa that she wanted to get away from. She had eighty-three days and a wake-up to go.

'I don't know why anyone would want to come here without being forced to,' she said.

He gave her a small self-deprecating smile, as if that were all the explanation that was needed. She wondered how far he thought he might go in life with that charming smile. All the way, she supposed, and he was probably right. He was good-looking, in a boyish sort of way, long and lean and very . . . English. But underneath the shy surface there was occasionally a flash of steel, and it made him both intriguing and a little dangerous. She had already decided to go to bed with him. There had been precious few opportunities for anything but work since she had been in Vietnam and she was too proud to surrender to the casual and arrogant invitations of the ER surgeons. Vietnam had had little enough to recommend it; she intended to take with her at least one pleasant interlude.

'I was eighteen years old when I realised I really didn't have any talent,' he said, suddenly and for no reason.

She stopped eating and stared at him. 'What makes you think you have no talent? Everyone has something they're good at.'

'That's different from talent. When you have a real talent things just happen for you. When you don't, you have to take risks. Try and be in the right place at the right time. Or else you're just . . . sentenced to mediocrity.'

'You have a talent,' she said.

'No, I have a camera. That doesn't make me a photographer. I don't have a talent, but I do have Vietnam.' He gave her another of those enigmatic smiles.

Mickey thought about the endless relay of helicopters that brought the bleeding remnants of the war to the emergency room and tried to think of it in his terms, as a stepping stone to a career. She couldn't. 'Was going back to that burning helicopter for the wounded lieutenant a part of the game plan?'

'Like I said, you shamed me into it. Anyway, enough of that. We agreed we weren't going to talk shop.'

She ignored that. Now they had started talking, she wanted to understand this a little better. 'Do you enjoy it, Hugh?'

'Funny, they told me I would. But no. No. You get used to it, in a way, but you don't enjoy it. At least I don't.'

'I guess that's good.'

'Is it? I have no idea.' He finished his steak and pushed the plate away. 'Do you think I'm a bastard?'

'I don't know you well enough.'

He grinned at that. 'Sometimes I think I am. When you're taking photographs of someone who's lying there with his legs . . . then there was this other time. I was on a medevac. There was a Marine lieutenant, holding a bloody compress to a chest wound, there was blood in his hair, caked in his ears, one eye bandaged up, and he leaned forward and tapped me on the shoulder. I thought he was going to swear at me. Know what he said? Could I take a photograph of him so he could send it to his wife.' He fidgeted with the ashtray on the tablecloth between them. 'We weren't going to talk about this.'

'It's my fault, I guess. I was the one asking the questions.'

'But did you want to hear the answers?'

She put her hand over his. 'Perhaps we both just need to forget about all of it for a while. Not talk at all.'

Another of the shy smiles. 'What would you like to do this afternoon, then?'

'I'll leave that to you,' she whispered.

A dusty yellow light filtered through the cane blinds. The room was steamy hot, perfumed with incense, tendrils of smoke drifting to the ceiling, stirred by the slow fan on the ceiling. A pale gekko darted along the wall.

Mickey pushed back the tangled sheet, raised her arms above her head, let the sweat cool on her body, her heart hammering in her chest. After a while she sat up, knelt astride his thighs. She leaned forward so that her hair grazed his face. His eyes blinked open and he smiled at her.

'You were wrong,' she whispered.

'About what?'

'You have an enormous talent,' she said. 'Absolutely enormous.'

# 10

'I have to see Soeur Odile,' Ryan said.

'*C'est impossible*,' the old nun said. '*Au revoir, monsieur*.' She shook her head and tried to close the heavy wooden door, but Ryan kept his foot there.

'Please.'

'*C'est impossible*,' Soeur Marie repeated, the wizened monkey face peering through the crack, her eyes bright and angry.

Ryan put his weight against the door and gently forced it open. Soeur Marie squealed in alarm. Ryan squeezed inside.

'You cannot!' she screamed at him.

Ryan grinned at her. 'Trust me. I'm a Catholic,' he said.

A man's voice had never before disturbed the crystal sanctity of the Vespers. Every face in the tiny chapel turned to stare at the intruder. Ryan strode in, Soeur Marie at his heels like a fussing hen. He stopped at the head of the aisle and looked straight at her.

There was no need for words. Odile looked back at him, and it seemed to her in that moment that the decision had been taken from her. He raised his hands in a helpless gesture as if he were saying *I can't help this. Neither can you.*

The canonesse rose from her knees to confront him. Ryan smiled, and after a few moments he backed slowly from the chapel. His eyes did not leave Odile's face. She felt the other novices staring, and her cheeks burned with embarrassment. But her heart bounded, and inside, mingled with the shame, was another emotion, something she had not felt since she was a child.

Joy.

She heard doors banging in the hooch, dragging her up from a pit of sleep. In the distance, through the receding mist of dreams, she heard the distant whump-whump-whump of the medevac rotors. She tried to focus on the green dial of her watch.

Someone hammered a fist on her door and threw it open. 'Mickey, we're on!' The light hurt her eyes. She heard running footsteps, rolled out of her cot and fumbled for her fatigues. 'Come on, kiddo, mas-cal!' another voice shouted at her.

I just want to sleep.

She stumbled out of the hooch, her boot laces dragging on the ground. The first Hueys were settling on the landing pads. The roar of the rotors was deafening; dirt and grit picked up by the downdraught stung her face and eyes.

I can't do this any more.

I can't face another boy with no legs.

'Mickey, c'mon!'

She saw a doctor and two nurses running towards one of the Hueys with a gurney. Instinctively she started running with them. Please God, get me through another night.

The canonesse looked out of the window to the courtyard below. The big Australian towered over the orphanage children, as happy and exuberant as a large dog, shouting and laughing with them as they kicked a plastic football around the quadrangle. He was as much a child as they were, she thought. And he had a good heart. But like a child he could cause a lot of damage without intention. That was the problem.

She turned back to the room with a sigh. Soeur Odile sat with her head bowed, in deference to the canonesse, but her posture and the set of her shoulders were rigid with determination.

'You intend to marry him?' the canonesse said.

'Yes, Mother.'

'When?'

Soeur Odile did not answer.

'I hope you have thought this through.'

'I trust him, Mother.'

'I do not speak against him. He has been one of our benefactors. But charity and responsibility are not always found in the same person.'

'I have made up my mind.'

'Yes, I was afraid of that.'

The canonesse sat down at her desk. Her study was plain; a wooden crucifix on the wall above the desk, three straight-backed wooden chairs, a prie-dieu in one corner, a black Bible open on the lectern. A rosary clicked softly between her fingers.

'Each of us must choose the way for ourselves, Soeur Odile. I only want you to make the right decision.'

'Yes, Mother.'

Beauty was a curse, she thought. It disguised so many other, more lasting imperfections. She wondered if Ryan really understood young Odile at all. The girl was sincere, and she too had a good heart, but she was not bright, and she had no knowledge of the world outside of her cloistered upbringing in Dalat. She had spent the last two years inside these four walls in Cholon. Perhaps Ryan had mistaken vacuity for mystery. She really was no match for such a man.

'When you leave us, you may never be able to return. You understand this?'

'I understand.'

'Do you really understand what you are doing, Odile? Do you really know this man?'

'I love him.'

The old woman sighed. The young fell in love so easily, and placed such store by it, yet they perhaps knew least about it. The canonesse had come late to her vocation and knew just how painful an emotion it could be. Her own parents had showed her that. 'May God go with you,' she said.

Ryan's voice echoed from the courtyard below, over the shouts of the children. Loud, ebullient, masculine. Everything Odile would not find in her cloistered life here.

'Would you like to pray with me?' the canonesse asked.

'Yes, Mother.'

And so they closed their eyes and prayed, but all the while she knew Odile was longing to flee for the door, like a schoolgirl detained to finish her homework. Only the canonesse prayed, truly prayed, that some good would come from this liaison, but she had known the world too long to feel confident that all life's stories ended well.

Webb spent two weeks up-country, living out of the Press Centre at Danang. When he got back to Saigon the Hashish Hilton had undergone a radical change. Nixon had gone. As Crosby told the story, Cochrane's Vietnamese girlfriend had been sitting in the room one night when the monkey had begun masturbating on the bookshelf behind her. At the inevitable conclusion of Nixon's performance the girl had felt something wet and warm on the back of her neck. She had screamed, grabbed the animal by the tail and tossed it out of the window.

He came, she got sore, he was conquered, as Crosby put it.

Crosby had moved into Ryan's top-floor room. Ryan's paraphernalia had all gone: the ashtray made from the shell casing, the NVA pith helmet with the red star, the Leica with the grenade fragment lodged in the lens, the meat safe where he kept his stock of marijuana. Crosby was sprawled on a hard divan chair, a can of Koors in one hand and a large joint in the other. He was stoned as well as drunk, red-eyed and remorselessly solemn.

He looked up as Webb walked in. 'The wanderer returns,' he said.

'Where's Sean?' Webb asked, experiencing a cold chill of alarm. 'He's okay?'

'Yeah, he's fine,' Crosby said. 'Moved out. Got himself a live-in girlfriend.'

'Sean?'

'Yep. I know it's hard to believe, but they do say fact is stranger than fiction. We've had some changes here while you've been gone. Cochrane got his ass transferred back to Washington DC. Hell, he was only here because he wanted it on his CV. Prescott moved on also.'

'Where did he go?'

'All over the place.' Crosby said.

'What?'

'He was with an ARVN company in the Delta. The guy in front of him stepped on a three-hundred-pound mine, man. They say there wasn't enough left of him to fit into a helmet.'

'Oh, Christ.'

'No one promised us a rose garden, boy. He didn't have to be here. None of us has to be here.' He blew smoke at the ceiling. 'Oh, man, I am going to miss him, though.'

Webb threw his duffel bag and cameras on the bed. He sat down, took the joint from Crosby and drew on it.

'We moved your gear into Cochrane's pad. If I rotate or step on a mine, the AC is yours.'

'I can live without air conditioning.'

'Easy to say this time of year.' He leaned forward. Webb could make out the thready streaks of the capillaries in his eyes. 'Ryan sure was pissed about Prescott. Said he owed him three hundred bucks and now he'll never collect.'

'Three hundred bucks? What for?'

'The nun, man. That bastard. He really made it with the nun.'

Webb hitched a ride out to Bien Hoa, arriving just before sunset. He walked across the compound to the hospital. Inside, the tech from Georgia was busy on one of the wards, changing wound dressings. Webb asked him where he could find Mickey, was told she was still over at the ER.

There was an orderly row of body bags outside the Emergency Room, lying on the dirt under a scraggly banana palm, lined up for their last inspection. Webb felt somehow indecent just walking past them as if they were just so much cordwood. He felt an insane impulse to salute, to bow his head, anything but just ignore them. They should get some show of respect, he thought, whatever good it would do them now.

He went inside.

It was quiet; the afternoon's casualties had been processed, two nurses were monitoring the last of the post-ops. Webb found Mickey in another room with the expectants – those soldiers who were too badly wounded to save. There was just one soldier left in there; he still had his fatigues and his jungle boots on, and his head was swathed in blood-soaked bandages so that it appeared to be almost twice its normal size. Mickey stood next to the gurney, holding his hand.

She looked up and saw Webb in the doorway. 'Another day in paradise,' she said. She looked down at the boy on the litter. 'We gave him one hundred and twenty units of blood. In the end he had so much new blood in him it just wouldn't clot. Now his whole head is leaking.'

She doesn't have to do this, Webb thought. The kid would be snowed with so much morphine he probably didn't even know she was there.

'It's not long now.'

'I'll wait outside,' he said.

When she came out, the quick tropical dark had fallen. There were flashes on the horizon, and Webb could feel vibrations underfoot as the B-52s carpet-bombed the jungle near the Cambodian border. Lights blazed on the apron as a Chinook dropped down from the night.

She stood in the doorway of the ER, a fragile silhouette. 'Well. Long time no see.'

'I've been up at Danang. Went out to Pleiku and the Highlands.'

'Get around, huh?'

'You know how it is. You have to hustle or you can miss some of the war.' He had meant it as a joke and it came out sounding trite and hollow. 'You okay?' he asked her.

'Sure I'm okay, I do this all the time. Walk me to the mess hall?' She reached for his fingers, held them. 'So. How have you been?'

'Cold and wet and muddy. How about you?'

'Hot and dry and clean. Want to change places?'

He thought about the young soldier in the expectants' room. 'Not really.'

'I got thirty-three days and a wake-up to go.'

He felt at once relieved for her, disappointed for himself. 'You're nearly there,' he said.

'Hey, I'll miss this place,' she said. He couldn't see her face in the darkness. He wished he could. She stopped walking. 'Look, Hugh, this isn't a good idea.'

'What isn't a good idea?'

'You and me.'

He felt suddenly sick as if he had swallowed cold oil. He knew whatever she wanted to say he didn't want to hear. 'I thought . . . I thought we were kind of good for each other. Didn't you?'

'Yeah, I feel that way too. But you know what's going to happen if you stick around. I'm going to get these feelings for you, not just when I'm horny, the other stuff, the stuff most guys hate. Then before you know it, I'm back in the world, and you're still here. And I spend the next God knows how long waiting to find out if you're going to end up like one of these sorry bastards I see in here every day. And you aren't here just for a tour. Are you? You could be here for years. Right?'

He didn't answer her. She was right. He had no plans to leave. He was only just starting to make a go of things.

'No, sorry, forget it. This hasn't got a future. Let's stop it now before it starts.'

'Mickey . . .'

'You want to come back with me to the world, maybe I'll think about it again. But you don't want to do that, do you?'

There was nothing he could think of to say.

'Please, please, please, don't do this to me. I've had enough for one war. A month from now I'm getting out of here and I don't want to remember a thing about this place. Not one damned thing.'

'So that's it?'

'Yeah, I guess so.'

She let go of his hand and started to walk away across the compound, towards the lights of the mess hall. But then she stopped and turned around. 'Don't let anyone ever tell you you don't have talent. Okay?'

'Will you send me a reference?'

'You don't need a reference, scout. Just put me on your CV, you'll get by.'

She walked back. For a moment he had the insane hope that she had changed her mind. Instead she stood on her toes and kissed him on the lips. 'Take care,' she said.

And then she was gone.

Webb stood in the darkness for a long time. What the hell, the soldiers always said. It don't mean nothin' to me. 'Shit,' he said under his breath. Well, that was the way it was, he supposed. Just forget it, Hugh. It was nice while it lasted but you won't see her again.

# 11

At night the roof of the Caravelle offered a ringside view of the war. Webb cradled his beer and watched as a violet dusk silhouetted the palm trees on the far bank of the Saigon River. The first wave of Phantoms roared over the jungle and he heard someone say: 'Show's about to start, folks.'

A magnesium-white flare dropped down the sky. Red and green fingers of tracers probed the jungle, and in the distance the orange muzzle flash of heavy artillery danced around the horizon like sheet lightning. The glasses on the table clinked to the earthquake rumble of battle.

Webb shook his head. The most expensive pyrotechnics show on earth.

His guts felt like lead. Mickey van Himst had caught her Freedom Bird that afternoon. *Don't mean nothin' to me.*

He nursed his beer and listened to the conversation around him. Crosby had told him you could get better information here than at the Five O'clock Follies. JUSPAO and MacVee officials, as well as Army and Marine headquarters staff, sat around on the rooftop bar with their wives or their Vietnamese girlfriends, watching the military's pyrotechnics and engaging in shop talk.

'Hey, did you hear we lost eight guys from the 25th to friendly fire in the Delta this morning?'

'Shoot, I heard it was an F-4 dropped short.'

'No, it was a Dakota, man. I was there. The pilot had the grid numbers screwed up. They lost two officers from Alpha company. Eight dead, fifteen wounded. Abrams went apeshit.'

Interesting, Webb thought. At the JUSPAO briefing the press officer had acknowledged that the 25th had taken losses from friendly fire, but described casualties as 'light'. But then, in this war, 'light' and 'heavy' were all a matter of perspective.

'Spider,' someone said. He looked up. It was Ryan. The sling and bandages were off his shoulder and he was hand in hand with a Eurasian woman, slim as a reed in an *ao dai* of violet silk. Webb stared; she was one of the most exotic, exquisite creatures he had ever seen, one of those women whose beauty is so perfect it is almost intimidating.

After a moment he remembered his manners, stood up and held out a chair for her.

Ryan grinned at him. 'Christ, you're such a gentleman, Spider. Is that for me?'

The woman smiled. 'Thank you, monsieur,' she said to Webb, sitting down.

'Watch me, you could learn something,' Webb said to him.

'Can't teach an old dog to change his spots,' Ryan grinned back. 'Odile, this is a friend of mine. Hugh Webb. One of Saigon's celebrated press corps. A pom, but never mind. Hugh, this is Miss Odile Ngai.'

Webb shook her hand. It was cool and soft. 'Pleased to meet you,' he said.

He was aware that heads had turned their way, and that a number of men were openly staring at Odile. Hard not to stare. Christ, typical of Ryan to land a woman like this. Some guys had all the luck.

Ryan ordered another round of drinks.

'How's the shoulder?' Webb said.

'Aches like buggery, but I'm back into the traces tomorrow. Thought I'd head down to the Delta for a couple of days, see how I go. I've had enough bludging around in Saigon. I'm bored out of my brains.' Webb saw a shadow of hurt pass across the girl's face. Ryan realised what he'd said, and reached for her hand. 'Only Odile here has kept me sane.'

'Odile. Pretty name. French?'

'*Bui doi*,' she said. Dust of life, the name the Vietnamese gave abandoned Eurasian children.

The deprecation hung in the awkward silence. A waiter brought two more beers, and a *citron pressé* for Odile.

'I've organised to go into the Cradle,' Ryan said. The Cradle; an area in the Mekong Delta totally controlled by the Viet Cong, infested with booby traps, rarely patrolled by government or American troops. 'The ARVN Seventh Division HQ is at My Tho. Probably take me a couple of days to get there. I'll have to get down by road the rest of the way to Ben Tre, then out on a chopper to Kien Hoa province.'

Webb listened to this madness without comment. Ryan made it sound so simple. To get to Kien Hoa itself would mean travelling by jeep through Viet Cong territory.

He saw the girl reach out and touch Ryan's hand, a proprietary gesture, as if trying to remind herself that he was really there, perhaps steeling herself for the time when he would be gone.

'How was Danang?' Ryan asked him.

'It's a beach resort. The Highlands are a little more interesting.'

'You are a photographer also?' Odile asked him.

Ryan grinned. 'He reckons he is. A few months ago he was still wet behind the ears. It was his fault I got this.' He patted his wounded shoulder. 'This black Marine sergeant shouted "Everybody get down!" and Spider stood up and started dancing.'

Webb smiled, but he had heard this joke from Ryan a hundred times before. 'My guardian angel was watching over me that day.'

'Bullshit. It was me saved your hide. Credit where credit's due.'

Odile ignored Ryan's outburst. 'You believe in God, then, Monsieur Webb?'

'Sometimes. Mostly just when it suits me, I'm afraid.' He noticed the gold crucifix at her throat. 'You're Catholic, Miss Ngai?'

She looked away. 'Not a good Catholic, I think.'

'She's being modest,' Ryan said. 'She was one of Rome's stormtroopers till I rescued her from the convent.'

He saw another flicker of pain on the girl's face, but Ryan did not notice. He's like a big dog in a china shop, Webb thought. He blunders about, meaning no real harm, destroying everything just by wagging his tail.

So, she had spent some time in the convent. It should have been obvious, by the way she sat, never crossing her legs, her hands folded demurely in her lap, her fingers toying with an imagined rosary. And then he suddenly remembered what Crosby had said about Prescott, and he felt a surge of disgust. The pieces fell into place. This was Ryan's nun.

'You all right, mate?' Ryan said.

Webb shook his head. 'You're unbelievable.'

'What's wrong?'

'Did you ever get your three hundred dollars?'

The smile froze on Ryan's face. Odile was staring at him, eyes bright, anticipating some new pain.

'That was a joke, Spider,' Ryan said, his voice hard. 'Let's leave it out.'

Odile knew this remark concerned her, and she was absorbed by Ryan's reaction. The guilt was etched on his face like graffiti. 'Sean?' she said, waiting for an explanation. But he refused to look at her.

'Thanks a lot,' he said to Webb.

Webb regretted the jibe now, but it was too late to retreat. Instead he said, 'I guess you must be bloody proud of yourself.'

'You know how it is, Spider. When Crosby told me Prescott was dead, I didn't know what to say. He was an old mate of mine. You don't go bursting into tears, so I said the first thing that came into my head.'

'What is this about, Sean?' Odile repeated. 'Why is he angry at you?'

Webb did not know what had made him say it. Perhaps outrage; he had expected more from Ryan. Ryan was his friend and his mentor and he had looked up to him. He felt almost personally betrayed and he wanted to punish him. He did not give a thought then to what effect the truth might have on Odile. What was it they said about the truth? It doesn't set people free, it just makes them miserable.

'Someone bet Ryan three hundred dollars he couldn't seduce a nun,' he heard himself say.

To give her her due, Webb thought later, Odile behaved with breathtaking dignity. He watched her gather herself, waiting for Ryan to contradict this version of events, and when he did not she carefully set her drink on the table, only the slight tremor in her hand betraying the turmoil of emotion inside. 'I see,' she said.

Ryan still would not look at her. He was staring at Webb, his face a mask of brutality.

Odile gathered her purse, and then, with the bearing of an aristocrat, stood up and walked away.

Ryan let her go. For a long time neither man said a word. Webb was the first to look away, returning his attention to other cruelties taking place in a more spectacular fashion on the far side of the river. The colours of battle were beautiful against the black velvet of night.

'Why did you do that?' Ryan said. He sounded surprised more than angry.

'I don't know.'

'You don't know,' Ryan repeated.

'It always amazes me what some people will do to stroke their own egos.'

'It wasn't like that at all, mate.'

'Wasn't it? It couldn't have been the three hundred dollars. Could it?'

Ryan pushed his drink away. 'I think it must be your shout. In the circumstances.'

He got up and left.

Webb ordered another beer and promised himself he would get drunk. Never any comfort in being a whistle-blower. What good had it done? He doubted it was a quest for truth and justice that had prompted him to do what he did.

Next time perhaps he would keep his big mouth shut.

## Seventh Regiment Armoury

'You think he did it for a bet?' Wendy Doyle said.

'No. He didn't give a damn about the bet,' Webb answered. 'It was the prestige. Another chapter in the Sean Ryan legend. He devoted his whole life to writing his own epitaph.'

Crosby helped himself to some more of the Bushmills and then made a round of the table. 'Hugh isn't being fair,' he said. 'I think he did love her, in his own way. At least, he told himself he did. He made a commitment to himself that he couldn't live with. Hey, we're all guilty of that, right?'

Webb frowned. 'You're always apologising for him.'

'I liked him.'

'We all liked him,' Cochrane said. 'But that's not the point.'

'He was always the great risk-taker,' Webb said. 'That was the way he painted himself. And yet away from the battlefield he was a coward. When he persuaded Odile to leave the novitiate she was the one who took all the risks. As soon as he got tired of her, he knew he could always leave. And what did he have to lose? Nothing.'

'I don't think he planned it that way,' Crosby said.

'I don't want to sound like an echo,' Cochrane said. 'But that's still not the point.'

Doyle picked up the bottle and looked at the poem that had been pasted to the back of the bottle. 'Perhaps this is the clue to why he did it.'

'Don't romanticise him,' Webb said. 'He doesn't deserve it.'

'So how long did it last?'

'Until he ran the first time? About four months. Then Nixon and Kissinger decided to order US troops over the border into Cambodia, and the hot news was in Phnom Penh for a while. All the talk in Saigon was about the Vietnamisation of the war. What that meant was that Nixon wanted out of the whole mess. As more and more US troops were sent home, Vietnam disappeared off the front pages. The war was escalating, with B-52 strikes over the border in Laos and Cambodia, but we couldn't film that, and with fewer and fewer American ground casualties public interest just faded away. It became somebody else's war. Even though we were still running it. It was a dead end for us. Battles sell newspapers, issues don't. Some of us transferred to Phnom Penh to pick up the front-line stuff there.'

'That's what Ryan did?'

Webb shrugged. 'It wasn't his decision. He was working for *Time* magazine and they just told him he was being transferred. But it was the easy way out for him. Odile told me later he left most of his things in the apartment and said to her he'd be away a week. And she didn't see him again for two years.'

'Sounds like a typical man,' Doyle said, and Cochrane laughed.

'You're probably right. But Odile wasn't a typical woman.'

The men tilted their whiskies and looked at the table. Doyle knew they had come to the part of the legend that didn't bear close examination. 'So what happened to Odile?'

'As you can imagine, I didn't see much of Ryan after the night at the Caravelle.'

'I can't imagine why,' Doyle said.

Webb gave a rueful smile. 'Before he left Vietnam we couldn't help running into each other, of course. The Continental, the Follies, the Press Centre in Danang. Once I literally bumped into him diving for a medevac chopper near Kontum. But we didn't talk to each other much. Obviously.'

'You heard about him, though?' Doyle asked.

'Sure. But the old guard split up. Lee here was back in the States. O'Leary was rotated back to London. It was just me and Croz.'

'You stayed on?'

'Croz had to, he was still with the AP. Me?' He shrugged. 'Like a dog with a bone. I wouldn't let go.'

'You were still freelancing for AP?'

'I was also selling some of my pieces to Time-Life and *Paris-Match*. It helped that I could take my own photographs to go with the stories. There weren't many warcos doing that.'

'So when did you run into Ryan again?'

'Croz picked up a bit of gossip occasionally. They went out drinking together whenever Ryan came back to Saigon. I didn't go. So I didn't see Ryan for a couple of years. It was Odile I found first. Purely by accident.'

# II

## Saigon, March 1972

'By showing war in its stinking reality, we have taken away the glory and shown that negotiation is the only way to solve international problems.'

– Howard Smith, ABC news presenter

'Take the glamour out of war? I mean, how the bloody hell can you do that? . . . Can you take the glamour out of a Cobra, or getting stoned at China Beach? . . . War is *good* for you, you can't take the glamour out of that. It's like trying to take the glamour out of sex, trying to take the glamour out of the Rolling Stones!'

– Tim Page, combat photographer, Vietnam War, in his autobiography *Page by Page*

# 12

There was a desperation about Saigon now. The grace once conferred by the French was all but gone, choked by overcrowding and pollution. Even the plane trees in the boulevards were dying. The American legacy had not been peace, but crowds of beggars and cripples and street children, and more war.

The Calley trial had created a groundswell of revulsion in the US, and now it was evident that America would ultimately turn its back on its disastrous Asian enterprise. The North Vietnamese were throwing more troops against the South, and the US military, with most of its ground forces now back in the United States, had reacted by hurling renewed waves of B-52s against Hanoi.

The desperation was most evident along the Tu Do; a Marine was becoming a rare sight around the Saigon streets and the competition among the prostitutes for the fewer and fewer American customers was fierce. As the russet and orange clouds of dusk broiled above the city – the pollution had made the Saigon sunsets remarkably beautiful – the strip came alive, the bars, nightclubs, restaurants, pizza and hamburger joints gaudily lit. The street pulsed with rock music, the shouts of bar girls, the laughter of crewcut soldiers, the buzz of Honda motorcycles adding to the din.

Most of the correspondents frequented the Melody Bar, where the girls were said to be younger, prettier and cheaper. But Crosby had fallen in lust with a girl who worked at the Chicago Bar, and Webb had arranged to meet him there. When he arrived, a group of bar girls were clustered under the hot pink neon sign at the door, smoking cigarettes.

They were all parodies of Times Square prostitutes: too-short miniskirts, high-heeled pumps, sweaters of electric pinks and greens one size too tight. They all wore too much lipstick. One of them tugged at Webb's shirt.

'Buy me ladies drink?' she said.

'No thanks,' he said.

She grabbed his crotch. 'I love you too much, baby.'

'Not right now.'

'Buy me drink, baby, love you too much.'

Webb disengaged himself. 'Maybe tomorrow.'

'Then you fuck off numbah ten cheap charlie!' she hissed in his ear.

He smiled and went inside.

Steppenwolf howling 'Born to be Wild', the bass on the jukebox almost overriding the lyric. Inside, a jostling crowd of crewcut soldiers in open-necked shirts and jeans, a handful of overweight Europeans, probably engineers, all of them surrounded by eager bar girls. He waited a moment for his eyes to adjust to the darkness. No sign of Crosby yet.

He went to the bar to get a beer. Over in the corner a huge black Marine was pawing one of the girls. Webb noticed her straight away; unlike the others she seemed reluctant, almost aloof, as if she had been led to the bar at the point of a gun. She was the only one not laughing too loud, shouting too much. But she was also much prettier than the other girls, and so perhaps, Webb decided, she did not have to try as hard.

He looked again. She was half turned away from him, staring into the mirror above the bar, not with vanity, but with horror, like a patient after a traumatic operation, examining the scars. She wore a red satin dress and stilettos, and her hair had been cut to her shoulders, leaving commas of black hair at her cheeks. She was wearing too much make-up, but it could not disguise her exceptional beauty. The Marine was running his fingers up and down her back, which was exposed by a plunging backline. He was laughing and whispering something in her ear.

'Christ,' Webb said aloud. He realised he knew her.

He moved closer, making sure.

'What you looking at, buddy?' the Marine growled at him.

'Odile,' Webb said. Her eyes widened. No recognition there, just surprise perhaps, at hearing her name spoken.

'You want something, man?'

The Marine was the size of a gorilla. Webb shook his head, took his beer and moved away. Another girl grabbed at him, but he pushed her away. *Odile*. Ryan's girlfriend, the novice. How had she ended up here? Not too difficult to guess. Why was he surprised?

Just walk away from this, he told himself. It wasn't his problem after all.

Instead he positioned himself behind the big Marine, waiting. He looked again, not trusting his instinct. Everything about her was different but it was her, he was sure of it. He saw her watching him in the mirror.

'GRENADE!'

Everyone hit the floor. Bar stools crashed over; the bar girls screamed. Tables crammed with bottles and glasses toppled over. Those closest to the door hurled themselves outside, others looked for shelter behind the bar. The big Marine lay prone at Webb's feet, his arms over his head.

Webb grabbed Odile's arm. He pulled her towards the door and she did not resist. In moments they were on the Tu Do, running.

As they ran, Webb told himself not to feel too smug. It had been clever. It had also been stupid.

They turned the corner into a side street. He wanted to put as much distance between themselves and the bar as he could. He knew that right now in the Chicago badly shaken soldiers would be slowly climbing to their feet, grateful to be alive, but wondering why there had been no explosion. When the first flush of relief had worn off, they would ask themselves and each other who had shouted the false warning, and then they would be very angry indeed.

Webb was still gripping Odile's upper arm. Unable to keep up with him in her stilettos, she tried to jerk her arm away, but he held her tighter. She shouted something at him in Vietnamese, and slapped his face.

Webb stopped. Eyes in the street were turned towards them now. 'I know you can speak English,' he said. 'Talk to me and I'll let you go.'

'Then please . . . let go of my arm,' she said. He released her. She looked up at him, her eyes sulky. 'Who are you?'

'Friend of Ryan's. Don't you remember?'

It was obvious that she didn't, but Ryan's name had her attention. 'You know where Ryan is?' she said.

'No, I don't.'

She rubbed her arm. His fingers had left angry red marks on her flesh.

'Sorry,' he said.

'What do you want?'

Good question. 'I don't know. I just wanted to get you out of there.'

'You want to sleep with me?'

He shook his head.

She had recovered her composure now, surprise and bewilderment transformed to outrage. 'Then what do you want? You crazy?'

'What the hell are you doing in that place?'

'It is not your problem, I think.'

'I suppose I just made it my problem.' They stared at each other. What insane impulse made me do that? he asked himself. What was I hoping to achieve? Sheer idiocy.

'You don't want to sleep with me, leave me alone.' She turned away, but he grabbed her wrist. She tried to wrench herself free. Passers-by stared at them; two Vietnamese military police stopped, but then moved on. Just another soldier having an argument with a prostitute over money perhaps.

'What do you want?' she repeated.

Webb wished he could tell her. All he knew was that this wasn't right, wasn't fair. All over Vietnam girls were being prostituted by circumstance, but he could accept that because he didn't know any of them personally. But this girl . . .

Was that really a rational basis for acting this way?

'Please,' he said, 'I have to talk to you. I just want to talk, okay? I'm a friend of Ryan's.'

She let her arm fall limp at her side. 'Monsieur Ryan is dead.'

'No. He's in Phnom Penh.'

'Phnom Penh,' she repeated slowly. She nodded, eyes closed, as if some great dilemma had finally been answered for her. 'You know where he is?'

'I haven't spoken to him . . . for a year. Perhaps more.'

'Then when you see Monsieur Ryan again . . . you will tell him how I live now. Yes?' She turned away.

'Wait . . .'

'Please. You cannot help me.'

Webb fumbled in his shirt, brought out a handful of piasters. 'How much do you want?'

She stared at the notes in his hand for a moment, then snatched them away and held them in front of his face, waiting for his approval. It was too much, way too much, but he nodded.

The alley was dirty and crowded. Old women squatted in the mud, hawking wicker pannikins of green bananas, durian and water melons. He followed her up a laneway, dodging the motorcycles and push bikes, picking his way carefully through the piles of rubbish in the gloom. In the light of a hurricane lamp he made out betel-nut stains in the dirt, like splashes of blood. There was a pervading stench of *nuoc mam*, kerosene and raw sewage, the staccato shouts of the night market and the whine of motorbikes. A man urinated against the wall.

She went ahead up a narrow flight of rotting wooden stairs. He followed her. An old woman with tombstone teeth stared at him as he passed.

They stopped outside a wooden door, and Odile removed the padlock with her key. She pulled him inside.

The only light came from a low-wattage bulb that hung from the ceiling on a frayed black flex. He looked around. The room was not much larger than his parents' bathroom back in London. There were rush mats on the floor, and a plastic bowl that he assumed was used for washing. In an alcove in the corner was a stove and a well from which she pumped her water. The only decoration on the peeling stucco walls was a wooden crucifix, the only furniture a child's cot.

Her bedroom was an area in the corner partitioned off with a torn curtain. Odile drew it back to reveal a narrow wooden bed. She sat down on the edge and started to unzip her dress.

Webb stopped her, shook his head.

'I only give you sexual intercourse,' she said, 'nothing else. I cannot do anything else.'

'I don't want sex,' he said.

Her shoulders sagged. 'You want your money back?'

'No, I don't want my money back.' He sat down beside her on the bed, his eyes still transfixed by the cot in the corner of the room. 'You have a baby now?'

She nodded.

'Ryan's baby?'

'A girl. She is fifteen months old. Her name is Phuong.' She put her head in her hands. 'What I said before. It is not true. I do not want you to tell Ryan how I live. I will have no face left. You understand?'

Webb shook his head. 'It's not your fault, it's his.'

'He does not love me.'

Webb did not understand his own outrage. There was no dearth of abandoned women and children in Saigon, as there was no shortage of men without legs in the military hospitals. It was just another cost of war. But somehow he had expected more of Ryan, because Ryan wasn't a soldier, he was one of his own. He had looked up to him. 'Where is your baby?'

'When I am . . . working . . . there is an old woman who takes care of her for me. I pay her money. Like an amah.'

'Can I see her – your baby?'

'Why?'

'Perhaps I can help you.'

'Why do you want to help me?'

'I don't know,' he said, and it was the truth. He supposed his motivations would make themselves clear to him later. For now he acted instinctively; later he would have time to think it through, to find his justifications.

She stood up, very slowly. It hurt him to look at her. She was a travesty of the woman he remembered from that evening at the Caravelle; the gaudy clothes, the lipstick, cosmetics plastered on like a mask. That night she had looked like a princess. Now she looked like a clown.

He followed her back down the steps to the alley.

She stopped outside a hole in the wall. 'In here,' she said.

It took a few moments for his eyes to grow accustomed to the gloom. No electric light here, just a kerosene lantern by the doorway. It was crushingly hot. The smells of cooking, sweat and urine. The small room housed a large family; a woman was cooking over a charcoal stove in the corner, three small children played on the dirt floor. A man in a white vest eyed him with unconcealed hostility. He said something to Odile, his voice sharp and angry.

'He is not happy that I bring you here,' she said. 'He says you will bring him bad luck. They do not like me. I pay double because I am *bui doi*.'

There was an old woman sitting on a stool, a small child playing at her feet. The child had the straight black hair of Asia but her features were European; she had round eyes and pale milk-coffee skin. She was naked except for a soiled T-shirt.

Odile bent to pick up the child, patted her bare bottom. She cooed something in Vietnamese, an endearment perhaps.

'So you have seen my little baby,' Odile said. 'Now if you do not want to sleep with me, I must go back to work.'

'I don't want to sleep with you. But you're not going back to the bar.'

'Tell me how else I can live.'

Webb hesitated. 'Perhaps there's a way,' he said.

# 13

The apartment was two blocks from the Tu Do, towards the Saigon River. A green wrought-iron balcony, wide enough for two chairs and a small iron table, looked out over the street. Just inside the green-painted and louvred french window was a plain wooden desk and Webb's prized Olympia typewriter. There was a small toilet room with a massive high-sided bath and brass taps.

In one corner of the room, opposite the window, was a single bed. It had a T-bar wooden frame covered with mosquito netting. There was a wash basin and an ancient armoire in the other corner. Webb's own black and white photographs had been tacked to the walls, along with a red Liberation Army flag with a yellow star which a drunken Marine had sold to Webb for ten dollars. A bookshelf contained mementos collected during his two years in South-East Asia: an opium pipe, a red and white Khmer scarf, an NVA pith helmet. His field gear – the pack, his cameras, a flak jacket – were on the floor beside the bed.

Odile looked around.

'It's not very big,' Webb said, 'but it's clean. And it won't cost you anything.'

She sat Phuong on the parquetry floor and perched uncertainly on the edge of the bed.

'I won't be here very often,' Webb said, quickly. 'It's just a base for me. A lot of the time you'd have the place to yourself.' He went to the wash basin. There was a wash cloth draining over the faucet. He wet it, and handed it to her. 'Here, wash your face.'

'Why?'

'Take off the lipstick. You don't have to be a whore any more.' He saw her flinch and realised how callous that had sounded.

But she went obediently to the wash basin and rinsed off the cosmetics. Her shame was painful to watch. He crouched down and smiled at Phuong, who stared back at him, fascinated with this new and strange face.

'Why do you want to do this?' Odile said.

'Should I just walk away and pretend it isn't my problem?'

'But it isn't.'

He could see on her face what she was thinking. This had to be some elaborate trap. Nothing was ever free; she could guess what the rent would be. But no doubt she had already calculated that this might be better than having the whole US Army as her landlord.

On a neighbouring rooftop an old Chinese practised his *tai qi*. A skyline of plane trees and flat roofs was silhouetted against the bright lights and neon of the Tu Do; in the distance could be heard the rumble of artillery.

They sat on the balcony. Phuong played inside, on the floor. The city sweltered, not a breath of air.

'Ryan is gone maybe two weeks when I think I am pregnant,' Odile was saying, staring into the darkness, her voice a monotone. 'First, I am worried that he will be unhappy. But I always think that he will come back.

'For a while he writes to me, sends me money. But then the letters stop, and there is no more money. Perhaps Ryan is killed, I do not know. So I write to my mother in Dalat, ask her for help, but she does not write back. I can never go back there with my baby. It will be too much shame. So I stay here. But after Phuong is born the money from Ryan is all gone. So I decide to go to the Tu Do.'

'Did you ever write to Ryan? Ask him for help?'

'Yes, I write often. Ask him why he does not write to me any more. But then I think, he does not answer so he must be dead. So then I do not write any more.'

'But does he know about the baby?'

She shook her head.

'If he'd known, he would have helped you.'

'Why would he help me, Monsieur Webb? He does not love me.'

'That doesn't matter.'

'To me, it matters very much. If he does not love me, I do not want his help.'

Phuong had begun to cry. Odile picked her up and sat down on the edge of the bed to offer the child her breast. Webb concentrated on the bottle of Johnnie Walker on the table in front of him. After a while the child slept quietly in Odile's arms. She laid her gently down on the bed.

She hesitated. The yellow lamp threw shadows across her face. Webb knew she was wondering if he wanted her to undress for him.

'I'm going outside to have a cigarette,' he said.

He shut the door behind him and went down the stairs to the street. He walked around for almost an hour, trying to sort it through in his mind. But by the time he got back to the apartment his motives were still no clearer.

Odile was in the bed, Phuong asleep beside her. He went to his field pack in the corner, and unrolled his sleeping bag on the floor.

'What are you doing?' she asked him.

'I've slept in worst places the last couple of years. At least it's dry and there're no snakes.'

'You do not want to sleep with me?'

'If I do you'll still feel like a prostitute. Won't you? Just with fewer customers.'

'It does not matter to me any more.'

'That's the point. I want it to matter to you again. Besides, I didn't offer to help you for that reason.' He sat down to take off his boots. 'You can stay here with me for as long as you want. No strings attached. We'll work something out. I'll write to Ryan myself.'

Whether Ryan would feel moved to do something about the situation, he didn't know.

He came over to the bed, picked up the scarlet dress from the floor and crumpled it in his fist. Then he went to the balcony and threw it into the street.

'What are you doing?'

'You won't need it any more.'

She stared at him as if he were crazy. Which perhaps he was. He had lived in a war zone for two years now, and the rules had changed for him. Life was too short and too fragile not to do whatever you felt like doing.

Perhaps that was where Ryan had gone wrong.

'You do not have to do this. I am not a nun. I never was.'

'I don't want you to be hurt any more, okay? Just accept that.'

She put her head back on his pillow. 'You are a very good man.'

A good man? Or a fool? He was not sure, he was never sure. Before he came to this country he had been so certain of what he was, what he could be.

He turned off the light, undressed and slid into his sleeping bag. He lay awake for a long time, hoping to hear her footfall on the timber floor, feel her warm body slip in beside him. But then he was aware of her soft, even breathing and he knew she was asleep. Of course, of course. She doesn't want to sleep with you! Sex was not an adventure for her. Tonight might be the first time in eighteen months she had gone to bed without having a stranger fall asleep across her body.

You're a good man, Webb, he told himself. You'll probably go to heaven.

But you'll be there all on your own, you silly bastard.

# 14

Webb was awake soon after dawn, the habit of two years in war zones, needing to be out on the street early, to test the mood of the city.

Odile was still asleep. She lay on her back, her arms above her head like a child. He stared at her. Exquisite, was the word that came immediately to his mind. Her beauty was almost too perfect, because it hid the person beneath. Her face has been her curse throughout her life, he thought. It made her at once a pariah and an object of desire, exotic to some, a creature to be shunned by others.

The sheet had fallen below her breast. Her body was creamy brown, slim, perfectly proportioned. He fought the desire to reach out and touch her. Instead he pulled the sheet gently up to her chin to cover her.

The child was already awake, playing on the floor. She was wearing a cheap pink nightdress probably purchased in the Central Market. She had short, very straight black hair, round eyes and a flat cherubic face. A pleasant, happy child but with none of the beauty of her parents. Not yet. Later perhaps. For all the good it might do her.

He went out, quietly closing the door behind him.

He had coffee on the Shelf and checked the gossip among the other correspondents. Crosby was there, and he wanted to know why Webb had not shown up at the Chicago. Webb muttered an apology and offered a lame excuse about feeling unwell. Crosby shrugged it off and proceeded to describe an incident that had taken place at the bar just before he got there.

'VC threw a fucking grenade in there,' Crosby said.

'No shit.'

'This Marine was telling me about it. Didn't go off, thank God. Probably some Chicom dud. Last time I'm going there.'

Webb smiled. 'Me too.'

He drank his coffee and left. Yesterday he had been planning to hitch a ride into the Delta to Can Tho. Instead he left the Shelf, crossed the square and bought fresh croissants at the Givral, and some green bananas from one of the street hawkers on the Tu Do. He took them back with him to the apartment.

When he opened the door, Odile was waiting for him, standing in the middle of the room, her hands behind her back, as if she were waiting to pass inspection. He realised with a pang that in forcing her to give up her role as a bar girl, he had also made her surrender her freedom. To him. He didn't want her subservience, but he had created it. Odile and her baby were both in his power now.

He held up the croissants. 'Breakfast,' he said. 'I bought some bananas for Phuong. She likes bananas?'

Odile nodded. 'Yes, but you will have banana all over your apartment.'

'Well, it needs redecorating. Yellow's a good colour.'

She had put on an *ao dai* of eggshell blue. She was almost as he remembered her the first time he saw her. Almost. If you didn't look too closely into her eyes.

They ate the croissants on the balcony. The city had clamoured to life. The street was a tumult of car horns and siclo bells; from a dozen windows and doorways came the tinny music of radios. In Saigon, Sunday was just like any other day.

They ate in silence.

'How long since you've been to church?' he asked her suddenly.

'To church? How can I go to church?'

'Why not? God forgives, doesn't he? Not that you did anything that needed forgiving. In my opinion. You had a child to feed.'

She concentrated on her croissant, which she held delicately, in two hands.

'We'll go to Mass this morning,' he said. 'I'm not one of your lot but I think I understand the way it works. You can go to confession, and you will receive absolution, and when you walk out you will leave the past behind. Okay?'

'I do not think it is so simple.'

'We'll go anyway,' he said.

* * *

The old canonesse was there, and Soeur Marie, a handful of the novices from the convent in Cholon. Odile saw their faces turned in her direction but she avoided their eyes. She tried to concentrate on the service, and on the tormented figure on the cross above the altar, but it was different from how it had been before. There was no comfort in the ceremony, no sense of sanctity or of belonging. She was an outsider now, locked out by her own perfidy.

When the priest sanctified the host, she did not approach the altar for Communion. But when the service was over, Webb urged her towards the confessional.

She obeyed.

Odile remained for a long time on her knees in the gloom of the Lady Chapel while Webb held little Phuong. She closed her eyes and tried to form the words of prayer in her mind, but they would not come. If she had suffered, it was because she had brought her suffering on herself. She had placed her own base longings over the natural order that God had created, had valued her own happiness over the duty that had been given her.

To think she had once considered committing *chat lam ba* – infanticide. It had been a traditional remedy for unwed mothers in Vietnam; chop the newborn child into three pieces, wrap the head, torso and legs in cloth and throw them in the river, so that the mistake is washed away by the tide. To have contemplated such evil! It proved to her that she was an evil person, and that God had made her suffer to correct her.

She tried again to form the words of her prayer, but the prayer would not come. Pointless. How could God forgive, when she could not forgive herself?

They stood on the cathedral steps, in the bright, hot morning. 'Did you receive your absolution?' Webb asked her.

'I could not tell the priest,' she murmured. 'There is too much shame.'

'You said nothing?'

'I accuse myself of the sin of envy. And once I think that I want to kill Monsieur Ryan. For that the curé gives me penance and absolution.'

'And that's all?'

'Please. You are very kind to me. But do not ask me to do what I cannot do.'

'You're not to blame!'

'You are not the judge,' she said quietly.

'Who is?'

How can I explain this to him? she thought. Her reasons were as foreign to him as his to her. He was not Vietnamese, he could not understand. Perhaps in his world there were no pariahs. He had the round-eye confidence, the unshakeable belief in easy answers. They struggled against God every day of their lives, as if fate was something that could be changed by force of will alone. Because he had taken her away from the Tu Do he thought he had expunged the shame that had seeped, like rust, into her soul.

He was a child.

For herself she knew there was nowhere to go on this hot morning but back into a hellish world where the beggars patrolled the streets like crabs and the homeless children roamed in packs, a world without sanctuary, a place where no grace could save her.

It was midday and inside Juliette's the heavy golden drapes were drawn against the sun. Through a gap in the curtains Webb could see over the rooftops of Saigon. The city looked tawdry and sad in the shimmering heat, a panorama of peeling hoardings and red-tiled roofs. He and Crosby were sitting on bar stools, drinking '33' beers, contemplating lunch, and discussing where the sirens of war might lead them after Vietnam. The conversation turned to Cambodia, and then, predictably, to Ryan.

'Have you heard from him recently?' Webb asked.

'A guy I know from UPI was in Phnom Penh last week, ran into him. Still the same.'

'You know where I can get in touch with him?'

'Does he owe you money?'

Webb shook his head. 'It's not for me. You remember the nun?'

Crosby grinned, as if in anticipation of the punchline of a favourite joke. 'Sure I remember.'

'He left her with a baby.'

Crosby did not seem quite sure how to react. Another chapter in the legend or did this smack of real scandal? 'Well, I'll be dipped in shit,' he said, finally.

'This wasn't just some bar girl, Croz. She deserves better treatment.' When Crosby offered no comment, he added: 'A lot of people seem to think he's a lovable rogue. He's an arsehole.'

'He saved your life once, man.'

'Is my life so important to the world that it's recompense for every outrage he cares to commit?'

Crosby sucked on his front teeth, thinking about this. 'There's a lot of it going around. Kids with no fathers, I mean.'

Webb felt himself getting angry. 'Ryan isn't some dumb nineteen-year-old Marine fresh out of the boonies. And she's not a whore. This is different.'

'Yeah. Yeah, I guess so.' Crosby played with the ends of his moustache, thinking it through. 'He know about this kid he's got?'

'I don't think so.'

'Maybe someone should let him know. One of my guys is flying to Phnom Penh on Friday. If you want to get him a message, I'll see it gets there.'

'Thanks, Croz.'

Crosby shook his head and chuckled. 'Shoot, but he's something else, ain't he?'

Webb started to compose his letter to Ryan, telling him about Odile's situation, but never quite finished.

Meanwhile his life took on a new texture. He anticipated his return to the apartment each evening with real pleasure. Phuong had for some reason found something pleasing about his presence and would smile at him as soon as he walked through the door. There was a domesticity to the arrangement that quickly became comfortable. Perhaps too comfortable.

In the evenings, instead of drinking in the Caravelle or the Melody or the Continental with his fellow correspondents, he took Odile and Phuong to dinner, in the Givral perhaps, or the Royale. For the first time he was aware of being envied. Crewcut young Americans stared at him and then at Odile and little Phuong and then grinned at each other. He knew what they were thinking.

Odile remained diffident. She had withdrawn inside herself, beyond his reach, had pulled a curtain across her soul. She spoke little. Occasionally she mentioned isolated incidents from her childhood in Dalat, but when he pressed her about her family or asked her about her life in the convent, she retreated to monosyllables and the blinds were again drawn on the past. She was attentive to Phuong, but nothing else in her life seemed to interest her.

Webb was quickly aware that his initial charity, if that was what it was, had become obsession, tainted with eroticism. Deep in his soul he saw her as some enchanted princess he kept locked away in a tower for her own protection. He guarded his secret life, like a child with some private treasure discovered in the mud. He felt a need to save her, to unravel her mystery. He thought about her constantly.

In the end the letter to Ryan was never finished, never sent.

# 15

Webb had rented the apartment because it had an air conditioner, but it broke down soon after he moved in, and his Tonkinese landlord had refused to repair it. Instead Webb threw the windows wide open to find relief from the heat. But tonight the breath of the city was still, airless and foul. He took his typewriter on to the balcony, labouring in the semi-darkness rather than endure the stifling heat inside. He heard Odile singing softly to little Phuong, settling her to sleep in her cot.

He fed a blank sheet of paper into the Remington, tried to find the right words to accompany the pictures he had taken that morning in the Delta. He was tired; it was a tired war. The photographs were unremarkable, and he doubted he would find an enthusiastic editor at Time-Life or *Paris-Match*. The world was not interested in stories of Vietnamese killing Vietnamese; it was only truly horrible if the dead bodies were white. The real war was going on in the sky across the border in Cambodia and Laos, away from prying eyes.

He was suddenly aware of her standing behind him. He felt her hands on his shoulders kneading his tense muscles. A warmth spread through his body to his groin, and he experienced the sudden collision of need and shame. Sex was not an expensive commodity in Saigon, but love and tenderness were in desperately short supply.

But this was not why he had brought her here, he reminded himself.

He stopped typing, reached up and laid his hands on hers. 'I have to go away tomorrow,' he said. 'Danang. I may be away for a week or two.'

'I will miss you. I will pray you are safe.'

'Will you?'

'You are a very good man.'

'No, I'm not.' He looked up at her face. For a moment she reminded him of PFC Judge that day at An Qanh; there was a wildness in her eyes which announced that a crime had been committed here that could not be undone. But while Judge had looked ugly with guilt, it only made Odile appear haunted and so more alluring. That was the curse of beauty; it turned even pain into something exotic.

'What would you do if you were free?' he asked her. 'If you could do whatever you wanted?'

'But I am not free. I was never free. I was born *bui doi*, in Vietnam. Immediately I am not free.'

'If you could leave Vietnam . . .'

She shrugged her shoulders, unable to imagine it. Damaged goods. Perhaps irreparably damaged, inside. For the first time he wondered if she had always been this way. Perhaps the fault was not just Ryan's.

'If you want to get out of Vietnam, I can help you.'

'Help me be a prostitute in America?'

'You don't have to go to America. And you don't have to be a prostitute.'

'I cannot stop being a Tu Do girl.' She held a hand to her breast. 'Not in here.'

'Am I supposed to be impressed? What atrocity did you commit exactly? Compared to murder? Compared to torture? Compared to dropping napalm on villages or burying a mine and blowing off another man's legs? For the last two years I've seen men do that to each other every day. Yours is such a small sin, Odile.'

'You cannot compare one sin with another like they are melons in the market.' She pulled her hands away. 'In my head I still hear myself say things I think I can never say, do things I think I can never do. I want to be like I was before but . . . it is like you are away from somewhere, the town you are born, and when you go back everything is changed. It can never be like it was before. Now when I pray, God does not want to listen.'

'All you did was find a way to feed your child.'

'Perhaps it is not the offence I committed against God, but what I did against myself.' She turned away from him. He did not know any way to continue the argument, and so he said nothing.

'What do you want from me?' she said, finally.

'I don't want anything from you.'

'Perhaps you would like to think that. But I have seen how you look at me.'

She went back inside. He heard the rustle of silk, and when he looked up she was standing beside the bed naked, the *ao dai* held in the fist of her right hand. The yellow lamp beside the bed threw shadows over her body.

Webb stood up, went inside. Exquisite. He reached out, touched the flesh of her shoulder, taut and silken. She was tiny beside him, her body so perfect she might have been fashioned from coffee-coloured marble, and her warmth and softness were almost a surprise. He had never imagined himself with a woman so beautiful.

He hesitated. If he did not love her, was he any better than Ryan? Or any of the soldiers in the Tu Do bars? Perhaps something else he still had not learned about himself.

'It's okay,' she whispered, and he could not decide if what he detected in her voice was tenderness or resignation.

He stepped towards her, cupped her breast in his palm, kissed her neck. The perfume of patchouli, silken hair against his cheek. A block away he could hear the traffic on the Tu Do, the barking cough of hundreds of Hondas, the heavy bass thump from the bars. A long way from London. A dream.

Webb was gone for two weeks. During long nights wrapped in a poncho, shivering with cold and fear on a firebase somewhere in the Highlands, or sweating it out on patrols with the ARVN in the jungles around Pleiku, he thought about her, sorting through the decision he knew he would have to make. He had eked out a living for two long years in Vietnam, perhaps two years longer than he had any right to expect when he had first arrived in Saigon. He had harboured dreams of death or glory, an ignominious end or a fast track to the top, but in the final course of events Vietnam had been neither. His photographs and stories had been used occasionally by some of the major international agencies and magazines, but he was still neither dead nor famous. He had perhaps arrived a year too late; Vietnam was no longer the war in which to see and be seen.

For the first time he had started to think about other career moves. It occurred to him that if he left Vietnam, he might perhaps take Odile with him.

He still had not written the letter to Ryan. If he did, he asked himself, what would Ryan do? There was no imperative on him to pick up the pieces.

And certainly none on me, Webb thought.

At first he had simply tried to help her because she had stirred some sense of moral outrage in him, an impulse to save at least one person from the misery he saw around him every day. He had put his money where his mouth was.

He had assumed she would want to leave Vietnam, and he had planned to secure a French passport for her, help her fight a way through the bureaucracy at the embassy. Then he could set her free, let her find her own way.

And what way was that, with no father for her child, alone in an alien culture?

She had refused all his offers of help in that direction. She did not want to leave, she had told him. Vietnam might not have been kind to her, but it was still her home, all she had.

Now he realised he had not been honest about his own motives; Odile was right about him, he might be a good man, but he was not that good. The moral compulsion to help her had been only part of it.

It was not love he felt for her, he was sure. Love was perhaps what had happened to him with Mickey, a feeling that everything fitted, dropping into place like tumblers in a lock. With Odile what he felt was something darker and far more compelling. It even went beyond sexual desire, a siren call for some phantom she inspired in his own imagination. Her beauty made her exotic, her pain made her mysterious, her mystery made her irresistible.

The image of her the night before he had left was imprinted on his memory like a brand. The shuddering moment of climax had been his possession of her and he relived the moment a hundred times in the following weeks. But he had told himself that he could not possess this spectre completely by loving her. It could only work if she loved him.

The night before he returned to Saigon he was sitting in the open-air cinema in Danang watching a rerun of *The Graduate* when the answer came to him. That she might not love him no longer mattered.

He would ask her to marry him.

# 16

Odile was in a siclo on Le Loi Boulevard, returning from the Central Market, when she saw him. He was sitting on the terrace, in one of those execrable Hawaiian shirts that he loved, smoking a cigarette. He was with some other journalists, in their tailor-made green safari jackets, laughing at some joke. But she was afforded only a glimpse of him, before he was lost again to the traffic and the mid-morning crowds.

She felt a stab of pain deep in her chest. She twisted around in the cracked leather seat but she could no longer see him. So she turned away, and put her arm more tightly around little Phuong. A *bui doi*, just like her, with the same terrible choices to make, one day.

At first the shock of recognition left her numb. But after a few moments the emotion he aroused in her was so powerful it made her gasp aloud; not regret, not shame, not longing – but hatred. She hated him then as she had never hated anyone, for his deceit, for his cruelty and for his betrayal.

When she got back to the apartment she settled Phuong on the floor with a plastic bottle of water and the wooden blocks that Webb had bought for her. Then she took the wooden-handled paring knife that Webb used to cut fruit, hid it in her purse and walked out of the door.

She waited for him in the Givral across the square from the Continental. She allowed her *café au lait* to get cold on the table in front of her. He was still there. Hard to miss him in that shirt.

She thought about the day he had left Saigon. He had told her that he had to go to Phnom Penh, but he had said it would only be for a week. He went away often, so his leaving that morning had been unremarkable. He had left money on the table and waved goodbye from the window of the taxi taking him to the airport.

In the following weeks she received letters saying he would have to stay in Cambodia a little longer than he had originally planned. There was money in the envelopes. But as weeks turned into months the letters became less frequent, and after a while the envelopes contained only money.

Then there were no letters at all.

Perhaps I should have told him about the child, she thought. But she had been too ashamed then; ashamed that she had allowed herself to be used and discarded. And a part of her felt that she should be punished, and so she accepted his abandonment as part of her penance.

But there was no absolution even in suffering. So if she was damned, then so was he. She would make sure of that.

She tensed. He had left his companions, was sauntering alone across Lam Son Square towards the Caravelle. She left money on the table for her coffee and rushed out of the door.

He was mobbed outside the Caravelle by the hordes of street children who made their living in the square, the shoeshine boys and cigarette vendors and flower girls, all descending on him like seagulls on an unguarded feast. He stopped, laughing, and reached into his pockets to give them his small change. They thrust their packets of Embassy and the handmade flower garlands at him even though he shook his head and said he didn't want them, just take the money. It was one of the things she had loved most about him, this easy-going generosity. Hard to imagine that there was another side to the man; that was what had fooled her.

She followed him into the foyer of the Caravelle.

A sixth sense must have made him stop and turn. There was a moment of astonishment and then he was coming towards her, laughing. 'Odile!'

He kissed her cheek.

She felt the point of the knife through her leather purse. It had been an impulse, the knife. She realised she had no plan. In the chest, in the stomach? How do you kill someone this way? And should I take his life here in the lobby, in front of everyone? Or in secret, and then try to escape?

If I am caught, what will happen to Phuong?

'You look fantastic,' he said, smiling.

She felt something snap inside her. She couldn't get her breath. This wasn't the way it was meant to be.

'Are you okay?'

'When did you get back to Saigon?' she managed.

'Couple of days ago.' The grin fell away. 'Guess you're mad at me, huh?' He didn't even begin to look contrite. He resembled a small child who had been found with his hand in a biscuit tin. *Aren't I a naughty boy? – but I can't help it.*

She opened her purse, felt the handle of the knife.

*How could you do this to me, Ryan?*

'You've been following me,' he said.

'I saw you . . . on the terrace.'

'You must think I'm a right bastard.'

She stared at him, confused and dumbfounded to hear her anguish so easily circumscribed.

'Look, I'm sorry. I should have written.' He shrugged his shoulders as if that explained everything. 'It's not done you any harm. You look great.'

There was not enough air in here. She felt faint. She couldn't just kill him. Not until he understood the enormity of what he had done. 'There's something I have to show you,' she said.

She turned and walked back through the doors. He ran after her. She found a siclo and jumped in. It was not too far to the apartment but she didn't trust her legs.

As Ryan climbed in beside her she gave the siclo driver her address.

'Where are we going?' he said.

'You have somewhere else to go?' she asked him.

'No,' he said. 'No, I guess not.'

She turned her face away, one arm gripping the edge of the canopy. The sun was fierce. 'You hurt me very much,' she said.

'Yeah, I'm sorry. I honestly tried. Us, I mean. I didn't set out to lie to you. It just . . . wasn't working for me. Then when I got to Phnom Penh . . . I guess I thought it was better that way.'

'Easier, at least.'

He had no answer for that.

'I give up everything for you.'

'You're better off. You were never meant to be a nun.'

*I was never meant to be a prostitute either.*

He touched her knee. 'Odile . . .'

She pushed his hand away. 'Please . . . don't do that.'

They turned off the Tu Do into a side street and stopped outside

Webb's apartment. Ryan looked puzzled but said nothing, and followed her inside, up the wrought-iron staircase.

She opened the door.

Phuong lay on her back on the floor, drinking from a bottle.

'Christ,' Ryan said.

They stood there, in the doorway, for a long time. Ryan sagged against the lintel, his jaw slack with astonishment.

'Her name is Phuong,' Odile said, finally.

Ryan appeared not to have heard. But then he surprised her. He bent down and picked the child up in his arms, very gently. Phuong did not cry at this huge stranger. She continued to drink from the bottle and stared at Ryan with huge brown eyes.

He took a deep breath. 'Well,' he said.

She had expected him to protest, to shake his head and say: 'She's not mine.' But he didn't. He did not even ask her assurance. Instead he sat down and bounced the little girl on his knee. Phuong gave a short hiccough of a laugh.

'You should have told me,' Ryan said. He looked around the room. He must have recognised Webb's photographs on the walls, she thought, but he just said: 'You've got another guy?'

How could she explain to him her relationship with Webb? 'He is very kind to me.'

He looked at the room's only bed and bit his lip, thinking. 'How did you get by?' he said.

She did not answer him. Enough shame, for now.

'Shit, I'm sorry,' he said.

In the siclo she had told herself that she would first show him the child, and then she would tell him, *This is what you did to me, this is what I had to do for us to survive*, and then she would push the knife into his heart. But it was a fantasy, not a plan. Where was all that hate now? Just dissolved, gone. Now there was just the sadness left. Sadness and the shame.

Phuong was still sucking on her water bottle, staring at Ryan. She would always go to strangers, this child, Odile thought. She was never afraid. There was some storehouse of trust in her that belied her birthright. And now Ryan was staring back at her, trying to come to grips with the fact that this small human was partly his own. 'How old?'

'Sixteen months.'

'She's beautiful.'

'She's too fat. She eats too much and her nose is too big.'

'No, she's wonderful.'

Odile realised she was crying. Not with her body, just with her eyes. The tears were hot, and fell off her cheeks like rain off the roof in the monsoon. This was how she had always pictured it would be, before he left. She had waited sixteen months for him to tell her she had given him a beautiful baby.

Then his arms were around her, and she tried to push him away, reminding herself that she hated him. But instead she found herself clinging to him, to the hugeness of him, drinking in his never-forgotten warm, masculine smell. He kissed her forehead, and then lifted her face with his fingertips and kissed her in the special, intimate way he had once told her was purely French.

She dropped the purse.

She felt him pull at the buttons of her *ao dai*. If this was to be another reckless mistake it no longer seemed to matter, and so she let him take off her clothes and lay her down on the bed. There was no physical need in her except the desire to feel him hold her again while she embraced the glimmer of a hope that he would somehow find a way to love her again and rescue her from this black cul de sac.

When Webb walked into the apartment they were both asleep. Odile had one arm around Ryan's broad, bare back, the fingers of her other hand entangled in his dark curls. His head lay on her breast. There was a sheen of sweat on their skins. The narrow bed was a crumpled mess.

Phuong looked up at him from the floor and grinned, four teeth, two top and two bottom.

Webb sagged against the wall, trying to marshal his feelings. Jealousy? Betrayal? Disappointment? In what, in whom? In her, for following her own desires? In Ryan, for doing what came naturally to him?

'Jesus,' he said aloud.

Odile's eyes blinked wide. She fumbled for the edge of the sheet.

'Another problem solved,' he said to her and went out, slamming the door.

# 17

The Cigale had curved iron bars on the windows and a boy on the door, whose job was to watch for any unwelcome parcels that the Viet Cong might think to toss through the door. Crosby and two of his fellow correspondents from the AP were sitting on bar stools, drinking brandies, watching the cowboys on their Hondas roaring up and down the Tu Do.

Webb heard them laughing from the street, but as he walked in there was a sudden stiff silence. Ryan was with them. Webb guessed the others knew what had happened. Gossip travelled fast in Saigon. News, of any sort, was why the city was there.

Ryan grinned at him and waved a hand. 'Drink, Spider?'

'Sure.'

Ryan shouted for another round of drinks. Webb sat down.

'We were just talking about the afternoon's Follies. Crosby's heard there's something big going on up at Que Trang.'

Que Trang sat astride the Ho Chi Minh trail, a bermed fort manned by a large Special Forces A-Team and over four hundred Sedang Strikers. The press officer at the Follies had claimed the fort had been coming under artillery bombardment and a company of ARVN had been sent in on a search and destroy mission.

'I was talking to a Green Beret colonel yesterday,' Crosby said. 'He told me the base is surrounded and two nights ago they were almost overrun. We're going up tomorrow to take a look. Interested?'

'Sure he'll come,' Ryan said. 'You'll do anything for a story. Won't you, Spider?'

It was a deliberate provocation. Ryan must be feeling guilty, Webb decided. In his experience the person you had to watch out for wasn't the one you had wronged, but the one who had done wrong to you. But he guessed there was some truth in what Ryan had said. No matter what else was happening in his life he still had a living to make and right now he would do almost anything for a story.

'Sure,' he said. 'I'll come.'

The next morning Crosby, Ryan and Webb jumped on a C–130 at Tan Son Nhut and flew up to Danang. From there they hitched a ride on a Chinook flying out to an LZ ten kilometres east of the Que Trang camp in the Highlands.

The moment the helicopter touched the ground, ARVN soldiers began racing towards them with wounded, crouching low under the propellers. The remnants of the company – the men that the press officer at the Follies had assured them would relieve the shelling at Que Trang – were sitting on the edge of the LZ, on half-tracks and ammunition boxes and sandbags, heads bowed, silent. The black panther shoulder flashes indicated they were from the élite *Huc Bao* battalion. Their faces were etched with the familiar hard stares of men who had just come from a long and bitter battle. They were stained with red laterite, some nursing field dressings on minor wounds.

They found a captain sitting on an ammunition box, his right arm strapped with a wound dressing. He was smoking a cigarette. Ryan went over, introduced himself as a reporter with *Time*.

'What happened here?' he said.

'What do you think happened?' the captain said, nodding towards the rows of body bags next to the LZ.

'You got through to Que Trang?'

'We walked into an NVA ambush, so we called in air support. Your air put their first strike right on top of us. I just lost half my company dead or wounded.'

All three of them were scribbling as fast as they could.

'What's the situation at Que Trang, Captain?' Crosby asked.

'The camp is totally encircled.' He drew on his cigarette. His hands were still shaking. 'There's three NVA battalions around Que Trang and the men inside are taking three hundred rounds a day.'

Webb looked at Ryan and Crosby. This was a different picture to the one they had had from JUSPAO, but that wasn't new. What the captain was describing was a Special Forces team and two companies of Montagnard mercenaries cut off and a company of ARVN regulars decimated by friendly fire. Crosby was eager to get it on the wire.

As they walked away he turned to Ryan. 'I'm going back to Danang and file.'

'We don't have the full story yet.'

'My deadline's tighter than yours. Besides, he says they're taking three hundred rounds a day.'

'Did we see the three hundred rounds?' Ryan asked him. 'Anyone been up there to count them? A thousand rounds is one every five minutes.'

'Shit, you still want to go into Que Trang after what he just said?'

'Don't you?'

'I've got my story.'

Ryan looked at Webb. Webb felt the cold creep of fear in his gut. Suddenly he wanted to walk away from this. He asked himself again, as he had asked himself countless times before, why he was fooling with his life this way.

Two Hueys were warming up on the LZ. A Marine colonel and two Vietnamese staff officers were loping towards them, crouched down under the rotors. Ryan saw them and intercepted them.

'Colonel, my name's Ryan, I'm a correspondent with *Time*,' he shouted over the roar of the Huey's engine, his face screwed up against the dust storm. 'Can you tell me what's happening at Que Trang, sir?'

The colonel looked irritated by the delay. 'The men in the fort are temporarily isolated by enemy movement. They'll be relieved in the next twenty-four hours.'

He tried to break away, but Ryan clung to his sleeve.

'Can we get transport to Que Trang?'

'I'm afraid that won't be possible. I can offer you a ride to Mae Son on my chaser if you want.'

He gave Ryan a pat on the shoulder and leaped into the Huey.

'Fuck him!' Ryan swore.

'Let's get on the chaser,' Crosby said.

The 'chaser' was a second helicopter that followed VIP politicians and military in case they were shot down; in this case it was an ancient CH-34.

Crosby jumped inside, and settled on the floor next to the door gunner. Webb and Ryan slid in beside him. Webb felt a curious mixture of disappointment and relief; he had no good pictures he could use, but at least he was alive. For Crosby it was different; he could file this as hot news.

Ryan grabbed Webb's shoulder. 'All we've got is a picture of a few blokes sitting on sandbags.'

Webb shrugged: if they couldn't get into Que Trang, there was nothing they could do.

The aircraft started to rise from the ground. Suddenly Ryan was scrambling towards the door on his knees. He jumped. Webb reacted without thinking, and leaped after him. The helicopter was a metre off the ground and he landed rolling in the dirt.

He looked up and saw Crosby's startled face at the gun door before the chopper rose and tilted away.

Ryan was already on his feet and running. Then Webb saw why; there was a medevac coming in from the north. It would be loaded with the wounded from Que Trang. And if the Huey had made it in, it sure as hell would be going back out to get others.

It was said that a combat spiral in a Huey could pull your brains out through your anus. Webb gasped as the chopper corkscrewed down, the wind rushing through the open doors, the door gunner firing wild bursts from his M-60. Ravines and green razorback ridges spun giddyingly across Webb's vision through the gunner's door. Fat blobs of red rose from the 50-calibre anti-aircraft guns, floating lazily towards them as if someone were lobbing beer cans at them from the trees, then suddenly they seemed to accelerate and whip-crack past them.

The Huey bounced as it hit the ground. They didn't wait for it to settle, throwing themselves clear and staggering immediately to their feet to weave through the storm of dust and debris, crouching low to avoid the rotor tips.

A mortar round thudded into the dirt not thirty metres away. Webb slipped and fell on his face. He wondered for a moment if he had been hit. Then a huge hand emerged from the ground and dragged him towards a trench. He toppled in and lay winded on his back.

A giant black man in tiger stripe camous crouched over him, his face stark with dirt, fear and exhaustion.

'Is it our reinforcements?' someone said.

'Hell, no,' the black giant said. 'It's just the fucking press.'

# 18

The Central Highlands of Vietnam scared even the Special Forces. At noon the sun barely filtered through the canopy of giant, gnarled hardwoods, and turned daylight into a furnace netherworld of shadows and silence and contrary mists. It was a place from the imagination of Conan Doyle, and was inhabited by the Montagnards, a strange and silent people who had become allies of the Americans and South Vietnamese by default. The northerners hated them and regarded them with a mixture of contempt and fear.

Que Trang itself was no more than a bermed dirt fort, a shambles of rusting barbed wire and rotting sandbags. The base had the look of a long siege; there were gaps in the rusted barbed wire where sappers had cut a way through, and in places their bodies still lay rotting in the sun. The ground was littered with spent shell casings, rusting ration cans, sodden pages from *Stars and Stripes* and blood-stained combat dressings. The monsoon had come, turning the red laterite into an ochre porridge. In a way the mud was a blessing; it soaked up the incoming and deadened the shrapnel.

The fort was manned by Montagnard mercenaries, under the command of a handful of American Special Forces and Vietnamese paratroopers. The Americans themselves had the look of men taken too far; their faces were gaunt from fear and exhaustion.

Everywhere there was the smell of death and dust and rancid sweat.

After the Huey had disappeared to the south, Ryan and Webb trotted away from the perimeter, picking their way along the red mud pathways, past the wreckage of the barracks. Most of the hooches inside the compound had been destroyed by mortar and rocket fire; the tin roofs of the few that remained were littered with shell holes. They finally located the headquarters, a bunker near the centre of the compound, the roof lined with rotting sandbags.

A lieutenant gave them thick, bitter coffee laced with Jack Daniels and two benzedrine tablets. They were assigned racks in a bunker near the perimeter of one of the hooches, and then handed an M–16 and three M–26 fragmentation grenades each.

'The enemy's right out there,' he said, 'in those trees.'

'The enemy?' Ryan said. 'You mean *Newsweek*?'

The lieutenant gave him a frigid smile. He had made it clear by his manner that he didn't like reporters. 'Cute,' he said. He nodded towards the surrounding mountains. 'There's maybe three battalions of NVA sitting in those hills. Sure as God made little green apples they are going to come deedley-boppin' through that wire some time this morning. Fact is, we're going to need all the help we can get.' The lieutenant pointed to the M–16s. 'You know how to use those mothers?'

'I know how to use one,' Webb told him. 'But I'm not going to.'

'Why not, son?'

*Son*. The lieutenant was probably only a year older than Webb. 'Because I'm a journalist, not a soldier.'

The lieutenant shrugged. 'That's up to you, I guess. It's your funeral.'

Webb and Ryan ate their C-rations in the bunker and watched the sun sink over the Highlands. Around them the Special Forces soldiers prepared for the night, smearing night fighter cosmetic under their eyes, clicking banana clips into their weapons and tucking grenades into the pockets of their camous. They threw sidelong glances at the Montagnards around them, wondering if they could trust them to hold their line, if they would still be there beside them on the berm in the morning.

Every few minutes a mortar round thudded into the camp.

Night fell quickly here. The air grew damp, and chill. Webb shivered inside his poncho. Fear crept through the lines, tangible, like a gas.

The radio in the bunker was tuned to the Armed Forces radio network.

*And for all you guys and girls at the 17th Evac, especially Mo in the Orderly Room, here's one from the fabulous Rolling Stones.*

'Why did you say you wouldn't use that?' Ryan said, pointing to the M-16 at Webb's side.

'We're not here to fight. If we start carrying guns then we become targets.'

'Oh sure, Charles is really hung up about shooting war correspondents by mistake.'

'It's a question of professional ethics. I haven't used a weapon yet. I don't intend to start now.'

'I'll give you an example of professional ethics, mate. In '68 I was with an ARVN platoon in the Delta and we were being overrun. One soldier died right there next to me and when I looked up there was this Charles running towards me with an AK. I was faced with an ethical dilemma then. The dilemma was: do I want to die right now? The answer, funnily enough, was no. So I picked up the dead bloke's M-16 and fired off a few rounds.'

'Did you kill him?'

'I never stuck around to find out. But I know I hit him because his head came off.'

*I see a red door and I want to paint it black . . .*

Webb shook his head. 'I don't believe in killing.'

'Then why the fuck are you here?'

'Because I don't believe in killing.'

Ryan shook his head. 'You amaze me sometimes, Spider.'

The moon rose, fat and yellow over the jagged trunk of a splintered tree. Through the flap of canvas Webb watched an illumination flare drop over the perimeter. He scraped the last of the cold ham stew from the can, listened to the rats scratching on the bunker floor. Ryan lit a cigarette, offered one to Webb. Webb didn't usually smoke, apart from the occasional opium pipe, but now he felt the need. Clean lungs wouldn't matter much if he was dead in the morning.

'Crosby'll be spitting chips he missed this,' Ryan said.

'Sure. He's back in Danang, he's filed his story, and he's eating T-bone steak and drinking chilled beer. Poor bastard.'

'But we've got the dateline. He hasn't.'

Webb coughed as he drew on the cigarette.

'You scared, Spider?'

'Of course I am. What kind of person would not be scared in this situation?'

'Just that . . . it's okay, you know.'

'I know it's okay.' He had never got to love the fear, as Ryan claimed to have done. He just got through the fear every time, for the story, because someone had to do it.

The lieutenant, doing his rounds of the perimeter, swore at them for breaking the blackout and dropped the canvas flap of the bunker shut. They lay back on their bunks in the darkness, fully clothed. The only light now was the burning orange tips of their cigarettes and the small, green glow from the radio valves.

*If you're going to San Francisco, be sure to wear some flowers in your hair.*

'About Odile . . .' Ryan said.

'I don't want to talk about her.'

'Are you in love with her, Spider?'

'No.'

'She reckons you are.'

'I can't help what she thinks.'

'I don't know what there was between the two of you but . . . I promised I'd look after her. She's my problem now, not yours.'

'Sure.'

'I didn't know she had a kid, mate. It's just that . . . I'm not the marrying kind. I couldn't imagine spending my life making love to one woman. You might as well put me in bloody prison.'

'Then why didn't you let her be?'

'I couldn't. I mean, I really thought this was different. But then, after a while, it . . . it turned out to be just the same. I got bored, I suppose.'

'Jesus, Ryan. It's not like there's a shortage of women in this country. You had to prove a point, didn't you? How many points did you give yourself for screwing a nun?'

'I know what I am. I don't need you to preach to me.'

Webb felt something sting the soft, tender flesh on the inside of his thigh. A leech had found its way there from the ooze around his ankles. He swung his legs up on to the bunk and closed his eyes. He waited for his other senses to kick in; he heard the soft pop of another illumination round, detected the smell of stale urine, mouldy canvas, and the sour odour of his own fear.

'Did you sleep with her, Spider?'

'No.'

'So what was it all about, then?'

'You wouldn't understand.'

'Try me.'

A mosquito whining around his head. *And this is Count Malaria here on AFVN reminding you to take your chloroquine phosphate pills . . .*

'I couldn't walk away and pretend I didn't know her,' Webb said. 'Oh, just another gook having a bad time. I didn't want to play at being compassionate. I wanted to do something over here besides take pictures.'

Ryan was silent.

'Now I've got a question for you,' Webb said. 'What are you going to do about her?'

'I don't know.'

'You don't love her.'

'I don't . . . I don't want to be responsible for anyone but me.'

'So why did you go back? If you'd left her with me you wouldn't have had to worry any more, would you?'

'I don't need any of this bullshit from you. I'll do the right thing, but I'll do it my way.'

Webb put the grenades and the rifle under his cot, flicked on a pencil light, checking that the first aid kit and his cameras and notebooks were within easy reach. Then they lay there in the dark listening to the terrible silence.

'What happens if you get blown away tonight?' Webb said, finally.

'Then I won't have to worry about it any more, will I?'

'This is not about you. It's about her. And the baby.'

'Yeah, well, life's a lottery, mate. We all take our chances. Maybe it's karma, like the Buddhists say.'

'Jesus, you're a callous bastard.'

'Look, I'll tell you something about me. Back home there was this creek. Big Moreton Bay Fig grew right next to it. Some older kids put a rope on one of the branches so they could swing across. My older brother dared me to join in. Thing was, I couldn't swim, but I didn't want any of the other kids to know I was scared, so I did it. Almost made it, too. Trouble was, the rope broke. The other kids laughed. They thought I was clowning around. I remember going under. It was like my chest was going to burst, then I couldn't hold on any more. I took this big mouthful of water and I started to black out. I knew I was going to die. As luck would have it, my brother pulled me out, and I woke up at home in my mum's bed. When I realised I was still alive and heaven wasn't a feather bed with jarrah corner posts, I remember thinking two things: one, I didn't ever have to be scared again, because I'd already been dead and it was okay. And two, I wasn't going to let anyone persuade me to do anything I didn't want to do ever again, no matter what they thought of me. So I'll play this my way, all right?'

'The only difference is, you were ten years old then. Every ten-year-old thinks the world was made just for them.'

'Well, maybe they're right.'

The silence was broken by the plop of a mortar round. Outgoing. A comforting sound, almost made you feel safe.

'What would you have done about Odile if I hadn't come back?' Ryan asked him.

'I don't know.'

'Yeah you do,' Ryan said. 'And I'll tell you something else. Maybe it's a good job I did.'

'Look, I don't give a damn about her, or about you. Do whatever the hell you want. Now go to sleep.'

# 19

It was two in the morning when the first 80-millimetre mortar rounds hit the camp. The noise and the concussion were like a physical blow. Webb was jolted awake, and instinctively rolled off his cot on to the floor. His whole body was shaking with the sudden adrenalin rush of fear. He fumbled for his cameras and notebooks and slopped outside through the mud to the nearest firing bunker.

Illumination rounds were streaking down the skyline, magnesium brilliant, silhouetting the jungle; blue-green tracers floated towards them, orange ones arced out. Death was beautiful by night.

Another mortar round thudded in, very close. He heard someone screaming.

'Ryan!' Webb shouted.

'Right here, mate,' a voice said beside him.

Silence. Webb stared across the perimeter, heard bamboo click in the wind, saw shadows flick through the mahogany trees. But there was no wind, and no moon to make shadows.

'Here we go,' Ryan said.

There was a series of explosions as NVA sappers took out the mines in the wire. Webb heard the distinctive popping sound of the NVA assault rifles, the answering bursts of Armalites; the stench of cordite drifted across the perimeter.

A parachute flare fell down a grey lowering sky. Bodies hung on the blown wire. The clouds meant there would be no air support. They were on their own.

He saw the shadowy figures of the NVA run through the wire, stagger and fall under a hail of machine gun fire. But others kept coming.

He heard someone screaming, 'Drop back! Drop back!' The NVA were inside the fort.

I don't have to do this any more, Webb told himself. I don't have to do this any more. 'We're being overrun,' he heard Ryan shouting. 'Hope you've got your M-16, mate. Or are you still feeling ethical?'

Webb answered his body's desperate need to run, scrambling over the lip of the bunker, slipping blindly through the mud. Flares and explosions lit the fort like strobe, warping all judgment of time and distance. He fell head first into a slit trench.

The bunker's only other occupant crouched next to him on the floor, bloodied teeth set in a mess of raw mincemeat. The man had taken a round in the face. His M-16 was still cradled in his arms.

'Ryan!'

'I'm hit,' he heard him groan somewhere in the darkness. 'I'm hit.'

Another flare illuminated the battlefield, almost directly overhead. Ryan was on his knees, a lone NVA soldier running towards him, his rifle resting on his hip. A quick burst into the back of Ryan's head and he would run on, looking for other targets.

Webb snatched the M-16 from the dead Montagnard, brought it to his shoulder. A moment's hesitation.

He wondered what Odile would do if Ryan did not come back to Saigon tomorrow morning.

He saw him clearly for that moment, the image burned into his brain, the details to be examined later, strand by strand. He was clad in a black shirt and shorts and he appeared very young, though Webb later decided that may just have been his imagination at work. The curious shape of the pith helmet was silhouetted against the dropping flare. He stood over Ryan, ready to fire from the hip.

Webb thought about Odile.

If he really wanted her he would have only to wait a few moments more.

His finger touched the trigger and he released the prescribed three rounds, the range no more than ten yards.

'Over here,' Webb said.

He reached for Ryan's hand, pulled him into the trench. A platoon of Strikers rushed past to fill the gap in front of them. The battle washed over them, like the ebb of a tide, and they were suddenly behind the lines again, beached and safe.

# 20

It was raining. The fort smelled of damp and death; drifting smoke carried with it the reek of the dump fire, the foul breath of the slaughterhouse. No smell more vile than death, Webb thought. And perhaps just as well. If it smelled good there would hardly be anybody left alive.

Ryan lay on a stretcher inside the sandbagged bunker that served as a hospital, a large M painted on his forehead with grease pencil. Other casualties from the night lay outside on the ground, swathed in blood-soaked dressings, eyes glazed from morphine and shock.

Webb strained for the sound of the medevac chopper.

He walked slowly back to the perimeter, to assure himself this awful thing was no dream. He found him, lying face down near the trench, his back blown apart by the exit of the high-velocity bullets. A swarm of green metallic flies rose in a cloud as he approached.

He flipped the body with his foot. There were three small bullet wounds stitched across the chest, what a professional soldier would have called a neat job. Webb felt no pride, but no regret either.

'Poor bastard,' he said.

He turned around, saw a Special Forces sergeant grinning at him. His face shone with a curious light, serene and wild at once. Combat gave a man licence to go beyond the dark edge into madness, Ryan had told him once. If he forgot to come back, no one noticed until he went home.

The man laughed, undid his fly and urinated into the mouth of one of the corpses. He was still laughing as Webb walked away.

The first Hueys were coming down the valley, to take out the wounded.

Webb mentally composed his copy, dateline, 3 April, 1972.

'Today I killed a man . . .'

But a magazine was not a confessional. And what was there to confess? If he had not fired his weapon, it would have meant the death of a fellow correspondent. And that death he could not have lived with, because he would have inflicted it in order to take Ryan's woman.

He went back to get his camera, captured the aftermath of Que Trang on three rolls of high-resolution colour film, for the vicarious thrill of a reader in London or Paris or Sydney. Death was a little like pornography, after all. The same shame and fascination mixed in together, inseparable.

As he climbed aboard the medevac chopper, he turned around and saw that the Special Forces sergeant had followed him. He was watching him, eyes burning under the poncho hood with messianic intensity. Webb tried to ignore him but the man suddenly came over, grabbed his arm, and jerked his face close to his. He could smell his breath, rank like a jackal's. 'Don't you got nothin' better to do with your life, man?' he whispered.

The Huey started to lift from the ground.

'I hope you die,' he shouted. 'You hear me? I hope you die!'

## Seventh Regiment Armoury

'So what happened to Ryan?' Doyle asked.

'They put him on a medevac to Pleiku and the surgeons picked thirty-four pieces of metal out of his butt.'

'They didn't get all the pieces,' Cochrane said. 'They used to say whenever he stepped through a metal detector he'd set the damn thing off with the metal that was still in his ass. Caught a plane with him once at JFK down to Guatemala and damn if it wasn't true.'

There were fond smiles around the table. The Sean Ryan legend always grew in the retelling. The fabric of the myth had become part of the tapestry of each man's own personal history.

'And what about Odile?'

Crosby looked at Webb, and their eyes locked. They would both have preferred the other to have told this part of the story. The question always hung there between them: perhaps I could have done more. No matter which way you told it, it always sounded, to their ears, as if they had failed.

Crosby was the first to look away. He reached across the table and took a cigarette from the packet Cochrane had left on the linen tablecloth. He lit it with Cochrane's lighter.

'We should have done something,' he said, looking at Webb.

'Like what?'

Crosby shrugged and looked at Doyle. 'It wasn't that he didn't care for her,' he said. 'I think his intentions were always good. At the beginning.'

'His intentions were always just to get laid,' Webb said.

'You're not being fair.'

'You're breaking my heart.'

'Ryan needed adrenalin like other people need oxygen. If he didn't get a constant rush I swear he would have died. A twenty-year relationship would last him about two weeks. Sex, danger, it was like breathing in and out to him. Some people said he was brave to the point of being reckless. But that wasn't the point. To be brave you have to be a little bit afraid to begin with. But Ryan got such a rush from all that shit. I swear he couldn't actually feel fear like the rest of us. At least, that's what I think.' He looked back at Webb. 'If he really didn't give a shit about Odile and the kid, he would not have stayed in Saigon.'

Webb shrugged. Maybe.

'He was still with her when you went back, at the end?' Doyle asked.

Webb nodded. 'He spent most of the next two years covering the war in Cambodia, from Phnom Penh. But he kept the apartment in Saigon for Odile and Phuong. Every few months he'd fly back and see them. I think he was hoping that in the meantime she'd find some American civil engineer to take her home to the States and off his hands. But she never did. She waited for him.'

'Perhaps she did it to punish him,' Wendy Doyle said.

Webb smiled at that. 'Maybe.'

'Where were you?'

'I sold the photographs and the story of the Que Trang fight to *Paris-Match*, and they turned it into a six-page spread. On the strength of it, the AP offered me a job with them. Croz here set it up for me. Not long after they asked me if I wanted to transfer to the Washington office. Frankly, I couldn't wait to get out. I kept thinking about what that Special Forces sergeant had said to me: *I hope you die*. I told myself I would never ever go back as long as I lived.'

'But you did.'

'Early in 1975 Thieu abandoned the Highlands to the NVA and

things moved fast after that. When Danang fell it was obvious to everyone that the communists were finally going to win. Vietnam had been such a big part of my life, I felt I had to be there, for the end. My bosses at the AP okayed the assignment at the beginning of April and I flew back to Saigon.

'And that was the last time I saw Odile.'

# III

## Saigon, April 1975

'If you have not seen a battle, your education has been somewhat neglected. For after all, war has been one of the primary functions of mankind, and unless you see men fight you miss something fundamental.'

– Herbert Matthews, war correspondent

'I just figured what with guns going off and things blowing up, there'd be plenty of deep truths and penetrating insights.'

– P.J. O'Rourke, *Holidays in Hell*

# 21

He had flown in to Tan Son Nhut many times before, but never like this. The pilot came in high, very high, before making a steep and rapid descent towards the airstrip. It was combat flying, and the 737 groaned and protested at the manoeuvre. Minutes later the airliner's wheels hammered on to the tarmac.

Webb looked out of the window. A blur of heavily camouflaged bombers and transports choked the aprons. As the scream of the engines' reverse thrust died away, the silky, breathless voice of the air hostess announced their safe arrival in Saigon. Even she sounded a little surprised that they had made it, Webb thought. His own fingers were clawed around the armrests, as if he were in a dentist's chair. Welcome to Saigon. A little jolt of fear just to get you started, get you used to it.

He had read about amputees experiencing phantom feelings from fingers and toes no longer there. That was the way it had been for him when he had left Vietnam. At first Washington had been new and dynamic and exciting; there had been the buzz of being so close to real power, feeling part of history. But after a few months it had all started to pall and there were times when he found himself actually missing Vietnam, missing the fear, the stench of the markets, the adrenalin rushes, sleeping with his camera under his pillow. The code was savage but simpler; hear a bang, hit the ground, haggle, hassle, trust no one except your fellow correspondents and sometimes even then . . .

In Saigon he had always had a little tingling of fear in the belly to let him know that he was alive. Everything was impermanent, so the present had been the most precious thing of all. By comparison Washington with its apartment blocks and traffic and TV dinners seemed like a wasteground.

As he stepped off the plane into the damp wall of heat he knew a part of his soul had been left here in Saigon. When he had first arrived he had brought with him a single change of clothes and his ambition; he had left overloaded with rage and guilt.

The rage and guilt were still there.

But this was a different Saigon from the one he remembered. Acres of refugee slums, shanties made of cardboard and flattened beer cans, had mushroomed on the outskirts of the city. All the government buildings bristled with barbed wire. There were checkpoints all the way along the road from the airport, keeping the hordes of refugees out of the city. The roads were clogged; everywhere fists were jammed on to horns. Small boys jabbed Coca-Cola bottles filled with petrol through the window of the cab.

'Petrol very expensive now,' his taxi driver explained. 'One Coca bottle same price as maybe five litre last month.'

It was a city in mindless panic. People seemed to be rushing everywhere, but where was there to go? The taxi crawled on into the city, past the sandbagged machine gun posts and the barbed wire barricades and the makeshift tank traps.

'Why you come to Saigon?' the taxi driver wanted to know.

'*Bao chi*,' Webb said. 'Journalist.'

The man fumbled in the breast pocket of his shirt and produced a folded, crumpled letter. He shoved it in Webb's hand. 'You read,' he said.

Webb unfolded the letter. *To whom it may concern. This is to certify that Tran van Minh, the bearer of this letter, served in the capacity of translator and adviser to the United States Army from April 1965 to February 1966, and proved himself a loyal friend of the United States. Please render him all assistance. Captain James Metherell. First Air Cavalry. Danang, 26 February, 1966.*

Webb handed the letter back.

'You help me get out of Saigon, okay?' the man said.

'I'll see what I can do,' Webb lied. It was like he had never been away.

# 22

'Well, look what the war dragged in,' a voice said.

Crosby and Ryan were sprawled in wicker chairs on the Shelf, in dust-stained Saigon jackets. Ryan had two Leicas slung around his neck, as if he were in the field. The love beads and the curling seventies moustache were gone, but otherwise he appeared untouched by the last three years, dark hair falling over one eye, grinning, unscathed.

'You boys must be going soft,' Webb said. 'Sun's been up nearly an hour. Why aren't you in the front line?'

'We are,' Crosby said. He pulled a chair towards the table with his foot. 'Sit down, and join the legion of the damned.'

Only Crosby looked older. His hair was still long but now there was a thin patch on the crown and several long silver strands in his moustache. Deep lines had been etched around his eyes. He had lived his life hard and now it was starting to show. Webb wondered what had made Ryan immune.

'When did you arrive back in sunny Saigon?' Ryan asked him.

'Yesterday afternoon. What about you?'

Crosby and Ryan exchanged a look that could have meant anything. 'We were in Phnom Penh until a few days ago. We decided to get out. Didn't care for the Khmer Rouge.'

'Butt still full of tin?' Webb said.

Ryan patted his backside. 'Last time I saw Spider,' he said to Crosby, 'I had an ass full of frags. I asked him to suck them out before they got infected, but he wouldn't do it. Right bloody mate he turned out to be.'

Webb had not heard from Ryan in three years, ever since the night in Que Trang, and in his more sanguine moments he imagined Ryan might be grateful to him for saving his life. He very possibly was, but he was not going to say so in front of Crosby. He could not let the legend down.

The Shelf faced Lam Son Square, and the hideous war monument, two giant Vietnamese soldiers cast in green cement. Loudspeakers had been hooked up around the statue, and martial music blared over the din of horns and traffic.

'You look like shit, Spider.'

'Thanks.'

'Croz says you're with his lot now.'

'Yeah. Washington.'

'How do you deal with all that shit? Shouting at press secretaries across the White House lawn, having Secret Service guys stick their elbows in your face when you get too close.'

'I did my time. I'm not a war junkie like you guys.'

'Sure. You got Vietnam on your CV. That's all that counts, right, Spider?'

Webb looked at Ryan, searching for malice in that boyish face but finding none. He wore the same ingenuous expression he had carried through Pleiku and the Delta and God knows where else, the eyes as black as a Leica lens, recording everything with impartial good humour.

'What brought you back?' Crosby said.

'Same reason as you, I suppose.'

'It's like Monopoly for us,' Ryan said. 'We did the fall of Phnom Penh. Now we're doing the fall of Saigon. All we need is the fall of Bangkok and we've got the set.'

At the next table there was a group of civil engineers, big crewcut men talking too loud. Their Vietnamese girlfriends were with them, smiles frozen into place. They clutched at the men's arms with something approaching desperation. This was their last drink in the Continental before Tan Son Nhut and a jet to America, Webb guessed. They were probably signed on to a flight as fiancées or spouses. It might not be everything these girls had once wished for themselves, but it was better than being left behind.

The white-jacketed waiter brought their breakfasts – boiled eggs, slices of paw paw, *café au lait*. Ryan took a hip flask from his pocket and tipped a little Mekong whisky into each of their cups. 'Here's health,' he said.

'How are things back in the world?' Crosby asked.

'Changing. Sometimes I think the sixties never happened.'

'I guess that's why I don't want to go back,' Crosby said. He waved an arm towards the square. 'Hell, I'll sure miss the ol' homestead,' he said in a mock Southern drawl, but Webb knew it wasn't a joke. 'This one's nearly done, Hugh. Some people say weeks, others say it's just a few days. Lenin's little brown stormtroopers are on their way. This time next month the old Shelf will be the Ho Chi Minh Inn.'

'We'll find another war,' Ryan said.

'Not like this one, baby. Not like this one.'

'They're all like this one,' Ryan said.

The question burned. He had wanted to ask it as soon as he saw him, had swallowed it down. Ryan knew what he was thinking, of course, or had guessed. But he just sat there, smiling, in that way of his. Giving no clues.

'How's Odile?' Webb asked him, at last, as casually as he could.

'Who?'

Their eyes locked.

Ryan grinned. 'Oh, she's fine.'

'Is she still in Saigon?'

'We've got an apartment in Cholon. Come round this evening. We'll have dinner.'

'Is Phuong with her?'

'With us. Yeah. Where else would she be?'

'Is she all right?'

'Why the hell don't you take up social work, Spider?'

Webb felt a rush of anger. He had hoped Ryan had found a way to get them out of Vietnam by now, put them on a flight to Australia or the States perhaps. 'When are you going to get them out of here?'

'I thought maybe I'd piss off and leave them behind,' Ryan said, a harder edge to his voice now. 'I'm a lot of things, mate, but I'm not as big a bastard as you seem to think.'

'I wouldn't count on it,' Crosby said.

'You should have found a way to get them out of Saigon a long time ago.'

Ryan made a face. 'Ever see *Pinocchio*?' he said to Crosby. 'There was this character, Jimminy Cricket. He used to sit on Pinocchio's shoulder and be his conscience. That's Spider, in my life. Jimminy Cricket.'

Webb ignored him. 'What the hell are you planning to do?'

'Don't worry, Spider. I'll get her out before the godless goons burst into Saigon.'

'How long are you going to wait? Until you see them running across the square? Why the hell don't you get her out now?'

Ryan raised an eyebrow. There was a long silence. 'She won't go.'

'Won't go?'

'Not without me. And I'm not going yet. So. Her choice, mate.'

'You could make her go.'

Ryan leaned forward, angry too, impatient with Webb's interrogation of his private life. 'What fucking business is it of yours?'

'Just don't let her down,' Webb said.

The grin returned as suddenly as it had disappeared. 'Would I ever let anyone down?'

Ryan's apartment was on the top floor of a two-storey house in Cholon, in a warren of alleys about half a mile from the Arroyo Chinois. Once it had perhaps been the home of some minor French administrator, but it had long ago fallen into disrepair, the whitewash flaking off the walls, the green-louvred windows hanging from their hinges. The house was sandwiched between a furniture maker and a noodle restaurant and the alley smelled of camphor and fish.

Webb pushed aside a sliding gate of horizontal wooden bars and went up a narrow wooden staircase. He rapped twice on the door. 'Viet Cong. Special delivery.'

Ryan opened the door. He was dressed in his own inimitable style, with a startling red and black paisley shirt over his jeans. Whatever women see in him, Webb thought, it's not his dress sense.

'Spider. You made it.'

'Sorry I'm late. I had to cross three different front lines and two border posts to get here. Tell me, what made you decide to live in the country?'

'Jesus, it's not that far. Humble journo like me can't afford to keep apartments in two different cities.'

The apartment was large, with a spacious living room and two bedrooms leading off from the main hallway. There was some wicker furniture, and a small sink and a stove in one corner. The walls had been decorated with some of Ryan's less macabre photographs: monks, smiling street kids, several of Ryan himself in his field gear, or perched in the doorways of helicopters. In one corner was a small candlelit altar, incense burning under a crucifix that had been affixed to the wall.

Odile emerged from one of the bedrooms, holding Phuong.

Her appearance was different somehow, in a way Webb was unable to define. Her beauty was still as overpowering as he remembered, and she was accompanied by a heady rush of expensive French eau de toilette. She wore a blue *ao dai*, her hair was freshly brushed and fell about her shoulders, and she was wearing lip gloss – to please Ryan, he guessed.

She seemed touchingly pleased to see him. 'Hugh,' she said, and conferred a broad smile.

'Hello, Odile.' They all waited for him to say something else, but he couldn't find the words. So the three of them stood in shuffling silence, until Odile indicated the child clinging tightly to her left hand.

'You remember Phuong,' she said.

The plump little girl with the sprouts of straight black hair was gone. This older Phuong was reed-thin with long glossy hair like her mother's, the same compromising round eyes and creamed-coffee skin. 'I remember a Goodyear blimp,' Webb said. 'Not this beautiful little girl.'

Phuong was shy, and clung to her mother's leg. She was staring at him, intrigued, but looked away quickly as soon as she caught his eye. She was dressed, like her mother, in a soft violet *ao dai*, and had been washed and preened for the occasion. Webb felt flattered.

Ryan studied his daughter with genuine affection. 'Great kid,' he said. 'Speaks English and French as well as Vietnamese. Unbelievable. But sometimes she mixes up her words so you have to know bits of all three languages to get it all.'

Webb bent down. He had brought Phuong a present, a doll he had bought at the Central Market. He held it out to her, but she turned away and hid her face in the silk trousers of her mother's *ao dai*.

'You always did have a way with women,' Ryan said. He took the doll and crouched down. 'Little Phuong,' he said, from the corner of his mouth, pretending it was the doll speaking. 'Little Phuong, why don't you come out to play?' The little girl turned around, immediately prepared to accept the illusion. 'Little Phuoooong!'

She giggled, at him, then at the doll.

'Your daddy feels pretty stupid making this funny voice, so you'd better come and get me!'

She snatched the doll away.

'Say thank you to Mr Webb for the nice doll,' Odile scolded.

'*Merci* very much,' Phuong mumbled.

'Thank you,' Odile said. 'I am sorry. She is just a little shy.'

'How do you reckon she'll go in Sydney, mate?' Ryan said.

'I'm sure they'll love her.'

Ryan smiled, but his eyes were hard. They both knew what he was thinking. 'Yeah,' he said. 'Sure they will.'

Odile had prepared a three-course dinner: Vietnamese spring rolls – rolls of rice paper filled with minced pork, crab, vermicelli and mushrooms, fried until they were crisp and brown; *cha ca* – fish slices braised over charcoal with noodles, roasted peanuts, lemon and *nuoc mam*, served with green salad; and for dessert *banh daui xanh*, mung bean cake accompanied by green Chinese tea, much more expensive than Vietnamese tea and reserved only for special occasions.

Odile was quiet, as always. Occasionally she asked Webb questions about his new life in America, and if he was married.

'No, no wife,' Webb said.

She gave a soft, sad smile.

'Who'd have him?' Ryan said.

Ryan, as usual, dominated the conversation, talking about his experiences in Cambodia, the barbarity of Khmer Rouge attacks on civilians, the indoctrination of the teenage soldiers and how it had turned them into crazed killers. But most of all he spoke about how fiercely the government soldiers had defended Phnom Penh, and how they had finally been defeated through lack of supplies and ammunition. 'Nixon got them into that war, and Kissinger said the Americans would back them. Then they pulled out and left them high and dry. Just like here.'

After the meal, Odile left the table to put Phuong to bed. Ryan and Webb went out on to the balcony with a bottle of Bushmills.

'I'm going to miss this place,' Ryan said. 'Be it ever so humble and the rest of it. I suppose your place in Washington is a little bit better.'

'It takes me an hour and a half to get to work.'

Ryan poured two glasses of whisky and raised his in toast. He gave Webb a knowing grin. 'Bet you thought Sean Ryan had left her.'

'I don't know what I thought.'

'You're a bloody liar, Spider.'

'All right, yes, I did think that.'

'One of the advantages of being a bastard, mate. You always have a margin to surprise people.'

'Why don't you marry her?'

'Why didn't you?'

Webb shook his head. What a stupid question.

'I'm serious,' Ryan said.

'She doesn't love me.'

'Yeah, she's like that. Most Vietnamese girls will love anyone who offers to get them out of Vietnam. Think she'd be the same . . . bitch.'

Webb glared at him, and the profanity hung in the silence between them. Ryan finally looked up, his expression contrite. 'She won't go, Spider. I've offered to send her anywhere she wants. I know I can fix it, but she won't leave without me. She thinks I won't come back for her once I know she's safe.'

'She's right.'

'That's got nothing to do with it, mate. She's got the kid to think about. She's just being perverse.'

'That's good coming from you.'

'I'm immoral, not perverse. There's a difference.'

Webb heard Odile singing Phuong a lullaby, in Vietnamese, a haunting melody he had never heard before. He saw her shadow on the wall of the bedroom, in the flicker of the gas lamp.

'What are you going to do?'

'They'll come with me when I leave. It's all arranged. I organised a visa through the Australian embassy. No worries.'

'And then?'

He took a long time to answer. 'Mate, I might try and make a go of it this time. I'm thirty years old. I've spent the last ten years in South-East Asia getting shot at. Old Hughie's looked after Sean Ryan pretty well but maybe it's time I gave him a break. Settle down, do a bit of surfing, the odd snap for the *Coolongatta Chronicle* or some such bloody thing.'

'Do you love her?'

'What's that Stephen Stills song – love the one you're with? When I was in Phnom Penh I was in love all the time. When I'm in Saigon I'm in love with Odile. I guess with me, love's just a matter of geography.' He saw Webb's expression. 'You're not like me, mate. Don't try and understand.'

'Why don't you get her out now, for God's sake? People are starting to panic. The whole thing could get out of control.'

'My job's here. Anyway, they say there could be a negotiated settlement.'

'That's crap and you know it.'

He laughed, in acknowledgment. 'Yeah, suppose I do. But this is still the biggest story around and I'm not shooting through until it's done. Then I'll think about kicking back for a bit, not before.'

They sat in silence for a while, listening to the distant rumble. Not B-52s, like the old days. This time it was NVA artillery, as the communists tightened their stranglehold.

'You ever think of settling down, getting out of this business?'

'Sometimes.'

'Yeah?'

'I promised myself once this is over I'm not going to do this any more. Funny. Sometimes in Washington I really missed this place, but now I'm back it scares the hell out of me.'

'Yeah, well, there you go. It's never scared me, not in all the time I've been out here. Only one thing really stirs me up. In fact it scares me so much, it keeps me awake at night.'

'Dying?'

'No, boredom. I don't mind pain, I don't mind fear, at least you know you're alive. No, I can't stand the thought of being bored.' He drained his glass and poured three more fingers. 'Why didn't you sleep with her?'

The sudden shift in the conversation caught Webb off guard. He didn't know what to say.

'You love her, don't you?'

Webb shook his head. 'No.'

Ryan raised an eyebrow to register his incredulity. 'No?'

'She's the most beautiful woman I've ever seen in my life. When she stayed with me, yes, I thought about it all the time. But I didn't love her. Not really.'

'And that's why you didn't sleep with her?'

Webb looked away so Ryan would not read the lie. 'I guess so.'

'Christ, I feel so dirty when I'm around you, mate. You're a fucking saint. I don't know how you've survived in this world as long as you have.'

Odile had finished the lullaby. She suddenly reappeared on the balcony, leaned on Ryan's shoulder and kissed him. 'Goodnight, *chérie*,' she whispered.

'You don't have to go to bed,' Ryan said.

'I have heard all your war stories and all your dirty jokes a hundred times. And I am tired.' She gave Webb a small smile. 'Goodnight, Hugh.' She held out her hand. He took it. 'It was wonderful to see you again.'

He stood up. 'It was wonderful to see you, too. And Phuong.'

'I owe you so much,' she said, and she stood on tiptoe and kissed him on the cheek. 'Be careful.'

She went back inside, shutting the balcony doors behind her.

Ryan looked at Webb. 'She always talks about you, you know.'

'Does she?'

'You must be proud of yourself. Every man's fantasy, saving a beautiful girl from prostitution.' He drained his glass and poured another. 'Sorry. I didn't mean that the way it sounded.' He turned away and looked across the alley at his neighbours in the apartment opposite. A Chinese man in a white undershirt was staring at a flickering black and white television, three small children clustered on the floor at his feet; his wife was sewing clothes under a bare bulb at the window. The harsh staccato voices of the television jumbled with the clamour of Chinese music on a radio from somewhere further down the alley, and two Vietnamese shouting at each other below.

'You didn't have to take her back.'

'No, I suppose not. But I always wonder what you would have done if I'd died that night at Que Trang.'

'I never thought about it.' Webb answered, too quickly.

'Then you would have been stuck with it, mate. You would have had to have taken care of her, whether you wanted to or not. You would have lost your out.' He grinned. 'So it was lucky for you too.'

'And you think you're not perverse.'

Ryan nodded, in acknowledgment. 'I never thanked you for what you did that night. I should have done. I guess I don't like thinking how close it was.'

'You would have done the same for me.'

'Not if I reckoned there was a good snap in it.' He smiled to show he was only joking. Perhaps. He refilled their glasses and raised his in toast. 'What will we drink to?'

'Saigon?'

Ryan nodded. 'Yeah. Goodnight, Saigon.'

They touched glasses.

'How long do you think?' Webb asked him.

'Before Charles gets here? Month at the outside.'

'People say there's going to be a bloodbath. I've heard stories that the Viet Cong beheaded half a dozen policemen in Danang.'

'That's bullshit.'

'But it could get ugly. Especially if the city comes under heavy shellfire, or there's door-to-door fighting.'

'Well, we'll be long gone.'

'Yeah, that's it, isn't it? The joy of being a correspondent. When the war gets too hot, we can always go home.' He thought again about McCague, and Judge, and the Special Forces sergeant in the poncho up at Que Trang. 'Do you think we did any good here?'

'I don't know, mate. I never think about it. It's not my job.'

'You've never been touched by any of this? By what's happened to these people, what's happened to the kids?'

Ryan shrugged. 'There's always going to be wars, there's always going to be people suffering, usually women and kids. You can't change that. Not with a few snaps.'

'What about the pictures Eddie Adams took of Loan shooting that VC during Tet? Or the girl with the napalm on her back, running down that road. They changed people's minds about this war back home.'

'Because they were ready to have their minds changed. Anyway, we both know that pictures lie. That one of Loan, for instance. One of his men had just had his wife and kids executed by the Viet Cong in his own home. The bloke Loan shot was the local VC area commander. So he was responsible for what had happened. But that picture put in people's minds that the South Vietnamese were the only ones committing atrocities. It was the truth, because atrocities were going on, but it wasn't all the truth, because the Viet Cong were doing it as well. Maybe two years before none of the papers in the States would have run it. But people had already changed their minds about the war, and that picture just gave them the justifications they wanted.'

'The war was wrong, and we showed it was wrong.'

'I won't cop that, mate. You weren't here in '66 and '67. Back then the editors at home were worried that we were giving comfort to the enemy and all that shit. They said the bloke in Martin Place or Piccadilly or Times Square might get the wrong idea about the war if we gave them too many different viewpoints, so they didn't want our photographs of young girls being tortured because they were suspected of being Viet Cong, or Marines setting fire to some poor bastard's hut, or some Special Forces psychopath with a string of human ears round his neck. But then came Tet and suddenly it was open season. The only thing that had really changed about the war was people's minds.'

'And who was it who changed those minds? Who was it brought Tet into people's living rooms and on to their breakfast tables?'

'Sure, that was us, Spider. And as usual, we were allowed to give a totally false impression. We made it look like the Americans lost that one, when it was the only battle with the Viet Cong that Westmoreland won. In the early days of the war the Marines and the Air Cav got massacred in the Ia Drang and at Dak To. We never got to change people's minds back then.'

'I don't understand you. You saw the atrocities committed in this country in the name of freedom and democracy.'

'And I'm not condoning them, all right? I just say we were hitting a soft target. We only had access to one side. The Americans provided the transport and the food so we could get a first-hand look at their stuff-ups and their massacres. Now that's true democracy, mate. Where were we when the NVA executed two and a half thousand civilians in Hue and dumped their bodies in mass graves? And anyhow, the real story about this war was how affluent Vietnamese arranged for their sons to avoid the draft while half the United States infantry that served over here consisted of black and Latino kids from American ghettos. We didn't really stop the war, Spider. We just shifted the focus to stuff they could show on television.'

'If you don't think it matters, why do you do it?'

'Taking snaps is one thing I'm good at. And anyway, when did you get to be so holy? You didn't come out here to save the world.

You came here because you were an ambitious little shit like the rest of us and you got lucky at Que Trang.'

'I didn't go back the same person.'

'None of us did, or will. But we were still here to write battle comics. It never changed a bloody thing.'

Webb didn't want to sit here and listen to this heresy. If what they wrote, what they recorded, did not make a difference, he'd rather be mending cars or building houses. 'I still think we did some good here.'

'The only good thing I'll do is get Phuong and Odile out of this shithole before Charles gets here. The rest is just an ego trip.'

'Then what? What happens after you get back to Australia? What if it doesn't work out between you and her?' He thought about Washington, and the sterility that was sometimes harder to deal with than the nightmares about McCague and Judge and Que Trang. 'What if you find you can't live a normal life any more?'

'Then I guess there'll always be other wars, mate. I don't think there's any danger world peace is going to break out in my lifetime.' He poured more of the Bushmills into his glass. 'Do you?'

# 23

Every day brought news of more government defeats, McNamara's domino theory in microcosm. Hue and Danang had been abandoned in March; in early April Cu Chi, in the infamous Zone C, fell to the communists, then the old US stronghold at Bien Hoa. Defeat followed defeat and the NVA swept south, the momentum of the advance inexorable now.

Panic.

The ARVN Eighteenth Division made a last-ditch stand at Xuan Loc, but when the garrison fell on 21 April, there was nothing standing between the North and Saigon. That evening Thieu tendered his resignation on television, and soon after rumours circulated in the city that he had fled the country with the Bank of Vietnam's gold.

It was evident that the end was no more than a few days away. Long queues formed outside banks as the Vietnamese spent all their life savings trying to get out. But only the very rich could afford it. An exit visa cost ten million piasters.

When Highway 4, the road to the Delta, was severed, Saigon was isolated, encircled by eighteen North Vietnamese divisions. Barbed wire and machine guns appeared outside the palace. A vigorous sunset curfew was put in place.

Webb and Crosby continued to file, Ryan recording the panicked death throes of the city with his camera, taking taxis to the front lines, which were getting closer to the city by the hour. Each morning they asked each other the same question: is it going to be today?

April wore on, and they shook their heads. No, one more day, we'll hang on one more day . . .

Odile said nothing to Ryan; it was as if the war did not exist. She waved to him from the balcony of the apartment as he left each morning; she was there when he returned at night. Her self-possession impressed him.

At night they could hear the NVA artillery. But she trusted him.

He felt the first gnawing of uncertainty. He had gone to the edge so many times he was no longer sure if he knew when he should draw back. And Vietnam had been his life for so long. He wondered if, at the very end, he would be able to make himself go. Even for their sake.

The flash of artillery danced around the horizon like sheet lightning. Ryan sat on the edge of the bed, watching. The night was hot; his body was slick with sweat. A fan creaked and laboured on the ceiling. Phuong whimpered in her sleep.

'What's the matter, *chérie*? Can't you sleep?'

'Can you?' he said. 'The NVA are just a few klicks away from the city. It's nearly over.'

She didn't answer him.

'I've got the tickets and passports for you and Phuong. The AP's arranged a special charter flight to take their people out tomorrow. I've booked you seats on it.'

'I cannot go without you.'

'Look, don't be so bloody stupid. Think about Phuong.'

'She is your responsibility also. You too must think about her.'

'This is my job, all right? I might have to stay in Saigon after the occupation. Do you understand?'

'Then we will stay with you.'

'You can't. It's different for me. I'm a foreigner. What do you think the cadres will do to you? Do you know what the Khmer Rouge did in Phnom Penh?'

'That is not my concern. My place is with you.'

'For Christ's sake!'

'I know you will do what is best for us.'

He had underestimated her, he realised. There was a steel in her he had not suspected at first. She had decided that if he left her she would have nothing, so she therefore had nothing to lose. In tying her fortunes with his she was forcing him to prove to her that he really loved her. In this ultimate game of brinkmanship she was even prepared to gamble with her child. She was using her own devotion as a weapon to beat him down, to show him the desert of his own commitment.

He fumbled in the pocket of his shirt, on the floor beside the bed. He found the envelope containing the documents and threw it on the bed. 'Take the bloody tickets!' he snapped.

'No,' she said, her voice calm. In losing his temper he realised he had lost face and to the Oriental in her mind he had diminished himself.

He got up and went to the window. The babble of voices and cassette music drifted along the alley. He looked at his watch. Almost midnight. Cholon never slept, even during curfew.

Bugger it, he thought. He owed her. There was no real choice. He would have to do it her way.

He would stay two more days. Perhaps three. He would know when it was time to go. When the other correspondents evacuated, he would go with them, and he would take Odile and Phuong. But he couldn't go yet.

Two more days.

Perhaps three.

# 24

In the early hours of the 28th the airport came under shellfire for the first time. Ryan woke to a smoky dawn, a cordite haze settling over the Saigon rooftops. He kissed Odile and Phuong goodbye, rushed down the stairs into the street and hired a siclo to take him into the city.

The streets were choked with traffic, trucks and vans and siclos piled high with furniture and suitcases. Everyone was outside, ignoring the curfew, on their bicycles and their Honda motorcycles, or in cars. Panic had overtaken the city. Where was everyone going? Where was there to go?

Perhaps they were all driving in circles around the city, Ryan decided, obeying the body's natural instinct to run from danger.

He went to the AP office opposite the palace to look for Crosby. Webb had already left to cover events inside the Doc Lap; there were rumours that the caretaker president, the ancient and enfeebled Hoang, was going to step aside and allow one of the generals, Big Minh, to take over and try to arrange a last-minute truce with the communists.

It was around mid-morning when the news came through. There was fighting at Newport Bridge, just half an hour from Saigon.

There was a fleet of ancient cars parked in front of the Caravelle, offering transport to the front lines. Crosby and Ryan negotiated an extravagant fee with the owner of a dilapidated old Dodge, both its rear doors and the exhaust manifold held on with bits of wire, and headed out on the old Bien Hoa road for the bridge.

The four-lane highway was jammed with cars and buses, bicycles and bullock carts, a swollen tide of refugees all heading for the city, seeking sanctuary from the war. A whole nation imploding on its centre. 'Where the fuck are all these people going?' Crosby murmured. 'There ain't nowhere to go.'

A Honda had spilled in the middle of the road, and a man lay on the ground beside it, blood forming a sticky pool around his head. His wife was crouched beside him screaming, her children standing behind her, their faces etched with the terrible blank expressions of dread and incomprehension Ryan had seen so many times before. They were all covered in blood, perhaps their father's, perhaps their own.

Traffic milled around them; a knot of bystanders stood in a group and stared. More death, more pain. It never seemed to stop.

'Now I know what a salmon feels like,' Crosby said.

The tide was all heading the other way. Old men in conical straw hats pushed handcarts loaded with cages of chickens and ducks and rice sacks and ancient wicker chairs; old women clutched the hands of small children as they ran; military trucks barrelled through it all, the drivers with their fists jammed on the horn. A pall of dust hung over the road as if over a stampede.

This terrible tide washed over them and around them. Ryan was struck by the faces; eyes wide, like animals running from a bushfire, faces etched with physical and emotional exhaustion. He finished one roll of film, reloaded his camera.

Another truck rumbled past. The soldiers in the tray all wore the snarling tiger patch of the Hac Bao battalion, one of the ARVN's élite units, the men who had fought so fiercely at Hue and Xuan Loc. When they saw Crosby and Ryan they shouted and shook their heads.

'This doesn't look good,' Crosby said.

The great span of the bridge appeared ahead. A black pillar of smoke spiralled into the sky. Their driver stopped the car, refused to go on. Crosby and Ryan jumped out.

Ryan could see the red and yellow liberation flag of the Viet Cong among the palms on the other side of the river. The NVA were that close. Shadowy figures moved among the burning warehouses on the far bank. There was the crackle of small-arms fire.

The government paratroopers who held the bridge were crawling up the rise of the span, preparing to counterattack. Ryan knew he had to get closer. He had to be able to photograph the faces. He started to run forward.

The mortar round landed without warning. Ryan heard a thud as it hit the road, and then he was sitting down, watching an olive-drab ARVN truck crackle into flames. A cloud of gritty dust drifted over him. He was aware of people screaming, some in panic, some in pain.

He had to get a shot of the truck. He groped for the cameras around his neck, tried to change the 25-millimetre lens on his Leica to a 105. But he didn't seem able to make his fingers do what he wanted. Everything was slowing down. He needed to stand up, to take the picture, but he suddenly felt just too tired. He couldn't focus his eyes properly.

'Sean! Oh, Jesus Christ, Sean!' He had trouble recognising Crosby's voice. He realised he must be hit. 'Sean. Christ! Oh, Christ!'

Something was obviously wrong. There was no pain, just an uncomfortable heat at the side of his head.

'Tell Spider to look out for Odile,' he said, but the words didn't seem to come out right at all.

The next thing he remembered was a bright light hanging in the air above his head and someone saying: 'I don't think he's going to make it.'

And after that he didn't remember anything at all.

# 25

The monsoon had come early, and from the restaurant on the top floor of the Caravelle the thunder and heat lightning was indistinguishable from the battle closing in around Saigon. Just two hours before, the city had been bombed from the air for the first time; three American A-37s, captured from Danang, had roared over the rooftops and attacked the airport at Tan Son Nhut, hitting the ammunition dump there.

The end was very close now.

It was ten o'clock. The guests at the Caravelle, all international journalists, had gathered in the restaurant. The atmosphere was festive, almost like a graduation party. They ordered *salade niçoise* with their trout almondine, and drank wine with their meals, each of them heady with the knowledge that they were witnessing history.

Webb had spent much of the day in a taxi, rushing to and from interviews at the palace and the US Embassy, heading out to the airport to cover the stalled evacuation, then a last walk along the Tu Do to interview the bar girls who remained. He was exhausted, his spirit wrung out like a cloth, and yet he knew he would not sleep. His body was flooded with adrenalin. He ordered a bottle of Montrachet and some *vichyssoise* and sorted through his scribbled notes, mentally composing his file story.

Then he went back to his room and sat down at his typewriter.

Ten minutes later there was a knock at the door. 'Who is it?'

No answer.

'Who is it?' Impatiently he got to his feet, and threw open the door. 'Croz.'

There was blood on his Saigon suit, a lot of it, and some had caked black into his hair. His face was a sickly grey colour.

At once Webb knew. 'Ryan?' he said.

Crosby nodded.

'How bad?' Webb said, but he wasn't thinking about Ryan. His thoughts were for Odile, and little Phuong.

Crosby shook his head. 'We went out to Newport Bridge. He was standing right there next to me. Then he kind of sat down, real hard, and when I looked at him it was like the whole side of his head was gone. It was just one fucking mess of blood.'

He staggered slightly. Webb pulled him through the door and sat him down in a chair. He fetched his supply of Johnnie Walker and splashed some into a glass.

Crosby took it. His hands were shaking.

'Where is he?'

Crosby appeared not to have heard.

'Croz, where is he?'

Crosby was still replaying the scene at the bridge in his mind. Reluctantly he brought himself back. 'I put him back in the taxi and brought him back to Saigon. It was a nightmare. We couldn't get through the traffic. Must have taken maybe two hours, I don't know. The doctors at the hospital say he's got shell fragments in his brain. I don't think he's going to make it.'

'Where is he now?' Webb repeated.

'I used my connections at the embassy. They flew him out of Tan Son Nhut on a Huey to a carrier in the bay. Shit, I never thought they'd get Ryan.' He ran a hand over his face. 'What a fucking mess.'

Webb was surprised to find there was no grief, none at all. Just anger. He turned around and punched the wall. A blinding white flash of pain. Christ, he'd split the knuckles, blood was oozing out. 'Shit.'

'He knew the risks.' Crosby said.

'I don't give a shit about Ryan. What about Odile? And the little girl?'

It was apparent Crosby had not thought about this angle. He nodded, slowly. 'We'll get over there in the morning. We can sort something out.'

Webb looked down at his hand. Blood was dripping everywhere. He pulled a handkerchief from a drawer and wrapped it around his knuckles. 'Let's get over there now.'

'No way, man! It's fucking insane out there. There's soldiers roaming everywhere, shooting at anything that moves. I didn't think we were going to make it back from the airport.' He finished his whisky. 'We'll wait till the morning, after the curfew. Okay?'

Webb knew Crosby was right. He shrugged his assent.

He slumped on his bed. I knew something like this would happen, he thought. Why didn't Ryan?

Well, that was done now. But tomorrow he would find Odile and Phuong and somehow he would find a way to take them with him out of this nightmare. Because he could not live with all the rest of it, if it finished this way. Something good had to come out of Vietnam. If after all the misery and death he had witnessed the two Vietnamese he cared most about were left behind, well, then Ryan would be right. Webb would know for certain that his own presence hadn't made any damned difference here at all.

'I got this,' Crosby said.

Webb looked around. It was one of Ryan's Leicas. There were blood stains on the casing. 'His camera,' he said, dully.

'I got some good shots of him. After he was hit.' He looked up at Webb, looking for sanction. 'He would have wanted it that way.'

Webb nodded. 'Yeah,' he said. 'He would.'

# 26

The 130-millimetre rockets were Russian-made, sleek and black; the Vietnamese called them 'hissing death'. There was no warning scream as they came in, as with artillery shells. Instead they came during the night, with a sigh, silent as death.

Just after four, Webb was sitting at the window of his room in the Caravelle watching a premature dawn. The orange glow he could see was a direct hit by one of these rockets on the ammunition store at Tan Son Nhut. He heard the rumble of other explosions as more rockets rained down into the slums of Cholon.

It wasn't only the Americans who made war on civilians, he thought; Ryan was right about that.

He cradled a bottle of Johnnie Walker in his lap. He wasn't drunk; impossible to get drunk anyway with this much adrenalin pumping through his body. He kept just enough whisky in his veins to get him through this last night in Saigon, to keep at bay the devils that always came out to torment him at night. He wasn't like Ryan, could never be like Ryan. He was afraid.

Tomorrow. They said it could all be over as soon as tomorrow.

He waited for the morning. Made his plans for Odile.

A single rocket had demolished every house on one side of the alley, and the ensuing holocaust had razed everything. A man stood among the twisted and blackened sheets of iron, jaw slack, face utterly blank. At his feet were two bodies, charred beyond recognition, arms petrified into the peculiar pugilistic stance of the burned corpse. The man's plimsoll shoes were smoking. He seemed oblivious.

Webb stumbled through the wreckage – the smashed crockery, the bits of family portraits with their incongruous smiling faces. Crosby followed behind him. 'They're gone, Hugh,' he said.

An overpowering smell of human fat and singed hair.

A policeman was shouting, twenty metres away, pointing at

something he had seen in the ruins. Webb ran over. It was a young girl.

Her face and shoulders were burned, her lips, ears, eyelids all gone. Her hair had been melded to a piece of corrugated iron by some burning plastic. What he had at first thought was a leaking gas pipe was actually the sound of her breathing.

'Odile,' he said.

The policeman was shaking his head, backing away. The woman should be dead. Impossible to survive, this badly burned. One hand, somehow untouched by the flames, clawed at the air.

Webb tore at the wreckage around her, bent down, tried to cradle her head. 'Odile!'

Crosby knelt down beside him. 'Hugh! Come away!'

Dear God. *Odile!*

'Hugh,' Crosby was saying, 'come away, it's not her.'

'Get some water!'

'It's not her!'

'Somebody get some water!'

'Look at her arm, man. Look at the skin! It's an old woman.'

Webb stared at the thing at his feet, wanting to believe. The uninjured arm was indeed not the arm of a young woman. The skin was loose on the flesh, the finger joints were gnarled with arthritis, the nails cracked and broken from menial work. Not her. Not Odile.

'Christ, why isn't she dead?' Crosby murmured. 'Why can't she just die?'

Webb stood up. The hand still clawed at the air, waving backwards and forwards, like a sea anenome in the tide. Two uniformed men stumbled through the hissing ruins with a stretcher. Webb heard the click and whirr of a camera. He looked around. Crosby was taking pictures.

'What the hell are you doing?'

'We're not tourists, Hugh. We didn't stay for the last day so we could talk about it at dinner parties.'

Webb tried to snatch the camera away. Crosby backed off.

'For God's sake,' Webb shouted.

'If we don't take the pictures, why the hell are we here?'

Webb realised his hands were hurting. He looked down. They were blistered from where he had pulled a remnant of hot tin away from the woman's body; a piece of skin had stripped away from his palm.

'Jesus, you're burned,' Crosby said. 'Let's get back to the Caravelle.'

'No,' Webb told him. 'We have to find Odile.'

The morning was still; the city sweated under a grey overcast. In the distance Webb and Crosby heard the crackle of small-arms fire. Deserters were roaming the streets. The police had disappeared.

The twenty-four-hour curfew had been ignored; the whole city was on the street. Webb saw entire families loaded on to tiny Honda motorcycles.

'Jesus, where are they all going?' Crosby said in wonderment. 'By this afternoon the whole population of Saigon will be doing laps around the roundabout on Ham Nghi Boulevard.'

They found a Renault taxi, drove through the chaos of the streets to the surrounding hospitals. The wards were overflowing with wounded from the rocket attacks. The doctors were harassed, frightened, overworked; they did not have the time or the inclination to talk to two crazed American *bao chi*. People everywhere in the corridors, shouting, angry and frightened and desperate; bodies lay on stretchers, crying; others were silent, already dead.

'We have to find Odile and Phuong.'

'They're dead, Hugh. They're under half a ton of smoking rubble. Let's get the hell out of here.'

'They can't be dead.'

'You saw the house. There's nothing left. For God's sake.'

'I have to find them.'

It was not until early in the afternoon that Crosby finally persuaded Webb to return with him to the Caravelle. By then the evacuation had already begun.

'I can't leave,' Webb said.

Crosby grabbed his arm. 'They're dead, Hugh. Okay? If they were alive we would have found them. There's nothing more you can do here.'

Webb suddenly felt tired. He knew Crosby was right. He sat down on the tiled floor of the foyer and put his head between his knees. 'Fuck,' he whispered.

'Get your stuff, Hugh. We've got to get out of here.'

Webb looked up. At the reception desk the Vietnamese cashier had his face in his hands. He was crying.

'Hugh.'

They were dead. They had to be. Hold on to that, believe it.

'Hugh . . .'

He nodded. Time to get out of Saigon. Nothing else to be done.

He stumbled up to his room, grabbed his typewriter, threw his clothes in a suitcase. Crosby was waiting for him in the foyer, clutching a carpet-bag.

Lam Son Square was empty, eerily quiet; even the bootblacks and the urchins selling cigarettes and pornographic pictures and flower garlands had disappeared. They picked a way through the coils of barbed wire that lay across the footpath. Three soldiers watched them from under a tree on the other side of the square. They were all armed. Webb thought he heard the grate of metal as one of the men jammed a new magazine into his Armalite.

'Run,' Crosby said.

A nightmare of cameo visions: angry faces shouting at them as they ran; a middle-aged man, dressed in a dark suit and tie, waving a wad of American dollars, as thick as a hamburger, in their faces.

Another man grabbed Crosby's arms and tried to pull him into a doorway. 'Take me with you! Take me with you!' he shouted. Webb pulled him away.

Someone grabbed Crosby's bag, wrenched it from his grip. 'Jesus, my bag! You crazy?' Crosby shouted.

He turned, ran up the alleyway after a street kid who was dragging the heavy carpet-bag behind him. Webb was about to follow, then saw a woman in a blue *ao dai* on the footpath on the other side of the road, making her way towards the embassy, clutching a small child by the hand.

'Odile!'

He scrambled through the press of traffic. A man appeared in front of him, a handful of American one-hundred-dollar bills fanned in his fist like playing cards. 'You take me, please!' he shouted. 'Please! You take me!'

Webb pushed him away. 'Odile!'

He could just see the woman's blue silk dress through the press of people. He used his strength and size to clear a path through the crowds. 'Odile!'

He grabbed her by the shoulders and spun her around.

Not Odile.

The young Vietnamese woman stared up at him in shock. Then her face underwent a transformation; first surprise, then relief, the dawning of hope. She picked up her child and held the small boy towards him. 'You take to America, please!'

Suddenly Crosby was beside him. He had the carpet-bag but there were long raking scratches down the side of his face.

'What the hell are you doing?' Crosby shouted. He pulled him away. 'For Christ's sake!'

The woman followed them. 'Please, you take him!'

'That kid tried to claw my eyes,' Crosby said. 'Jesus. Who's that woman? What were you doing?'

'I thought I saw Odile,' Webb said.

The woman was still following them.

'The embassy's just a block from here. We've got to get out of this shit.'

Webb turned back once, saw the woman staring after him. He looked at the child. He had round eyes.

Then they were both lost in the crowds.

It was almost dusk when the last of the giant Chinooks landed on the heaving deck of the *Blue Ridge*. Crosby and Webb leaned on the rail, side by side, staring at the grey churning water, the coast of Vietnam a fading violet shadow in the distance. The warm salt air was mixed with the taints of grease and aviation fuel.

'Well,' Crosby murmured, 'and so on to the next war.'

It was always hard to tell if Crosby was serious. 'Not me,' Webb said. 'I'm going back to my job in Washington and I intend to forget all about Vietnam.'

'You'll never forget,' Crosby said, and Webb knew he was right.

Two Marines, crewcut, starched white T-shirts under their uniforms, appeared on the deck beside them. 'Look at that,' one of them said, laughing. 'Reckon I could just about zap that gook from here.'

Webb saw what they were pointing at. An old fishing boat was wallowing in the water below, crowded with Vietnamese. A woman stood at the stern, holding up her small child, imploring someone on the carrier to take the infant with them.

'Oh, for God's sake,' Webb said.

He closed his eyes. When he looked again, the woman was gone. Crosby told him she had fallen over the stern into the water, still holding the child. They had quickly disappeared into the oily grey swell.

The carrier moved away through the water, almost capsizing the tiny boat in the massive wash from its engines. It was soon a fading silhouette against the backdrop of the hot green coast.

'Well, folks,' the admiral said over the ship's PA, 'that just about wraps up Vietnam.'

For some of us, Webb thought. But it would never be over for him. He felt sick and dirty and ashamed. The war might finally be over but he knew he would relive it every day for the rest of his life; and the last scene would always be Odile standing in the middle of the flames, holding her daughter towards him in outstretched arms before she vanished, swallowed up by the gathering darkness.

## Seventh Regiment Armoury

When Webb finished there was silence around the table. At the back of the hall one of the British guests had apparently ingested a restricted substance in the gentleman's washroom during the interval and had become boisterous. He was being coaxed towards the exits by friends.

Cochrane and Crosby refilled their glasses. The Bushmills had almost gone. Cochrane picked up the bottle, reread the poem on the back and smiled. There was no eye contact around the table for a long while. Then Crosby said: 'It really wasn't Sean's fault. The guy wasn't planning on getting zapped.'

'The point is he should have got her out long before the end,' Webb said. 'He was so wrapped up in himself he never gave a thought about what might happen to her or her child. Death or injury was an everyday reality in a war zone. We all knew that.'

Cochrane shook his head. 'I think you're being a bit tough on him. It was bad luck, that's all.'

'It was bad luck for Odile, that's for sure. Seven years' bad luck. But Ryan didn't let himself get too fazed by it. He was out of hospital in three months and back in Angola in six.'

Crosby shook his head. 'You're doing him an injustice. He loved her, in his own way. Besides, she was partly to blame. He wanted to get her out of Saigon. She wouldn't go.'

Doyle leaned forward. 'I didn't know him as well as you fellows. But I did know him.' She smiled. 'In the biblical sense. And it seems to me . . .'

'Yeah, when was that?' Cochrane asked her.

'The Gulf War. Dhahran. Must be something about hot desert nights. And if you ask me, as a woman, I'd have to say he never loved anyone except himself.'

Crosby looked at Cochrane. 'Help me out here, Lee. They're beating up on my friend.'

# IV

## El Salvador, October 1982

'When one's nation is at war, reporting becomes an extension of the war effort.'

– Max Hastings

'I wouldn't tell the people anything until the war was over – and then I'd tell them who won.'

– military censor at a meeting in Washington

# 27

They were almost a tourist attraction, in their own way, the bodies of the disappeared. They turned up everywhere, at bus stations, on vacant lots, in the ravines behind San Benito and Escalón. One of the most popular repositories was the lava field at El Playón. The previous year the panorama of rotting flesh had featured regularly on the evening news across the United States.

Their job lately, it seemed to Webb, was to drive around each morning photographing the new bodies that had appeared at the roadsides or on the garbage tips or dumped between the graves in the cemeteries where they were picked over by wandering dogs. One day, for a change of pace, Webb and his photographer, Mike Daniels, hired a VW Golf at the Avis desk in the Camino Real and drove up to Puerto del Diablo.

The route took them past the Casa Presidencial, and up a winding road narrowed by landslides and deep gullies that had eaten away the roadbed. When they reached the top, Daniels stopped the car and they sat for a few moments looking back towards San Salvador, the distant city framed by the walls of the gorge. The morning was grey, the lowering sky as suffocating as a blanket. As they got out of the Golf, Daniels shuddered.

'This place gives me the creeps,' he said.

Webb had been told that the executions took place at night, at the top of the cliff, and the bodies were then rolled over the lip into the Puerto del Diablo. They started to climb down. The way down the steep walls of the cliff was not easy, the stones slick with moss and damp, the air thin. An overcast sky, ferns dripping water, the deafening buzz of cicadas.

The first bodies began to appear, maggoty mounds of flesh and bone and hair. The vultures had already been busy. Webb had been told that they went for the eyes and mouth and genitals first.

Daniels started to take photographs. His face was sickly grey. You could never get hardened to this, Webb thought, no matter how many times you saw it. If you were a veteran you kept your breakfast.

Further down the gorge they found more bodies. Most of them had been there a long time. They stared over a landscape of stripped spines, blood-caked scraps of clothes, heads rotted to skulls beneath a tonsure of hair.

'Look at this,' Daniels said.

He handed Webb an identity card. A schoolboy in a badly knotted tie grinned from the photograph. He wondered which mouldering pile of bones was his. He stooped to pick up a shoelace, held it between his fingers, overcome with sadness and revulsion. Difficult to breathe down here. The sky seemed to be drowning them.

They worked in silence. This was worse than anything he had seen before, even in Vietnam. He had thought before he came to El Salvador that he was inured to death and killing, but here was something beyond brutality. Down here he felt as if he was in the presence of the Devil himself.

Hard to accept that his adopted country condoned and supported this.

Daniels focused on an empty ribcage, a woman's shoe.

By now they should be running out of politically suspect victims, Webb thought. The Puerto del Diablo and the lava flows at El Playón were choked with the mouldering remains of priests, teachers, journalists, students, writers and doctors; so many had been murdered that all possibilities for rational democracy had been eradicated. But the United States continued to support President d'Aubuisson and his death squads because they were committed to fighting Marxists, although these days a Marxist was just anyone who was opposed to the government. By now every dictator in Latin America knew that the fight against communism was a bait the United States administration could not resist. If you wanted arms, if you wanted money, you honeyed the hook with the Cubans, and the US came snapping on the line every time.

Daniels had found an upturned palm, a skull stripped of flesh except for the hair. His Canon clicked and whirred.

There was no proof that the government was involved, as there was no proof that the current president of the country, Roberto 'Uncle Bob' d'Aubuisson had ordered Archbishop Romero murdered as he said Mass in the Metropolitan Cathedral in San Salvador. There was no proof; even though d'Aubuisson's diary with the date of the assassination ringed had been produced in evidence, with a list of the armaments required for the job listed on the same page. There was no proof because one of d'Aubuisson's judges said there wasn't.

Daniels changed film, fired off half a dozen frames of the bones littered along the rocks.

Every morning in the national daily, *El Diario del Hoy*, there were full-face photographs of the disappeared, often appearing jarringly alongside grainy photographs of mutilated bodies found the previous day by the side of the road. Officially the government blamed the *desconocidos*, the 'unknown men', claiming their victims were casualties in a clandestine war being waged between the right and the left. But everyone knew who the death squads supported. One of the best known, ORDEN, had links with the current president, and its members were paid off by one of the country's leading businessmen, Fabian Ventura.

Daniels was standing over a disjointed spine. He raised his camera, changed his mind, lowered it again. He seemed overcome.

When he first arrived in El Salvador, Webb had interviewed an ORDEN member. The man had claimed that if you were asked to join one of the death squads, and you refused, you were immediately labelled a subversive and became their next victim. But there were other reasons men joined, besides fear. He had been promised year-round employment on Ventura's coffee plantation, and offered an interest-free loan. The choice was simple. If you did not want to become one of the oppressed, then you joined the oppressors.

Did he enjoy killing? Webb had asked him.

The man had stared at his hands, trying to frame an answer to this difficult question. Once a victim is chosen, he said haltingly, everyone has to join in, so that the guilt is shared equally. Everyone must have a little of the victim's blood on their hands. It is not death but brutality that makes people afraid. That is what they teach us.

But did you enjoy it? Webb asked him.

'It is like sex with a prostitute,' the man said. 'Afterwards you feel dirty. But at the time . . .'

Daniels put down his camera and turned away.

'Look too long into the abyss and the abyss looks into you,' he murmured. 'That's Nietzsche.'

'And I think to myself, what a wonderful world. That's Louis Armstrong.'

The atmosphere was oppressive. Mist rose from the ground like corpse gas.

'Let's get out of here,' Daniels said.

'Got everything you needed?'

'There's only so many ways you can do death through a lens,' Daniels said, 'and I think I did them all the first day I got here.'

When they reached the car park at the top of the cliff they saw a battered Toyota pick-up truck, without plates, half a dozen men sitting on the bonnet and the tray. They all wore aviator sunglasses and cowboy boots, and had machetes or revolvers tucked into the thick leather belts of their jeans.

ORDEN.

The pick-up was parked directly behind their car. 'Oh shit,' Daniels said.

'It's going to be all right,' Webb said.

He walked over to one of the men sitting on the bonnet of the pick-up. He was wearing a cowboy hat, his paunch swelling his golf shirt and bulging over his jeans. '*Buenos días, señores*,' Webb said, smiling, and then, still in Spanish: 'Do you think you could move your truck? We have to return to San Salvador.'

The men grinned at each other. No one spoke.

'Oh Jesus,' Webb heard Daniels say.

The man in the cowboy hat hawked deep in his throat and spat on the ground.

Webb turned away and went back to Daniels.

'They know who we are,' Daniels whispered. 'This is a fucking set-up!' His face was shining with sweat, not all of it from the exertion of their climb back up the gorge.

'Keep calm,' Webb said.

'We've been set up! Let's just walk. Leave the fucking car right here.'

'I'm not walking all the way back to San Salvador.'

The men were grinning at them. This was a good game, a little light entertainment on a slow morning. Webb checked the clearance between the cars. A foot, perhaps a foot and a half.

He climbed in behind the wheel of the Golf. Daniels leaned in the window. Webb could smell the sweat on him. 'What the fuck are you going to do? Drive over the cliff?'

'I used to live in a terraced house in Hammersmith. I know a thing or two about getting a car in and out of tight spaces.'

'For Christ's sake, Hugh! You dent their truck, what the hell do you think they'll do to us?'

'I'm not walking and I'm not waiting.' He started the engine.

He reversed three times, wrestling with the wheel to get full lock on each forward turn. The *desconocidos* watched intently from the bed of the truck, leaning forward with rapt attention as if they were watching a soccer game. They grinned at each other; bad teeth, stubble and toothpicks.

Each time Webb inched forward he forced himself to forget the giddying drop in front. He left the door open. If the Golf started to topple he hoped he would have time to jump.

Daniels hit his fist hard on the boot. He came to the open door. 'You're about an inch from the front bumper.'

Webb nodded and the Golf crept forward again. He thought he could do it this time. He heard the truck roar to life behind him. Perhaps the *desconocidos* had tired of their game.

Not a bit of it. The truck drew forward and the space behind him was gone, trapping him against the edge of the cliff.

Daniels came back to the window. 'Let's just get the fuck out of here,' he breathed.

Webb glanced in his mirror. He remembered something Ryan had told him once, that he'd seen more men killed running blindly from a battle than staying behind and using their reason and their instincts to get them out of danger. He was surprised to find himself icy calm. There had been worse times than this.

The men in the pick-up truck were not going to let them walk off the mountain. If they tried to walk away, they would follow them in the truck. And the game would then continue to its deadly, if not premeditated, conclusion.

Webb left the engine running and walked around to the front of the car. The wheels were at full lock; there was just inches between the left front wheel and the edge of the cliff. But it was perhaps enough.

And really, there was no choice.

He went back to the Golf, threw open the back door, then got behind the wheel and gunned the motor. If he was going to do it, there was no point in being prissy about it. 'Get ready to jump in,' he said to Daniels. 'If I don't make it, you're on your own. See if you can win them over with a few jokes.'

'What are you going to do?'

Webb put the car in gear, keeping his body weight on the wheel, holding the lock as far to the right as it would go.

*Now!*

He released the clutch. The tyres shrieked, and Webb felt the passenger-side front wheel lose traction for a moment, but then the car swung around, through 180 degrees. He slammed on the brake.

Daniels jumped into the back seat and Webb immediately gunned the car back on to the highway, the rear door still flapping.

He put his foot to the floor and headed back towards San Salvador.

Daniels slammed the door shut, then wound down all the windows. There was a ripe and overpowering smell in the car.

'Sorry,' he said. 'I shat.'

# 28

Among the correspondents it was known as the number four war, numbers one to three being Beirut, the Iran-Iraq conflict, and the Falklands. The American public had grown bored with the bodies on El Playón, and it was fast becoming stale news. So many reporters had abandoned the Camino Real that the dining room had discontinued its breakfast buffet. In fact Webb had propounded a theory that the political climate of El Salvador could be gauged by the Camino Real's breakfast menu. *A la carte* meant no action, no bang-bang and complete editorial indifference in New York.

In some ways the routine of his life reminded him of his time in Saigon. Every morning he presented himself at COPREFA, the press office at the Ministry of Defence, to listen to their spokesman exaggerate the number of rebel casualties claimed by their forces in the surrounding provinces, much as the JUSPAO PIOs subverted their reports at the Five O'clock Follies at the Rex. Each day officials from the COPREFA office taped 'urgent' notices to the front desk at the Camino Real announcing staged press events, such as the ritual display of 'defectors', thin and unshaven men with the demeanour of beaten dogs who were seldom allowed to speak more than a few words.

Like Saigon the city of San Salvador was a sour cocktail of excess and fear, an island of imported Americana surrounded by enemies. On the Boulevard de los Héroes, directly opposite the Camino Real, was the Metrocenter, claimed as 'Central America's Largest Shopping Mall'. Inside, plump Escalón matrons in too-tight Levi jeans trailed their maids and babies behind them and shopped for beach towels printed with maps of Manhattan featuring Bloomingdale's and Sachs, and the muzak played 'I Left My Heart in San Francisco'. Outside, National Guardsmen patrolled the entrance clutching M-3 machine guns.

On Wednesday nights at the Camino Real wealthy middle-aged couples shuffled past the oysters and spare ribs at the poolside buffet, dancing stiff rumbas before hurrying home for the 9.30 curfew when the crackle of small-arms fire again echoed around the city. In the discotheque off the lobby, waiters in black cowboy hats darted around the strobe-lit dance floor carrying pina coladas to the rich sons and daughters of San Benito, until their shrieks of laughter were cut short by the FMLN cutting the power lines to the city, leaving the room in black silence.

Webb had heard Vietnam's name invoked many times since he arrived in El Salvador. One night in the bar of the Sheraton he overheard a tall crewcut American in a tan suit giving a fellow journalist from a provincial Mid-West newspaper his view of the war: 'Yes, sir, we sure as hell are not losing this one. This is no Vietnam. Make sure your folks back home understand that, loud and clear. We can *win* this one. Yes, sir.'

Unlike Vietnam there were no free helicopter rides to the front, so that the press contingent could see for themselves how the government's war against the rebel coalitions was being fought, could confirm that the United States' allies really could win this one. For an opposing viewpoint Webb and his fellow correspondents had to content themselves with transcripts from the rebel radio station, Venceremos, prepared by the CIA in Panama and made available every day at the US Embassy.

The only other option was to speak to the dead at El Playón.

Daniels was unsettled after the previous day's incident at Puerto del Diablo. Webb noticed the tremor in his hand as he picked up his coffee cup. He stared out of the window at the volcano of San Salvador, but Webb guessed that what he was seeing was his own bones mouldering in the gorge with the other disappeareds.

Webb did not feel this same fear. The brush with ORDEN had left him only with a residue of anger, like grit in the bottom of a coffee cup. He understood the mechanics of terror, and these latest efforts to intimidate him had only strengthened his resolve.

Daniels put down his coffee cup. It rattled in the saucer.

'You okay?' Webb asked him.

'I didn't sleep very well.' He was antsy, Webb noted, continually shuffling in his seat, like a man troubled by fleas. 'Are we out to El Playón again this morning?'

'Change of pace. I've arranged an interview with Ricardo Beltrán.'

'Who's he?'

'He's a guiding light in the Fourteen Families. A *finquera*, and one of d'Aubuisson's staunchest supporters. He's also said to be ORDEN's paymaster.'

Daniels nodded. 'Okay. Just be careful where you park the car this morning. All right?'

Webb had heard someone say that San Salvador reminded them of Los Angeles, except the slums were built of cardboard instead of concrete. There was a little truth in that, he thought. As they drove through the streets that morning they passed automobile showrooms, Coke billboards and air-conditioned shopping malls. The worst of American freeway culture transferred to the malaria belt.

It was only around the plaza that you were reminded that you were after all in Latin America; vendors squatted beside panniers of oranges and young corn, shoeshine boys haunted the outdoor cafés, toothless old women with arthritic fingers sat on the sidewalks begging; all around them the lottery ticket sellers and the newspaper vendors, the drunk and the mad, so many faces hungry and hopeless. The ones they called *la chusma* – the rabble.

Black and white police cars patrolled in pairs, rifle barrels bristling from the windows, National Guardsmen patrolled the streets cradling their M-3 machine guns, fidgeting, clicking the safeties on and off. Violence and despair simmered in the heat.

The crossroads at the Avenida Roosevelt and the Avenida Gustavo Guerrero was the divide between the raucous and treeless downtown and the pleasant hills and avenues of the residential areas. Here the houses were insulated from *la chusma* by high walls and luxuriant gardens. They passed a small park surrounded by expensive fashion boutiques, a supermarket and a busy McDonald's. Above it presided the statue of Jesus, his arms outstretched, balanced on a tiny globe. The city's namesake. *El Salvador del Mundo* – Saviour of the World.

'Christ on the ball,' Daniels observed.

'I wish He was,' Webb said.

San Benito was hushed and leafy quiet, the preserve of only the most privileged. It was here, and in Colonia Escalón, that most of the members of the so-called Fourteen Families had their homes.

The Fourteen Families were supposedly El Salvador's ruling élite, but this was a fallacy as power was shared between two to three hundred families, and almost all of them had built their wealth on coffee. Ricardo Beltrán was the patriarch of one of the most influential of these clans, one of the right's illuminati.

Webb stopped the car. The street was deserted. The original twenty-foot-high stone walls of Beltrán's house had been reinforced with an extra ten feet of brick, and when Webb looked up he saw concertina wire and the eye of a closed circuit camera looking down at them. As they got out they heard the metallic click of a safety catch on an automatic weapon, the crackle of a handheld radio as the security moved into action.

A plain-clothes guard with an automatic pistol tucked into his belt checked their COPREFA identity tags and whispered into his radio. He reluctantly opened the gate and Webb and Daniels were ushered into a courtyard fragrant with cannas and oleander. In front of them was a colonial-style two-storey house, *copa de oro* and bougainvillea creeper climbing the whitewashed walls, pools of blossom undisturbed on the paving below. Two Mercedes were parked in the driveway beside a marble fountain. Mozart drifted from an open window.

The home of Ricardo Beltrán.

'I am an anti-communist,' Beltrán said. 'The United States is also anti-communist. Ronald Reagan is anti-communist. Therefore if I am extreme right, so is the president of your country. So are all Americans. So are you.'

Beltrán spoke his twisted logic softly, like a reasonable man, ice clinking in a glass of imported Johnnie Walker. An Alsatian slept on the carpet at his feet. On the other side of the room, Beltrán's daughter lounged on a brocade sofa, filing her nails, watching an episode of *Starsky and Hutch* that had been dubbed into Spanish. A parrot squawked in its cage on the terrace.

It was the 9-millimetre pistol on the cushion at Beltrán's side that made Webb nervous.

He returned his attention to his notebook. 'Sir, yesterday we went out to Puerto del Diablo.' He glanced up at Beltrán. At the mention of the gorge a muscle rippled in his jaw. 'Who is responsible for the deaths in San Salvador?'

Beltrán spread his hands, the helpless gesture of a civilized man. 'I must tell you I do not know. The leftist guerrillas have destabilised our country to such an extent that it is no longer clear who is doing what to whom. Some people are very angry with them and perhaps a few vigilantes have taken the law into their own hands. Then, of course, you have the leftists committing some of these murders for their own ends. So who is to say who is responsible for what?'

'What do groups like the FMLN have to gain by killing peasants?'

'To understand the mind of a communist you have to be one.'

Webb and Daniels exchanged glances.

Webb leaned forward, checked that the small cassette recorder he had placed on the coffee table still had plenty of tape, and returned his attention to the interview. 'There seems to be a consensus of opinion elsewhere that almost all of these killings can be attributed to the so-called death squads, and that these groups are made up of the government's own security forces dressed in plain clothes who are doing the government's dirty work for them.'

Beltrán seemed at ease with this sort of speculation. 'You are just repeating propaganda from the leftists, dreamed up by the Cubans and Marxists who are trying to destabilise our government.'

'But what exactly is a communist, by your definition, Señor Beltrán? Someone who resents having a member of his family taken from his bedroom in the middle of the night and murdered?'

Beltrán picked up the pistol and started to play with it. 'You have to understand, Señor Webb, this country is not like your country. We cannot be America. How long have you been here?'

'Is this relevant?'

Daniels shot him a warning glance.

'One month? Two months?' Beltrán continued. 'And you think you understand El Salvador?'

'Perhaps you're right, sir. I don't understand a country that makes war on its own people and murders all the doctors, priests and professors.'

Daniels coughed nervously. But Webb had no intention of backing down now. He sensed that Beltrán's urbane façade was starting to crack. Besides, he did not think Beltrán was going to use the pistol here in his own house, if for no other reason than he did not want blood stains on the new carpets. He felt safer here than he had at Puerto del Diablo, at least.

'Señor Beltrán, what is your opinion of land reform?'

'It is an evil that will destroy free enterprise in my country. How will it benefit El Salvador if we take away the land from the very men who made it prosper? We blame your former president, Jimmy Carter, for exporting this nonsense. He forced it on us, in return for the money and arms we needed to defend ourselves from the Marxists. He did what they had failed to do – he brought communism to El Salvador.'

Webb again experienced an unsettling sense of déjà vu. He had heard these same arguments propounded by President Thieu about social reform in South Vietnam. He supposed that King George III would have said the same thing to Washington and Adams.

'El Salvador exports five hundred million dollars' worth of coffee a year. The coffee growers stash the profits in Swiss bank accounts rather than pay taxes on it.'

'Does the United States government tell your companies what to do with their profits? And what if we did pay our taxes here? What would happen to the money? The National Bank would give it to the Marxists for land reform.'

Beltrán's expression had changed. There was an edge to his voice now, and his eyes were bright with venom.

Webb ploughed on. 'Most wage earners in this country get less than one dollar a day. Surely they don't need a Marxist to tell them they're hungry. They don't need a Cuban to tell them their children are dying of starvation.'

Beltrán was silent for a long time, and the silence became deadly. He cocked and uncocked the pistol several times. Finally he looked up at Daniels. 'You,' he said. 'You put away your camera and I will show you something.'

Webb shrugged and Daniels replaced the camera in its metal case.

Beltrán left the room. Daniels and Webb looked at each other, but did not speak. Daniels was pale.

Beltrán returned with a small sugar sack. He emptied the contents on to the table. At first Webb thought the sack contained dried peach halves but then he realised what these objects were. He remembered these trophies from Vietnam.

They were human ears.

'This is what we do to those who will not listen to the voice of reason and moderation in this country.'

Webb stared back at him.

'These once belonged to your beloved Marxist guerrillas,' Beltrán went on. 'Now I will answer your question, señor, and I will answer the Marxists at the same time.' He picked up one of the ears and held it to his mouth. 'Go fuck yourself!' he shouted. 'There, I think he heard that, señor. Now, I think our interview is over. I will advise you to be very careful in El Salvador. You are a guest in our country. When you are a guest in a man's home and you piss on his carpet he is no longer required to be the genial host, no? Remember that.'

The maid showed them out of the house. When they reached the courtyard Daniels was already sweating despite the air conditioning inside the house. He got into the car and did not speak until they reached the forecourt of the Camino Real. Then he said: 'Everyone in this country is a fucking psychopath,' and he went straight to the bar and got drunk for the rest of the afternoon.

At the opposite end of the Avenida Roosevelt, in the hub of the downtown area, is the Metropolitan Cathedral, El Salvador's main place of worship, notorious since 1980 as the scene of Archbishop Romero's murder. It faces a small, dusty plaza and the sombre grey façade of the National Palace. A few supplicants move through the square soliciting contributions for the families of the disappeared.

Webb and Daniels paused in front of the cathedral. A flock of raucous parakeets wheeled overhead. Webb checked his watch. Almost five o'clock.

They went up the grey concrete steps and through the barricades. Something made Webb look up and he saw two olive-clad National Guardsmen watching him from the balcony of the palace, a forbidding presence in their black helmets and shiny black Prussian boots.

The atmosphere inside the cathedral was that of a construction site abandoned because of a labour dispute. High walls of concrete bristled with rusting structural rods that wept brown stains down the grey concrete. The ends of unfinished wiring were exposed, fluorescent light fixtures hung askew, and the high altar was backed by a piece of warped plyboard. There were no frescoes on the walls, no representations of the Stations of the Cross, because Señor Romero had halted the expensive refurbishment of his church. He had said that the money should be spent on the people and not on display.

Webb and Daniels sat in the pews to wait. It was dark inside; there were no candles burning on the high altar, no illumination behind the globe of the world, *El Salvador del Mundo*. Some flowers that had been placed there had long since died.

Webb studied the linoleum on the cathedral floor, saw dark stains near the altar, splashes of blood perhaps. He wondered if it was the Archbishop's. Romero's tomb was in a transept off to the right, and in contrast to the altar it was surrounded by offerings of fresh flowers and notes decorated with motifs cut from greetings cards. Three women, their heads covered in white lace veils, were praying at the sarcophagus. A needlepoint tapestry had been placed on the tomb. Webb silently translated: *Praise to Monsignor Romero from the Mothers of the Imprisoned, the Disappeared and the Murdered.*

A figure appeared from the shadows and sat down beside him. 'Señor Webb?'

'Father Hernandez?'

'Thank you for coming.'

'Thank you for agreeing to speak with us. I realise the risk you are taking.'

'My life belongs to God. There is no risk greater than the loss of one's soul. Follow me, please.'

A car was waiting for them at a side door. They got in. Their driver touched the rosary hanging from the rear-vision mirror and crossed himself. Then they drove out of the city into the *barrancas*.

'La Fosa'. It means The Grave. It was one of the city's most desperate slums, where the *mozo* – the truly poor – lived in cardboard boxes, under pieces of tin and black plastic held down with rocks. Webb stared out of the window, saw filthy children teeming over wrecked cars, playing in sewage. Any spare expanse of wall had been plastered with graffiti.

They stopped outside an undertaker's parlour, a wooden shack with cheap wooden coffins stacked inside like firewood. Father Hernandez led them inside, past the hordes of near-naked children who had come to stare.

The corpses of a young man and woman lay on the cement floor.

Daniels brought up his camera and started to take pictures.

A woman was kneeling over one of the bodies, rocking backwards and forwards, her arms clutched to her stomach as if she had been stabbed. She was wailing, helpless with her grief. Another young man was trying to comfort her, and she clung to his arm as if it were a lifeline.

Webb felt the blood drain out of his face. He had seen a lot of death in his profession, and he could endure it while it remained impersonal. It was grief he could not tolerate.

'What happened here?' he said to the priest, his voice hoarse.

Father Hernandez spoke quickly to the undertaker. After the interchange he turned back to Webb.

'That is her son. Some men came, took them both away to a barn. They tied his thumbs behind him with barbed wire, then put some rope through the wire and threw the other end over the rafters. They lifted him until his feet were clear of the ground. Then they tied a bucket to his genitals and every half an hour they threw a heavy stone into the bucket. It took him sixteen hours to die. They made her watch.'

Webb thought he was going to be sick. He turned away.

He wondered at his capacity for outrage. After all, wasn't this the same as Vietnam, the same scenes played out with different faces? In that war both sides had used torture and terror as a matter of routine. And the Americans had had their own death squads; their operations even had a codename – Phoenix. The rules of the Geneva Convention were not observed anywhere any more. If they ever were.

'So you see, señor, death is not the problem here,' the priest was saying. 'It's the terror. Finding heads lying in the street, men with their genitals stuffed in their mouths. One thing I saw with my own eyes, in this very *barranca*, will haunt me for the rest of my life. I found a young man lying in the street. They had just chopped him up. First his hands and arms, then his feet and legs, then they removed his eyes, ears and tongue.'

'He was dead?' Webb asked, almost afraid to ask.

'No, señor.'

Daniels put his camera down. 'I'm all done here,' he said.

The priest said some words over the bodies and followed them outside. Daniels excused himself. Webb heard him retching in the alleyway beside the undertaker's shop. Webb got back in the car, staring straight ahead, oblivious of the children that had gathered around the window, laughing and shouting.

Father Hernandez climbed in beside him. 'I am sorry if you found it distressing, señor.'

'How can you do this?' Webb whispered to him. 'How can you come here day after day and not lose your faith?'

'Evil will always be with us. It has always been this way. You think crucifixion is not a cruel way to die?'

Daniels got back in the car without a word. As they drove back through the streets of the *barranca*, Webb composed his story.

*Ricardo Beltrán threw the bag of human ears on the table. 'This is what we do,' he said, 'to those who will not listen to the voice of reason.'*

*I did not ask Señor Beltrán how he came by the ears. I did not dare. Señor Beltrán is a leading figure in the government here, a respected businessman, and a close friend of the president, Roberto d'Aubuisson. He is also considered a close friend of the US administration in San Salvador, who have described him as 'a man committed to bringing democracy to Central America'.*

*Señor Beltrán lives in a privileged and leafy suburb of San Salvador, his palatial home protected by security guards wielding shotguns and automatic weapons. In the valley below, almost within view, tens of thousands of people live in cardboard boxes, in filth and squalor. And each day more and more bodies pile up on the lava flows at El Playón; most show signs that they were tortured before being killed. Their murderers are never found. The reason for this is that the death squads are believed to be either off-duty soldiers and policemen or thugs directly in the pay of the government.*

*That this is a brutal and evil regime is without question.*

*The more pertinent questions regard our own country. From what are we protecting the people of El Salvador? What government could possibly be more brutal than the incumbents? Why is the Reagan administration supporting a government perhaps as murderous as the one that ruled Nazi Germany in the thirties, one that may even be compared in its barbarous intent towards its own people to that of Stalin's Russia?*

*Last financial year our president's apocalyptic obsessions led us to squander one hundred and forty-four million dollars on shoring up this tyranny.*

*Do we hear the ghosts of Washington and Lincoln in the Capitol tonight, asking: When did* our *country lose its way?*

* * *

When he finished Webb was sweating. He had written three thousand words, in a rush, without even pausing for rest. The story had poured out of him in a torrent, the first time he had not struggled over copy. Together with Daniels' photographs, he was sure the piece would make the front pages across the country.

# 29

San Salvador's Sheraton Hotel boasted the largest swimming pool in Central America. It was surrounded by tennis courts and gardens lush with bougainvillea and lavender orchids and was built on the slopes of Colonia Escalón, commanding a breathtaking view of the surrounding volcanoes.

Its lobbies and bars had become a favourite meeting place for San Salvador's élite. It is apparently also favoured by the death squads, Webb thought as he climbed out of his Avis car and noted the trademark black Cherokee Chiefs parked in the forecourt. They were all fitted with reinforced steel and plexiglass windows an inch thick.

Three days after the interview with Beltrán he received a phone call at his hotel from someone who claimed to work for the United States Embassy. Someone over there wanted to meet him. No, he could not have their name or their rank. Be in the coffee shop at the Sheraton at five o'clock. That was all.

Webb had agonised over whether to ignore the summons. The Sheraton was not exactly a safe haven. Two years before an American freelance journalist, John Sullivan, had disappeared from the lobby, and a year later two US officials, who had come to the country to advise on agrarian reform, had been gunned down in the dining room. The killer had then calmly walked out through the lobby, unchallenged, and driven away.

As soon as he went through the doors, Webb saw a man striding across the foyer to meet him. He had copper hair, cut very short, a square jaw, and looked fit and very tanned. He held out his hand but he did not smile. 'Hugh Webb?'

The man's handshake was like a vice.

'I don't think we've met,' Webb said.

'Smith. John Smith,' the man said. He led Webb to a table in the lobby. Webb noticed several groups of men sitting around, drinking, holding the zippered purses that in San Salvador were not used to carry money or passports or Amex cards but usually contained Browning 9-millimetre pistols.

'Drink?' John Smith asked him.

'Just coffee.'

Smith ordered two coffees. Webb studied him a little more closely. The haircut, the straight back, the hard, muscled body, delineated a military man. The tan suit and crocodile-skin loafers were as out of place on John Smith as a tuxedo on a squad sergeant. Webb guessed that whatever post he held inside the United States Embassy, it wasn't a clerical position.

'Can I ask what rank you hold at the mission here, Mr Smith?'

'It's classified.'

'Then how do I know you are with the embassy?'

'You don't,' he said.

The coffees arrived. Smith stirred three sugars into his and leaned forward. 'I'll make this brief, Mr Webb. We've had some complaints about your performance here.'

'Who's we? And who's making the complaint?'

He ignored the question. 'The thing is, we expect you guys to play ball with us on this one. We don't want the press compromising our war effort here the way it did in Vietnam. Do I make myself clear?'

'Well, that depends on your point of view.'

'There is only one point of view. You either support the United States or you support the communists. It's quite simple. Who do you support, Mr Webb?' He smiled, but there was no humour in it. He looked uncomfortable with this. Webb guessed he might be more accustomed to other forms of persuasion.

'I don't accept that the situation here in El Salvador is as simple as the one you've just painted for me. That's the job of the journalist, Mr Smith. To present all sides of the picture.'

Smith toyed with his coffee cup. 'You weren't born in America, were you, Mr Webb?'

'Did my accent give me away or have you been checking on me?'

'Both.'

'Well, then . . . Mr Smith . . . if you have been checking you should be aware that I am neither pro-communist nor pro-Reagan. I would like to take the side of truth and justice in this argument, but as yet I haven't found any.'

Smith stirred his coffee and seemed to be considering one of several replies. Finally he said: 'You guys make me sick.'

Now they were getting down to basics. 'That doesn't bother me.'

Another smile. The effect was not pleasant. Webb imagined someone had told Smith to take a softly, softly approach with him, but add just the right amount of menace. Smith could manage the menace; it was the rest he was having a hard time with. 'Mr Webb, I don't think the issues here are complex at all. I'll admit that right now El Salvador does not have a perfect system in place, but you are just not going to bring democracy to a country like this overnight. Right now we are trying to do the best we can with what we have.'

'And what do you have?'

'We have a pro-American government pledged to bring democracy to this country, fighting against externally supported guerrillas committed to turning El Salvador into a Marxist state. We just cannot afford another Vietnam right here on our doorstep.'

'I agree with you. We can't. That's why I can't believe you people are here making the same mistakes you made last time.'

'The only mistake we made last time was letting you guys lose that war for us. That is what I'm trying to make clear to you, Mr Webb. We are asking you nicely to get with the team and support your adopted country.'

'You talk about Vietnam as if it was a war we should have won. The fact is it was a war we should not even have fought. There's a difference there, but I wonder if it's a little too subtle for you. I also wonder if perhaps the humiliation of that defeat hasn't warped a few minds. It seems to me a few generals in the Pentagon have been looking for someone to push around ever since, someone maybe a little smaller we *know* we can beat up. Foreign policy by revenge.'

'What we are talking about here is fighting communism.'

'What you are talking about here is exporting fascism. You talk about democracy as if it's some magical antidote to the Russians. So let me remind you what democracy is. It's the right, enshrined in law, to speak out openly even if your opinion opposes that of the government of the day. In San Salvador, speaking out against the government is tantamount to signing your own death warrant.'

'You don't have democracy without stability. We have to save this country before we can free it.'

'You can't fuck for virginity and you can't stand up for democracy by violating human rights. Let me tell you something else: the reason the United States is a free and a democratic country is not because of the military. It is because of the free press. In short I am the one that stands for democracy here. You don't.'

A chill smile. 'I'll convey your remarks through the proper channels.'

'You do that,' Webb said.

He had talked tough, but in truth he was scared now. Scared of Smith, scared of this country. He wondered what sort of pressures might now be brought to bear on the free and democratic press he had so ardently deified a few moments ago. But he would not let Smith see his doubts. Instead he threw some money on the table. 'Coffees are on me. My contribution towards bringing democracy to the free world. Keep up the good work.'

And he walked out.

When he got back to his hotel he took a phone call from his editor in New York. His last story was good, the man said, but too emotive. It would have to be cut. Especially his remarks about Ricardo Beltrán, which were possibly defamatory. Also any criticism of Reagan and the United States itself would not be received kindly, especially from a foreign-born journalist.

And tell Daniels to tone it down a little. Most of his shots were too explicit for the national press.

But you're doing a good job. Just try and be a little more even-handed in your approach.

When Webb hung up he tore the connection out of the wall and threw the telephone across the room.

# 30

Webb and Daniels were sitting on the canopied porch of a Mexican restaurant in Escalón. The FMLN had blacked out the city again, and the candles on the table provided the only light. Both men only picked at their food, their attention focused on the Cherokee Chief with smoked glass windows that was parked in the Esso station across the road, its headlights extinguished.

'I thought you ought to know,' Webb said. 'I think I was threatened this afternoon.'

Daniels was on his fourth beer. The last few days, Webb had noticed, he had been drinking too much and eating very little. In the guttering light of the candle he looked sallow and ill.

'Threatened? Who by?'

'A man who may or may not be called John Smith and who may or may not work for the United States government. He may or may not have threatened me. I thought about the conversation later and he made no direct statements to the effect that my safety was in question. I just got the feeling. You know?'

Daniels shifted in his chair. 'You think maybe it's time we suggested a transfer? I think we've done all the stories we can here.'

Webb shrugged his shoulders and did not answer.

'New York is mutilating your copy. Nothing we say or do is going to make any fucking difference.'

'I don't want to go yet. I'm certainly not going to be chased out.'

'You're willing to risk our lives to prove a point?'

'Not your life, Mike. If you want out, go. I mean it.'

Daniels considered this offer. 'Okay,' he said, finally.

There was not much more to say after that. Webb had suspected Daniels wanted out, but having it confirmed disappointed him.

They paid their bill and left. They caught a taxi back to the Camino Real. Several times they saw the driver glance anxiously in his rear-view mirror and cross himself. Webb turned around in his seat. The Jeep Cherokee had followed them, still without lights.

When they climbed out of the taxi in the forecourt of the Camino Real, the Cherokee parked a hundred metres back up the boulevard. They hurried inside the lobby.

Daniels grabbed Webb's arm. 'Fuck this. Come out with me. You can't fucking stay here.'

'No wonder you're a photographer,' Webb said. 'Your language is terrible.'

He pulled away. It wasn't Daniels' fault. Besides, he was probably doing the smart thing. Webb suspected that his own stubborn pride in journalistic integrity was overriding his reason. Yes, he was frightened. But he was also angry. Angrier than he'd ever been in his whole life.

The highway to the airport snaked through lush hills green with jungle and banana groves. Children prodded cows along the side of the road with sticks; squads of brown-skinned men laboured over roadside culverts. Every few kilometres there were army checkpoints where National Guardsmen in tight tunics and high leather boots waved down his car to paw through his passport and check his COPREFA credentials with sullen hostility.

El Salvador's international airport was barely two years old, a legacy of Molina's National Transformation, a glass mausoleum carved from the lonely jungle. Webb parked the Avis Golf and went inside. The arrivals hall was all marble, the air conditioning frigid. Two soldiers, armed with M-3 machine guns with flash suppressors, followed him with their eyes. An Escalón matron cruised the airport gift shop, trying on silk scarves.

Daniels had flown out the previous evening. When Webb had got back to the Camino Real there was a message for him from the IPA office in New York telling him that his replacement would be arriving this morning. Webb was confident he could do the job just as well on his own – after all, he had earned his spurs as a photo-journalist in Vietnam – but it was agency policy that two was the minimum staffing for any bureau, for safety reasons. Webb hoped Daniels' replacement was someone he had worked with before, preferably someone who knew a little more Spanish than he did.

The morning flight from Miami disgorged its human cargo –

wealthy businessmen who had been looking for investments for their coffee or cattle money, or their designer-dressed sons and daughters who had spent the last two weeks in Florida spending it. Webb's new photographer did not fit in with this crowd; he was taller, not as well dressed, and without the ubiquitous gold ropes at his neck and his wrists.

Webb glimpsed a horrendous Hawaiian shirt, with lavender-coloured slacks and an expression of complete enchantment. This was a man who was immediately enamoured of the sight of so many soldiers and police with guns.

It was Sean Ryan.

# 31

Ryan and Webb were driving north along the Suchitoto highway. Ryan was eager to get some pictures of government soldiers in action, and COPREFA had been issuing communiqués describing offensives under way in Chalatenango province. That morning they had headed in that direction, despite military warnings that the area was strictly off limits.

After an hour they saw smoke rising from the distant hills and saw US-made A-37s swoop overhead. 'Here we go,' Ryan said. 'Just like old times.'

'Why don't I feel nostalgic? Oh, shit.'

There was a roadblock just ahead. Webb pulled the Golf over to the side of the road, and they both reached into the pockets of their jackets for their passports and COPREFA cards. They did this very slowly; it was not considered wise to startle a teenager holding an M-16.

The soldiers wore crucifixes, wrapped with green yarn, and their olive-drab uniforms were stained with sweat and ochre dust. One of them, a boy with badly pockmarked skin, indicated they should get out while the car was searched for weapons.

When the search was completed the scar-faced boy handed them back their papers and shook his head to indicate that they would have to go back to the capital. 'Not allowed,' he said.

Webb nodded to Ryan. Up ahead he could see a handful of farmers – *campesinos* – running down the road. He thought at first they were dragging a sack, but this turned out to be an old man with blood on his shirt. They were shouting in Spanish.

'What are they saying?' Ryan asked him.

'They said they were being bombed by government planes.'

'What do you want to do?'

'I want to see for myself.'

'That's the spirit, Spider. Wave goodbye to the nice soldiers and let's see what we can do.'

Webb turned the car around and they headed back up the road towards San Salvador. They turned a bend a hundred metres from the roadblock and stopped the car. They jumped out and ran into the forest and then headed back the way they had come.

It took them three hours to circle around the roadblock through the thick jungle, and rejoin the Suchitoto road. As the day wore on the heat seemed to suck all the moisture from their bodies, and the dust from the road found its way into their eyes and throats. The jets were still patrolling the skies, far in the distance.

'Christ, it's hot,' Ryan said. 'Reminds me of Queensland.'

'Do you get bombed in Queensland?'

'Every Saturday night, mate.'

There was corn stubble and deserted bean fields on either side of the road. They passed several houses that had been gutted by bombs. A cow lay in a ditch with its feet in the air. As they approached, a black swarm of flies rose into the air.

They held their hands over their noses until they had passed.

'The air force have done a job here,' Ryan said. He finished a roll of film and began to load another.

Suddenly Webb grabbed his arm. 'I don't like the look of that,' he said.

The fuselage of the A-37 flashed in the sun against the dark backdrop of the volcano. It banked sharply, and began a low swooping dive towards the road. Webb had known many jet jockeys in Vietnam who had boasted about strafing civilians for fun on the way back to base after an operation. He realised they might appear to be a tempting target.

They ran towards the ruins of a farmhouse fifty yards away on the edge of the jungle and threw themselves inside. The jet roared overhead, treetop high, before wheeling away.

'Bastard,' Ryan hissed.

Webb sat up. He looked over his right shoulder and found himself staring into the black and stubby muzzle of an Uzi sub-machine gun.

There were six of them, an FMLN patrol sheltering from the same A-37 that had sent Ryan and Webb scurrying off the road. They wore an odd assortment of uniforms, a mixture of cowboy hats and forage caps, UCLA sweatshirts and olive utilities, but they were well armed, each of them carrying a Galil or Uzi assault rifle.

The *comandante* introduced himself in English as Salvador. He was grossly fat, his belly protruding over the leather belt of his jeans, his face dark and cratered, eyes no more than slits above plump cheeks. He wore aviator sunglasses and a beret with a little red star. His vast chest was criss-crossed with banderillos.

He grinned at them with bad teeth. 'Tourists?' His voice belied his size; it was high-pitched, almost feminine.

'Yeah. We're looking for the local Club Med,' Ryan said.

Webb handed Salvador their press credentials and passports. Salvador shook his head. 'Gringos,' he said. 'You crazy?'

'Yeah,' Ryan said. 'Aren't you?'

Salvador considered the situation, tapping the passports against his palm. 'You must come with us,' he said at last.

Webb looked at Ryan and shrugged his shoulders. 'In the circumstances I think it might be churlish to refuse.'

They set off through the jungle, along the narrow, winding trail that snaked north-west towards the forbidding black presence of the volcano. Occasionally they passed small settlements, *caserios*, several adobe houses still smouldering from recent aerial attacks. The air was hazy and thick with the stench of smoke.

'You want to take photograph now?' Salvador said to Ryan, pointing to the ruins of a *caserio*.

He sounded as casual as a tour guide. Ryan nodded and dutifully moved through the smoking ruins, documenting the results of the bombing with his Leica. Flies rose from a decomposing body inside one of the houses. A child.

'We were seen here. So they bombed the village.' Salvador spoke casually, as if the logic of this was irrefutable.

When Ryan had finished they moved off again, single file. The guerrillas spoke little, to them or to each other, and there were few rest stops. Dusk fell quickly but the pace did not falter. An impenetrably black tropical night descended. To keep from getting lost they had to hold on to the pack of the man in front. Around midnight a fat yellow moon rose over the volcano and the march became easier.

Webb reached what he considered the point of exhaustion, far beyond what he thought he could endure. Even then there was no choice but to keep going. By the early hours of the morning putting one foot in front of the other seemed to be a reflex action, like blinking and breathing. Like a heartbeat. He imagined that he slept as he walked – there were bright, vivid dreams that were over in seconds – before he stumbled and was jarred back to reality.

He wondered how long it would be before their Golf would be found abandoned on the Suchitoto road. It would probably be assumed that they had been kidnapped by death squads, and the agency might even distribute their obituaries. The prospect excited him. The story they might get from this could lead to a major feature. Only a handful of Western journalists had so far been willing or able to report on the war from the FMLN viewpoint. The title came to him: *Back from the Dead.* His editor in New York would like that.

It might even make them famous.

All they had to do was stay alive.

Finally, as the sun rose behind them, they saw their first tiled roof.

'We're here,' Salvador said. 'La Esperanza.'

La Esperanza consisted of thirty or forty adobe huts clustered under the broad canopies of oak and ceiba trees that provided shade as well as camouflage against the government jet bombers and helicopter gunships. As they got closer, Webb could see that they had not always been successful; several of the huts had shellholes in the walls and roofs.

The air was clamorous with insects, redolent with the taints of woodsmoke and sweat and human waste.

As they entered the village half-naked children seemed to emerge from everywhere, and clustered around, staring in frank curiosity at these *yanqui* strangers. Webb was too exhausted to do more than give them a cursory glance.

Salvador stopped in front of one of the huts. It was apparent to Webb that it was some kind of aid station; mouldering dressings, discarded syringes and broken glass ampoules were strewn on the ground outside.

'Our hospital,' Salvador announced, lending the building more grandeur than it perhaps deserved. 'We have a gringo nurse. Perhaps you will like to meet her.'

He went inside and reappeared a few moments later with a slender and fair-haired American girl.

Webb stared.

'Mickey,' he said.

# 32

'Jesus,' she whispered.

'Hello, Mickey,' Webb said.

She was wearing a khaki workshirt and shorts, her hair unkempt and tied back in a ponytail. She looked thin, her face gaunt with fatigue and, probably, malnourishment. Webb calculated that it had been twelve years since he had last seen her.

'Well.'

She shook her head. 'Well.'

'You haven't changed,' he said.

'Yeah. I looked like hell in Vietnam as well.'

He smiled. There was some truth in that, he supposed. The years had been kind; it was the present that had been cruel.

'You still chasing ambulances?'

'These days I try and get there first and let the ambulances follow me.'

A flicker of a smile. She looked at Ryan. 'You brought your pal.'

'Colleague. Let's get it right.'

'Sean Ryan.' Ryan nodded, too tired to do more. 'I'm sure I'd remember you if we'd met before. If you were in Vietnam you probably picked some metal out of me some time or another.'

Mickey turned to Salvador and asked him, in Spanish, where he had found the two gringos.

'These idiots were just walking up the road,' he said. 'We were going to shoot them.'

'I bet you couldn't hit a cow with a shotgun if it was standing on your foot,' Webb said in Spanish, and Salvador flushed with embarrassment and his men laughed. Even Mickey smiled.

'He didn't know you spoke Spanish.'

'Obviously.'

She came down the steps and looked up at him. 'So you've come looking for a story?'

'Looks like we found it.'

'One thing I'd like to clear up,' Ryan said to her. 'Are we prisoners?'

'Of course not,' Salvador interrupted. 'Why? Do you want to leave?'

'I guess not.'

'Come with me,' Salvador said.

Webb looked at Mickey. He had a hundred questions he wanted to ask her, but he guessed they'd have to wait. Right now he just wanted to sleep.

Salvador led the way to a hut at the edge of the village. There were shellholes in the roof and in one of the walls. The floors were hard-packed dirt.

'Nice place,' Ryan said. 'Is there a bond?'

'The last family who lived here was killed by the same bomb that made the hole in that wall,' Salvador said. 'Besides, we don't bother to fix the houses any more. Once you put the fire out it looks just like any other ruin and so they don't bother to bomb it.'

Two hammocks were strung across the roof from the rafters. The floor was beaten earth.

'A few pictures on the walls,' Ryan said, 'and it will look just like home.'

'I'll get you something to eat,' Salvador said.

'Two steakburgers. Hold the onion.'

Salvador didn't smile. He went out.

They looked at each other.

'Gee, Ollie, this is another fine mess you've gotten me into,' Ryan said. He swung his legs up into the hammock, lay back and groaned. He closed his eyes. 'God Almighty.'

Webb leaned against the hammock. He barely had the strength to raise his legs from the dirt floor.

Suddenly Ryan's eyes blinked open and he sat up, clawing at his calf. He rolled up one leg of his jeans and slapped at something that was feeding on him. 'Christ, fleas.' He picked the insect off his skin and flicked it on to the ground, and then began a minute inspection of his legs for its companions. 'Who the hell is the girl?'

'She was one of the nurses at Bien Hoa in '70. She was there the day you were wounded in the shoulder.'

'Shit, but you've got an amazing memory.'

'Well, some people are hard to forget.'

Ryan caught the edge in Webb's voice. 'Run the Union Jack up that particular flagpole, did you?'

'Christ, you're a crude bastard,' Webb muttered, and he crawled into his own hammock. His feet were numb, beyond pain.

Ryan gasped as he removed his jungle boots and settled in the hammock. 'I think I'd prefer a water bed. I'm getting too old for this.'

'I wonder what the hell she's doing here?' Webb murmured. He felt giddyingly tired; it was as if his eyes were full of grit. His belly growled with hunger but he knew he could not wait for the food. He just wanted to sleep.

When Webb woke the sun was high in the sky. His head ached and he felt as if he were suffering from a massive hangover. Ryan was still sprawled open-mouthed, snoring. Webb struggled out of his hammock, staggering, light-headed. He clutched the hammock ropes, feeling slightly nauseous, while he sorted the tattered memories of the last twelve hours into order. He went out into the bright sunlight, saw the adobe 'hospital' fifty yards away on the other side of the compound. He made his way over.

The hospital consisted of six rustic beds and a few hammocks slung from the rafters on the open verandah. Part of the roof was missing; there appeared to be no plumbing or electricity and the operating table was a wooden door supported on trestles. There were dark and sinister stains on the beaten earth floor.

Mickey was examining an old man, a stethoscope pressed against his chest. He was so thin Webb could count his ribs, and his skin had the sickly grey pallor of approaching death.

Webb stood in the doorway and watched her. A doctor with a crisp thin moustache and a polished dome of skull eyed him suspiciously from the corner.

Mickey looked up and saw him. 'Salvador said you were both snoring like pigs,' she said.

'That was Ryan.'

She returned her attention to the old man. 'Marquez is fifty years old. He has congestive cardiac disease. For five dollars a month I could get him digitalis and diuretics and keep his heart beating for years. Hundreds of thousands of people in the United States have lived to old age with the same complaint. Marquez will not live until Christmas.'

Marquez put his shirt back on. Mickey gave him a phial containing some red capsules. He thanked her, in Spanish, and hobbled away.

'Placebos,' she explained. 'Sugar pills. They won't help his condition but perhaps he'll feel better.'

She went out on to the verandah. Webb followed her.

'I often wondered what had happened to you,' he said. 'I thought about you a lot when I got back to the States. I even looked you up in the phone book once.'

'Yeah? I was in the Yellow Pages. Under "E" for "Easy".'

'That wasn't it.'

'Yeah?'

'Yeah.'

There was a long and difficult silence. 'So,' she said, finally.

'So.'

'I guess you did something with that talent of yours. You're not freelance any more.'

'I'm working with a news group called IPA. I've done okay.'

'Still doing wars?'

'I did presidents trading as criminals for a while but it wasn't as much fun. Washington's too dangerous for me.'

She smiled. 'I'm glad you done okay,' she said.

'What about you?' He tried to make a joke of it. 'What's a pretty girl like you doing in a place like this?'

'It's a long story.'

'I'm sure I can edit it down.'

'I don't want to end up another feel-good weekend magazine feature.'

'That really wasn't why I was asking.'

'But you're a journalist. You'll file it away for later anyway.' She lit a cigarette and offered him one.

He shook his head. 'I don't remember you smoked.'

'I didn't before I came here. It keeps the insects away. And you don't feel as hungry.' She leaned back against one of the verandah posts, studying him. 'Fate, huh?'

He nodded. 'Fate.'

There was a burst of laughter. They looked around. Salvador and his men were squatting under a nearby oak tree, cleaning their weapons, their transistor radio tuned to Radio Venceremos. They started singing in tune with a pop song:

*I yes call to sigh I lof you . . .*

Mickey turned back to Webb. 'Salvador thinks you are a great public relations coup for the Front.'

'Perhaps he's right.'

She shook her head. 'You guys mean well. But do you really think anyone in America gives a damn? Or in Britain? People can sustain outrage for a week at the most. Then they get bored. When the elections roll around they still vote for the government that offers them the lowest taxes.'

'That didn't happen in Vietnam. We made a difference there.'

'Because it was Americans dying. Because it was Americans killing babies. But who gives a damn about a few spics and Indians, right?' She turned away, embarrassed by her own vehemence. 'But it's good that you try.'

'What about you? What difference are you trying to make? You didn't get here by accident either.'

'I can feel an interview coming on. Have you got your notebook there?'

'This is strictly off the record.'

She shook her head. 'When you're talking to a journalist, there's no such thing, right?' She grinned, unexpectedly. It was like the sun coming out from behind a cloud. 'Was my number in the book?'

'I couldn't remember which city you were from,' he lied.

She shrugged and threw her cigarette in the dirt. 'I'd better get back to work. Ramón is giving me the evil eye.'

'Ramón?'

'He's the doctor. I goof off too long he'll accuse me of betraying the revolution. You'd better go get something to eat. They do great crabmeat enchiladas with asparagus here. Tell the maître d' I sent you.'

'Can I get a pina colada?'

'Anything you want. Just put it on my tab. I'll talk to you later.'

She went back inside.

# 33

They were in what was known as a controlled zone; the death squads could not operate here, but the villagers faced dangers of a different kind, being subject to attack from the air and the occasional ground offensives by government troops. Webb realised this was what the Americans used to call a 'free fire zone' in Vietnam. For the first time he might find out what it was like to be on the receiving end.

The *compas*, which was how the guerrillas referred to themselves, had fixed outposts that served as an early warning system against invasion, and used radios and runners – young boys known as *correos* – to communicate with each other. The guerrilla patrols were constantly on the move. One day Webb would see a group of FMLN camped under the trees, their webbing belts and bandoleros slung from the branches, but by early the next morning they would be gone.

Only Salvador, as regional commander, kept a base in the village. He was a figure of some importance in the guerrilla movement, and as such his bodyguard was better armed than some of the other combat groups, who sported anything from modern Russian or Chinese-made AK-47s to ancient Mausers or Hodgkiss machine guns.

'If you want action, you will have to be patient,' he told Webb and Ryan. 'We don't seek out the *chuchos*.' *Chuchos*, or 'little dogs', was the FMLN's contemptuous name for the government soldiers. 'We let them come to us.'

'Remember Vietnam?' Ryan said to Webb.

In fact Webb had the uncomfortable sensation of reporting the same war all over again, but this time from the other point of view. This time they would witness how small bands of poorly armed but highly motivated young men and women used guerrilla tactics against American technology. Ryan even made a joke of it; he referred to the rebels as Carlos, the Spanish name for Charlie.

'There's no point in us hanging around here if we're not going to see any fighting,' Ryan told Salvador.

Salvador just shrugged. 'It is your choice. But the air raids are becoming more frequent and d'Aubuisson has boasted on the radio that he will send the Ramón Belloso battalion to annihilate us, that we will all be dead in six months. If you stay with us a little longer, I guarantee you will see all the action you want.' He gave Ryan a small, sardonic smile.

'I'm not waiting six months for one firefight,' Ryan said.

'Well, you are free to go at any time. Unlike us.'

They decided to stay.

They settled into the rhythms of the village, a cadence that beat to the gentle slapping sounds of the women sitting around the blackened griddles patting the *maizillo* into tortillas, the thwack-thwack from the river as they beat their washing on the rocks.

The *campesinos* accepted their arrival among them without curiosity. The villagers did not ask questions about them, did not seem interested in where they had come from nor how long they would stay. Resignation had set into these people's souls like rust. There were no toys for the children, no books for the adults. All thought, all energy, was attuned to personal survival. Sickness, particularly malaria, took such a toll that thirty was considered the onset of old age.

Even the children appeared lethargic, their bellies swollen by malnutrition. Invading government soldiers had burned the previous season's corn crops and now the villagers were living off their reserves of sorghum.

Compassion was not as easily summoned as revulsion, and the perceived romance of the revolutionaries did not stand close examination. Webb watched the *campesinos* clear their noses on their hands and wipe the results on the walls, spit on the dirt floors where the babies were playing, defecate in the water upstream from where the women collected water for drinking. The smoke that hung around the village continually irritated his eyes, the large fat flies harassed him, tiny fleas and mosquitoes made his life a torment, the stench of rotting vegetation and human waste made him continually nauseous.

And then there was the food.

On that first day Salvador himself brought them their first meal: two brown-green tortillas topped with red pinto beans and a little salt. Ryan stared at it, depressed.

'In another month,' Salvador said, 'there won't even be this.' He scowled and walked out.

They chewed their tortillas. They were half an inch thick and made not from corn but from sorghum. They tasted foul.

Ryan ate half and threw the rest out of the window into the undergrowth where the children and the dogs squabbled over it.

The nights were a different kind of torment. The only light came from candles, and after an hour or two of darkness these were extinguished and everyone slept. The *compas* simply put a piece of plastic on the hard ground, lay down, and tucked themselves in with a thin blanket. Every part of the body had to be covered because at night the bats would descend, looking for a meal. Their saliva contained an anaesthetic as well as an anti-coagulant, so you did not feel their bite. They simply opened a vein and lapped up the flow. If you fell victim you would wake in the morning to find yourself covered in fresh blood.

Webb was told that the bats preferred animal blood, but the *chuchos* had killed all the livestock during the last invasion so now life was even difficult for the parasites.

Webb's own nighttime ritual consisted of balancing on his hammock, then shaking out his jeans and socks to get rid of the fleas. After checking them by the light of his torch he would carefully put them back on, taking care not to let them touch the dirt floor and become reinfested. Then he would fastidiously tuck a blanket around his body and pull it up over his head. Before sleep finally came he would hear the bats stretch their wings in the rafters overhead while the malarial mosquitoes hummed around his head looking for the smallest piece of unprotected skin.

It was almost a relief when the first killings came to break the famished and tortuous routine of their lives.

In Vietnam the sound of helicopter rotors always meant a friend; it was either extra firepower or more supplies or a medevac. Here helicopters meant death.

Webb ran outside and watched the Huey closing in; he was familiar with this particular 'flight profile' from Vietnam, a full-tilt treetop boogie with machine guns blazing. If you were caught out in the open there was no time to do anything except pray.

It occurred to him as he watched that he had once been on board a Cobra as it had done the same thing in a 'free fire zone' in Chu Lai province; the pilot had come in low, hitting every target he could see, as if playing a frenetic arcade video game. Here was another camouflaged Huey doing the same thing.

Now he knew why the Vietnamese had hated the Americans so much.

He heard the heavy-calibre bullets thud across the compound, kicking up devils of dust. Several rounds slapped into an adobe wall just behind him. And then it was gone, the chop-chop of the rotors disappearing beyond the forest canopy before the *compas*' small-arms fire could be sustained. Webb stood quite still, gasping with shock, amazed to find himself unharmed.

Then he heard the screaming.

A woman lay on her side in front of one of the houses. There was blood on her blouse. She was holding a small child in her right arm, limp as a rag doll. She held out her hand, cried out to him in Spanish.

When Ryan had run out of the house, he had automatically grabbed his camera. He brought the viewfinder to his eye, focused the lens, but hesitated. He could take the shot, or he could take the child.

He made his decision.

*The woman's hand, dark stains in the dust, face creased in anguish and pain, eyes big as saucers.*

Frame.

*Bullet holes behind her in the adobe wall. The child's jaw slack, eyes shut in the tiny face.*

Frame.

Someone brushed past him. Salvador knelt down beside the woman, put his arms around her. He looked around at Ryan – and at the camera – appealing for help with the child.

*Blood smeared on his forearms. The expression frozen between anger and utter despair.*

Frame.

'Help me here,' he shouted in English. 'For the love of God help me with the child!'

Frame.

A woman, Anaya, one of the *compas*, rushed past him and grabbed the child. Salvador picked up the woman. Running backwards, Ryan kept them in focus as they stumbled up the path towards the hospital.

Frame.

Webb heard screams and ran in the direction of the hospital. They were dragging the first casualty in by his arms. It was Marquez, the old farmer he had seen Mickey treating when they first arrived. His shirt was sodden with blood. Webb saw Ryan standing to one side, with his cameras.

'Get the shots,' he said.

Everyone was shouting. The doctor and two of the nurses, the *sanitarios*, rushed out of the hospital to help two *compas* carry the old man inside. Ryan ran beside them with the camera. Mickey tried to push him away but he kept firing off one frame after another.

'Get out the way!' she shouted at him.

Ryan backed against the wall, finished one roll, changed the film, put the used roll into his pocket. This was good. He was in close, there was good light, he had the expressions on the faces. This would sell to *Time* or *Newsweek* or one of the Sunday newspaper magazines.

They lay Marquez on the makeshift operating table. There were three entry wounds in his chest, but most of the blood was coming from his back. He was dead, no worries, Ryan thought. He had seen enough of death to know. Ramón felt for a pulse, shone a penlight into the old man's eyes. He shook his head and the *sanitarios* lifted him quickly from the table and dropped him to the floor, like a heavy sack. Time for the dead later.

High-pitched screams, like those of a child. Ryan looked around. The boy was perhaps fourteen or fifteen. He was supported by two *campesinos*, his left leg dangling, attached to his hip by just the sinews. Ryan started shooting again. The leg, the blood wasn't important. Get the faces, he heard his old editor saying, the *faces*.

'For Christ's sake, get out of the way!' Mickey screamed at him.

She shoved him back against the wall.

The camera slipped out of his fingers; the strap at his neck took the weight. He wiped the sweat on his shirt, picked up the camera again. For a moment he glimpsed Webb standing in the doorway, watching. No accusation in those eyes, just the understanding of a co-conspirator.

Ryan finished the second roll and stumbled outside. Webb was sitting on the steps, waiting. Gouts of blood in the dirt.

Ryan fumbled in his pockets for his cigarettes.

'You okay?' Webb asked him.

Ryan shook his head. 'Sometimes,' he said, 'I feel like a right shit.'

The Huey's strafing run had been productive; an old man, a child, and one of the *correos* had been killed, and a woman and a young boy had been badly wounded. The boy would lose his leg. Ryan stood in the doorway with his cameras as Mickey assisted the doctor in the amputation, which was done without benefit of anaesthetic.

Another roll of film.

That evening the three dead were buried on a hill overlooking La Esperanza – delay was undesirable as decomposition was rapid in the tropical heat. There was no priest to perform the ceremony. Salvador spoke a few words from a heavy black Bible and everyone walked away. Ryan was there with his cameras but found no grief to record on the faces of the survivors. By now they were numb to that.

Mickey sat on a stool beside the bed, holding the boy's hand. He lay quite still, staring at the ceiling. He could have been dead except for the slow blinking of his eyes.

The only light came from a candle in a corner of the room. Grotesque shadows danced on the bare, stained walls. The woman whose child had been killed was crying, softly. The only other sound was the buzzing of insects.

Ryan stood in the doorway for a long time, watching.

'What Salvador cannot understand,' Mickey said at last, 'is not that you are immune to human suffering but that you can ignore it.'

He was surprised. He did not think she had seen him. She still had her back to him. Perhaps she had only sensed his presence. 'What does he think I should have done?' he said.

'He told me that Marguerita held her arms out to you. She was pleading with you to help her.'

'My job's to record what happens here for the outside world. One photograph could help a thousand Margueritas.'

'Is that how you see it?'

'I'm not a doctor. I'm a photographer, a combat photographer. It's what I do. If I don't take photographs I might just as well be a tourist.'

She turned her face. He watched her, in profile. She looked so pale in this light, he thought. Almost opaque. All the life seemed to have been squeezed out of her body; even her voice was thin. He felt as if he could pass a hand through her, as if through vapour.

'I remember a few years back,' he said. 'I was in Biafra. There was this woman. She looked ancient, but she couldn't have been that old because she was nursing a little kid. We were in this village and she followed me around for hours while I took photographs, just kept touching me on the shoulder, on the arm, whispering something, Christ knows what. I knew I wanted to do something for her but I couldn't think of anything that would make that much difference. I gave her something in the end, though.'

'What?'

'Her picture on the front page of *Time*.'

Mickey shook her head.

'You don't like me very much, do you?' he said.

'Not really.'

'Neither do I, sometimes.'

'Where's Hugh?'

'He's borrowed a typewriter from Salvador and he's tapping away by candlelight, every flying insect God made crawling over his head. It's what he does for his living. Me, I take my snaps and that's it. He saves his up for later. Like a squirrel with nuts.'

'If he's a squirrel, what does that make you?'

He shrugged. 'A jackal, I suppose?' He moved away from the door, came and stood at the foot of the bed. 'Don't mind me saying this, but you look like shit.'

'I bet you say that to all the girls.'

'How long have you been in this dump?'

'All my life. Or maybe it's just thirteen months. I can't remember.'

'What the hell made you come here?'

'I wouldn't know how to start to explain. Why don't you tell me why you're here?'

'I'll show you mine if you show me yours?'

'Right,' she said. The boy moaned and twitched, semi-conscious. She stroked his forehead. He moaned again and subsided. 'You enjoy this?' she asked him.

'I must do.'

She shook her head.

'You want some hypocritical bullshit about wanting to change the world? I like the danger. I get a buzz out of it.'

'Did you enjoy today?'

Ryan felt a door slam inside him. 'If I'd stopped filming to pick up the kid, would he have lived?'

She shook her head. 'Half his brain was missing.'

'There you are, then. All right, now it's your turn.'

'My turn?'

'I've showed you mine. A deal's a deal.'

She took a deep breath. 'When I got back from Vietnam I tried to pretend that that part of my life had never happened. I wanted to block it out, forget everyone I ever knew there, everything I'd seen and heard. I did a year in Walter Reed, left the army, got a job in New Orleans. For some reason I found myself back working in emergency rooms. Just couldn't leave that shit alone, you know? I was drinking a lot, but what the hell, right? Spent a lot of time in singles bars, put a few notches on my lipstick case. Then one day, I guess I took my eye off the ball or something. I met a real nice guy. Jesus, don't know how that happened. And glory be, he was a paramedic. Match made in heaven, right?'

'What happened?'

'We got divorced in 1980.' She made a face. 'Maybe it would have lasted if we could have had kids. But probably just as well. I would only have screwed them up.'

'So you're running away, Mickey?'

She gave him a look of contempt. 'Oh, please.'

'You mean you're not?'

'This is running away? Frag wounds? Traumatic amputations?'

'All right, explain it to me.'

'Every night for maybe a year after I got back from Vietnam I had this same dream. It was a mas-cal at Bien Hoa, and there was this guy, real bad head wounds, he was put with the expectants. I gave him the speech. You know, I'm Mickey van Himst, you're at Bien Hoa Field Hospital, we are going to make you as comfortable as possible. Jack 'em up with morphine, put them in the room, come back later to tag 'em and bag 'em. The mas-cal was ten, maybe twelve hours, and when I came back that kid was still alive. He was looking at me with these eyes – darkest, darkest damn eyes I ever seen. I called one of the surgeons but when he got there he said the kid was dead.' She stopped, wiped the sweat off her face.

'Perhaps you imagined it,' Ryan said.

'Maybe I did. What's worse?'

'I don't get it.'

'I can't . . . I can't get through it, all right? I just can't get back to a normal life. It's been twelve years and I still can't turn it off.' Another deep breath, as she tried to stay in control. 'I was following what was happening here in the papers. Oh God, I thought. Another Vietnam. Then after the divorce I decided maybe this time I'd join the good guys. I applied to the Peace Corps but they said it was too dangerous here for a woman. Like Vietnam wasn't dangerous. So, all right. Okay. I took a crash course in Spanish, went down to Cuernavaca in Mexico, got in touch with the FDR, and they smuggled me into El Salvador. So I'm not running away. I'm running back. Okay?'

Ryan did not know what to say to her.

'I guess you think I'm crazy,' she said.

'No, I don't think you're crazy.'

'Liar . . . Damn, I never meant to tell you all that. I've got a big mouth.'

'Your secrets are safe with me. When I don't have a camera I'm harmless.'

'Yeah?'

'Yeah.'

'So, what about you? Are you all finished up here now? Wash the blood off, go back to the States, sell your pictures, pick up a Pulitzer?'

Ryan turned away. He was feeling a little too raw for this sort of treatment. 'You know what?'

'What?'

'I don't think I like you either.'

# 34

There were four boys playing with a plastic football in the dust outside the hospital. Ryan had joined in. The children were shrieking and laughing, trying to get the ball away from him. Ryan was slapping his chest, shouting. 'Pelé – the white Pelé!'

He stopped when he saw Rogelio, and let one of the boys take the ball. The child ran off, the others chasing after him.

'Hey, Rogelio,' Ryan said. 'Want to play?'

Rogelio sat on the hospital steps, staring straight ahead.

'What do you think, Rogelio? Pretty good, aren't I?'

The large black eyes were fixed on the ground.

He saw Mickey on the verandah.

'What's his problem?'

'He's an orphan.'

'Does he talk?'

She shook her head.

'Why not?'

'His mother and father were murdered by the *chuchos* right in front of him. Great photographic opportunity. Pity you missed it.'

She went back inside the hospital.

Ryan knelt down. 'Hey, Rogelio, you play *fútbol*? Pelé. Paolo Rossi. Bobby Charlton. All that good shit.' He took the little boy's arm, but Rogelio pulled away. 'I'll show you.'

Ryan ran after the four boys, won back the ball by shouldering the biggest into the dirt. The boy laughed, got up and kicked Ryan in the leg. Ryan pretended to be hurt. The others shrieked with excitement and chased after him. Ryan dribbled the ball to where Rogelio was sitting. 'Try and get it off me!'

The other boys descended on him. Ryan fended them away, showing off. 'Rogelio!'

The boy did not move.

Ryan kicked the ball as hard as he could, into the bushes. He raised both arms. 'Australia one, El Salvador nil!' He bent down again in front of Rogelio. 'Hey, Rogelio. *Jogo bonito*, all right! Come on.'

Nothing.

'He likes playing with kids,' Webb said. 'He knows he can win.'

Mickey turned from the window. 'Rogelio's mother was raped and murdered in front of his eyes. Then his father was shot in the stomach and left to die. He saw all of it. He hasn't spoken since he got here.'

Webb smiled. She saw him watching her and turned away, embarrassed.

'So,' she said. 'How's life been for you?'

'Up and down.'

'Not married?'

He shook his head.

'Girl in every bureau?'

'These days I live mostly in New York. I asked for this assignment.'

Ryan was still trying to convince Rogelio to play football with him. 'He's still twittering away to the kid. Does he speak Spanish?'

'Not much.'

'Rogelio sure as hell doesn't speak any English.'

'It's okay. Ryan could listen to himself for hours.'

'He's not everything he looks, is he?'

Webb recognised the grudging admiration in her voice and felt a familiar resentment. Even women who hated him were somehow attracted to him. Another of the world's injustices. He had charm like sticky honey.

Webb watched her. She was not the most beautiful girl he had known in his life; she was not Odile. But then he had never loved Odile, only desired her. He remembered the tight pain in his chest when Mickey had walked away from him that evening at Bien Hoa, and he experienced that same pang once more. She was not the first girl he had loved, or the last, but he had told himself he remembered her more than any of the others because of Vietnam, because life had been so sharp and vivid then, and perhaps also because she had been the one to end it. But the old embers were not cold. This time he did not want to leave her behind.

'I've been talking with Ryan,' he said. 'We want to try and get back to San Salvador first chance we can. Why don't you come out with us?'

'Why?'

'Why not?'

'Because I make a difference here. Back in the States . . .' She shrugged her shoulders. 'What is there to go back to? Daytime television. Weather reports. Shopping malls. I'm close to life here. I get one good cup of coffee a week, and I've learned to appreciate it. And I'm needed.' She pointed to a line of *campesinos*, men and women, waiting for the morning clinic that was being conducted by two of the *sanitarios*. 'It doesn't take a lot to help them. When I got here most of these people were suffering badly from anaemia. Their diet, too many pregnancies, malarial fevers, parasites, all drain the iron out of them. So I made them a special medicine. You know what I did? I cleaned some nails with pieces of lemon, soaked them overnight and then made the people drink the rusty water. No more anaemia.'

'But you can't stay here for ever. You're not one of them.'

'I'm not an American either. I haven't felt like a normal American – whatever the hell that is – since I got back from Vietnam.'

He was suddenly aware of the gulf between them, and he didn't know what to say to her. She still looked much the same on the outside, but the girl he had met twelve years ago was long gone.

Ramón called to her. He was changing the dressings on the boy with the amputated leg and he wanted her help.

'See, I'm needed,' she said, and turned away.

Salvador's command post was a one-room house that he shared with his brother and his brother's wife and several of his bodyguards. They all slept together on the floor. On the verandah was a wooden trestle table with a handset radio and typewriter and an old wicker rocking chair. A slogan had been scrawled on the wall in red paint: *Por la Sangre Derramada, de Adelante Camarada*. For the spilled blood, onwards comrades!

Webb conducted the interview while Ryan moved around taking photographs. Salvador's sister-in-law lay in a hammock, breastfeeding an infant. A few scruffy chickens clucked in the yard.

'We have no schools, no hospitals, no land, no art, no culture,' Salvador was saying in his strange falsetto. 'Most of all we have no dignity. We watch our children die of hunger because our wages are so low. And then when we protest, the government calls us Marxists and rebels and their soldiers murder us like dogs. Finally, after so much violence, you realise these people do not understand words. Or they do not care to understand. So we have no choice but to go to war against them. It is the only language they comprehend. Look what they did to Monsignor Romero. A gentle man, a humble man, a man of peace.'

One of the bodyguards brought them coffee, hot, black and very sweet, in earthen mugs.

'In the early days it was not easy to make war. On my very first night watch I remember they gave me some firecrackers because they did not have a gun to spare. If I saw the enemy I was to light them, to make the *chuchos* think it was an ambush, and also to wake my companions, my *muchachos*. These days we have Israeli assault rifles and M-60 machine guns.'

He leaned to one side and broke wind.

He noticed Webb's grin. 'So I fart. My brother farts. My sister-in-law farts. Even the baby farts. What do you expect from a diet of beans?' He scratched irritably at his groin. The fleas loved the body's hidden places, secreting themselves away in the creases of a tight pair of jeans. 'Once we all had a little land to grow corn or beans. But the *dueños* stole the land to grow coffee or to graze their cattle, driving many *campesinos* into the city where they starve in the slums or are disappeared by the death squads. What they do not understand is that if you take everything away from a man, he will eventually turn around and fight you to the death, because he has nothing left to lose. Tell them that in America.'

Webb ended the interview. Ryan had finished taking photographs and was sitting in one of the wicker chairs, tapping his foot impatiently in a rhythmless tattoo.

'We believe that very soon the government troops will be starting another campaign against us,' Salvador said. 'You are welcome to stay with us for as long as you want, but it is dangerous and we have little food.'

'I don't have much film left,' Ryan said to Webb, 'and the stuff I've taken is growing several types of fungus.'

'It is your choice,' Salvador said. 'But I hope that when you get back to the United States you will tell the world what is happening here in my country.'

'We'll tell the story,' Webb said. 'I cannot guarantee that anyone will listen.'

Salvador stared at him, and his expression betrayed his disbelief that people would not care, if they knew. He stood up suddenly, unhitched his belt and dropped his jeans to his knees.

'Jesus Christ,' Ryan said.

'They did this to me when I was fourteen years old,' Salvador said. 'Now you see why I hate them so much.'

Webb lay in his hammock, his arm over his eyes to shield them from the light. His bones ached, and he had not slept for days. Nausea made it impossible to eat. He thought he knew what the problem might be and that morning he had swallowed a handful of quinine pills in a desperate attempt to halt the progress of the fever through his body.

He groaned. He felt as if his eyes were going to push themselves out of his head. His hands would not stop shaking.

'You all right, Spider?'

'Just tired,' Webb said.

'Better get some sleep then, mate. Salvador has promised to get us an escort back to the Suchitoto road in the morning.'

But next morning, when the sun rose, Webb could not rise from his hammock. His body burned with fever in the chill morning air. Mickey hurried over from the hospital to examine him.

'Malaria,' she said.

# 35

Ryan was standing in the dusty compound in front of the hospital, tapping the ball on his foot, keeping it off the ground, counting. Thirty-seven, thirty-eight, thirty-nine . . . Rogelio sat on the steps a few yards away with his hands between his knees, staring at the ground.

The ball bounced away, through the dirt. Ryan retrieved it, held it out to him. 'Your turn, mate.'

'You never give up, do you?'

He looked up. It was Mickey. 'He could learn a lot from me.'

'I'm sure. I didn't think Australians played soccer.'

'They don't. But I had these Italian mates where I grew up. They taught me. I was pretty good at all ball sports.'

'Why aren't I surprised?'

Ryan left the ball at Rogelio's feet and followed Mickey inside the hospital.

'Don't misunderstand me,' she said. 'I approve of what you're trying to do with Rogelio. Just don't get your hopes too high. We've been trying to get him to talk for three months. You've been here a week.'

Webb tossed on one of the bunks, lathered in sweat. Ryan had sat with him through the night, while he shivered and babbled and sweated. His skin was a sickly yellow and his eyes had already sunken into his cheeks as the fever gnawed at his body.

Mickey took a thermometer from a jar.

'Want me to insert that for you?' Ryan asked her.

'I'd only use that method if I was taking your temperature.'

She slipped it under Webb's arm, held it there, counted the pulse rate as she waited. 'Hugh. Can you hear me. Hugh?'

Webb muttered something neither of them could understand. She retrieved the thermometer.

'How's he doing?'

'He's pretty sick. He's not going anywhere for a while. Don't you guys take your tablets?'

'He got careless, I guess. I missed my weekly dose too. I took two last night to make up for it.'

'You don't look too good yourself,' she said.

'I didn't get much sleep. I was here all night.'

'I know. The *sanitarios* told me.'

'Got to look after the bastard. He'd do the same for me.'

She smiled. 'You're full of surprises.'

He smiled back. 'I think you're a pretty remarkable woman, too.'

She looked embarrassed. 'I didn't mean it that way.'

'I did. I haven't met a lot of women that I've really admired. I mean, not just for their looks.' He shrugged. 'It takes a very special kind of woman to do what you're doing.'

She brushed a wisp of hair from her face, a self-conscious gesture. She seemed about to say something, changed her mind.

He moved closer.

There was a noise from the doorway. They both looked around. Rogelio was standing there, watching. Something rolled across the floor. Ryan looked down.

It was a football.

'Look. He's got Rogelio playing soccer with him.'

Salvador nodded, slowly. He didn't like the big gringo, could never forgive him for his behaviour the day of the attack by the government helicopter. But he grudgingly conceded that he had worked a miracle with the orphan boy.

'What happens when he goes?' he said.

Mickey folded her arms, said nothing.

'How is the other gringo? He is ready to travel?'

'Soon.'

'Did I do the right thing letting them come here?'

'They will tell your story, Salvador. But I don't think it will stop the war.'

'So what good did it do?'

He walked away.

Ryan was juggling the ball on his foot. He looked up and saw Mickey. 'What's come and get it off me in Spanish?'

The little boy lunged at him, but he turned away, pivoting on his left leg, moving the ball with his right foot. The boy kicked and kicked, growing increasingly frustrated. Ryan laughed. Finally Rogelio pushed him, catching him off balance. Ryan fell on his back.

Now it was Rogelio's turn to laugh.

'That's the first time I've heard him do that since he's been here,' Mickey said.

Ryan sat up, breathing hard. 'Maybe I should teach you to play soccer.'

'Me?'

'I haven't seen you laugh yet.'

'There hasn't been a lot to laugh about.'

'Moping around with a long Latin expression doesn't do any bloody good either. Can I take a snap of you now?'

'For the newspapers?'

'No, for me. Something to remember you by.'

She ignored him. 'Your friend's better.'

'As soon as he's got some strength back, you'll be leaving.'

'When will that be?'

'Salvador says the day after tomorrow.' Rogelio was shouting something. 'He wants you to come and play with him,' she said. 'He'll miss you when you go.'

'Reckon he'll be all right?'

'I don't know.'

He grinned. 'What about you. Will you miss me?'

'I hardly know you.'

'Yeah. Bloody shame.'

She went up the verandah steps and into the hospital. Ryan watched her go, feeling strangely depressed. Cheer up, son. What's the matter with you? He could feel the onset of another of the black moods that had dogged him over the last few years. Sometimes they lasted a few days, sometimes weeks. He called them his black monkey. Sometimes the little bastard just climbed on his back and wouldn't let go. Christ, what did he have to feel bad about?

Rogelio was grinning at him, gap-toothed. 'Pelé, Bobby Charlton!' he shouted, and dribbled past him.

'Paolo Rossi!' Ryan shouted. He took the ball off him and ran as fast as he could the other way, Rogelio and two of the village dogs in pursuit.

# 36

Ryan lay in his hammock, staring at the moon through the shellhole in the roof, listening to the sounds from the jungle. At night the forests sounded like a drunken party in a brothel, the animals and bats and night birds hooting and screaming, and at first it had been a little unnerving. But after sunset all fears were illusory, because the *chuchos* were hiding in their barracks, and the jet planes and helicopters could not fly. It was like the Nam. The night belonged to the guerrillas.

He heard a movement outside, thought it was rat, or perhaps a snake. His hand reached for the flashlight under his pillow. Then he saw a face illuminated for a moment by the flare of a match.

'I used to do this all the time,' Mickey said, lighting her cigarette, 'then I figured there was no value in it.'

'It depends what you were looking for, I suppose.'

'Something of value. Something permanent.'

'And what are you looking for now?'

'Damned if I know.' The glow of her cigarette was suddenly extinguished and then she was standing beside the hammock.

Her hand reached for his in the darkness. 'Be nice.'

'Look . . . I don't want to sound inexperienced . . . but I've never done it in a hammock.'

She laughed. 'God, just when I need a man who knows what he's doing.'

He swung his legs out of the hammock. She stood between his thighs. 'I'm told it's easier if one of us keeps their feet on the ground,' she said. 'The trick after that is all in the rhythm.'

Sweat trickled between their bodies. She lay on top of him, one leg resting either side of the hammock for balance. As her breathing slowed she heard the pulsing of his heart in his chest.

'I've been bitten,' he said.

'It's never like the movies. Hot tropical nights, I mean. The reality is mosquitoes and vampire bats. And hammocks. The thing I miss more than proper food and hot water is making love in a real bed.'

He laughed, a deep, rich sound. She laughed with him. He was right. It was a long time since she'd laughed. Perhaps there was more of the war-damaged child in her than she realised. 'When you first came here,' she said, 'I hated you on sight.'

'I have that effect on people.'

'I put you down as the sort of guy who sleeps with a girl then immediately demands a score out of ten for his performance.'

'Yeah, I was going to ask you about that. What do you reckon? Eleven?'

'No offence, but you need to work on your hammock skills.' She sat up, so that she was astride his chest. 'I can't believe I just did this.'

'Why? Was this the wrong thing to do?'

'I promised myself I'd never do this again. You know what I mean. It's not love, is it? It's just sex.'

'Don't say "just sex" like that. It's not good for a bloke's ego.'

She began to button her blouse. 'Would you have done this if we'd been in Chicago or New York?'

'Have sex in a hammock?'

'Would you even have thought of hitting on me?' He did not seem to know how to answer her. 'It's funny,' she said, 'my big sister's the one with the looks. I was always just her gawky little kid sister. I guess I always wanted to be the one the guys looked at, but I never was. Now she's thirty-four, she's got three kids and she's fat. And I'm still here, making out with guys in uncomfortable places. I still don't know which one of us I'd rather be.'

Unexpectedly he reached out and took her hand. 'Don't stay here. Come back with us, Mickey.'

'Sure. We can buy a little cottage with a white picket fence and live happily ever after.'

'Don't you reckon you've had about as much as you can take here?'

'I don't know. They never told me how long the tour would be when I was drafted.'

'Even if it was Vietnam you would have been home by now.'

'Well, you know what they say. You can take the girl out of the war, but you can't take war out of the girl.'

'Mickey . . . did you ever talk to anyone? When you got back from Vietnam.'

'Like a shrink, you mean?' She fumbled in the darkness for her shorts, shook them out and tried to balance on the hammock as she wriggled back into them. 'Every ink blot looks like a blood stain to me. This is the only thing that works, Ryan. At least I can sleep at night. Back in San Diego nothing I did meant anything. And it wasn't getting any better.'

'This is no way to live, Mickey.'

'Look who's talking.'

'That's different. This is my job.'

'And this is my job, okay? It may not be as glamorous as yours, hot shot, but it's still my choice.'

'You can't stay in this bloody jungle the rest of your life.'

'Look, Ryan, I remember meeting guys in the Nam who'd done two, three tours of duty. They kept volunteering to come back because a normal life just didn't have anything for them any more. I didn't understand them back then. I thought they were crazy. Now I don't.'

'How long do you think you can keep this up?'

Mickey felt herself getting angry. She let a man sleep with her, he thought he could run her whole life. They were all the same. 'What do you care what I do? I stay here, I come with you, whatever I do, you'll still be gone in the morning. Right?'

She waited a moment for confirmation, her reasoning affirmed by his silence.

'Thanks for the ride,' she said.

# 37

Webb watched her change the dressings on the boy with the amputated limb. Strange that fate had brought them both here to this same place at the same time. He had imagined her married with babies, nursing in some provincial hospital as the children grew. He had never expected to see her again, thought he might not recognise her even if he did. Yet she seemed hardly changed at all. As she bent over the boy, he remembered how she had looked those times at Bien Hoa, holding that young man's hands in the expectants' room, or examining a field dressing in the triage the day he had wandered into the hospital in the middle of a mas-cal. A lock of hair fell in front of her eyes, as it had done that day, and she brushed it away quickly with an impatient flick of her right forefinger, a gesture he found almost poignant. He smiled.

She looked up, saw him smiling at her. 'So, you're awake. Feeling better?'

She put a hand on his forehead to check his temperature, took his pulse. Now the fever in his bones had gone, he felt lighter, the colours around him seemed more vivid than they ever had before. Like waking from a nightmare to the solid contours of reality. 'How long have I been in here?' he asked her.

'Four days.'

'Malaria?'

'You should have taken your tablets.'

'I forgot a dose here and there.'

'It was the Negroes who invented rock music, but it was the anopheles mosquito that really showed people how to shake, rattle and roll. We should be able to start you on solids today.'

'Not tortilla and beans. I'd rather be sick again.'

'How is he?' a voice said.

Webb looked around. It was Ryan.

'He must be better,' Mickey said. 'He's complaining about the food.'

'How you going, Spider?'

Webb smiled, raised a hand weakly.

'He's been worried about you,' Mickey said.

Ryan made a face. 'Bullshit. I don't give a stuff.'

'Sorry about this,' Webb said. 'You must be itching to get back.'

'Not really,' Ryan said.

Webb saw the look that passed between Ryan and Mickey, and immediately he knew, he knew with complete certainty what had happened.

Ryan. Fucking Ryan. As if all the women in the world weren't enough, he had to take Mickey as well. But what else did he expect?

Inside, the shutters came rasping down, with a terrible finality. What the hell. If she was so stupid and naîve, she was welcome to him. He didn't give a damn.

'You'll be here another couple of days,' Mickey was saying, 'until you get your strength back. It's a long walk back down the mountain.'

'Bloody hell, he's making a meal out of this, isn't he?' Ryan said, grinning.

'Can you do me a favour?' Webb said.

They both looked at him.

'Just leave me the hell alone.'

Sunlight flashed on the cockpit of the A-37 as it banked over the Guazapa volcano. Ryan ran inside for his camera. When he got back outside he saw a plume of black and orange smoke broiling up the horizon, and the white trails of phosphorous marker rockets.

He looked around desperately.

Oh, Jesus Christ Almighty.

He saw the winking of the Gatlings and the dust kicked up by the heavy 7.62-calibre bullets. Then the jet was past him, the pilot banking out of his strafing run, the roar of the guns echoing around the hills. An illusion, of course; light travels faster than sound. It was why some of the *campesinos* thought the pilots could fire backwards.

Even as he ran he knew what he was going to find, knew what the target had been. Some of the children had been playing *fútbol* in the dirt compound behind the hospital.

When he got there he found a litter of small bodies lying in the dirt.

'Rogelio!'

He was lying in the awkward broken-puppet attitude that death sometimes confers. Blood everywhere; impossible to make out where it was all coming from. Ryan stood over him, staring.

Around him, the plaintive mewling of the wounded.

'Rogelio!'

He bent down to pick him up. He felt a jelly-like mass inside the boy's T-shirt; something was terribly wrong. He realised with dumb horror that Rogelio had been eviscerated. He dropped him, staring at the mess on his hands.

He looked up. Salvador was standing over him. It was not a smile that he saw on his face, for of course he took no pleasure in this. But it appeared to Ryan that there was some appearance of satisfaction. Perhaps because he thought Ryan now knew a little of what he felt.

Because of the sudden extra workload at the hospital, they transferred Webb to the ruined house he had been sharing with Ryan. Ryan went to help with the wounded at the hospital. He returned, later that afternoon, with Salvador.

'So, gringo. You missed the big show today. The pilot of that plane must be very proud. He made three kills in just one run. Four other children wounded. One is crippled.'

Webb said nothing. There were no words for this.

Salvador lit a cigarette and leaned against the wall. 'They are moving against us, as d'Aubuisson promised. They have increased their patrols along the highway, and reinforced the garrison at Suchitoto. These bombings are just a way of trying to soften us up.'

Webb knew their hopes of getting back to San Salvador the way they had come were rapidly diminishing. 'What are you going to do?' he said.

'We must evacuate. We cannot fight a war against planes and regular army battalions. We have to protect the civilians.'

'Then we will come with you.'

'In this you have no choice.' He grinned at them, as if it were all a big joke. Which perhaps it was, only the joke was on them. 'You will have plenty to tell people in the United States of America when you return,' Salvador added, '*si Dios quiere*. God willing.'

He went out. Webb looked at Ryan, who seemed strangely subdued. His head was bowed and he looked exhausted.

'You okay?'

'Sure.'

'Bastards.'

Ryan did not respond.

'I didn't see any of it. I heard the scream of the jet and a few minutes later they started bringing the injured into the hospital.' When Ryan still did not answer, he said, 'Did you get pictures?'

'No.'

'Why not? That's what you're here for.'

'I forgot.'

'Christ Almighty.'

'Anyway, I'm nearly out of film, mate. Good job I didn't use it all up today, right? Looks like we're going to be around for a while longer.'

'As long as you keep your mind on your job.'

'What's that supposed to mean?'

'It doesn't matter.'

Ryan shrugged and went outside. He walked slowly back to the hospital. Mickey was sitting on the steps, her head between her knees. From inside he heard a soft mewing sound, like a wounded animal, or a baby.

'Mickey.'

She did not look up.

'Mickey . . .'

He realised she couldn't hear him. She had her hands over her ears. He touched her arm and she started, uttered a small sob of surprise. 'Ryan.'

'You okay?'

She shook her head. 'Can't you hear that?'

He made a face. *What is it?*

'We have no morphine,' she said. 'We took both that boy's legs off and we have no morphine to give him.'

He sat down on the step beside her. He put his arm around her and she moved closer. The trees threw long shadows across the ochre dirt; mosquitoes whined in the air as evening fell.

'You're right,' she whispered.

'About what?'

'About me. I think I've had enough.'

'Maybe I have too,' he said.

Her knuckles were pressed hard against her temples. 'It'll pass,' she said.

'I mean it, Mickey. I've been in every bloody war going in the last ten years; Vietnam, Cambodia, Angola, now here. I've lost some good mates, and Christ knows how many times I thought I was going to get it. Then today, for the first time, I thought, bugger it. I've had enough. I don't want to see any more.' The child was still crying. It grated on his nerves, impossible to shut it out. 'I don't want to hear any more.'

'You're lucky. You can say when you've had enough. These people can't.'

'Maybe that's it. I'm lucky, I can have a normal life. At least I'd like to find out what a normal life is. What about you?'

'What about me?' she said.

And suddenly Ryan thought: what about you? Perhaps it's just the black monkey, he thought. Or perhaps *what about you?* was the question he had been asking himself all along.

# 38

By now the *guinda* – the evacuation of the village – was routine. When the soldiers came the *compañeros* and the guerrillas would retreat together, then come back and rebuild what was left of the village when the soldiers had withdrawn. Like a boxer pitted against a taller, stronger opponent, they were always shuffling back, leaving the *chuchos* punching air.

The next morning the old men and the children drove the few remaining cows and goats out of the village and into the hills to fend for themselves. Any livestock the soldiers found in the village would be shot. Meanwhile the women buried the seed stocks and any personal items of value in underground caches called *buzones*, hidden outside the village, safe from the looting soldiers. Webb saw one woman carrying a turn-of-the-century sewing machine wrapped in heavy cloth.

It was afternoon when they heard the crackle of small-arms fire in the distance, and the first hollow thump of a landmine. As in Vietnam, the guerrillas had sown the jungle trails with landmines and *trampas* – booby traps. The *compas* would harass the soldiers as they advanced, laying ambushes, then retreating quickly.

Webb and Ryan were summoned to Salvador's command post. He and his bodyguard were gathered around a radio. One of the *compas* was monitoring the radio traffic with a United States-manufactured Bearcat scanner. As he turned the dials they both heard quite distinctly the voice of an American calling out coded orders. Although he spoke in Spanish, the downhome Texan drawl was distinctive.

Salvador looked up at them, in accusation.

'You write in your story how the Americans are helping to kill innocent civilians,' he said.

'What's happening?' Ryan asked.

Salvador squatted on the floor and drew a few strokes in the dirt with a finger. 'The soldiers are from the Ramón Belloso battalion.

They are fresh from training in your Fort Bragg. They have been trucked here from the capital and are sweeping west through the hills from the highway. To fight a whole battalion we have just three hundred *muchachos*.' He drew a circle in the dirt, then a cross. 'The lake is behind us, on two sides, an army garrison is here on the other side of the volcano. The *chuchos* are squeezing us in a vice. We can escape across the lake but we do not have enough boats. We can take out only the hammock cases, those too sick to walk. Miguelito will lead this group.' Miguelito was the name the *compas* had given to Mickey. 'But it will be dangerous for them, they must arrive in San Lorenzo before morning or the jets will find them.'

'And the others?'

'We cannot drive the soldiers back, there are too many and they are too well armed. But we can slow them and dictate the way they must come.' He made a snaking motion with his hand to show how the enemy vanguard could be deflected right and left by attacks from the flanks. 'Then tonight we will walk out, straight past them.'

Webb stared at him in disbelief.

'How will you do that?' Ryan said.

'At night the *chuchos* make camp, form a perimeter, entrap themselves. Up here in the mountains, the night is ours. We do what we want.'

Webb remembered, and nodded. Another echo of that other faraway war.

Salvador turned to him. 'You must go with Miguelito,' he said.

Webb started to protest.

Salvador shook his head. 'There is no dishonour in this. You are still weak from the malaria, you will slow our pace and endanger us all. There is no choice.' He turned to Ryan. 'Your friend Bobby Charlton can come with us, if he wishes. Perhaps you will get your big story after all.'

Ryan grinned. 'Maybe I'll bring you luck,' he said. Salvador shook his head and in his distinctive falsetto said, 'I doubt it.'

Webb was pale and his hands shook as he taped his notebooks into a watertight plastic bag. There was a sheen of sweat on his skin.

'You okay, mate?' Ryan asked him.

'I'm okay.'

'Here. You better take this.' Ryan held out another plastic bag. 'Half the film. If something happens to one of us, at least we've still got some film.'

Webb took it without comment.

'What is it, Spider?'

'Nothing.'

'You're pissed at me for something.'

Webb taped the package to his chest. Even that small effort left him exhausted. How the hell am I going to get off this damn mountain in this state? he thought. He lay back on the hammock. 'You're like a dog, Ryan. No matter how hard I kick you, you keep coming back for more. Get it through your fucking head. I don't like you. I've never liked you. You've got the soul of a mannikin. Everything you do is for show. What you did to that girl in Saigon was unforgivable. The only thing you have going for you is you're a good photographer and you've got guts. But I suspect even the courage is just lack of imagination. You're too stupid and too fucking vain to ever contemplate that one day you might actually die. So, yeah, I am pissed at you. For being born.'

A shuffling silence.

'Okay, let's stop beating around the bush, mate,' Ryan said. 'I want you to be straight with me.'

'That's the other thing that really pisses me off. Your pathetic sense of humour.'

Ryan leaned against the wall. 'It's Mickey, isn't it?'

'Go and screw yourself.'

'I mean if it's Mickey, just say so.'

'It's not just Mickey.'

'I really like her, Spider. I mean it. It's different this time.'

Webb pointedly looked at his watch. 'It's only six o'clock. Let's check how you're feeling again in another hour.'

'Very funny.'

'You've had a great week. A war, a woman, plus a few kids to show off to, give the caring side of Sean Ryan a bit of an airing. The last bit's important, isn't it? Just in case anyone gets the wrong idea and thinks you're a totally selfish piece of shit.'

'Careful, Spider.'

'Getting close to the bone, am I?'

'I'm going to try and forget you said all that.'

'I don't want you to forget. I want you to remember. I'll write it down for you if you want.'

Almost sunset. Shadows creeping swiftly across the room, the sound of small-arms fire getting louder. Ryan stared at the jungle, the forbidding silhouette of the Guazapa volcano looming over La Esperanza like a marauding giant. He took something out of his pocket and wrapped it around his neck. 'My lucky green towel.'

'You've been badly wounded seven times wearing that stupid fucking thing. How can it be lucky?'

'I'm still alive, mate.'

Webb muttered an obscenity under his breath.

'I'm going to say goodbye to Mickey now,' Ryan said. 'I suppose I'll see you before you move out. If not, I'll catch you in San Lorenzo in a couple of days.'

Webb said nothing.

'Wish me luck, mate?'

'I don't give a damn if they catch you and cut your heart out.'

'Yeah. Right. Best of luck to you too, Spider.'

Night closing in. The hum of mosquitoes, the rattle of automatic weapons, the fetid breath of the jungle, the proximity of death.

Ryan chewed a cold tortilla, watched Mickey supervise the loading of the 'Salvadorean ambulances', hammocks slung between two bamboo poles. In one of them a boy injured in that morning's A-37 attack was barely clinging to life. Besides those with traumatic wounds there were also two heavily pregnant women and an old man. The medical supplies were loaded into boxes to be carried with them. Anything they could not carry would be destroyed.

Mickey moved along the line of makeshift stretchers, whispering to each of the patients in turn, encouraging them, preparing them for the ordeal ahead. She knelt beside the small boy with the chest wound, held his hand as he moaned and jerked.

Ryan crouched down beside her. She looked up, but did not recognise him immediately in the darkness.

'Come to wish you luck,' he said.

'You're going with Salvador?'

'I never liked boats. I get seasick.'

'What about your friend?'

'I don't think he'd like you calling me that. He's dirty on me.'

'What for?'

'You, I suppose.'

There were urgent shouts around them in the gathering darkness as the villagers hurried to finish the preparations to *guindar*. Torches flashed in the gloom. Ryan put a hand on Mickey's shoulder, felt the answering pressure of her fingers. There was something special about this woman, he told himself. He wondered why he should feel differently about her than all the other women there had been in his life. Perhaps, he thought, it's because the others had just been decoration, had always been peripheral to the news he had been chasing. This one was a part of it. Easy to think of her now as a kindred spirit.

'Stay out of trouble,' he whispered.

'You too.'

He wanted to say more. He felt a sudden need to make promises, but old fears stood in the way. Commitments were too easy to make and too easy to regret. Perhaps Webb was right. He would wait and see how he felt about things at seven o'clock. It was still only quarter to.

# 39

The path was uneven, slippery with mud and rugged with stones and roots. The pace was slow, and no one spoke. They walked to the rhythmic creaking of bamboo, the soft cries of the wounded. Several of the *sanitarios* had torches, but after an hour or so the batteries were exhausted, and now they stayed together by clinging to each others' clothes in the darkness.

Mickey walked in front with one of the *compitas*, the women guerrillas who had been chosen to escort them down. They were not expecting trouble. The *chuchos* were attacking from the other direction.

Webb's mind was wholly concentrated on his legs. He would not let them carry him in one of their makeshift stretchers, his pride would not allow it, and when they had first set out he had felt strong, was sure he could make it. But for the last half an hour he had been struggling to stay upright; his muscles felt like rubber, and there was no strength in his knees.

Suddenly it was as if his body had been lathered in cold grease. He did not remember falling.

Now he was cradled in someone's arms, and he heard Mickey's voice. 'Hugh. Hugh, can you hear me?'

He tried to answer her but his tongue seemed unable to form the words. He grunted an acknowledgment.

'You must get up. You have to keep going.'

He felt the soft warmth of her breast next to his cheek. So tired, so very tired. Easy to stay here, just sleep.

'Please, Hugh, you have to get up. It's not far.'

He tried to stand up, but his arms and legs felt as if they were in the control of some amateur puppeteer.

'Take some of this,' Mickey said. Suddenly her finger was in his mouth, and it was sweet and warm. Honey. He licked it off hungrily.

'A glucose fix,' she said. 'It will help you.' She gave him more, smearing it along the insides of his cheek.

In his semi-delirious state he found it almost funny, mildly erotic. 'Can we do this again tonight?' he wanted to say, but it came out an incoherent mumble.

'Please, Hugh,' she said, and he recognised the impatience in her voice. 'Please get up.'

Mickey and two of her *sanitarios* helped him struggle to his feet. Distant stars were a blur of light, spinning through the sky.

'Hold my shoulder,' Mickey said to him.

They started walking. Only a little further, she had said. All right. He thought he could go on just a little further.

It was imperative that the small children be kept quiet when they passed through the soldiers' lines and so the surgeon, Ramón, had crushed his remaining store of tranquilliser tablets, mixed them with honey and had the mothers feed the concoction to their infants. He had to guess how much to give each child, knowing that too little or too much might prove equally deadly. In previous *guindas* mothers had suffocated a wakeful and crying child rather than have it betray the whole column to their enemy; but if the dose he gave a child was too large the drug would depress the child's respiratory system and it would die.

As soon as all the children were asleep the *guinda* had begun.

Fires were lit in the village and dogs tied to porches to bark through the night in an effort to persuade the *chuchos* that the villagers were still in their homes. When all was done, Salvador and his remaining fighters led the silent column of refugees into the jungle.

Salvador set a devastating pace, but no one complained. They clung to each others' knapsacks, the mud sucking at their legs, bare skin sliced by the sharp *zacata* grass. They climbed higher and higher into the mountains. The lights of the giant Fifth of November and Cerrón Grande dams appeared in the distance. The rest of the Guazapa controlled zone was in utter darkness.

*The chuchos play their radios at night*, Salvador had told him, *so we will know where they are and not blunder into them by accident. They don't want to fight us in the dark.*

It was true.

They had been marching for about an hour when Ryan heard it. Music. After a while he realised he recognised the song. Stevie Wonder.

He could smell the camp. The soldiers were cooking their dinner. He thought he detected the aroma of coffee and stewed meat. His mouth flooded with saliva. For weeks his diet had consisted almost exclusively of the grim maize tortillas, and now, even as he anticipated the dangers of the next hours, his body became preoccupied by thoughts of food. Madness.

He heard laughter and the tinny crackle of Spanish over a command radio.

The pace slowed.

They were very close now.

Ramón, the surgeon, was in front of him. He could hear his breathing, very fast, almost hyperventilating. Ryan could almost feel the buzzing in his own veins, excitement and dread pulsing together in a delicious cocktail.

They must be just yards from the soldiers' lines.

# 40

The skeletons of two adobe houses were silhouetted against the lake. Phosphor ash from marker rockets glistened on the ground like frost. Beyond the ruins, silver against the black shallows of the lake, a dozen aluminium canoes were pulled up on the beach.

The *sanitarios* loaded their patients. Mickey paddled through the water, examining her charges with the one remaining flashlight. The boy with the chest wound was dead. His skin was cold, his pupils dilated. He must have died soon after they left La Esperanza, she guessed. She told two of the *sanitarios* to take him back to the shore and bury him.

She picked her way back up the beach to find Webb. He was sitting on his haunches, against the wall of one of the shelled-out houses, his head between his knees. She had not thought he would be strong enough to make the trip down the mountain unaided, and he had collapsed twice and had been partly delirious for the last part of the journey. But he had refused to let them carry him.

She shone the torch on his face. 'You're all right?'

He nodded.

'You were saying some strange things coming down.'

'I'm okay.'

She squatted beside him. 'The boy died.'

'Boy?'

'The young boy with the chest wound. Rogelio's friend. He died.'

Webb ran a hand through his hair. 'One more's not going to make any difference.'

'What?'

'Sorry, but I'm on compassion overload right now. I just want to get out of this bloody place.'

A long silence. Further along the beach the *sanitarios* were scrabbling at the dirt with their bare hands, preparing a shallow grave.

'Why Ryan, for God's sake?'

'What?'

'Why Ryan? He's such a prick.'

'For God's sake, a ten-year-old boy has just died from bullet wounds. Our personal lives don't count for anything in all of this.'

'I've been trying to save the world for a long time, Mickey. Maybe as long as you have. Suddenly it all seems so bloody futile.'

She stood up. 'We have to get going. I'll help you into one of the boats.'

'No thanks. I'll get there myself.'

He struggled to his feet, almost overbalanced, then staggered away down the beach. Mickey stared after him. What he had said echoed inside her head. *Suddenly it all seems so bloody futile.* Futile. Ryan had been right about her. She was just replaying the same scenes of her life over and over to try to understand them, and she never would. Her life had stalled in 1970.

Why Ryan? Why not Webb?

She looked up at the sky, saw a part of herself arc away, free-falling.

Ryan heard the child's cry, and every muscle in his body froze rigid. The infant had woken from its drugged sleep; perhaps Ramón had misjudged this one dose, erring on the side of caution. A second whimpering shout, quickly muffled as the mother stifled the cry. Then silence. For a moment he even thought they would get away with it.

Webb heard it, in the distance, the staccato crack of small-arms fire. He knew, they all knew, what it was. The *chuchos* never fought at night unless they had to, so the *guinda* must have walked straight into their camp.

They finished loading the boats in silence. There was nothing they could do. The gunfire went on and on.

Nothing they could do.

Webb waded to one of the canoes, was helped aboard. He sat with his head in his hands. He remembered something his father had told him when he was a small boy. If you wished hard enough for something . . .

He saw Ryan lying dead in the jungle.

A stab of guilt. Almost as if he were responsible.

# 41

Ryan heard shouts in Spanish, and then a frightened *chucho* on the camp perimeter fired blindly into the jungle. He recognised the familiar booming of an M-60 machine gun, the sound reverberating around the forest, blue flashes slicing overhead as the tracers ripped through the darkness. There were screams of panic and pain all around him.

*Mamá, mamá!*

The familiar instincts returned, as comfortable as an old friend. Ryan had been through this a hundred times before, knew exactly what to do. He had seen too many men die running blindly from a battle. What you did was wait, bide your time. He grabbed Ramón, pulled him down to the ground.

The frightened sentry kept his finger on the trigger until the barrel overheated and jammed.

Ryan looked up, saw a flare falling down the sky, silhouetting a dozen terrified *campesinos* as they ran down the trail. Then came the yammer of an M-3 and they were scythed down.

Ryan stayed down, clung to the earth, breathing it in, the hot, corrupt smell of it. He heard the gabble of voices on the soldiers' radios, recognised that same Texan drawl from a few hours before on Salvador's scanner. The tracers were so pretty at night, he thought. Easy to forget that those deadly fingers were looking for you.

Ramón was crying, a sound he had heard many times before, the long *aaah-aaah-aaaah* of a wounded man, unable to catch his breath.

He put an arm around his shoulders and dragged him through the undergrowth, away from the shouts and the deadly rattle of small-arms fire. Bullets sliced over their heads, slapping the leaves and branches like a torrent of rain, and hammered into the trees, showering them with bark. He found a fallen tree trunk, crawled over it, dragging Ramón with him, and slumped into the mush of leaves and mud on the far side.

Another flare arced overhead. Ryan waited.

He saw a woman running towards where they lay. She staggered, ran on, tumbled forward. There was a child in her arms. Now she was trying to crawl, blood spilling out of her mouth.

'Stay down!' he screamed at her.

He left Ramón in the mud hollow, started to crawl towards her. At that same instant he felt a numbing blow to his left side, knew he had been hit. He kept going, reached the injured woman, pulled her over. In the darkness he felt a sodden mess on the front of her dress. She was not breathing. He groped for the child. The back of its head was gone.

He swore, rolled on to his back, grimacing with pain.

His whole left side felt as if it had been hit with a hammer. Something warm and sticky seeped into the waistband of his trousers. He felt for his arm. It was still there, still attached.

Ramón was groaning. He crawled back to him, cursing himself for a fool. Futile heroics.

'Shut up!' he hissed at Ramón. '*Silencio!*'

But Ramón could not, would not hear him. There was a sucking noise each time he breathed, and one side of his chest would not expand. One of the worst kinds of wound, Ryan thought. He took the green towel from around his neck to seal the entry and it seemed to help a little.

The numbness on his left side gave way to fierce electric bolts of pain in his shoulder. Between the spasms he tried to make his plans. He was sure the soldiers would not venture beyond their perimeter until morning. They had perhaps even convinced themselves that they had beaten off a concerted attack by the FMLN.

If they were to escape they had until morning when the patrols would be sent out to find them. Salvador had been leading them north. But which way was that? He could not see the stars under the high canopy of the jungle.

*Aaah-aaah*, Ramón said. Something bubbled deep in his throat.

Ryan felt his body prickle with cold sweat. He vomited.

Safe here, he thought. So good to be able to rest. Just for a few minutes, wait for the firing to die down, then crawl again, get away.

Blackness came suddenly, a warm buzzing gelatin swallowed him up, and he couldn't fight it off.

Just sleep. For a few minutes.

A boot in the ribs woke him. It was what the medics called 'response to pain'.

The force of the kick rolled him on his back. He looked up into a scowling peasant face. It could have been one of Salvador's *compas*, except this one had on the camouflage uniform of a government soldier, and he was carrying a US-made Armalite. He saw the surprise on the man's face when he realised he had captured a *gringo*.

Another of the soldiers had rolled Ramón on to his back. His eyes were half open, the face grey in death. Rigor mortis had set in; he had been dead a few hours. The soldiers looked disappointed.

Ryan stared into the brutal young faces. Suddenly he understood what fear really was; not the gamble of death or injury in combat, but the cold, cold emptiness deep in the gut, the terror of being utterly helpless. He remembered Salvador's stories of FMLN prisoners who had been skinned alive with knives. Perhaps it was just guerrilla propaganda; or perhaps it was true.

One of the men made a jerking motion with his rifle, indicating that he wanted Ryan to stand. Ryan tried to move, gasped with pain. His whole left side above the waist felt as if it were frozen, and any movement was agony.

The soldiers kicked him again, crowded in on him, shouting.

*Either you sit here, Sean, old son, and let them kick you to death, or you get on your bloody feet somehow and bugger the pain.*

He managed to shift his weight to his right elbow, twisted, got up on to one knee. He launched himself to his feet, cannoned into one of the soldiers, who pushed him backwards with his M-16. The barrel jarred his wounded arm, and he screamed.

One of the soldiers laughed, a crazy sound.

Another of them moved in, tore the camera off his neck. He screamed again, almost fainted from pain, willed himself to stay on his feet. That's my only chance, he thought. If they think they will have to carry me, they won't bother taking me prisoner.

He looked down at his shoulder, examined the wound. There were two ragged holes. Blood had soaked into his shirt down to the waist, but it didn't look too bad. Perhaps his luck was still holding.

One of the soldiers was ripping through his camera bag, found the spare film and the lenses. They shouted something at him in Spanish.

'*No hablo español*,' he said. '*Inglés*.'

English. They probably hadn't heard of Australia; they might think it's a state in America.

A gun barrel hit him in his ribs, the universal sign language for put your hands on top of your head, shitface. Ryan took this as a good omen. With each passing second he knew his odds of survival were improving. They weren't going to shoot him here in the jungle after all.

He hoped he wouldn't regret that thought later.

'Can't put my hands on my head, sport,' he said. 'My arm's buggered.'

One of the soldiers became very angry. He shouted and hammered his rifle into Ryan's side.

'Okay, okay!' Ryan yelled back at him. He put one hand on his head, tried to move the other, by an effort of will. It suddenly reminded him of the time they had had tuberculosis vaccinations at school. He couldn't move his bloody arm then either; there was a great green scab on the place where the needle had gone in and Michael Kennedy had deliberately punched him there. It had all been a game then.

He had to reach right over his left shoulder, grab his other hand, and pull it up into place on top of his head.

They liked that. It made them laugh.

He laughed along with them. See. They were all mates now. He was sure it was going to be all right.

# 42

There were seven of them gathered around the hurricane lamps in the command post at San Lorenzo; Salvador, one of his lieutenants from La Esperanza, three other *comandantes* from Chalate province, and Webb and Mickey. They leaned on the crumbling adobe walls, lounged on wooden chairs around the trestle table, smoked, drank coffee. The mood was sombre.

They had lost so many.

On the government radio it had been announced that the Ramón Belloso battalion had slaughtered the rebels to the last man. In fact, from the column of over three hundred that had left La Esperanza, more than one hundred and eighty had straggled into San Lorenzo that afternoon. The rear of the column had borne the brunt of the casualties. Of the approximately one hundred and twenty who were missing, only twenty were *compas*. The rest were women, children, old men.

On the Bearcat scanner they overheard the soldiers talking about a captured gringo. Webb knew what that meant. They had Ryan.

Mickey broke the oppressive silence. 'What is going to happen to him?' she said.

Salvador looked around at the other men. A lot of coughing, spitting, smoking.

'If he was a *compa*,' Salvador said at last, 'I could tell you with complete certainty what they would do. But he is a gringo. So how can I say? Perhpas they will send him back to San Salvador and deport him. Perhaps they will let him take pictures of their great victory at La Esperanza. Or perhaps they will gouge out his eyes and skin him alive, like they did to Ricardo Cayetano.'

'We have to get him back,' Mickey said.

'There are fifteen hundred men in the Ramón Belloso battalion. They have helicopters, grenade launchers and M-16 machine guns. We could perhaps amass three hundred *compas*. We should waste all those lives for one gringo?'

'What if they kill him?'

'Then Señor Webb here will write about his murder in his newspaper and all America will understand the crimes your country commits here.'

Webb listened to the discussion without comment. He doubted the soldiers would content themselves with having Ryan deported, not after what he had seen. Easier to shoot him, say they had found his body in the village after the offensive, claim that the guerrillas had murdered him. A political point scored, and they hid their own dirty laundry.

You should be pleased. You never liked the bastard.

And there's Mickey . . .

'But he has the pictures,' he heard himself say.

Salvador looked up at him, his face creased in confusion. 'I do not understand.'

'He has all the photographs, the proof of what you want us to tell the world. The pictures of the time the helicopter flew over your village and killed María Montez and her child. The time the A-37 strafed the compound near the hospital and Rogelio and the others were killed. It was our record of how you live here, with your wives and your parents and your children, proof that you are not an army, that you are people like people everywhere. Without Ryan's film I have no proof of what I want to say, and no one will take any notice. No national newspaper or magazine will buy my story because it is pictures that sell newspapers and magazines.'

Salvador shook his head. 'As soon as the soldiers find his camera and his film they will destroy them.'

'His camera, yes. But not the film. He has hidden it.'

'They will find it.'

'Only after they've skinned him.'

Salvador looked up suddenly. He translated what he thought this meant for the others in the room.

Webb felt Mickey's eyes on him.

It was a lie, of course. Webb had half the film in his own pack.

Salvador looked around the room. 'We cannot risk so many men.'

'He took risks for you.'

That was a lie too. How could you explain to these men that Ryan actually liked war, that he came not only because of principle or because he got paid but because he enjoyed it? These people whose only devout wish was for an end to war?

'Perhaps,' Salvador conceded.

There was an argument in Spanish. Webb did not understand all that was said, but two of the *comandantes* suggested that a small but heavily armed task force should go back for Ryan. The plan they mooted was a diversionary attack, at night, while a rescue team infiltrated the perimeter and got Ryan out.

'They will never expect us to risk our lives for one gringo,' one of the other *comandantes* said. 'And they will not expect us to attack them. They will shit themselves like children until the officers get control again.'

Salvador shrugged, conceding that the advantage of such a surprise had merit. He smiled grimly, his soldier's instincts excited at the prospect of striking such a psychological blow against the hated *chuchos*. 'But we must ask for volunteers,' he said. 'I cannot order any of my *compas* to do this. If you can find thirty volunteers, I will lead them myself.'

Webb knew that Mickey was still watching him. He could not fathom the expression on her face. He wondered if she knew, or had guessed, about the six rolls of film taped to his chest. He shrugged at her. What else could he have done? He might despise Ryan's morals but he was still one of his own, and besides, he had to live with himself later.

Finding no humans to slaughter, the soldiers had contented themselves with massacring the dogs that had been left behind. The village reeked now of their corpses. Dozens of them lay in the sun, stiff and bloated and covered with the black iridescence of flies. One of them had been nailed to a picture of Archbishop Romero, in the attitude of crucifixion, and flung in the dust.

A group of women and children stood in the compound outside the hospital surrounded by a ring of soldiers. The children were crying, many of them hiding their faces in their mothers' laps. The women tried to comfort them but their faces betrayed their fear. Ryan felt their eyes on him, knew they were hoping that his appearance somehow meant they would be saved.

When the soldiers led Ryan into the village an officer was standing on the hospital verandah, studying his prisoners, but when he saw Ryan he immediately marched over, apparently even more delighted with this new prize. He had the look of a West Point colonel, the brass at his belt and the buttons on his tunic spit-polished, and he wore a silk cravat and an olive-green forage cap. A major, Ryan guessed, by the pips on his shoulder. He had black, Spanish eyes, intelligent and cruel.

'American?' he asked, in heavily accented English.

'English,' Ryan said, deciding to keep to his story.

The major surveyed his wounds with detached interest. One of the soldiers threw his camera and backpack on the ground.

'Who are you?'

'My name's Sean Ryan. I'm a photo-journalist. I'm on assignment for the BBC.' People who had never heard of *Newsweek* or Dan Rather or even *Time* magazine had heard of the BBC. Ryan had borrowed the credentials of this august organisation on more than one occasion when he needed to save his hide.

But the major did not appear to be as impressed as he had hoped. 'What are you doing here?'

'I have been doing a story on the *compas*.'

'The terrorists.'

'Yeah, the terrorists. I got caught up in the firefight last night.'

There was a quick exchange in Spanish between the major and one of the soldiers.

'You were fighting with the terrorists?'

'No, I was taking photographs of them.'

The major did not appear convinced but seemed unsure how to proceed. He was no doubt weighing his choices, one of which, Ryan supposed, was to stand him against the hospital wall and shoot him.

'Your papers?' the major asked.

'In my jacket.'

The major nodded to one of the soldiers, who patted him down and found his passport and COPREFOR press accreditation. The major glanced at them, then slipped them into the breast pocket of his tunic. 'How long have you been with the terrorists?'

'Three weeks.'

'Three weeks? Alone?'

Ryan decided to keep quiet about Webb. No point in alerting them to another potential source of trouble. Not yet. Perhaps keep that ace in the hole. 'Alone.'

'It is illegal to consort with communists. You have placed yourself outside government protection.'

Ryan knew what he meant by that. 'I was doing a story on their activities, that's all.'

The major nodded and turned away. Ryan knew that for the moment his fate had been deferred. The major had more pressing matters to attend to – the women and children his men had captured that morning. He rapped an order to his sergeant, who relayed the instructions to his soldiers. Immediately his squad barged among the women, tearing the screaming children from their mothers' arms. The women shrieked in terror; the soldiers used their rifle butts to fend them off. It took long minutes before the prisoners had been coralled into two groups.

Ryan felt sick to his stomach. He knew what was coming.

The women were herded against the hospital wall. The major nodded to his sergeant, and the soldiers removed the safeties on their M-16s. A rasp of metal as ammunition clips were jammed into rifles.

'Wait,' Ryan said.

The major turned around, a smile playing on his face.

'You can't do this.'

'These people are terrorists.'

'They're just women.'

'The women are sometimes worse than the men.'

The major waited. Ryan's mind raced through endless bargains, all of them useless. I shall report this, he almost said. But then he knew the simple answer to that. They would shoot him too.

'You're just creating another generation of terrorists,' he said.

'No. We are destroying their wombs.'

Ryan shook his head. 'Look at the children. They'll remember how you murdered their mothers in front of their eyes and they'll come back and kill you when they're older. Let the women go, for God's sake!'

The major nodded. His face creased into a frown of thoughtful concentration, as if they were debating philosophy in some book-lined study. 'Perhaps you are right,' he said, finally.

'Let them go. For mercy's sake, let them go. They're just innocent bloody peasants.'

'No one is innocent, *inglés*. Only God can take away our sins and make us innocent.' He rapped another order to the sergeant.

The soldiers broke the cordon and ushered the children back to their relieved and sobbing mothers, who bent to hug them as they reached the safety of their arms.

Another clash of metal as the soldiers raised their rifles to their shoulders.

'No,' Ryan said.

The M-16s were set to automatic fire. It took just a few seconds for the dozen soldiers assigned to this duty to empty their clips, and in that time the huddle of women and children became just a sprawl of bloodied and twitching limbs in the red dirt.

Silence.

The major turned away, satisfied. 'Thank you for your advice, *inglés*. You were right. Unless we are thorough, we will just make another generation of terrorists and murderers.'

Ryan heard the enfeebled cries of a child, still alive among the bodies. He knew as well as the major that bullets did not always kill straight away. Dying took time, unless the executioner was precise.

The major took an automatic pistol from his belt and walked among the bodies dispensing this precision. He reloaded the clip twice before he was finished.

# 43

A company medic stripped off Ryan's shirt and examined him. After he had dressed the wounds he spoke rapidly in Spanish to the major and left.

'He says you are lucky. They are just minor wounds. One bullet merely removed a little muscle from your shoulder, the other went through the bicep and grazed the humerus.'

'Yeah, I feel lucky,' Ryan said.

There was a sonorous buzzing of flies from outside the window as the insects descended on the freshly slaughtered bodies. Ryan guessed they would be left unburied, one further humiliation. The metallic smell of blood hung heavy on the air, cloying sweet.

'What are we going to do with you?'

'You could drive me back to the Camino Real, get me some breakfast and a hot bath, and put me on the first plane out.'

The major laughed easily. 'Yes, we could do that,' he said. He sat down on a stool beside the bed and crossed his legs, searching for his own reflection in his polished boots. Too much mud on them for his liking. He rubbed fretfully at the leather. 'But that is not my decision.' He stood up. 'Did you enjoy this morning's show?'

'Did you?'

The major laughed again. He got up and left, leaving two unsmiling guards with M-3 machine guns guarding the door.

Ryan curled up on the cot. He felt numb; not from his wounds, or from fatigue, because the numbness was not in his bones or in his muscles.

*I am responsible for the deaths of those children. Not in the same way as the major is responsible, perhaps. But responsible.*

He tried to push the memory from his mind, because the events of that morning did not gel with his own perception of Sean Ryan. He had made a mistake, broken his own golden rule; he had got involved again. He had never wanted to be responsible for the destiny of another human being, but somehow events always contrived to trap him, to draw him in. He was ashamed. Somehow he would have to lock this away, bury the morning's events in the same private vault where he had lain the bodies of Odile and her child.

Some time early in the afternoon he heard a helicopter land nearby. Heavy boots stamped on to the verandah, and he sat up. The major entered, followed by another man wearing camouflage fatigues, heavy jungle boots and a forage cap. He was chewing gum. There was no insignia on his uniform but Ryan thought he recognised him. Long ago, in a Strikers' camp on the Cambodia border. He remembered the place well. He should – he still had some souvenirs in his backside from that memorable evening.

It was the lieutenant at Que Trang.

He was older now, but he looked just as hard, and his skin was tanned the colour of old tobacco. 'My, my, my. What have we here?'

'The Marines are here,' Ryan said. 'Thank Christ. I'm saved.'

'Not quite, son. I know you, don't I?'

Ryan recognised the Texan drawl from the radio.

'I think we've met. But the name escapes me.'

'Name's Buford. Don't go botherin' yourself about things like rank and such. You can just call me sir.'

'Thanks, Buford.'

A thin smile, a slit of a mouth like a shark's, no lips. Buford stood beside the cot, hands on hips, shaking his head.

'You know this man?' the major asked.

'Sure do. His old man was a real live movie star. Where do I know you from, boy? Was it in the Nam?'

'Que Trang.'

Buford shook his head. 'Damned if I remember it, but if you say so.' He sat on the cot beside Ryan's bed. 'Well, I knows if you go deedly-boppin' through the jungle you gonna get some crap on your boots, but I didn't expect to find real deep crap like you.' He looked at the bloody dressings on Ryan's shoulder. 'My, my, you got holes in you, boy. You really got yourself in the middle of some shit this time.'

'You missed a great show this afternoon, Buford. The major here blew away two dozen women and children.' The sun was hot outside and the bodies were already starting to decompose. The stench in the room was tangible. For God's sake, he asked himself, how could the soldiers stand this? *Why didn't they bury them?*

'You saw all that, did you?'

'Makes you feel proud to be American.'

'There's always collateral damage when you're fighting a war, boy. Besides, the women terrorists are just as bad as the men. You should remember that about old Charlie Cong. Women as bad as the men, the kids as bad as the women. Today you got some snot-nose shittin' in their pants, as soon as they can walk and run they shit on you. No need to crack sentimental, Ryan.'

'Still fighting the same old war, right, Buford?'

'No, son. We're winning this sucker.'

'Don't expect me to stand on the sideline and cheer.'

'You sound like one of them damn communist sympathisers to me, Ryan. Press is full of them. Your daddy would be turning in his grave like a goddamn top. Your daddy was a hero, boy.'

'My old man drank two bottles of vodka a day and screwed blondes who wanted to be Jean Harlow. The closest he ever got to a war was on an MGM back lot.'

'I don't pay no never-mind to that. He stood for somethin'. He made people believe in what was right. Maybe he wasn't a soldier, but at least he wasn't a traitor, like you, son. He stood for the free world. He stood for democracy.'

'You couldn't even begin to understand what democracy is, you asshole.'

'I know democracy is whatever communism ain't. Communism is folks not having enough food to eat and being afraid to go to sleep at night without having someone banging on their door and taking them away someplace.'

'Just like the people here. You don't get it, do you? We're the fucking bad guys here, sport. We're the Nazis.'

'Well, maybe this war ain't pretty to bleeding-heart liberals like you, but if we don't fight the communists right here in El Salvador, we'll have to fight them in Charleston.'

'Maybe we could beat them in Charleston.'

Buford bent down. His face creased into a grin. 'Tell me something, Ryan. If you're so fucking smart how come you're sitting here, all fucked up, a prime fucking candidate for a bullet in the head?'

He jabbed a forefinger into Ryan's shoulder. Ryan cried out in pain, and jerked away. The shock took his breath away and he felt the bandages getting wet again as the wound reopened.

After a while his breathing returned to normal. 'Are you going to murder me, Buford?'

Buford grimaced. 'I'm a soldier, Ryan. Murder's just a matter of geography. I shot a whole shitload of people in Vietnam. Now that was my duty. I do that outside a McDonald's in Washington, that's murder. You catch my drift here?'

'You're a piece of shit.'

He did not see the next blow coming. There was a flash of white light in front of his eyes as Buford hit him round the side of the head, sending him crashing on to the floor. His legs kicked desperately against the pain from his shoulder.

He recovered slowly, raised himself on his knees. There was fresh blood on the dirt floor. He looked up.

Buford was standing over him. 'Now why did you make me do that?'

The room was spinning. Ryan thought he was going to be sick.

'Like I was saying,' Buford continued, his tone once again conversational, 'we do have a problem here. Well, check that. You are the one that's got the problem. We just got a choice. Whether we take you back with us to San Salvador or we don't. What do you think about that, Major?'

The major's eyes glittered. Ryan knew what he thought.

Buford took out a pearl-handled .38 from a holster on his hip. He flicked back the hammer with his thumb.

Ryan had never been frightened to die before. In contacts he had always felt that his experience would get him out of anything. It was only the inexperienced or the unlucky who died. And he was experienced and he was lucky. But experience and luck counted for nothing here. This was personal, as well as tactical. If he were Buford, he knew what he'd do.

'I'm not up here on my own,' he said.

'You trying to deal with me, boy?'

'You know we never work on our own. There was another journo travelling with me. If I don't get back, he's going to tell the whole fucking story to the *Washington Post.*'

Buford was quiet a moment. 'Shit happens, Ryan. Like Romero. Like the nuns. It's a war zone.'

All right. Fuck it, then, Ryan thought. He wasn't going to beg.

If Buford really wanted him out of the way, he'd do it and let the politicians double-talk their way out of the shit-storm later. It really wasn't Buford's problem, he supposed.

Buford crouched down, grabbed Ryan's hair and held the revolver against his head. 'Bang,' he whispered.

Ryan didn't say anything.

He was thinking about Mickey. Maybe I missed out on something there, he thought. Thirty-seven years on this earth and I never really had a normal life. I wonder what it would have been like; children, a home, roots. And what am I leaving behind? When I'm gone there'll be a few guys – other journos, a few women – who'll remember me, fondly or bitterly, and maybe I'll merit a few lines of obituary in one of the papers I work for. After a few weeks when missing becomes probably dead. But that's it. And I don't know if I'm happy with that.

I always promised myself one day I'd do it another way.

Suddenly he wanted to scream: *No, not yet! Give me one more chance. Maybe I want to die in bed after all.*

Too late now.

'You disappoint me, Ryan,' Buford said.

'Yeah?' His voice was hoarse, but it sounded strong. He was pleased with that. Don't give the bastard the satisfaction. That was the code. Don't ever cry out when you're wounded. He had seen a lot of battles and he knew everybody cried out when they were wounded. Except a rare few. That was the real test.

'Thought you'd do a little blubberin' before you went. Yes, sir, I picked you for a blubberer.'

'I picked you for a first-class asshole the first time I saw you, Buford. Guess I'm just a better judge of character.'

Buford pulled his hair a little harder, stretching his head further back. Ryan could feel the pulse in his neck against the metal barrel of the gun. His shoulder hurt so fucking much . . .

'Off to commie heaven, boy. You ready?'

Ryan thought about Mickey again. He wondered what it would have been like. If he had his chances again, perhaps he would like to walk up that road. Christ, fifteen years spent in war zones. What did he have to show for it at the end? What a waste.

Too late now. Perhaps just as well. After what had happened to Odile. He did not deserve better than this anyway.

'No one's ever going to find the body, boy. You got mixed up in a firefight someplace, just bad luck. Won't look too good on the record, I guess, but better than have you go back home to tell all the nice people some shit-heel story about us massacring babies and all.'

'Just do it, Buford.'

Out of the corner of his eye Ryan saw the major staring at him, like a man looking at a woman he wanted. Blood lust. He probably had a hard-on.

'Nighty-night . . .'

# 44

The hammer hit the chamber with a dull click. Buford laughed. 'Boy, if you ain't covered with cold grease like a new rifle,' he said.

Ryan blinked, but couldn't speak. He had lost control of his bladder after all and he was ashamed.

'I know it's a bitch but I can't just go and do this without checking, son. Army red tape, drives you crazy, don't it? Maybe somebody somewhere will figure this was a mistake, and they'll go looking for someone to blame, and I'm not going to spend the rest of my life counting bird shit on Guam on account of you. So I'm going to get on the radio right now and get someone else to take the fall. Personally I figure you just ain't worth a ladle of dog shit, but there you are.'

He stood up.

'You pissed your pants, boy.'

Ryan said nothing. The world had stopped.

'Now don't get too excited. I'll be back in the morning, I dare say.'

They tied his good arm to the cot, and left him alone in the darkness with his fear and the cold. The bats shrieked in the rafters, the mosquitoes would not let him rest. Tiny flies drank from the mucus in his nose and at the corners of his eyes. His shoulder pulsed with pain.

The dead outside were really starting to stink.

Through the window he could see the stars over the Guazapa volcano. They were so close; tomorrow he would be catapulted out there with them into the unknown, to oblivion or to something else, perhaps some reckoning to be truly feared. But whatever it was, he was there on the edge now, separate from other men, hand in hand with whatever he had been running from all his life, his own death.

He had despised those foxhole prayers he had heard so many

times. *If you get me through this.* But now here he was, the words were on his own lips.

*If you just get me through this I'll do the rest of it different. I'll do something worthwhile with the rest of my time. I'll really make it count for something.*

Easy to say now, when there wasn't going to be a rest of it.

But even then there was another part of him, still gnawing away, refusing to accept his final judgment of his life.

It kept on replaying the moment when the women and children were gunned down, in freeze-frame.

And kept on wishing he had had his camera.

Finally he slept, exhaustion taking him under, swallowed by a vortex of vivid and violent dreams that finally shook him awake in the middle of the night to find the vampire bats clustered at his injured shoulder, the rest of his body covered with hard lumps from mosquito bites, more blood on his legs where other bats were feasting.

He kicked them away with a shrill scream of disgust, sat upright in the bed, wide-eyed, sweating.

Corpse gas leaked through the windows. Death everywhere around him.

Why didn't they just come and shoot him and get it over with? Let's do it, let's get it done!

He searched the night sky, eager for the dawn. Let's get the night out of the way, get Buford back in here with his six-gun and finish this. Anything but this torment of waiting.

*If you just get me through this.*

An explosion . . .

. . . an explosion.

His body jerked in surprise. A grenade.

Then another.

He heard the answering chatter of small-arms fire and then the screams, a babble of fear as men were dragged from sleep and brought face to face with death. What was it? Had another *guinda* stumbled into the camp?

Surely there was no one left. They had all run from the *chuchos*.

He listened to the sounds of the battle from the northern perimeter, saw a flare pop over the jungle, trailing green towards a ragged fringe of palms. The soldiers' shouts were panicked, they sounded unnerved; they were unaccustomed to night fighting. Buford was yelling orders in bad Spanish.

He felt a flare of hope. Fight it down, beat it down.

He remade his bargain.

*If you just get me out of this . . .*

The sounds of combat were at a distance, a hundred metres, perhaps a hundred and fifty, somewhere out on the perimeter. Then without warning he heard a sharp, short burst of automatic weapons fire, very close, right outside the door. Someone had taken out the guards.

Suddenly Ryan knew; they had come for him. He wrenched at the rope that secured him to the cot, but the knots bit tighter into his wrist.

Another burst of gunfire and then the sound of heavy boots running on the verandah.

Two figures stood silhouetted in the doorway. 'Gringo?' He recognised Salvador's falsetto.

'Over here!'

Salvador lumbered into the room, sawed through the rope with three slashes of the knife in his belt. He pulled Ryan to his feet and dragged him to the doorway. Bullets slapped into the adobe wall and they both threw themselves on their faces. Ryan heard someone gasping in pain, very close. Salvador's partner was hit.

The *comandante* swore in Spanish, crawled towards the wounded man. He was making a gurgling sound, like a child sucking milk through a straw. There was a single gunshot and Ryan felt something warm spray across his face.

Christ, he's shot him, Ryan thought.

Shapes milled blindly in the darkness, more bullets smacked into the wall behind him. 'We are one hundred yards from the perimeter,' Salvador said in his ear. 'Run very fast, but do not run straight.'

At that moment the moon disappeared behind the clouds.

'Now!'

# 45

## Tegucigalpa, Honduras

Mickey stood in front of the bathroom mirror, one of the hotel towels wrapped around her body, her hair damp from the shower and uncombed. She surveyed the damage of fourteen months in El Salvador. Her face looked thinner than she remembered it and there were dark hollows under her cheeks. She wondered what Ryan had found so attractive.

She dropped the towel and looked more closely at her body. She could see her ribs through her skin. But at least she was clean again, her skin flushed and pink after the luxury of soap and hot water. She had stood under the shower for almost half an hour, letting the hot needles of water sting her skin.

She could not stop thinking about Ryan.

She wondered why she could not cry for him. He deserved a few tears, at least. A long time since she had felt that way about a man, any man. Why Ryan? She thought she knew the answer. Because there had been something wild about him, something she could not resist. Something dangerous.

Well, that was a fact. You couldn't get more dangerous than dead.

Salvador and thirty *compas* had gone back for him, but they all knew it was too late. Meanwhile, at Salvador's insistence, Webb had been escorted back across the border into Honduras. She had gone with him, ostensibly to ensure that he did not suffer a recurrence of the malaria, but in reality she knew she needed to rest. She was emotionally and physically exhausted. A few weeks in Tegucigalpa and then she would go back.

There was a knock at the door.

* * *

Ryan.

He looked very pale, and much thinner. A ghost. 'Can I come in?' he said.

She stood aside, gripping the towel to her shoulders. He stood in the middle of the room, a beggar at the feast, stinking shirt and trousers, mud tracked across the plush carpet from his jungle boots. His hair was lank and unwashed and he smelled of the jungle, of vegetation and mud.

She gaped at him. His arm was in a sling, but the bandages were filthy.

'I thought you were dead,' she said.

He made a face: I thought so too.

'Are you okay?' It sounded hollow, hopelessly inadequate. She moved towards him very slowly, as if he were an illusion, as if at any moment he would disappear.

'I'm okay,' he said, but his eyes were focused elsewhere.

She touched him, the palms of her hands held gently against his chest. 'You stink,' she said.

The glimmer of a smile. 'I bet you say that to all the boys.'

'Get your clothes off.'

'That's more like it.' It sounded false, an actor with a badly rehearsed line.

'You need a wash.'

She went into the bathroom and ran the shower. When she came back he was still there in the middle of the room, staring. He let her peel the clothes off his body and lead him to the bathroom. She let the towel drop on to the tiles and climbed in beside him, helped to soap him down. 'It was Hugh,' she said.

He frowned, as if trying to remember the name.

'He persuaded them to go back for you.'

'Salvador told me. Good old Spider.'

'What happened?'

'Oh, the usual shit.'

The dressings on his arm were rank. She unwrapped the bandages, dropped them on the floor of the shower stall. The professional in her carefully assessed the damage: a T & T bullet wound on his upper arm, another surface laceration on the shoulder. The wounds were suppurating; they would require sterilising, debriding. He needed a good hospital.

She felt him fall against her. The weight of him was too much for her, and she sat down hard on the tiles. His face was ashen. 'Sean?'

'Sorry.'

'I'll get you a doctor.'

'I'm all right. Just a bit dizzy, that's all. Had the runs the last couple of days.'

Probably dysentery, she thought. Plus blood loss, hunger, exhaustion. Unexpectedly he grinned, and the light seemed to come back on in his eyes. 'You look great.'

'I look like shit, Ryan.'

'Not to me.'

'Oh, no.' She looked down. He was coming back to life. 'You can't, you idiot. Get an erection right now and you'll go into shock. You need all the blood somewhere else.'

'I've got a proposition for you.'

'Not now. Absolutely not. It's for your own good.'

'No, listen.'

'You're in no state to do anything but get on a drip.'

He reached up with his good arm and stroked her hair. 'You've got the most beautiful eyes I've ever seen. They're like looking into the ocean.'

She knew what he was doing. When a man said she had beautiful eyes it meant he wanted to take her to bed. She didn't want this again. There was no future in it. Not with Ryan.

'You're coming back with me,' he said.

'Don't do this, Ryan.'

'It's Sean.'

'I don't want to get that intimate.'

He kissed her, kneeling between her legs. 'If I pass out halfway through, don't stop. Please don't stop.'

Suddenly she found she was crying. The tears had come, after all. She wept with relief; not just that he was alive, but that they were both alive, and because it was so good to have a warm human body against hers again, and so good to feel safe. 'But I never liked you,' she said.

'I never liked you either. See, we have more in common than we thought.'

He lay on the bed while she dressed the wounds on his shoulder. They were bleeding again. 'We need to get you to a hospital,' she said.

'Just want to sleep,' he mumbled.

'You sleep. I'll be back soon.'

She dressed quickly and slipped out, closing the door quietly behind her. Ryan lay asleep on the bed, his hair tousled, like a little boy.

Well, a boy perhaps. But certainly not little.

Ryan opened his eyes as soon as he heard the door close. He was tired, tired to the marrow of his bones, but he knew he would not sleep. They had come to him again, in the drawn darkness of the room, the murdered women and children of the plaza in La Esperanza, and Salvador's two dozen good men, all clustered around his bedside.

And there, towering over them all, his hands on their shoulders, was the castrato, Salvador.

'Two dozen good men,' he said. 'Two dozen good men for one life. Your life. For you, gringo. I hope it was worth it.'

He had never had nightmares before, not in fifteen years of reporting. It will pass, he thought. Just delayed shock.

It will pass.

Besides, it will be different from now on. I've got my second chance and I have promises to keep. I have to make it worth it.

For Salvador.

It will be different from now on.

# 46

They had arranged to meet in the coffee shop across the road from the hotel. She ordered coffee and waited. He arrived half an hour late, looking pleased with himself.

'The film's freighted out,' Webb said, as he sat down. 'I filed the story this morning from the hotel. It will be in all the nationals before we get back.' Then he noticed the look on her face. His expression changed, and his excitement was replaced by resignation. 'Ryan's back.'

She nodded.

'Where is he?'

'He's resting. In my room.'

Pain like a shadow on his face. She supposed she should be flattered, two men fighting over her, but she was just sad. She wondered if she had made the right choice.

'I've booked to catch a flight back to the States this evening,' he said.

She nodded. 'Do you want to see him before you leave?'

'Not really.'

'You saved his life.'

'Great.'

'You didn't have to do that. You could have told the truth about the film.'

'Salvador would have gone back anyway. It was a question of pride.'

She moved the cold dregs of her coffee with her spoon. 'I'm sorry.'

'Don't be. You're not the reason I hate his guts. Not the only reason anyway.' He smiled. 'I'll get over it.'

'I have to get him to a hospital.'

'He's in pain, then?' Webb asked, hopefully.

'Yes.'

'Then the day hasn't been a complete disaster.'

'He's asked me to come back to the States with him.'

'Will you go?'

She nodded.

'That's good.'

'You're happy about that?'

'It's better than going back with the *compas*. You wouldn't have lasted another six months.'

'And what about me and Ryan? How long do you give me there?'

'About that long. But Ryan's not fatal. At least I don't think so.' He threw an air ticket on the table. 'It's only as far as Miami. The agency has already paid for it. I'll figure out how to claim for it later. You earned it, I guess.'

'Come and see him before you leave.'

'Give him my best.'

'Please.'

He held out his hand. 'Take care. If you're ever in New York, and Ryan isn't with you, look me up.'

'You're wrong about him.'

'I don't think so.' He stood up, hesitated, leaned across the table. 'I love you, Mickey,' he said. 'I think I always will.'

And he walked away.

## Seventh Regiment Armoury

Many of the guests had left. Those that remained had drifted down to the Colonel's Reception Room, on the ground floor. It was a large room, sombre with black walnut and oak, the atmosphere inside stale and heavy with tobacco smoke. It was dominated by a huge Rembrandt Peale oil portrait of Washington. George VI glared back at him in eternal enmity from the opposite wall, down the length of his aristocratic nose.

They stood by the marble fireplace, on Washington's side of the room. Cochrane selected their drinks from a passing waiter. They all chose cognacs except for Wendy Doyle, who wanted a Strega.

'Back to the story,' she said, turning back to Webb. 'What did you do when you got back to New York?'

'I'd had enough. I decided no one really cared what I was writing about. You can show them war, famine, torture. People shrug and turn to the funny pages. Some people just want to read the sports anyway. I figured America was afflicted with compassion fatigue. And so was I.'

'You quit IPA?'

'The previous year I'd written a book about my experiences in Vietnam, and it had done quite well. My publishers were encouraging me to write another one. I decided to retire to Long Island, buy a pipe and one of those cardigans with leather patches on the elbows and become a famous author.'

'So you'd already written *Goodnight, Saigon* by this stage,' Doyle said.

He nodded. 'I'd decided on a sequel. I wanted to tell the story of the Vietnamese refugees, in two parts. In the first half of the book I was going to interview boat people who had been trying to get to America, in the second half I'd talk to some of the Vietnamese who were already here, about their experiences. The royalties I'd earned from *Goodnight, Saigon* and the advance for the sequel were just about enough to live on for a year, with a little left over for research expenses. And I planned to do some freelancing on the side.'

'Did you keep in touch with Mickey?'

He shook his head. 'I told myself that was a closed chapter. I knew what Ryan was doing, of course. He was a minor celebrity for a while, as you know. But he was a closed chapter, too, as far as I was concerned. I had a new direction in my life, and I just wanted to turn my back on the rest of it.'

'Funny how life messes you around when you think you've finally made a break,' Cochrane said. 'Isn't it?'

'Maybe it's fate,' Doyle said.

'I don't believe in fate,' Webb told her. 'I suspect, in some unconscious way, we make these things happen.'

# V

## Philippines and the United States, March 1983

'You see these things, these terrible things. But in an odd way they're good stories.'

– Charles Mohr, war correspondent

# 47

## Vietnamese Refugee Camp Number U-5
## Puerto Princesa, Philippines

A navy jeep had been sent to escort Webb from the small airport to the Philippines Western Command Headquarters – WESCOM – which was situated a few kilometres away up a dusty red-dirt road. Grandiose in name, it turned out to be no more than a few rows of wooden bungalows and access roads shaded by drooping palm fronds. A handful of young mango trees grew from the shallows beyond the beach.

Commodore Sergio Garcia, WESCOM's commander-in-chief, rose to greet him as he was escorted into his office. He was dressed in a crisp khaki uniform, a handsome man with a mane of thick black hair, flecked with silver, with black spectacles and a boyish grin.

'Mr Hugh Webb. I am Commodore Garcia. We have been expecting you. Please take a seat.' He spoke perfect English but with an American accent.

'Commodore.' They shook hands. 'Thank you for arranging my visit.'

Webb sat down and took in his surroundings; a small, neat office, cooled by an electric fan. There was a map on the wall behind the commodore's head that delineated his command: the Sulu Sea and the eastern reaches of the South China Sea including large areas of disputed but largely uninhabited reefs and islands.

'We are always pleased to entertain gentlemen from the American press. Would you like refreshment?'

'Something cold.'

Garcia turned to the aide who had ushered him into the office and spoke quickly in Tagalog. He turned back to Webb, still smiling. 'So, what can we do for you?'

'Well, to clarify something, I'm not actually with the American press. I am engaged in writing a book.'

'Ah, you are an author. That is very good.' Garcia seemed impressed. He beamed even harder.

'I was a journalist for many years and I spent several years in Vietnam. The book I am writing is about the Vietnamese experience of that war, during and after. Naturally a great part of that experience includes the so-called boat people.'

'And you wish to talk to some of these people in our camp?'

'That's right.'

'Of course. I believe you have already obtained a clearance from the government?'

Webb nodded, opened his briefcase and took out a letter signed by the Philippines Minister for Foreign Affairs. Garcia examined it briefly, then handed it back, still smiling. 'You have been to other camps?'

'Not in your country. I spent a few days in Hong Kong, and then Malaysia, at Pulau Bidong.'

Garcia stopped smiling. 'You will find the conditions here a little better, I think. But then we have not had to deal with such large numbers.'

Webb sensed he had found a man of some compassion; on his travels around the refugee camps of South-East Asia he had found such men in short supply.

The aide returned with two glasses of Coca-Cola on a metal tray. He set them down on Garcia's desk and left. Ah, the exotic world of Americana, Webb thought. Hard to escape it. But he sipped the cold drink gratefully.

'What is it you are looking for, Mr Webb?' Garcia asked.

'To be honest with you, Commodore, I don't know. I find all the refugees have an extraordinary story to tell. I think I would like people in America simply to understand what they have gone through. We fought a war, supposedly on their behalf, but we never really understood them.'

Garcia considered for a moment. 'If it is the extraordinary that you are looking for, there is one young girl you must talk to here. The truth of her survival is remarkable, truly remarkable. She must definitely be in your book.' He stood up. 'Come along, we will find her. You will require an interpreter?'

'I have a little of the language from my time there. Since I began my research I have learned a little more. But I am by no means an expert.'

Garcia nodded. 'Then we will bring Lieutenant Marquez with us. Come with me, please.'

The camp was situated at the end of the airport runway, overlooking the sea. It was a flat, sandy wasteland, cordoned off with barbed wire, and a handful of scrubby trees provided the only shade. A BAC-111 roared overhead, destined for Manila.

Webb considered it well organised, especially in comparison to some of the other camps he had seen. There appeared to be no overcrowding and the refugees were housed in solid wooden huts. Opposite the guard room, he noticed, there was even a kiosk selling canned drinks and ice-cream and cigarettes. Next to Pulau Bidong this was a resort. Garcia noted his glance of approval and smiled.

Marquez crossed the compound, past a knot of youths playing volleyball on a hard dirt pitch. A young girl was drawing water at a hand pump. The lieutenant spoke to her, and the girl put down the bucket of water and followed Marquez back to where they were standing.

The child wore a ragged T-shirt with the bizarre decal of Mishka the Bear from the 1980 Moscow Olympics, and a pair of tattered bell-bottom jeans. He imagined she had bought them on the island. She was as thin as a stick, and this made her brown eyes seem even more huge. Her skin had been burned nearly black by the sun, and there were fresh scars on her arms and legs. Webb smiled at her, and the little girl smiled back. More a grimace really, he thought, like some alien trying to imitate his own expression.

'Her name is Phuong,' Garcia said.

Phuong. He felt a sharp stab of guilt, almost like a physical pain. It was a common Vietnamese name for a girl, and he had heard it many times during the last few weeks. But every time he heard the name spoken he said to himself: *I should have done more*.

'She was found on the McAdam Reef nearly seven hundred kilometres from the coast of Vietnam,' Garcia was saying. 'Some fishermen discovered her and brought her back to their village on an outlying island. When one of my patrol vessels called at the island a few weeks later they handed her on to us. She was brought back here to the navy hospital in a very poor condition.'

'What happened to her arms and legs?' Webb asked him.

'She says that when her boat was thrown on to the McAdam Reef, she had to crawl across the coral to reach the island. The cuts have taken a long time to heal. In fact, when she was brought here, they were still very badly infected.'

'How long was she on the island?'

'We estimate about four months.'

'How did she survive for so long without food?'

'We don't know. We imagine she took shellfish and snails from the reef. She stored rainwater in plastic containers thrown up on the beach by the wreck. I suspect there is more to her story, but that is all she will tell us.'

Webb looked down at the little girl. Her left hand was balled into a tight fist.

'Is there something in her hand?'

Garcia spoke quickly to Marquez, then turned back to Webb. 'Lieutenant Marquez says he doesn't know. He thinks so but she will not show him and he has not the heart to make her.'

'Perhaps there's physical damage to her hand.'

Another quick exchange with the lieutenant.

'The lieutenant doesn't think so. He says the doctor examined her when she first arrived here, and that she became quite distressed when he tried to prise open her fingers. But he believes there is no injury. Do you wish Lieutenant Marquez to use force?'

Webb shook his head. 'No. No, don't do that.' He crouched down. The little girl was still grinning back at him, ingratiatingly. He wondered how old she was. He guessed somewhere between ten and twelve years.

'*Con am com chua?*' he said in Vietnamese, the traditional greeting: Have you eaten?

'*Da con an com roi, ba.*' Thank you, but I have already eaten, Uncle.

For some reason Webb felt uneasy. The hair rose on the back of his neck. He did not know why. It was as if he were in a dark room, and could feel but not see the presence of another person.

'You would like to hear her story?' Garcia asked.

Webb stared at the little girl, his face creased into a frown.

'Mr Webb?'

Webb looked up, shaken from the reverie.

'She can come back to my office. We will be more comfortable there.'

'Thank you. Yes. I'd like that.'

* * *

Marquez pulled up a straight-backed chair and indicated that Phuong should sit down. He gave her a glass of Coca-Cola, which she accepted without a word, gulping down the whole glass in one swallow.

Marquez brought up a chair and sat down beside her.

'Tell her there is nothing to be afraid of,' Garcia said, and Marquez translated. The girl accepted this information without expression. Her eyes were silent and watchful.

'Can you ask her when she was born?' Webb said.

The girl spoke slowly in her own language.

'She says she was born in the Year of the Dog,' Marquez said.

Webb calculated quickly. The previous year had also been the Year of the Dog, on the Chinese calendar, and the calendar had a twelve-year cycle. So the girl was a little older than he had anticipated, around thirteen.

'Tell her I am a writer, a *bao chi*, from America. I would like the people in America to know her story, and the story of the other Vietnamese people who were forced to flee her country. Tell her I would like to know what happened to her, so I can write it down.'

Marquez translated this.

The girl murmured something and Marquez interpreted. 'She wants to know if you will take her with you to America.'

It was a question they all asked at some time. He felt Garcia watching him, curious as to how he would answer. 'Tell her I have no power over what happens to her here. Tell her eventually she will be resettled in another country but her fate is quite out of my hands.'

She said something to Marquez. 'She has asked me why she should help you, if you cannot help her.'

Webb was a little startled by this reply, but he said: 'Tell her there is no reason.'

The little girl stared at him, as if deciding for herself whether he could be trusted. Finally she turned back to Marquez.

'She asks if American people realise what is happening in her country, will they try and stop it?'

'Perhaps they will do more to help you and the other people in this camp,' Webb said.

This seemed to satisfy her. She held out her glass for more Coca-Cola.

'The first thing I remember,' Marquez translated, 'I was living with my mother in Cholon . . .'

# 48

*My mother was a very fine lady, very beautiful. Everyone loved her and respected her. She always wore very beautiful clothes, and she was very kind and gentle. My father was a big businessman with lots of money. We had a beautiful villa right in the middle of Saigon, with a beautiful garden, and green shutters on all the windows. My father drove everywhere in a big car and he was very, very important.*

*He was also a very brave man and he decided to stay in Saigon when the communists came, to try and protect the people. But of course as soon as they took over the city they threw him in prison and used our fine house as a barracks for their soldiers. We never saw my father again.*

*My mother and I were forced to live on the streets, begging for food.*

*But the communists did not want people to live on the streets, everyone was supposed to have work in their new utopia, so eventually we were sent to an SEZ, a Special Economic Zone, in the countryside. It was at a place called Le Minh Xuan and it was one of the first and largest of the SEZs, ten kilometres from Saigon. Here we were sent out to work, digging irrigation canals, building mud into walls with our bare hands. The communists gave us nothing in return; no food and no shelter. We had to do everything for ourselves, starting from nothing. We had to build our own huts and grow our own food as best we could. If we were able to raise any pigs or chickens they had to be sold back to the state at ridiculously low prices. Life was very terrible. Those who did not starve were killed or maimed by unexploded mines while working in the fields.*

*We survived there for two monsoons, but the harvests were disastrous and one night my mother whispered to me that we certainly would not survive another season. So like many others we returned to Saigon, once again sleeping in parks and on sidewalks, begging and stealing to survive.*

*We began new lives as pavement hawkers. My mother would buy one packet of cigarettes on the black market, then sell the cigarettes one at a time to realise a small profit. We squatted on the sidewalk from dawn to sunset every day, peddling cigarettes. But still we could not make enough money even to eat properly, so my mother finally sold her wedding ring. She had kept this hidden from the communists all the time we were in the SEZ, clinging to the hope that somewhere my father was still alive. But now she pawned it and used the money to buy a big bundle of old clothes from a Chinese woman in the Cholon district. Then we resold the items one by one on the pavement outside the Central Market. But it was very dangerous to be found doing this and we had to move on quickly if we saw the police or the soldiers.*

*For a while everything was all right. But then one day the police arrested us and we were sent back to the Zones.*

*This time it was the SEZ at Rach Gia. The camp was much worse even than Le Minh Xuan. It was run like an army regiment. The people were divided into five battalions of four companies, each consisting of one hundred people. A communist cadre was appointed to each 'company', and it was his job to interrogate everyone about their past. They were looking for people who had sympathised with the Americans.*

*The worst thing about Rach Gia was that there was little potable water. We could not irrigate the crops, and anything that did grow was quickly consumed by insects. Most of the children there suffered from anaemia and malnutrition and many others died of disease.*

*Fortunately it was not a very difficult camp to escape from – everyone who had been sent to Rach Gia zone eventually returned, like us, to the city. We walked all the way back to Saigon, and went back to living on the street.*

*My mother still had a little gold, tiny ingots, which she had kept hidden. Do not ask me how, it is very private, how she did it. When we got back to Saigon she sold the gold bars and then we went back to Cholon, found the same old Chinese woman who had sold us the clothes. Now she was selling china plates and my mother bought a big box from her and again we went back to being hawkers, dodging the soldiers, selling the plates on the street. There was very big money doing this, as long as we could keep away from being arrested. My mother sold the plates and I was the lookout.*

*One day my mother told me she had decided we must escape from Vietnam, that our life was never going to get any better. Now the only way you could escape was by living near the sea where the boats were, but to move to another city you had to have the right papers. My mother used the money we had made selling the plates to bribe an official from the government to forge some documents for us. The cadres made a lot of money doing this.*

*My mother then paid two yaels to a man who had a boat and the next day we went to Vung Tau. But the boat never came. I remember my mother cried and cried. I had never seen her cry so much, even in the Zones. I was very frightened. I thought she was going to die from crying.*

*But my mother was a strong person, she was never sad for long. She said we would just have to sell more dishes and make back all the money we had lost.*

*And that is what we did. One day my mother told me she had met a man who had a boat and it would take us away, to freedom, to America. We still did not have quite enough money but my mother said the man who owned the boat was very kind and he was taking some people even though they could not pay.*

*So we went back to Vung Tau.*

*We got on the boat late one night. I remember there were a lot of people on board and the boat was very small. No one had any food, and I was very hungry. But I did not mind so much any more. I was very happy because my mother told me we were going to America and we would have a fine house and a nice car and live a good life and be happy. She was very excited and I was very excited too. I thought everything was going to be all right.*

*When we set off the sea was rough and everyone was very sick so it did not matter there was no food. But then we ran out of water. It seemed we had only brought enough for a few days. We were supposed to sail to Thailand, but the man who was in charge of the boat knew very little about navigation and a week went by and still we had seen no sight of land. Some people became delirious with thirst and committed suicide by jumping overboard.*

*To make matters worse our boat developed a list, and then one night there was a terrible storm. I woke up to feel our little boat tossing on the sea like an angry water buffalo. I heard screaming. Some people had fallen out of the boat.*

*My mother held on to me very tight but I could feel her trembling and I knew she was as afraid as I was. When the morning came the sky was still very dark and our boat was lying right over on its side in the water. Another big wave crashed over us and I was sure we were all going to die.*

*Then someone cried out that they could see land. We thought we were saved. But then there was a jolt and a terrible noise came from underneath the boat. Everyone started screaming again. Big waves shook our boat as if some giant dog was shaking us in its teeth. Then the deck pitched right over and I fell in the water. I reached out for my mother but she was not there.*

*I cannot swim. I felt myself go under and my mouth filled up with water. Then someone grabbed me and held my head above the surface. All I remember is kicking and screaming. All the time these big waves kept breaking over our heads. I was still shouting for my mother. I could see the hull of the boat turned right over on top of the water and heads bobbing up and down between the waves. But my mother had disappeared.*

*I saw a big piece of wood and wrapped my arms around it. I clung on as tightly as I could. The person who was holding on to me – I don't know who it was – let me go. I never even thanked them for saving my life. I had no thought of anything else, just hanging on to the wood and screaming for my mother.*

*The waves dragged me over some coral. The pain was very bad and I screamed and screamed but there was nothing I could do. Suddenly the sea became much calmer and I saw a tiny island very close by. I realised the water was much shallower and that I could stand up.*

*When I reached the shore I sat there on the beach all that day, and the next, looking for my mother. Some other people were washed up on the sand but they were all dead. Bits and pieces from the boat were thrown up by the waves and I draped them over bushes to make some shade. There was also a big tin drum. That night there was another storm and the drum filled up with rain. If it was not for this drum I would not have survived.*

*Then finally I found my mother, lying face down in the shallows. I dragged her up on to the sand and I sat next to her all that day and the day after, talking to her, hoping she will come alive. But then the smell of her body, and of all the other bodies, is too bad and I have to go and sit on another part of the island.*

*And that is how I lived until the fishermen found me.*

When she had finished the three men sat for a long time in shuffling silence.

'It's a terrible story,' Garcia said. 'These people have endured unspeakable misery. Even,' he added, 'for this part of the world.'

Webb studied the little girl. There was something wrong here, something that didn't quite make sense. It had not registered with him at first but now he realised that the little girl had round eyes, that she was Eurasian. Yet she had claimed that both her parents were Vietnamese. Also, there was something about her home as she had described it. A child would surely remember how it looked from the inside, her toys, the garden, the smells. Phuong had described only the exterior.

'Ask her which of her parents had round eyes,' he said to Marquez.

The lieutenant looked uncomfortable with such a question, but dutifully translated it. Webb watched the girl's reaction, and he knew immediately that his suspicions were correct.

She looked down at her lap and refused to answer.

There were tens of thousands of round-eye children left behind by American servicemen during the war, he reminded himself. And yet there was something about her face, or her eyes, that . . . or was he seeing just what he wanted to see? Was the guilt about what had happened eight years ago still pressing on him so heavily that he could not escape it? Was he determined to see that woman and that child wherever he went?

'Do you know her mother's name?' He asked Garcia.

Garcia shook his head. 'She claims not to know.' He arched one eyebrow in curiosity. 'Should this be important?'

'No, it's not important.' No, this could not be *that* Phuong. That girl and her mother had been killed by rocket fire in Saigon on 28 April 1975. A name, a faint similarity, Eurasian features, a small lie in a child's past; it amounted to nothing.

But the feeling of unease would not leave him. It was a part of that same instinct that Ryan had taught him to respect in combat, the hair-trigger tingling along the spine that warned you when a sniper had you in his cross-hairs, that made you hug the ground a moment before the grenade exploded or a contact was made. There was no sense to it, no logical reason.

But surely this was different.

No, that little girl was dead. She had to be.

He leaned forward. 'Lieutenant Marquez, will you ask her again what nationality her father was, please?'

Marquez shrugged his shoulders and translated the question.

The little girl shook her head. 'She says she would like to go now.'

Webb wanted to shake her. *Tell me the truth about you, please!* He had known all along, of course, that this book, this pilgrimage through the refugee camps, was partly atonement, and yes, also a last vain search. And now here it was again, this same doubt that had been with him for the last eight years. What if they had survived the rocket attack? What if they were still alive?

If they were still alive they were Ryan's responsibility, not his. What had Ryan called him? Jimminy Cricket. The voice of his conscience. Here he was, still harping, turning over rocks, wondering if Ryan still had debts to pay.

'You wish to talk to this girl any more?' Garcia asked him.

Webb shook his head. He thanked her in her own language, but she did not reply. She stood up and left, without a word. He knew that he had shamed her; it was not the Asian way to reveal a lie so blatantly. He had made her lose face.

*The dust of life*, the Vietnamese called them. She was twice an alien; she did not belong in her own country, and she did not belong in the West. Of course a child would try to deny her own past in such circumstances.

More doubts. He could not get that one thought from his mind.

What if she had survived?

He spoke to four others that afternoon, more flotsam thrown up on the Filipino beaches eight years after the war: a woman who had seen her two sons drown in front of her eyes; an old man who had lost his sons, his daughters, his wife and his grandchildren, one by one, first to the war, then to the Zones and finally to the sea; a young boy hoping to find his sister in Australia; another young girl, around the same age as Phuong, whose parents had fallen from their leaking boat during a storm, leaving her orphaned and alone.

More tales of misery and grief, equally as harrowing as Phuong's. And yet when he flew back to Manila later that afternoon the one face he could not shake from his memory was that of a bony little girl in a ragged T-shirt who had reawakened the past for him yet again.

* * *

A week later he was back in New York. But it was another week after that before he bowed to the inevitable and picked up the phone to dial the number of the Philippines Embassy in Washington to ask for sponsorship forms. The chances that it was her were beyond imagining, but he had realised it no longer mattered.

The point was it *could* have been her. And now he was finally bringing her home.

# 49

From Manila, Phuong was flown to Camp Pendleton in California, where American soldiers sprinkled DDT powder on her head, and immigration officials gave her a form stating that she was a refugee with parole status. From there she was transferred to an internal flight to New York via Chicago.

She was given food on a plastic tray. She put some into her mouth but promptly spat it back on her plate. Inedible. She returned her attention to the magazine in the little pocket in front of her, stared open-mouthed at the glossy photographs of animals she had never seen before, who lived in a place called Africa. The advertisements left her completely overawed, a treasure trove of expensive watches, cameras and motor cars.

A middle-aged American businessman who was sitting in the seat next to her gave her a book. On the front cover was a picture of a man with a beard standing on top of a very tall building. The American told her the man's name was Jesus. Phuong remembered this name. Her mother had told her that Jesus was God. The American also claimed that he spoke to Jesus every day and that if she did the same thing this man with the beard would help her with anything she needed, anything at all.

Perhaps this is why they all have expensive watches and cameras and motor cars in America, Phuong thought. All they have to do is ask Jesus for one. But then why didn't they also get Jesus to help them beat the communists in Saigon?

The man asked her for some money to give to Jesus and she gave him the only money she had, the ten United States dollars that Commander Garcia had given her when she left Puerto Princesa.

They hit turbulence an hour out of Chicago and she hid under her seat. Jesus's good friend vomited noisily in a bag. A lady in a uniform came and coaxed Phuong from the floor and buckled her back into her seat. Then she held her hand until the turbulence subsided. When it was over Phuong felt ashamed to have been so frightened. It was not anywhere near as bad as the boat.

The hostess then escorted her on to another plane at O'Hare. When she arrived at JFK International in New York she was holding a copy of *Watchtower* in her right hand, her left fist was still clenched tight at her side, and everything she possessed was zipped into a flight bag over her shoulder.

She emerged from the arrivals hall wearing the same Mishka the Bear T-shirt she had been wearing the day he first saw her on Puerto Princesa. Her bell-bottom jeans were torn and frayed at the cuffs. She was shivering with cold and looked utterly lost in the crowd of shouting, laughing people.

Their eyes met, but this time she did not smile.

What if I've made a terrible mistake, Webb thought. How much of her mind had been permanently damaged by war and poverty and malnutrition and deprivation? Are you really ready to take on this responsibility? For the first time the enormity of the task he had set himself really hit him.

He crouched down. 'Hello, Phuong,' he said.

She did not answer. He had been told she had been learning English at the school at Puerto Princesa and that she had proved an exceptional student. But perhaps she simply did not know how to address him. He knew he could never ask her to call him Father. And calling him by his first name would be considered impolite by a Vietnamese. 'You can call me Uncle,' he said.

She nodded, her brown eyes huge. 'Hello, Uncle, how do you do today?'

He embraced her and felt her stiffen. The wrong thing to do. 'Are you cold?' he said.

'Yes, it is cold today,' Phuong said. 'I think it may rain.'

Webb smiled at her schoolroom English. He took off his leather jacket and wrapped it around her shoulders.

'Let's go home,' he said.

A watery April sun hung low over the potato fields. Phuong sat quietly in the passenger seat, gaping at the cars and the flat, empty fields. She was astonished that there were no buffalo and no one tilling the fields.

They turned on to the Lincoln Cove turnpike and ten minutes later they were in the main street.

Lincoln Cove was an old whaling village, now mostly a tourist town. It was still early in the season and there was just a handful of tourists on the sidewalks, braving the cold in shorts and sweatshirts that bore the ubiquitous Lincoln Cove cartoon whale.

Webb drove with the window down. A salt wind jangled the halyards of the yachts in the marina, and he heard laughter from the verandah of the Whalers Hotel where a group of yachtsmen were drinking beer in bentwood rockers. He turned down a narrow lane towards Bayberry Cove and pulled over a hundred yards from the point.

'Home,' he said.

A white picket fence and a mailbox with *Webb* hand-painted on the tin in black paint. An old cedar shaded an unkempt lawn, its branches concealing most of the house from the road. He led the way through a creaking gate and up a shell-grit path. The house was white clapboard, with cedar shingles on the roof. The tangle of mimosa that grew over the verandah was just coming into bloom.

Phuong hesitated, then followed him inside. Cedar panelling on the walls, french windows the length of another wall, a view looking out over the cove. The oak floors were covered with oriental rugs and there was a coal fire burning in the stone fireplace.

She stood in the middle of the room, gazing around, mouth open. She looked so tiny; the leather jacket he had put around her shoulders in the terminal hung almost to her knees, a pair of sparrow-thin shins protruding. There was a pair of cheap rubber sandals on her feet. She looked as if she had just fallen through the roof from outer space.

He noticed that her left hand was still balled into a tiny fist.

He waited a moment, let her gather her composure. Then he stepped forward and took the flight bag off her shoulder. It was very light. He looked inside. Her lifetime's possessions amounted to a tin spoon, an in-flight magazine and the torn half of a file card stamped by the United States Immigration Service. There was also a dossier form provided by UNHCR that was supposed to contain her family history, but most of the names and dates were recorded as 'unknown'.

He took a deep breath. Too late for regrets now. So many variables. He might not like her. She might not like *him*. Well, if it did prove to be a mistake, it would not be as bad as if he had taken on a small child. Five years and she would be an adult, able to make her own choices. Just think of her as a long-term house guest.

He was giving her a second chance at life and even if it turned out to be a disaster he could always take some comfort in that. Assuming, of course, that her life, and perhaps her mind, were retrievable. And that was perhaps an assumption he should not have made.

Phuong just stood at the window and stared at the gulls.

'Are you hungry?' he asked her.

She shook her head. 'I am very tired,' she said.

'Okay,' he said. 'I'll show you your room.'

# 50

When Phuong woke the next morning Webb was already awake and sitting out on the deck, holding a cup of steaming black coffee. His breath left wispy clouds on the damp air. Gulls and jays wheeled over the water and disappeared, screeching, through the mist.

'Good morning,' he said.

'Good morning, Uncle, how are you?'

He smiled. 'I am very well, thank you, Phuong. Did you sleep well?'

'Yes, thank you.'

He had a bowl in front of him, Phuong noticed, and in the bowl was some gooey brown slop and some milk. 'Do you want breakfast?' he asked her.

She was starving. 'No, thank you, I have just eaten,' she said, remembering a phrase from her lessons at Puerto Princesa. She saw the surprise on his face.

'What have you just eaten?'

'I am sorry. My English is not so good. I mean I do not have hunger.'

'I'm not hungry,' he coached her.

'Yes, sorry, I am not hungry.' She gave him a hesitant smile. She had forgotten so much of her English. She remembered a time when it was all she spoke at home, before the communists came. It was a painful language to use; it reminded her too much of that other time.

'This must be very hard for you,' he said. 'I cannot imagine what it must be like.' He put down his coffee cup. 'Phuong, you must try and think of me as your family now. I know that won't be easy, and it won't happen today or next week. But eventually perhaps. This is your home now, do you understand?'

'Yes, I understand, Uncle,' she answered, but she thought: You can never be my parent. I will never show you my heart. Perhaps you are a nice person, but one day you will leave me or you will get hurt. I don't want any more parents, I just want to live here in America and have an easy life, like my mother said.

She looked around, at the garden, at the big house, the water. It was all so unreal. Last night she had thought: When I wake in the morning I will be back sleeping under a tree in Saigon or alone on the island, with only the stink of the dead for company. I will find it is all just a dream. Or any moment someone will come, someone in a uniform, and they will say: *Sorry, this is all a mistake, you must come back to Saigon now. You are a criminal and you must go to a Zone.*

'You're quite safe here,' Webb told her.

She lowered her face, appalled that her thoughts could be written so plainly on her face.

'Did you sleep in those clothes?'

Well, of course, she thought. How else should one sleep?

He stood up suddenly. He seemed irritated with her. 'Come with me.'

She followed him back inside the house. He went into her bedroom. She looked up at him, expecting approval. Everything was as it had been the night before. She had been careful to make no mess or dirt.

'You didn't sleep in the bed,' he said.

She had tried. But the soft Western bed with its mattress and pillow had been too uncomfortable and so she had curled up on the rug on the floor.

He picked up the clothes that were still neatly laid out at the foot of the bed, where she had found them. 'I left a nightgown for you on the bed. These are for you too. A T-shirt and jeans and some underwear. I had to guess your size.'

'This clothes belong to me now?'

'Not this clothes, *these* clothes. And yes, they're yours. You can't wear these old things any more. Take them off and give them to me. I'll throw them away.'

'Take them off . . . now?'

'Well, no, not now. Later. After you've had a wash.' He went into the little bathroom that led from the guest bedroom and turned on the shower. 'Look, this tap makes the water hotter, this one makes it colder. Okay?'

Phuong stared at the steam rising from the shower cubicle. Another miracle.

'Here's some soap.'

He unwrapped the soap and gave it to her. She held it to her nose, inhaled the sweet bouquet. Perfumed soap. A luxury beyond imagining. Surely this was how people lived in palaces.

'I'll wait outside. Okay?'

She searched her memory for the right phrase from her English book on Puerto Princesa. 'Thank you very much, kind sir.'

He grinned at her, as if she had made a joke. 'Oh, that's quite all right, good lady,' he said, and went out.

They climbed in his mandarin-red Jeep Wagoneer and drove into town. There was a flagpole in the centre of the lawned traffic circle at the end of Main Street and Old Glory snapped in a brisk morning breeze. They drove over the bridge and headed north on Scrub Pine Road.

Phuong stared out of the passenger side window, amazed by the beautiful houses and shiny new cars. But the people were so ugly. Everyone was so fat! They passed a man running up the hill, his face flushed as red as betel-nut juice, his belly shaking like jelly under his T-shirt as he ran. The women were worse. You could see their bottoms wobbling in their tight jeans . . .

Webb parked the jeep on a bluff overlooking the cove. The wind had raised white caps on the surface of the water. Below them a ketch, its hull painted sky blue, cut through the bay towards the narrows.

After he had turned off the engine Webb sat for a long time in fidgeting silence. Phuong sensed there was something very difficult that he needed to say to her, and she waited for the blow to fall. Perhaps he had changed his mind about her and now he wanted to send her back to U-5. She suddenly remembered how he had asked her, on that first meeting, about her parents not being Vietnamese. Even a foreigner knew she was *bui doi*, the dust of life.

Why had he chosen her, then?

'Will you tell me about your mother?' he said.

She was right. He knew she had lied. But she would lose too much face to change her story now. 'She was very beautiful lady,' she recited, 'very kind. From a very rich family . . .'

'No, tell me the truth about her, Phuong. Please.'

Phuong smiled at him, in the oriental manner, the accepted

response to a question that was too difficult or too embarrassing to answer. 'I do not understand, Uncle.'

'You understand.'

She looked at his hands on the steering wheel of the jeep. The knuckles were white. She had done something wrong. She had made him angry.

'Please, you are going to send me back to U-5?'

'No, of course not. No one's going to send you back. This is your home now. I'm your family. But I must know the truth about you.'

Phuong lowered her head. 'My father was an American,' she mumbled.

'You're sure?'

'He was very bad. My mother was very unhappy. He went back to America and never come back for her.'

'He was a soldier?'

'I don't know.'

'Please. Try to remember.'

'He worked for the government, I think.'

Webb's fingers drummed on the wheel. She stared into her lap, hoping this interrogation would soon be over. Why had he shamed her this way?

'Do you remember when the communists came?'

What was the correct answer to such a question? She knew he wanted to hear something from her, but what? If she told him everything she knew, it might be wrong, and he would send her back to U-5 anyway. Why so many questions? She just wanted to forget that time.

'I don't remember,' she said.

His fingers drummed on the wheel.

'To hell with it,' he said, finally. 'Are you hungry?'

She nodded.

He looked at his watch. 'You've been in America nearly eighteen hours and you still haven't had a hamburger. We'd better fix that.'

He started the engine and they drove back into town.

She had never been inside a McDonald's before so Webb ordered for her, a Big Mac and a large fries. She unwrapped the hamburger with elaborate care and suspicion, as if she were defusing a bomb.

She took one mouthful, made a face and put it back in its box. The fries grew cold on the tray. Instead of eating she contented herself with drinking her Coke and most of his as well.

'You have to eat something,' he said.

She shrugged her shoulders.

Time to bite the bullet, Webb thought. He had bought a Vietnamese cookbook; after two weeks of practice the only dish he had managed successfully was *pho* – Vietnamese noodle soup. 'All right, let's see if you can take some of my home cooking,' he said.

While Webb was in the kitchen, Phuong wandered out on to the deck and made her way down the steps to the yard. He watched her from the window. Seagulls had gathered on the lawn, near the bulkhead rocks at the foot of the garden. One stood separate from the others, its head turned into the breeze. Phuong had moved very slowly across the grass until she was just a few yards away, crouched directly behind it.

What the hell is she doing? Webb wondered.

She inched imperceptibly closer to the bird. Webb felt the hairs rise on the back of his neck.

God Almighty.

She moved so quickly that he did not realise what she had done until it was over. He heard the panicked screeching of the other gulls as they took off, saw Phuong rolling over and over on the lawn. When she stood up she was holding the gull's beak in one hand, its wings in the other.

He ran out on to the deck.

'No. Let it go. Let it go!'

She stared up at him, bewildered. There were flecks of blood on her hands where the gull had bitten her. It was still screeching and writhing in her fist.

'Let it go!'

Phuong obediently opened her hands and the bird fluttered to the ground. It flew off, bouncing once, twice, across the grass before taking to the air in wounded and ragged flight.

Webb ran down the stairs to the lawn. 'What were you doing?' he shouted.

Phuong did not answer. There was something in her mouth. She spat it back into her left fist and closed it.

'I was hungry, Uncle.'

He stared at her. My God, what sort of creature have I allowed into my house? She's practically feral. She had stalked the bird with the instincts of a wild animal.

'If you're hungry I'll cook you lunch inside,' he said.

He put his arm around her and led her back to the house. Good God.

At least now he knew how she had survived for so long without food on McAdam Reef.

She ate two bowlfuls of the *pho* without comment. Afterwards she stood at the window watching the grey clouds gather over the cove. She seemed lost in some dark reverie of her own and he did not try to intrude. He imagined she was turning over in her mind the questions he had asked her earlier that morning, and he prepared himself for her revelation.

At last she opened her mouth to speak and he braced himself. 'I think it is going to rain, is it not?' she said.

'Yes, it looks like it could rain.'

Another long silence. 'You . . . very rich?'

He smiled. 'No, not really.'

He knew she did not believe him. A house like this, a big car; it would take a long time for her to understand that in America these were things that many people accepted as their birthright.

'You are a businessman, isn't it?'

'Not really. I write books.'

She frowned. This was something beyond her comprehension.

'I'll show you,' he said. 'Come on.'

From the living room a wrought-iron spiral staircase led to a loft area which Webb had added to the original cottage a year before. At the top of the landing one door led to his bedroom at the rear of the house, another to a study with dormer windows overlooking the cove.

He opened the study door. Two of the walls were lined with bookshelves, the third was hung with perhaps two dozen framed photographs, colour and monochrome. In the middle of the room was a desk with a PC, a printer, and a phone fax, crowded on to a desktop that was already overflowing with loose sheets of paper.

Phuong looked around, perplexed.

'I used to be a journalist, okay – *bao chi*. These days I write books.'

He took a hardback book from one of the bookshelves and showed it to her. The front cover photograph showed a helicopter lifting from the roof of the United States Embassy in Saigon in 1975. The title was embossed in red and gold: *Goodnight, Saigon*. Hugh Webb.

She turned the book in her hands. A black and white photograph of Webb was on the back of the dust cover.

'I got sick of chasing ambulances.'

She frowned at him, not understanding.

He pointed to the scattered typewritten papers on his desk. 'My next book. *Voices from America*. It's about Vietnamese living in America. People like you.'

'You write this book about me, please?' she asked him, frowning.

'No, not just about you. About . . . many Vietnamese in America.'

She looked up at the framed photographs on the far wall and was drawn towards them, as he knew she would be. Most of them were from his Vietnam days: one of him sitting on an APC at Chu Lai, another crouched in the door of a Huey, another with Cochrane and Crosby and Ryan in a Saigon street.

He held his breath.

'You?' she asked him, pointing to one of the photographs.

'I looked a bit different then. No grey hair.'

'Soldier?'

He shook his head. 'No, no, *bao chi*.' He pointed out the photograph Ryan had taken of him, out on patrol somewhere in the Delta, a camera slung around his neck.

'*Bao chi*,' she repeated.

He stood back and watched her as she studied the rest of the photographs. He waited for some sign of recognition on her face.

Nothing.

It's not her, he thought. If it was her she would have recognised Ryan straight away. Perhaps. Even though she was just five years old when Saigon fell, even though he was hardly ever there.

No, it still proved nothing.

It could not possibly be her, he told himself. On the UNHCR form her mother's name was given as Ngai, Ngai Dieu-Quynh. Ryan had introduced them once, but he could not remember Odile's surname, had never learned her real name, her Vietnamese name, the one she would have reverted to when the communists took over.

Phuong examined each of the photographs carefully. He dropped his gaze to her fist, still tightly closed.

'Have a good look around. As long as you like.'

He left her alone in the room and went downstairs.

He went into the kitchen to make coffee. When he looked up, she was standing on the stairs watching him. 'You like coffee?' he said, holding up a jar of instant.

She shook her head.

'There's Coke in the refrigerator. Help yourself whenever you want.'

The previous evening, using a Vietnamese dictionary, he had made a number of handwritten signs and had tacked them around the house: above the telephone he wrote *telephone* on a piece of cardboard, and the Vietnamese equivalent, *diên thoai*, underneath. He did the same on the oven, the refrigerator, the table, the doors, walls, chairs and so on around the room.

Phuong went to the refrigerator, peered intently at the sign. 'Refrigerator,' she repeated. She went to the oven. 'Oven.' She leaned over the range. 'Hot pl —'

She let out a shrill scream and jumped back.

Webb spun around. She was clutching her left hand, her mouth open in shock and pain. He realised immediately what she had done. He pulled her towards the sink, turned on the cold tap and put her hand under the running water. There was a pink burn along all the knuckles of her left hand.

'It's okay,' he said, 'it's okay, it's not a bad burn. It's okay, Phuong.'

She was crying, her whole body trembling with shock. He put the plug in the sink, kept her injured hand in the water, put his other arm around her shoulders and held her. 'That's why they call it a hot plate, I guess. You're okay.'

Something caught his eye and he looked down. Whatever Phuong had been holding in her fist had dropped to the floor. A soft glint of gold. A cross. Gently he turned over her burned hand. She had been gripping the crucifix so tightly for so long that it had formed a bruised imprint in the flesh of her palm.

She tried to pull away from him, to retrieve her treasure from the floor. He held her tighter. 'No one's going to take it away from you, Phuong. Let's fix this burn first. No one's going to steal it.' She would not be comforted. She tore herself away from him, grabbed the cross with her uninjured hand.

'Was it your mother's?' he said, more gently.

She nodded.

'She was a good Catholic, wasn't she?'

She sank to her haunches on the floor, cradling her injured hand in her lap.

'It's okay,' he said. He knelt down on the floor beside her and rocked her in his arms. Enough questions. He wasn't sure he wanted to know the truth himself any more.

The next morning he drove to the shops to get milk and bread. When he got back he found her in the kitchen, reading the signs he had put up for her, committing each object to memory. She did not hear him walk in and spun around, startled.

'Hey, it's just me,' he said. He put the grocery bags on the counter top. 'How's your hand?'

She held it out for his inspection. Two of the knuckles had blistered.

'That will be okay. Just don't break the blisters.' He walked over to the range. 'What's this?'

'Hot plate,' she said.

He grinned. 'Right.'

He reached into his pocket, took out a small velvet-lined box. 'I've got something for you,' he said.

Her face registered only suspicion.

He shrugged and opened the box. Inside was a gold chain. 'Twenty-two carat,' he said. When she still did not respond, he undid the clasp and laid it on the counter top. 'It's a cross chain,' he said. 'Like your mother would have worn. You put the cross over the link here, and thread it down. Then you wear it around your neck. It saves wear and tear on your hands.'

She did not move.

'Phuong, trust me. You think this is all an elaborate hoax? Some kind of sick practical joke? No one is going to try to take your mother's crucifix away from you. Please. It's a gift. Take it.'

'I don't understand, Uncle.'

'Yes you do. You understand.'

She was staring at the gold chain as if it were a snake, as if it might at any moment rear up and strike at her. But then she slowly opened her fist. She carefully took the crucifix and fixed the chain through the eye.

Their eyes met.

'You want me to put it on for you?'

She nodded.

He picked up the chain and fastened the clasp behind her neck. She ran to her bedroom. After a few seconds he followed. The bedroom door was open, and she was standing in front of the dressing table staring at herself in the mirror. The cross glinted at her throat.

She was crying.

'Thank you very much, kind sir,' she said.

He shrugged his shoulders. 'That's all right, good lady,' he said, and went back to the kitchen to finish unpacking the groceries.

## Seventh Regiment Armoury

'A gold cross doesn't prove anything,' Doyle said.

'No,' Webb agreed, 'it doesn't.'

'But you thought it was her, right from the beginning.'

'Because I was looking for her. I suppose.'

'Did you ever think of getting in touch with Ryan?' Crosby asked him.

'Why?'

Crosby shrugged. 'He would have known the right questions to ask.'

'I knew the right questions to ask.'

'But you didn't want to ask them,' Doyle said.

He smiled at her perspicacity.

'Where was Ryan anyway?'

'He was in Washington. Lee here decided he'd look good in front of the camera instead of behind it.'

Cochrane shrugged. 'He came to me and said he wanted a job that would keep him in one place. We'd just lost our White House correspondent to another network and I had this idea of giving Ryan a screen test. He was a natural.'

'He made him a star overnight.'

'He was good,' Cochrane said, a little defensively.

'Where was Mickey?' Doyle asked.

'She was with him. They got married soon after they got back from the El Salvador jaunt.'

Crosby shook his head. 'Ryan told me once he could never imagine sleeping with just one person for the rest of his life.'

'I think that says more about Ryan than it does about marriage.'

'Then why did he marry her?' Doyle asked.

Cochrane leaned forward. 'In my opinion he genuinely thought he'd had enough. The thing in El Salvador shook him up, badly. For all his recklessness he never believed he was ever in danger. He always thought it would happen to someone else. He even talked about the wounds he took like a small boy boasting about breaking a collarbone. But after Central America he was different. For a while, anyway. He came face to face with his own mortality, really for the first time. I hate to say it, but marriage was just his way of dealing with that.'

'Thank you, Dr Freud,' Crosby said, with a grimace. 'But Ryan was always reckless. That he'd rush into a quick marriage doesn't surprise me in the least. That's not the part I find intriguing. The question is: why did Mickey marry him?'

Webb's face was blank. 'I can't answer that.'

'Women.' Crosby said.

Doyle looked around the group. 'So none of you big, tough guys have ever fallen in love with a woman you knew was totally wrong, had no future for you, and was an utter bitch?'

Crosby grinned, taking the point. 'No, not this week. But last Wednesday when I was in Denver . . .'

Webb was silent, staring into his cognac. 'She loved him.'

'And you?' Doyle said.

'I *didn't* love him,' Webb said, and smiled.

'You loved her.'

'It didn't matter about me. I was the Invisible Man when he came on the scene. He was dangerous. He also had a lot of charm. But that was the trouble with Sean. Women came too easily. It's like being born with money. You never get to value it because you've never had to work for it.'

'Anyone here go to his wedding?' Doyle asked.

'I got an invitation,' Webb said, 'but I had a prior engagement.'

'I went,' Cochrane said. 'So did Croz.'

'Registry office affair,' Crosby said. 'It was like they were both frightened that if there were long-drawn-out arrangements they would change their minds.'

'What happened?' Doyle asked.

Webb shook his head. 'I don't know this part,' he said. He looked at Cochrane. 'You'd better tell the story.'

# VI

## Washington, DC, and Long Island, New York, May 1984

'War is the ambulance chaser's wet dream . . .
the visions of misery and suffering
can also provide a convenient reference point
for putting aside one's own damaged emotions.'

– Paul Harris, freelance photo-journalist, from *Someone Else's War*

# 51

The President of the United States emerged from the diplomatic entrance of the White House and strode towards the helicopter that was waiting for him on the South Lawn. He was greeted with a barrage of questions from the waiting reporters, all of them trying to shout over the roar of the rotors.

'Mr President, what's your reaction to the murder charges being laid against members of the military in El Salvador?'

'Mr President, is the United States still going to support the regime in El Salvador?'

'Mr President, what's your reaction to the news of free elections in Nicaragua?'

Reagan grinned in his good-natured-uncle manner and cupped a hand to his ear to indicate that he couldn't quite hear the questions over the sound of the helicopter engines. Then he pointed to his watch to indicate he was running a little behind schedule.

He saluted the white-gloved Marine at the foot of the helicopter steps and turned at the door to wave expansively, as if to a large crowd of admirers, instead of a huddle of shouting reporters and a clutch of television cameras.

'Jesus Christ!' Ryan swore.

'That's what he *wants* us to think,' a voice said. Ryan turned. It was Mike Nesbitt, the NBC Washington reporter.

'This isn't news, mate. We might as well be doing commercials for the bloke. We're just the film crew. These bastards are writing the script.'

'Did you see what they called you in today's *Post*? The human bullhorn.'

'Yeah, right, they make out the joke is on me, but the joke is on the American public. He makes it look like he's accessible, and he isn't. He hears the questions all right. If he gets one he thinks he can answer, he shouts back his sound-bite soon enough. Shithead!'

'Whoa, boy. That's the President of the United States you're talking about.'

'He's just an out-of-work actor, mate. You would have done better electing Jack Benny. When was the last time this bastard gave us a press conference?'

'Take it easy, Sean. It's all part of the game.'

The helicopter lifted off the lawn and was gone. The gathered news crews began to pack away their equipment. 'They're stuffing us around, Mike. We have to show this on the news because it's the only film we've got and they bloody know it. But what have we got? The President looking busy. And it's all bullshit. I bet right now he's strapped in the dickie seat with his cardie over his knees, snoring. My guess is they fly him up and down the bay all day to keep him out of the fucking way.'

'Take it easy, Sean. You'll give yourself an ulcer.'

Ryan scowled. His cameraman, Danny, looked at him questioningly. 'What now? The usual stand-up shot with the White House in the background?'

Ryan shrugged. Why not? What else was there to do on another frustrating spring morning in Washington?

# 52

The Four Seasons was one of Washington's most elegant hotels, with an address in the fashionable Georgetown district. Lee Cochrane was sprawled in an armchair in the air-conditioned hush of the Garden Terrace lounge. Ryan was escorted to his table by a waitress who took the bottle of Chardonnay from the cooler on the table and poured some of the chilled straw-coloured liquid into a wine glass.

She departed with a longing smile in Ryan's direction.

'I don't know what it is you've got,' Cochrane grunted, 'but she wants some of it.'

'Money,' Ryan said.

Cochrane grinned. 'How's things?'

'Fine.'

'Mickey?'

'Yeah,' Ryan smiled, 'she's good too.'

He settled back in his chair and regarded his new boss and mentor. His most vivid memories of Lee Cochrane were of a scrawny young hippy in a camouflage jacket clutching the floor of their Saigon apartment because he was afraid he was about to fall off it. That Lee Cochrane had somehow metamorphosed into a senior news editor in the New York headquarters of a national television network. He now boasted a power haircut, manicured nails and a Rolex Oyster Perpetual on his wrist. He wore a button-down two-tone silk shirt, a Sulka tie, and an Armani double-breasted wool suit. His leather shoes were Italian and very expensive. Even the grey now appearing at his temples had the appearance of an executive accessory.

Ryan no longer felt comfortable around Lee Cochrane. They were still good friends; it was Cochrane who had got him this job, as well as an exorbitant salary. But Cochrane was also his boss, and was part of the establishment now. Ryan still saw himself as the rebel, the nonconformist, the hard-ass liberal.

When he got back from El Salvador he had asked for, and got, a transfer to the staff at IPA headquarters in Rockefeller Plaza. But being on the news team at a domestic bureau was vastly different to the hot-shot independence he had enjoyed at a tightly manned foreign bureau. He didn't know how to power-dress, his hair was always a little too long, his attitudes too far to the left. He knew from the beginning he would not fit in.

For a while he was content to do the stories about schoolchildren being mugged for their Big Macs, talk his way into crack houses, spend nights in fortress apartment blocks on the Upper West Side with old people besieged by crime. There were week-long assignments to Canada, Mexico, Boston.

But inside two months he found himself staring at the latest news reports from El Salvador and Lebanon and wishing he was back in the game.

It was Cochrane who had rescued him from all that, given him a new challenge and celebrity status in his own industry, real money for the first time in his career. But he was too proud to feel grateful, and so he made jokes about Cochrane behind his back and had nicknamed him Lee Cocaine.

'How you settling in here?' Cochrane asked.

'Fine,' Ryan said. He shifted uneasily in the lounge chair. He had the feeling he was being interrogated. 'Look, mate, where's all this leading?'

'I just wanted to touch base with you, Sean. How long have you been in Washington now?'

'Eleven months.'

'It's a big change from the war zones.'

'I don't miss it. Look, don't bullshit me. You didn't get me here to talk about the weather. You got something to say to me, spit it out. The suits in New York don't like what I'm doing?'

'I told you, Sean, you look good in front of a camera. You've got a natural presence.'

'Well that's good. Right?'

Cochrane swirled the wine around his glass. 'It's just that, well, you're right, there are some things management is worried about.'

'Such as?'

'I don't want you to feel pressured by this.'

'Tell me what it is and I'll let you know if I feel pressured.'

'We've been taking some heat from Washington.'

'The whole of Washington?'

Cochrane smiled. 'Some people in the White House press office.'

'That's good, isn't it? Shows I'm doing my job.'

'To a certain extent. But you've got to remember this isn't a foreign potentate you're dealing with here.'

'No, this is *our* potentate.'

'I'm not saying I agree with the criticism. But this isn't Vietnam or even Central America. You can't deal with Reagan like he was some petty dictator.'

'Even if he behaves like one.'

'This is America. We have to have a little bit of give and take here.'

'Yeah, we give 'em an inch, they'll take a mile.'

'You know what I'm saying.'

'You want me to take a softer line on Reagan. Is that it?'

'The network is worried that your reporting is not showing the proper balance. There's a difference between being tough and being antagonistic. Just lately the Sean Ryan charm has been a bit thin on the ground. You're coming across pretty sour.'

'Well, maybe I should go back to just taking the pictures.'

'Maybe you should. But I thought this was what you wanted.'

Ryan looked away. He watched a young and very attractive blonde in a black cocktail dress glide across the lounge to another table. He had never seen so many beautiful women as he had since being in Washington. Perhaps that old saw about power being the most powerful aphrodisiac was true.

'Can I talk to you as a friend, Sean?'

'I'm listening.'

'I guess I shouldn't be saying this, but what the hell are you doing in this job?'

'Mate, you should know. You gave it to me.'

Cochrane raised a hand in acknowledgment. 'Because you said you wanted it. And I wouldn't have given it to you if I didn't think you had the talent for it. But . . . maybe what you want and what you think you want are two different things.' His fingers beat a tattoo on the armrests of the chair. 'I saw Croz the other day.'

'What's that got to do with anything?'

'He's back working for IPA. He's going to be running their

Far East bureau. He needs a photographer to cover the war in Afghanistan.'

'If you want me out, mate, just say so.'

'When I want you out, I will.'

'So what are you saying, then?'

'You told me when you took this on that you'd had enough of covering combat zones.'

'I have. That's a young bloke's game.'

'Then lighten up, Sean. The White House isn't a combat posting. Take off the flak jacket for the stand-ups and stop treating the President as if he's Joseph Stalin.'

'I think I'd prefer Joseph Stalin.' Ryan took a deep breath, considered what Cochrane had said to him. 'Okay. I'll try and tone things down a bit, all right?'

Cochrane shrugged.

'Mate, remember the Hashish Hilton? I never knew anyone could smoke as much dope as you and still get their stories out on time.'

Cochrane gave him a tight smile. 'Sometimes I miss all that. But the world turns.'

'I guess it does.'

'The thing that bugs me the most,' Cochrane said, 'is that you still don't look a day older.'

'I put it down to clean living. Are you in town overnight? I'll call Mickey. We'll go some place and get a feed.'

Cochrane shook his head. 'I have to get the evening shuttle back to New York. Maybe next time.'

'Yeah, maybe next time.' Ryan looked at his watch. 'I'd better get back to the sweatshop. Schultz is giving a press conference at three o'clock.'

'Think about what I said.'

'Sure. Smile more on camera, don't mention Central America, and kiss Reagan's ass.'

'That's not quite it but it will do.'

'I'll do my best.'

Ryan got up and walked out through the lobby. Editors. They were all bastards. He thought he had been doing well, as well as he knew how. But there seemed to be some sort of conspiracy to get him back out there. Even people like Cochrane couldn't seem to accept the fact that he had changed. He'd given him a lifeline and now he was trying to snatch it back again. The fact that he no longer wanted to play the same old tune seemed to upset them personally, as if the world had shifted on its axis.

Well, bugger them, he wasn't going to do Afghanistan for Crosby, and he wasn't going to give up his job. He'd kiss Reagan's ass if he had to. And Schultz's, even Larry Speakes'. Who could tell? After a while he might even get used to the taste, if not the smell.

# 53

Ryan brought a glass and a bottle of Bushmills out to the green wrought-iron table on his Georgetown patio and sat down. A yellow carriage lamp threw shadows across the paving. The evening was cool, ripe with the scent of flowering jasmine.

He poured a slug of the whisky into his glass and swallowed it down, closing his eyes as the liquor burned the back of his throat. What a day.

He picked up the ashtray on the table, a souvenir from the Continental in Saigon, and stared at it for a long time. He remembered the evenings he and Crosby and Cochrane and Webb had spent on the Shelf, drinking coffee, talking over Saigon politics or their most recent contact in the boonies. The best of times, the worst of times. From inside the house came another fragment of the memory, the electric buzz of Jimi Hendrix on the record player.

He couldn't help it. Cochrane had got to him today. He was right, he did miss the excitement, the danger of the war zones. He had been consumed more and more by his recollections of the rougher, rawer days of Saigon. It was becoming harder to disassemble the component parts of those memories, whether it was nostalgia for his youth or nostalgia for the war itself. The trouble with peace, he decided, is that it's dull. What was there to give you that same buzz you had when you were living out on the edge? He missed the Lee Cochrane he had known in Saigon, despised the Lee Cochrane he now had to deal with as part of his daily life. These days loneliness and longing and emptiness stalked him through the nights, patient and mean-eyed and ruthless.

But he was not going back. He had made a commitment, not only to Mickey, not only to himself, but to Salvador and the dead women and children in the plaza at La Esperanza.

He heard Mickey at the front door. A few moments later Hendrix was abruptly silenced and replaced by a CD. Compact disc technology, something else he hated about the eighties. He preferred his LPs. He liked the dust and the scratching, so evocative of other times.

Mickey appeared, holding a Stoli and orange.

'What's this shit you're listening to?' he said.

'It's the Police.'

'Sounds more like the riot squad.'

'Planet Earth calling Sean Ryan. We have a message for you. The sixties are over. Do you receive?'

He scowled at her.

'Have a bad day?' she asked.

She was still in her nurse's uniform. She looked pale and tired, and when she leaned over his chair to kiss him her clothes smelled of sweat and antiseptic. He didn't like it; it reminded him of too many bad times spent in hospitals.

'I saw Cochrane today.'

'And?'

'And nothing.' He hesitated. She raised an eyebrow. 'He thinks I look too sour lately. Whatever that bloody means. Like charm is everything for a journo, right? Tell that to the boys at the *Sydney Morning Herald*. I mean, what am I, a stand-up comic? I could do El Salvador jokes, right? How many death squads does it take to change a lightbulb?'

'You did have a bad day.'

'Schultz gave a press conference on Central America. Evidently the Russians are going to invade New Mexico some time in August. Helping the El Salvador government massacre half the urban population is a diversionary tactic.'

She poured him another Bushmills.

'How was your day?'

'One T&T gunshot wound, a stabbing, a road trauma DOA, two drug ODs, one of them a twelve-year-old black kid. The usual.'

'You okay?'

'It's cold out here. Let's go inside.'

Ryan went into the kitchen and made coffee. Mickey sat at the breakfast bar. She worked a long strand of hair loose from her ponytail and started to chew it. Ryan watched her for as long as he could stand it.

'What's up?' he said.

'I don't know how to tell you this.'

'What, you're sick? You lost your job? What? Tell me.'

'I think I'm pregnant.'

He stared at her, his expression unchanged. 'Are you sure?'

'No, I'm not sure. I missed my period. I saw the doctor today. I'll get the results back tomorrow.'

He nodded slowly.

'Are you pleased?'

'I'm not sure.'

'Well. Well, that's honest, I guess.'

'The thought of being responsible for another life terrifies me.'

'Me too.'

He made no move towards her. They stood looking at each other, like two total strangers, trapped in the same lift.

'Going down,' she said aloud.

'What?'

'Nothing. It doesn't matter.'

The television was on in the lounge room, a news report of the latest fighting between the Russians and the *mujahideen* in Afghanistan. His eyes moved away from her to the screen.

'How come you never look at me like that?' she said.

'Say again?'

'You just look so horny when you see a Pathan with a handheld missile launcher. I can't compete.'

'Not that again.'

'Look, Sean, I have to know. I mean, if you're not interested in this baby . . .'

The kettle boiled on the stove. He turned away, took it off the range. 'I thought you wanted a kid,' he said.

'But I have to know if you're going to be around when it's born. When it's growing up.'

'Of course I'll be around. Where else would I be?'

'That's the burning question of the hour. Get it right and you win the car.'

'Translation?'

'It means I know more about what's going on in your head than you do.' She stood up. 'I don't want any coffee. I'm bushed. I'm going to have a shower and an early night. I've got another early shift tomorrow. Are you coming to bed?'

He looked vague. 'I'll be up in a while.'

'Don't worry,' she said. 'It may just be a false alarm.'

She went upstairs, decided she would shower in the morning

instead. She stripped off her clothes and fell into bed. It would have been nice to have had him slip between the sheets beside her, just to hold him, have him hold her. It had been so long since she had felt really close to him. She put a hand on her belly, wondered if she could feel a seed growing in there, or if it was all just her imagination. She had wanted a baby so much.

She had thought he had wanted it too; but perhaps she had been wrong. Hard to know what her husband wanted any more.

# 54

The EMTs were running with the gurney towards the emergency room. They had put an inflatable MAST suit on the boy's legs, and had an intravenous line running a unit of plasma into his arm, but the boy had started convulsing. It didn't look good.

Two of the residents were running with them, while the lead EMT shouted the handover.

'He's still breathing!' a nurse shouted.

'I got a pulse!'

'Notify the OR and get me eight units of O neg,' one of the residents screamed.

Mickey ran to the phone, called in the order to the blood bank and put a page on the chief resident. When she got back to the emergency room, two doctors and three nurses were transferring the boy from the gurney to the table.

'Ventilating!'

'Multiple gun shot wounds to the abdomen, chest and legs.'

'Pulse one sixty and thready.'

As Mickey cut away the boy's T-shirt she looked at his face for the first time. Vietnamese.

She froze.

'He's hyperresonant on the right side. I'll decompress.'

'Let's intubate him. Suction!'

*Once she had had a mild concussion when her car was rear-ended at a set of lights on Wisconsin. Witnesses said that she had sat behind the wheel for more than two minutes, not moving, not speaking. The only thing she remembered of the incident was looking up and seeing a traffic cop banging on the car window, asking her to unlock the doors.*

'Suction! I can't see a thing here!'

Now she was back there again. The resident was screaming at her for suction and she had no idea how long she had just been standing there, staring at him. She fumbled around the Mayo stand, but she couldn't think where the suction tubing was, or even what it looked like. As if it were her first time there. She stumbled away from the table.

Suddenly Kath, one of her fellow nurses, was beside her. 'You okay?'

'Suction,' she said.

Kath pushed past her, grabbed the suction and handed it to the resident, who was staring at Mickey wide-eyed in frustration. People were shouting, moving around her. She stared at this scene, numb and out of focus. She looked back at the boy on the gurney, the dark skin, the high cheekbones, almond eyes, the black mop of hair.

*We shouldn't be wasting our fucking time on gooks. There's our own boys dying out there.*

She turned and ran out of the ER.

Kath waited with her in the chow line at the cafeteria. They got coffees and sat down at a table in the corner, on their own.

'Are you okay?'

'Yeah, I'm okay. I'm sorry about what happened in there.'

'It's okay.'

'I froze. I've never done that before.'

'Hey, sometimes . . .' Kath shrugged. '. . . it happens.' But they both knew it didn't, not to an ex-army nurse with fifteen years of triage and ER experience.

How can I explain this? Mickey wondered. I can't just let it go. The chief resident won't just say 'it happens', he'll want a better explanation that that. 'I think I'm pregnant,' she said.

Kath looked almost relieved. 'Mickey . . . that's great . . . does Sean know?'

'Yeah. Yeah, he's really pleased.'

She was pregnant, that was it. It was the hormones. This was the third time something like this had happened to her in as many weeks, but the first time it had affected her work. The other two occasions she had covered up, no one had noticed. She felt she was losing control. It had to be the hormones.

'Maybe you should ask for a little time off.'

'I don't need time off.'

Kath bit her lip. 'You don't look so good.'

Mickey felt the tears come, fat and hot. She hadn't cried in years.

A little in '76, when her father died, but even then she had held back the dam waters. Some of the flood had spilled over the top, but the walls had held. Now she could feel those same walls creaking and groaning. No, I can't let this happen. When they break I have to be at home in my own house, doors and windows locked shut. I can't let anyone see this. A wave of panic reared at her from a calm sea and she wanted to run.

She sipped her coffee, took control again, fought it back. 'What I said about Sean, being pleased. That wasn't true.'

'He doesn't want the baby?'

'He says he wants a baby. We've been trying, you know. I mean, when he's not too tired and I'm not too tired.' A brittle laugh. 'But then when I said I thought I was . . .' She shrugged. '. . . you should have been there. Seen his face.'

Kath reached out and took her hand. 'Mickey . . .'

Mickey took her hand away and wiped at her eyes, a quick, impatient gesture. 'Well. No one ever said it was going to be easy.'

Deep breaths. Win back control.

'Maybe he's finding it hard, dealing with the pressure,' Kath said. 'Did you see the cartoon in the *Post* this morning?'

'Yeah, I saw it.' Ryan had been depicted clinging to the wing of an airborne America One with one hand, while with the other he thrust a microphone towards the President through the window. *Mr President, what do you think of the current situation in El Salvador?*

'Next thing he'll be in *Doonesbury*.'

'I don't think any of that bothers him. I honestly don't believe he gives a damn what anyone says. I wish he did care. I wish he would play up to it a little. At least then I would know what he wanted.'

She looked into Kath's eyes, saw both sympathy and the special kind of satisfaction that comes when envy dies. She knew having Sean Ryan as a husband had conferred on her a vicarious celebrity and that many of the nurses – and perhaps even a couple of the female doctors – envied her.

'I guess it ain't that easy being you, huh?' Kath said.

'It shouldn't be this damned hard.' She realised she had raised her voice and that a couple of the interns were staring at her. She stared back and they turned away, embarrassed.

Could she trust Kath with her private feelings? Probably not. But what the hell, she needed to let off a little of the steam. She leaned across the table, lowered her voice. 'I don't know what he wants. I have no idea. He doesn't talk to me.'

Kath shrugged. 'Maybe you're lucky. My Bob tells me everything. He'd give me a blow-by-blow of his bowel movements if I let him.' She was trying to be light, perhaps uncomfortable with this new level of intimacy, but Mickey was not in the mood to let her off the hook. After all, Kath was the one who had volunteered to listen.

'What do I do, Kath? How do I get him to talk to me?' She let the question hang, knowing it was unfathomable. 'I don't think he's ever opened up to anyone. His deepest thoughts and feelings just stay bottled up in there. He's a human camera. He sees, he records, but I don't know if he feels anything.'

Kath, who had nurtured a number of her own romantic fantasies around Mickey's story of how she had met Sean Ryan, how he had gone on to become one of Washington's hot-shot television reporters, swallowed hard and tried to absorb this new perspective. Mickey and Sean had seemed to be the happiest, wildest couple she knew, and up to this moment she had been insanely jealous of Mickey Ryan. Now she had been allowed a glimpse behind the façade and she was stunned, and even a little angry, that her illusions had been torn down.

'Have you thought of talking to anyone about this?'

'You mean counselling? Can you imagine a guy like Sean going to counselling?' She thought: *It's the last thing I want, anyone going near my head. One thing leads to another*.

'So what are you going to do?'

'I don't know,' Mickey said. But the truth was, she did know what she would do. She would build the dam walls a little higher and try to pretend the last fifteen years had not happened to her. She would try to forget about Nam, forget about the wasted years in Walter Reed and San Francisco, forget about the year in the Central American jungle. But if she trashed all that, how much of her life was left to remember, to validate as worthwhile? A few years of adolescence spent in awe and envy of her sister, and a decade of childhood. Well, at least her childhood had been good.

Better start living soon, Mickey, or it will all be gone.

'He's going to leave me, Kath.'

'What? Has he said anything?'

'I just feel it.'

'Mickey, not every guy is happy about children at first. That doesn't mean he's going to —'

'I know Ryan. I know what goes on in his head.'

Kath touched her hand. 'Look, you've got to talk to someone about this.'

Mickey ignored her. 'It was a mistake from the beginning. We were like survivors in a shipwreck. We were worn out and exhausted and we saw this bit of driftwood coming by so we reached out and hung on. The bit of driftwood was each other.'

'Mickey, you need a few days out of here.'

'Maybe.' She could be right, Mickey thought. Perhaps I need more than just a few days away. Why am I still in ER rooms after all these years? We rush them in on gurneys and some of them die and some survive and then they go upstairs to surgery and mostly we never hear from them again. Every day is like reading the first chapter of a book and throwing it away. So what am I looking for? Why am I still replaying the same scenes over and over?

They looked at each other, neither of them knowing what to say. Kath shrugged helplessly.

'I'll work it out,' Mickey said.

She was stopped at a red light on Wisconsin. It was late and she was tired and she had a pulsing headache. The radio was playing 'Mrs Robinson'. Some hidden memory made the connection between the song and one of the parties at Bien Hoa and her mind inevitably returned to Vietnam. For a moment she could even smell the familiar odours of the base hospital: aviation fuel from the helicopters, rotting vegetation from the jungle, the starker taints of urine and antiseptics. She wound down the window for some fresh air.

Overhead she heard the whump-whump-whump of helicopter blades. Just an aerial police patrol, she reminded herself. But her body reacted to another memory, and again, from the calm sea, the big wave came in broiling whitewater panic. She saw two teenagers running towards her Prelude. They were holding Chicom rifles and shouting to each other excitedly in a high-pitched babble of Vietnamese. Viet Cong.

She fumbled with the door, jumped out of the car and started to run.

She heard the helicopter circle overhead, a government gunship on the lookout for FMLN. They had seen her running across the open ground and they were coming back for her. She weaved across the road in a low, crouching run, heard the blaring of a car horn, waited for the impact of the bullets.

For some reason they held off firing. She found cover behind a wall. She peered back down the street but the two VC were gone. She had lost them. She looked up, searching the sky for the Huey, saw the white arc of its floodlights two blocks away.

Now the whine of a cherry-top as it turned off Wisconsin, red beacons flashing. A uniformed patrol officer ran across the road, holding a flashlight. He saw her crouching behind the wall and stopped, one hand on his service revolver.

'Are you all right, ma'am?'

She fumbled in her pockets for her identity papers. She had to prove she was American. She tried to think what time the curfew was in this city.

The patrolman's partner was at the cherry-top talking quietly into his radio. Perhaps calling up air support.

'Ma'am, are you okay?' the patrolman repeated. He had stopped, wary now. The beam from his flashlight blinded her for a moment. She shielded her eyes and turned away. She realised she was sweating. She imagined someone finding her body in the morning, out on the base perimeter, on the wire, or on the lava flow at El Playón. She wondered what her father would say. It would kill him.

'I can't find the suction,' she said.

'Ma'am? What did you say, ma'am?'

The curtain lifted. She started, as if waking from a dream. Suddenly the night was cool again and the sweat dried rapidly on her skin. She felt foolish. Like that time she had been rear-ended on Wisconsin. Ma'am, are you okay? Can you unlock the door, please? Her heart was banging in her chest, her mouth was dry, her tongue gummed to the roof of her mouth.

'Ma'am, please come out from behind that wall.'

Mickey stood up, her hands limp at her side. 'I'm sorry, Officer,' she said. 'I'm quite all right. Really.'

'I saw you run out of your car back there. Someone chasing you?'

How could she explain to him?

The helicopter was still around somewhere. She heard the thump of the rotors in the distance, saw a beam of light heading east towards the Capitol. 'Have you ever heard of Vietnam?'

He seemed to relax. 'Shoot, is that what's bothering you? I get the same feeling sometimes when I hear those damn things.' He took his hand away from his revolver and took a few steps closer. 'You were there?'

'I was a nurse at Bien Hoa in '69.'

He nodded, as if he understood. 'You all right now, ma'am?'

'I've made a fool of myself.'

He chuckled. 'You got out of that car like a scalded cat.' He called to his partner in the cherry-top. 'It's okay, Ray!' He turned back to her. 'Live far from here?'

'Not far. I've got a townhouse on P Street.'

'I'll walk you back to your car, ma'am.'

'No, really, it's all right. I'm sorry I've been a nuisance.'

'It's no problem, ma'am.'

He walked her back to the corner. The Prelude was still parked at the lights, the driver's door swinging open. She felt humiliated. You're losing it, Mickey. You're heading for a breakdown.

She took deep breaths. Calm down, Mickey, calm down.

'You take it easy now,' the policeman said. 'Wind up the windows and turn on the radio. A little jazz is good for the soul.'

She felt outrageously grateful to the man for his kindness. Embarrassed, she jumped into the car, shut the door, snapped the belt buckle and almost drove straight off through the red light.

The patrolman leaned in through the window. 'Now you just take it easy, okay?' he said.

'I'll be fine,' she assured him.

For God's sake. Just let me get home!

She ran up the stoop, the old-fashioned gaslights throwing yellow pools of light on the steps. As she fumbled for her keys she heard the rustling of leaves in the night wind, like the murmurings of distant voices. She imagined there were people watching her, soldiers in olive fatigues. She looked quickly up and down the street. Empty.

She locked the door and rushed up to the bathroom. She turned on the jacuzzi, undressed, and lowered herself into the hot, swirling, eucalyptus-scented water. She lay back and rested her head on the marble rim of the tub. Rivulets of sweat started to run down her face.

She imagined her life, an intricate maze of sandcastles painstakingly constructed by a child on an empty beach. The seas crashing in, battering them away.

# 55

They drove out through Loudon County towards Leesburg, past the trim white fences of thoroughbred horse studs. Huntingdon Lodge was a mid-nineteenth-century plantation house set in fifty-six acres of rolling hills. As Ryan drove through the gates he saw a line of cars stretched along the gravel drive, waiting to be parked. He pulled up behind a new Volvo; in the rear-vision mirror he saw a red BMW 525i. Here he was in a white Mercedes coupé. To think he had spent a large part of his life getting around in a Mini Moke with bullet holes in the coachwork.

'What's wrong?' Mickey asked.

He didn't answer her. He didn't know the answer himself. Instead he quickly checked his appearance in the driving mirror; a full head of dark hair, straying over his collar, a clean-shaven face that somehow contrived to look much the same as it had ten years before. Next year he would be forty and his colleagues all told him he looked ten years younger. Dorian Gray, some of them called him. His contemporaries were losing their hair and their bellies were sagging, but Sean Ryan was unaltered by the passing years. Something in the genes, he supposed. He guessed his father might have worn well, too, if he hadn't drunk himself to death.

He brushed some imagined lint from his tuxedo, consulted the Rolex on his wrist. By all accounts a successful man, he supposed. Not outrageously so – he had never grown accustomed to spending the obscene amounts of money they now paid him. Still. It was a long way from an outback wheat town in Queensland. He had taken a lot of risks to get here and he knew he deserved all of it. So why this restlessness, why did he feel as if he had thrown it all away?

'It's all bullshit,' he said.

'What?'

'Life. It's all bullshit.'

Mickey raised her eyebrows. 'You should write that thought

down. One day it might find itself in a book of quotations. That's not going to be the theme of your speech tonight? These ladies are from North Neck, remember. They might not appreciate that kind of language.'

He looked at her out of the corner of his eye. A sky-blue silk gown, blonde hair teased with mousse, lips wet with pale pink gloss. Radiant; on the surface at least. Earlier, before the application of the make-up, she had appeared pale and fractious. Perhaps the baby, he remembered. The baby. Another suffocating dose of reality.

But this was what he wanted, wasn't it? When Buford had held the gun to his head that night in La Esperanza, this was what he had told himself he wanted. This was the bargain he had made. So why was he so scared?

If it wasn't for the baby, perhaps they could rethink this. But he could not back out now. He owed her that much.

Spider would like this, if he knew. He would probably think there was some symmetry to it.

'You'd think they'd let the guest of honour park first,' Mickey said.

'I may be the guest of honour tonight but they don't want me to forget I'm still just a journo the rest of the time.'

They pulled up at the forecourt, and a door opened for Mickey. A valet came around the car to Ryan's side and handed him a chit. A liveried footman in a black top hat led them inside. 'Welcome to Huntingdon Lodge, Mr Ryan,' he said, and then, *sotto voce*, 'I watch you on the television all the time.'

'What's it like being married to a celebrity?' Ryan whispered to Mickey as they stepped inside.

'It sucks,' she said, and he laughed, but then he saw the look on her face and he realised she meant it.

They walked into the cocktail bar. Mickey sat down on a bar stool and Ryan stood beside her. She ordered Stoli and orange, he ordered Bushmills with ice. There was a long silence.

'Are you nervous?' she asked him.

'I hate talking in front of crowds.'

'You've got an audience of fifty million every night of the week.'

'No, I have an audience of two, my cameraman and my soundman. If the other fifty million yawn or pick their noses or fall asleep with their heads in their dinner I don't have to watch.'

She grinned. 'You'll charm the pants off them.'

'Just the women, I hope.'

He looked around the room; the house had been decorated to resemble a colonial inn, warmly lit with lamps. There were hunting prints on the wall, a few Victorian antiques and a stone fireplace with a log fire.

He turned his attention back to Mickey. Something not right there. He noticed a tremor in her hand as she held her glass, and she was drinking too fast. She was always uncomfortable in these surroundings; she had never grown accustomed to playing the Washington socialite. 'You're the star,' she had told him more than once. 'I'm just a nurse.' But then he had not married her because she was glamorous. Which begged the question: why had he married her?

But he suspected it was more than just the occasion that had unsettled her. Perhaps it was being pregnant. Hormones.

'What about you?' he said. 'Are you nervous?'

'Why should I be nervous? I don't have to stand up and bare my soul to a couple of hundred blue-rinsed Loudon County matrons.'

'I'm not going to bare anything.'

'That's a relief.'

'I'm here to talk about my life as a correspondent in the world's trouble spots. Including Washington.'

'Tracing the trouble back to its source.'

He smiled. 'Very good.'

She put her glass on the counter. 'One more before we go in.'

He was still only halfway through his Scotch. 'I thought it was my breed that were supposed to be the drinkers.'

'Australians are all pussies. Same again.'

He caught the barman's eye and ordered another Stoli. He decided to sit on his Bushmills. He didn't want to slur his words. Not good for the public image.

'Can I ask you a personal question?'

He braced himself. 'Sure.'

'Are you having an affair?'

'Oh, that personal.'

'I don't mean to pry. But I guess being the wife of a celebrity has made me a little audacious.'

'No.'

'No what?'

'No, sir.'

'Don't be cute with me, Sean. I have to know. Is that a no, not at the moment, or a no, not ever. Or is it a no, but I'm thinking about it?'

'This is not a good time to discuss this.'

'I'm not mad at you, Sean,' she said, softly. 'I just need to work a few things out right now.'

He looked at his watch. 'I'm wanted elsewhere.'

'What I mean is, before you came to Washington you were dangerous, you were charming, you were good-looking. Now you're all those things and you're a highly paid television star as well. I can understand that puts a lot of strain on the best of intentions.'

'You're missing the point.'

'What is the point?'

'I don't know. I think I missed it too.'

Mickey finished her drink and they crossed the lobby and went into the dining hall; Irish linen on heavy oak tables, the clink of crystal, heavy silver. White jacketed waiters moved among the crowd.

Mrs Carson, president of the Loudon County Literary Guild, swept towards him, arms open.

'Abandon hope, all ye who enter here,' Mickey whispered, and slipped away.

'Well. Sean Ryan! I'm so delighted you could be with us tonight. Everyone is so excited to meet you.' She embraced him as if he were a long-lost nephew, and his nose twitched at the cloying scent of perfume. You can have too much of a good thing, he thought. 'You look even more handsome than you do on television.' She indicated a plump, expensively dressed woman at her side. 'This is Mrs Havermeyer, our treasurer. She's your greatest fan.'

Oh, Christ.

'You are a naughty boy though,' Mrs Havermeyer said.

'Why's that?' he said, feeling his features set into a death's head mask.

'You have been saying some very unkind things about our Mr Reagan lately.' It was as if he had insulted one of the family, Ryan thought. Which in a way he had. 'But we forgive you.'

Ryan looked up, panicked. Mickey was talking to an olive-skinned waiter with a designer ponytail. She took a flute of *cuvée brute* from the tray, raised her glass in a toast and smiled.

There was salmon and scallop mousse with lobster sauce, followed by venison game pie and *crêpes flambées*. Afterwards Ryan spoke for half an hour, drawing on a well-rehearsed store of anecdotes filed away for occasions such as this, sprinkling his monologue with names such as Sihanouk and Carter, Schultz and Begin, Cao Ky and Reagan, and with place-names as evocative as Beirut and Saigon and Peshawar and Jerusalem. Then he fielded their questions for almost an hour and finally sat down, exhausted, to rapturous applause.

Now the waiters were drifting among the tables, clearing away the empty coffee cups and wine glasses and creased linen napkins. As guest of honour Ryan felt obliged to stay until at least half of the guests had departed, after first graciously receiving their personal thanks and admiration and small platitudes. He had strategically positioned himself at the door, and was looking desperately around the room for Mickey so that he could make his escape.

'Mr Ryan.'

He looked around, saw a small dark-haired woman in a rather plain blue woollen dress. She had a tired look about her. There were flecks of grey in her hair, and she had large sad eyes that were accentuated by her thick spectacles. She wore little jewellery, just a pair of pearl earrings and a small emerald brooch. In fact Ryan thought she seemed rather underdressed, considering the tone set by many of her contemporaries that evening.

'I did enjoy your talk.'

'Thank you,' Ryan said, and surreptitiously checked his watch. Where was Mickey?

'I especially enjoyed what you said about Vietnam. I think it was important what you and your fellow correspondents did. It meant a lot to the boys over there.'

Ryan was tired of the small talk. 'I think people see the war in a different perspective now,' he said.

'I think all you people were very brave. You must have been so relieved when it was all over.'

'Not really. I enjoyed it.'

She stared at him, her confusion very evident.

Ryan felt suddenly rebellious and belligerent. He was sick of his own empty posturing. He had an urgent need to shock someone. With the truth. 'I'd go back there tomorrow if they decided to have a rematch.'

'Why would you want to go back to a place like that?'

'I had a good time. We got to play with guns, ride in helicopters, see things getting blown up. If you've never done a combat landing in a C-130 you haven't lived. Major pucker factor. It's like riding the biggest rollercoaster in the world with the most fantastic firework display ever staged going on around you. To be brutally frank with you, I loved every minute of it.'

'My son died in Vietnam,' the woman said, and walked away.

Mickey emerged from the ladies' rest room. 'What's the matter?' she said.

'What?'

'You look like you've seen a ghost.'

'I'm fine. Where the hell have you been?'

'Sorry, did I miss something here? Have I done something wrong?'

'Let's just get out of here.'

'Are you upset?'

'Why the fuck would I be upset?' Oh, this is wrong, he thought. Why was it, when a man felt like shit, he always took it out on his wife? Perhaps that was why he had never got married before, the very same reason he did not want to look after other people when he was out in the field. Sometimes it was hard enough just taking care of yourself. 'Let's just leave, please.'

That was stupid, Sean. Lie to them, lie to yourself. But don't ever say you enjoy it. That wasn't the only reason you were there. You and Spider and Cochrane and Crosby and the rest *did* make a difference. Someone had to be there to record the war and show up the lies for what they were and help turn the tide of opinion in America. But don't tell people the rest of it. Don't try to explain how you get off on the taste of your own fear, and that the fact of your own survival afterwards is the biggest high there is.

Don't tell people that part of it.

*Stupid!*

# 56

Ryan threw back the bedclothes, swung his legs out of bed and padded across the carpet to the window. Outside, the street lamps were still on, but the sun had risen over Washington, throwing a weak and dappled light through the trees. On Wisconsin cars were already heading towards the parkways and train stations. Washington was on the move.

Mickey was dead to the world. She had worked late again at the hospital. God knows why. They didn't need the money; he had told her that.

He sat down on the edge of the bed and watched her as she slept. She was wearing a white T-shirt as a nightgown. She said she never felt comfortable in lingerie but would never sleep naked. She had told him that when she first got to Vietnam they had sent her up to the 71st Evac at Pleiku, and one night they had come under mortar fire. She had leaped out of bed and run straight into the nearest bunker, and was then forced to spend the entire twenty minutes of the bombardment crouched in the dark stark naked, surrounded by a dozen sweating soldiers and doctors. Since then she had vowed never to sleep in the raw again.

She mumbled something in her sleep, and then he heard her grinding her teeth. Another nightmare. She frowned, and a lock of hair fell across her face. He brushed it away and shook her gently to rouse her from the bad dream. Her eyes opened for a moment, she frowned again, then rolled on her side and went back to sleep, but more peacefully now.

He kissed her lightly on the forehead, then got up and slipped on his dressing gown. He went downstairs and made a cup of strong black coffee. While it was filtering he found and stripped the *Washington Post* and the *New York Times* from their plastic wrappers.

He took his coffee on to the patio. The surface was wet with dew.

He shivered in the chill morning air. He held steaming coffee close to his face and opened the *Times*.

*US CONSIDERING*
*EMERGENCY ARMS FOR EL SALVADOR*

*IPA, Washington: Secretary of State George Schultz said today the Reagan administration is considering giving El Salvador emergency military aid, without waiting for Congress to act, so its army can maintain pressure on the insurgents in the coming election period . . .*

He finished the article and threw the newspaper on the table in disgust. Whoever had written the story, or whoever had edited it, had made no attempt to balance Schultz's view of the world with a less partisan viewpoint. They had given the Reagan administration exactly the story they wanted.

Everything he had told himself in Loudon County about the Vietnam experience was wrong. He and his fellow correspondents had changed nothing, and nothing had changed. They were going down the same road as Vietnam, making the same mistakes, committing the same unpardonable sins. The irony of modern America; here was a country founded on the principles of democracy, yet it was exporting right-wing politics around the world because it did not believe democracy was strong enough to stand on its own. But his adopted countrymen didn't like to hear that, especially from an outsider. Perhaps that was his disadvantage here. No matter how long he lived and worked in this country he had still been born somewhere else, and Americans didn't like to hear criticisms of themselves from their own commentators, never mind from a wild colonial boy like himself.

He abandoned his coffee and went back upstairs to shower. He stood with his back against the cold tiles and let the hot needles of water play on his scalp. He thought about his day. Start in Larry Speakes' office, 9.15, for the press briefing, then spend the rest of the day digging around for the real story, which would be everything Speakes hadn't told them. Just like the Five O'clock Follies.

He didn't think he could do this any more.

* * *

She was back in Bien Hoa. They had just finished a mas-cal, and Mickey stumbled bone-weary from the ER into the room where they had put the expectants. In the dream the room stretched for ever, row upon row of gurneys, jungle boots, and torn and bloodied fatigues. She looked down at one of the litters and there was the Vietnamese boy from a few days before. His eyes blinked open and he smiled. He was holding a grenade.

He took out the pin.

She sat bolt upright in the bed, her body slick with cold sweat. It took her a few moments to remember where she was. She looked out of the window at the dirty stain of dawn creeping up the Georgetown sky, heard the muted roar of the traffic.

A thud of rotors overhead. She heard someone in the hallway. *Mickey, hurry, mas-cal.* She swung her legs out of bed and threw open the door, expecting to see the other nurses rushing past in their olive-green uniforms. But the landing was empty.

She heard Ryan in the shower.

She remembered. She was in Washington. It was 1984. The helicopter she had heard overhead was just the police traffic control.

Her heart was racing. She leaned on the hallway railing and took a deep breath. Calm down.

Christ, she was coming apart.

She went downstairs to the kitchen. There was coffee on the range. She poured some, straight and black, into a china mug and took two muffins out of the refrigerator. Her head was pounding. She felt as if she hadn't slept at all.

Why now? Why were the dreams coming back now, after all these years? She thought she was through all that. The war was years ago.

She put the muffins in the toaster.

They wouldn't go down. They wouldn't go down. *They wouldn't go down!*

Ryan stared at the orderly rows of suits and shirts hanging in the wardrobe, a regiment of respectability arrayed for his inspection. He felt the soft blossoming of contempt. A talking head in a suit. Everything he had once despised. We become what we hate.

He heard a crash from downstairs, the sound of breaking crockery, splintering glass.

Mickey.

He ran out on to the landing, took the stairs two at a time, stood gaping in the kitchen doorway.

Mickey stood in the middle of the kitchen in her T-shirt, her arms folded, biting her lip. She was staring at the floor, eyes huge, like a gawker at a bad road accident. The toaster lay at her feet; the coffee percolator and her coffee cup had been swept from the counter and lay in a litter of glass and splintered china and coffee grounds on the tiled floor.

'What happened?' he said.

'The muffins wouldn't go down,' she said. 'I can't stand it when the muffins won't go down.'

He took a cautious step towards her, gently wrapped his arms around her. She was stiff and unyielding. It was like holding a storefront mannikin. 'The muffins won't go down,' she repeated, in a voice that betrayed both wonderment and fear at what she had done.

'Shh, it's all right,' he said, knowing that it was not all right. He hoped this was just the baby. Just hormones. He hoped it was not what he thought it was; because if it was still Vietnam, then Mickey was in big trouble.

# 57

They had built the press room over what had once been President Franklin Delano Roosevelt's indoor swimming pool. Over the years the press contingent had expanded and now the room was very cramped indeed. All the networks had booths at the back of the room, originally designed for two people, but now they all accommodated at least four, seated side by side along narrow counter tops crammed with typewriters, word processors, printers, newspapers, press releases, make-up kits, books, televisions, radios and empty coffee cups. Every morning the reporters and their crews had to pick their way over video cameras, thick television cables and recording equipment to find a seat in the briefing room.

Normally it was bedlam, but when Ryan got to work that morning there was a funereal hush around the room, knots of people talking in tight-knit groups. He found his soundman, Larry Norstadt. 'Who died?' he said.

'Nobody died. Yet.'

'What's going on?'

'It's Lee.'

'Cochrane? What happened?'

'He's in ICU in Mount Sinai. Massive coronary. They had to resuscitate him twice in the ER.'

'Oh Christ.'

Larry shook his head. 'He's only thirty-nine. Same as you.'

'Yeah. Right. Thanks.' He looked around. The news had stunned everyone. Everyone knew Lee Cochrane; he had been around a long time. A few of them were staring at Ryan, waiting to see how he would react. Cochrane was not only his boss. It was common knowledge that they had been close once, that they had been in Vietnam together.

Well, screw them. He wasn't a show.

He looked at his watch. Larry Speakes would be holding the first press briefing of the day just after nine and Ryan wanted to nail him on the latest developments in El Salvador. Speakes was also expected to announce a presidential press conference for that evening.

'I'll call the office and make sure someone sends him some flowers from us,' he said, loud enough for them all to hear. 'Okay, let's get to work.'

Reagan always held his press conferences in the evening. It gave him a larger, more immediate audience and prevented the networks from analysing what he had said and then presenting it to the public in their own way in the early evening news. His press aides argued that this prevented network bias; the truth of it was that in the live conferences only Reagan's downhome charm came through. In any edited version the substance of what he was saying was more evident, and could not be disguised by his style.

Reagan gave far fewer press conferences than his predecessor, Carter, and they had therefore become a major event. Some suggested more cynically that they were the best theatre they had seen all year.

The demands of television meant that the room was lit like a sports stadium. There was a battery of lights across the top of the stage, two more banks on aluminium standards to the left and right of the rostrum. In front of the lectern were crammed twenty rows of seats, rising towards the rear where the camera crews fought for space among the cables and scaffolding. Ryan took his place in the very front row, which was reserved for the media VIPs: the talking heads from the major television networks and the reporters from the four major wire services, Reuters, AP, UPI and IPA, and other luminaries such as Sam Donaldson, Andrea Mitchell and Bob Scheiffer.

Ryan was finding it hard to concentrate on the job. He kept thinking about Cochrane. He had phoned his assistant at the network office in town and arranged for her to send him a packet of cigarettes and a hamburger from McDonald's along with a get well card. Inside the card he told her to write *You're fired* above Ted Turner's name. Hell, if it was him lying in hospital the last thing he would want is to be treated like an invalid. He would want one of his mates to give him a hard time and make him want to get well again so he could give them the finger.

But the news had shaken him. As Larry had said, Cochrane was the same age as he was. Dying in a war was one thing; that was fate or whatever. You took calculated risks and sometimes your luck ran out. But a heart attack was different. He had never considered death sneaking up in that way. No bullets, no mortar explosions, nothing; just whack, one day a pain in the chest and you're down and that's it, that's all you ever get.

And where would he be when that happened? Standing on a White House lawn doing stand-ups to a nation that didn't give a damn about anything except abortion and lower taxes? Or on the way to work, worrying about the mortgage on his apartment in Georgetown and the loan for the new baby furniture?

He realised he didn't want that, didn't want the responsibility of another living creature depending on him. He didn't want to be reluctant to take risks because he had someone to worry about at home. If he was going to die he wanted it to be on his own terms, not taken from behind by a blocked artery or some bubble floating around in his brain.

He didn't want to die bored.

He forced his attention back to the job at hand. There was an air of expectancy in the auditorium. Perhaps the people still loved Reagan, but it would be a poor night if they could not rely on the Teflon President for at least one major gaffe.

A voice boomed over the loudspeaker: 'Ladies and gentlemen, the President of the United States.'

A doorway opened halfway down the main hall and Reagan emerged, dressed in a dark grey suit, entering the auditorium along a long carpeted hallway and through a set of double doors. Another wonderful piece of theatre, Ryan thought.

He found it hard to concentrate on Reagan's speech, which consisted mainly of a policy statement on Central America. He delivered it with an actor's faultless style, lending some dignity to rhetoric that painted Latin American politics as a shooting match between the cowboys and the Indians.

When the President indicated that he would field questions, Ryan patiently waited his turn. Reagan finally smiled and pointed in his direction.

He stood up. 'Mr President, why is this administration supporting a regime in El Salvador that routinely tortures and terrorises and murders its own civilians and leaves their bodies lying in the street?'

He heard a sharp intake of breath from the reporters around him. It was not the sort of question any president wanted levelled at him on live prime-time national television. He saw Reagan's minders and press aides glaring at him. If looks could kill? But then they could not kill him, however much they might like to. Freedom of speech and freedom of the press was what democracy was all about. Some of the people on the other side of the podium might have preferred it otherwise, but they were stuck with it.

Reagan stumbled on his answer, as he often did, responding with the usual mumbling, incoherent phrases that the American electorate appeared to love. He mentioned the forthcoming national elections in El Salvador and quantitative progress in human rights and the threat posed by Cuban-backed guerrillas. Ryan felt his frustrations boiling over. He did the unthinkable.

He shouted him down.

'Mr Reagan, this is all bull and you know it. We are going down the same blind path as we did in Vietnam. We are backing a blatantly fascist regime for our own imagined short-term political gains. Is this or is this not true?'

A breathless moment, flashbulbs popping, consternation on either side of the podium. Reagan blinked and stared, looking for all the world like an old man being asked to get off the bus because he did not have enough money for the fare. Ryan saw one of the senior press aides pull a Secret Service agent aside and point to him. They were going to try to throw him out. Well, that would make good television, especially if he resisted.

'You've really screwed up this time, Ryan,' one of the print journalists from the *Post* hissed in his ear.

'This is all crap,' he said, loud enough for the microphones to hear, and he stood up and walked out of the room. Even as he did it he knew he would never be back. He didn't think he would miss it at all.

# 58

Mickey stood in the middle of the living room, staring at the television. She was still in her nurse's uniform. She backed into the kitchen, keeping her eyes on the screen. It was the Reagan press conference, and she knew Ryan would be there somewhere. She unscrewed the cap from a bottle of Stoli, found a carton of orange juice in the refrigerator. Finally she recognised Sean's voice, noticed the badgering tone creeping in, saw the consternation on the President's face.

'Oh, Jesus,' she said.

She heard a commotion off camera, but the news editor kept with the President. She couldn't watch any more. She flicked off the remote control and went upstairs to the bathroom.

She turned on the hot tub, let her clothes slide to the floor.

It had happened to her again, in the People's Drug on Wisconsin. She had heard a car backfire in the street, and immediately she was on her face in the aisle, waiting for the mortar rounds to hit. When she looked up the rest of the customers were just standing and staring at her, mouths agape.

She couldn't ignore this any more. She would have to do something.

The fact was, she couldn't get past this, she didn't think she could be normal again. She had seen too much, done too much, hoped for too much. She had seen men and women at their best and at their very worst, had held young men's hands as they died, held other nurses in her arms as they wept for some young soul they had lost after perhaps long weeks suffering with burns or terrible wounds. She had formed friendships with complete strangers of an intensity she had never experienced before, and had found more in herself than she ever dreamed existed.

Now everything she had ever done outside Vietnam seemed totally worthless and false. Fourteen years ago she had stepped from a freefire zone to the twilight zone. She had made it back, but as an alien, and she had never again found anywhere in her own country where she could fit in. She had spent all those intervening years running away from that.

She had made it back to the peace only to find mortgages and trim lawns and shopping centres and singles bars and loneliness, a place where no one really gave a damn about anyone else. No one really wanted to listen to her war stories, which were, in essence, the story of her life. She was utterly confused by the dilemma in her soul; she had hated Vietnam, but now she wanted to go back, just for one hour, to experience again that communion with her fellow men and women she had never been able to regain.

But there was no way to go back, and so all that remained for her from that war were the scars and the terrible, terrible guilt.

When Ryan got home he found Mickey in the hot tub, an empty bottle of Stoli rolling across the green marble tiles. Her hair was loose around her face, her eyes heavy-lidded, her cheeks flushed. 'Way to go, you son of a gun,' she said, slurring the words.

Drunk. Never mind, let it go. 'You saw it?'

'Just like *High Noon*. The showdown between the bad guy in the grey suit and the good guy with the notebook and the harassed expression. A man's gotta do what a man's gotta do.'

'I really showed him, right?'

'You sure got him good and pissed. We'll probably get nuked in our sleep. You don't mess around with Ronnie, you know.'

'Fuck Reagan.' He dropped his jacket to the floor, looped his tie over his head, and sat down on the edge of the jacuzzi to rip off his shoes and socks.

'Think you better send in your I quit letter before the acceptance letter gets here.'

'I already did.'

'What did Lee say?'

'Lee wasn't there. He's in Mount Sinai hooked up to a life support machine.' Ryan peeled off his shirt and pants and shorts. 'Why do they call it a cardiac infarct? I hate that word. Why not a heart attack? Then everyone knows what they fucking mean.'

He got into the scented and bubbling water, put both arms along the cool marble and laid his head back, resting it on the rim.

'You're kidding.'

'They don't joke about heart attacks. Not even in New York. *Especially* not in New York.'

'Christ, he was . . .'

'Yeah, same age as me. The point's been made.'

'Is that what this evening was all about?'

'Partly.'

He felt her toes stroke his groin under the water. 'I was proud of you tonight.' When he did not respond she added: 'I like a man who can stand up to the President of the United States.'

He pushed her foot away.

'Uh-oh. I did something wrong again.'

'It's not you.'

'Why do guys always say that when they can't get it up for you any more? If it was Nastassia Kinski lying here in the hot tub naked and you couldn't get it up for her, would you still say "It's not you" in that condescending voice?'

He closed his eyes. 'I don't need this.'

She splashed some of the water on to her face. 'I have a confession.'

'You do?'

'My pregnancy test. It was negative.'

He looked at her in wonderment. 'What?'

'Sorry.'

'You mean all this time . . .'

'I wanted to know how you'd react.'

He was silent for a moment, absorbing this information. 'And how did I react?'

'Like an asshole.'

'Right.'

'I wish you'd put your fist through the door. Hit your head against a wall. Pulled out a revolver and shot yourself in the head. That would have been more honest.'

'I was trying to accommodate your feelings.'

'Sorry. Is English your second language?'

'I knew you wanted a baby, all right?'

'I thought you wanted a baby too,' she said.

'I did. I did think that.'

'But now you don't?'

'Now I don't. I'm sorry.'

'Well then, maybe we should have a little celebration. You got what you wanted. I got what I didn't need.' She fumbled for the bottle of Stoli. 'Shit, it's empty. Look at me. A hot tub, an empty bottle of Stoli, and sterility. Life doesn't get any better than this, does it? Unless you count having your husband fired from a top-rating network news programme. How the hell are we going to pay the mortgage?'

'We'll survive.'

'How?'

Their eyes met and locked.

She should have known, she realised. Ryan never got into a firefight without mentally marking out cover. He had told her that many times, and breaking house rules in the White House was the same as knowingly walking into an ambush. Yeah, he'd already had his cover staked out, that was obvious.

'Who have you been talking to, Sean?'

'Croz was in town last week.'

'Croz?'

'Dave Crosby. We knew each other in Saigon. He's at IPA these days. They want someone to go to Afghanistan for them. Cover the war.'

She closed her eyes. 'Jesus. Don't do this, Sean.'

'I have to.'

'No, you don't have to! You *want* to. You're a journalist, you should know the correct usage of these words.'

'I'm dying here.'

'No chance of that over there, of course.'

'You knew the kind of bloke I was when you married me.'

'Yes, but you said you wanted to change.' Here came the tears again; she swallowed them back. Oh, don't give him the satisfaction. She felt as if she were standing on the edge of a tall building, swaying in the wind. Didn't he realise she needed him right now? The flashbacks and the nightmares were getting worse; she was right out there, and she needed a hand, any hand, to drag her back in.

She had always thought that hand would be Sean's.

'It will only be for a while,' he said.

'Sure. How long can a war of attrition last anyway?'

'It's a three-month tour.'

'Which you'll extend when you start having fun again.'

'Wars aren't meant to be fun.'

'Sure. But they are, aren't they?'

They stared at each other. First one to blink loses, she thought. Ryan looked away. So you won the argument and lost . . . a husband. Such as he was. Funny how it had all crumbled away so quickly. Fifteen months. Not a record, not in America, but still screwed up much faster than she would have believed possible.

'The break away from each other will do us good,' he said.

'Goes without saying.'

'Mickey, I need some time on my own right now. I need time to recharge my batteries.'

'What are you, a torch?'

'You think I want out of the marriage.'

'Don't you?'

'No.'

'You've spent too long at the White House. You can lie almost as good as they can. I could imagine George Schultz when you said that.'

Well, crazy to think she could keep him. She watched him as he stood up, the water streaming off his hard, muscled body. Too damned attractive, that was Sean Ryan's trouble.

'Well, I guess that's a wrap, then, as they say in the business.'

'Mickey, it's only three months.'

'You already told me that.' She stood up too, put her hands behind her head, coquettishly ran one foot along the inside of her other leg. 'Take a good look, Sean. Something to think about when you're curled up in a shellhole in the Hindu Kush in the middle of winter. All right, it's not Nastassia Kinski, but there's a couple of interns who still don't think it's all that bad.'

'Mickey . . .'

'Don't Mickey me, you son of a bitch.' She grabbed a towel, wrapped it around her. 'When are you leaving?'

'Monday.'

'Jesus Christ. How long have you known about this?'

'I didn't make up my mind until this afternoon. That's the truth.'

'Tick, tick, tick.'

'What?'

'It's my biological clock.'

'Oh, for God's sake.'

'It's not your problem, Sean. But I do want a baby. I know in post-feminist fucking Washington it sounds dopey, but I want to be normal and have kids. Tick, tick, tick, there goes that clock. One day, brinnnng! Forty-five. *Wake up! What the hell did you do with your life*? What do I say? I waited for my husband to come back from the front?'

'I have to do this. I can't cut it in Washington any more. I'm going crazy.'

'Yeah, me too.' She went out trailing wet footprints across the landing carpet. She left the bedroom door open. Just in case.

# 59

## Lincoln Cove, Long Island

They were in the kitchen making spring rolls. It was a skill Phuong had learned as a small child from her mother and had never forgotten. Now Webb had persuaded her to pass on the secret to him. He stood beside her at the kitchen bench, surrounded by the detritus of pastry, bean shoots, shrimp and diced vegetables.

His first several attempts split and spilled on to the counter top.

'This is impossible.'

'You're not making a hamburger! You have to be gentle.'

'I don't have the fingers for it.'

'Your pastry is too wet. Like this. See?'

Webb shook his head. 'Perhaps I'll stick to pizza.'

'No way! You just keep at it! All right?'

He smiled. Those were the exact words he had used on her every day for the last twelve months, when she found her English lessons too hard, or when she was having trouble making new friends, or even just baiting a fishing hook. *Keep at it. Don't let it beat you. You can do it.*

And she hadn't let it beat her. She had a good ear for language and after just a few months her stilted phrase-book English had been replaced by all manner of New York idioms. She had overcome the initial racial and cultural barriers to make many new friends at school, and she had become a better fisherman than he was. The last accomplishment, he conceded, was perhaps not as great as the others.

She had dropped her Vietnamese name and had chosen Jenny as her adopted English name. In fact he had been a little dismayed at how eagerly she had tried to banish all traces of her heritage and assume the customs and manners of her adopted country. She had even become an aficionado of McDonald's, though he suspected that she still hated hamburgers and forced herself to eat her Big Macs so that she would be accepted by her new friends.

He picked up a red chilli from the bowl on the counter. 'I'm feeling lucky.'

She laughed. 'You'll need more than luck.'

She selected a chilli from the same bowl, and they faced each other, duellists waiting for the other to set the contest in motion.

She giggled. 'You're a wimp.'

He bit into the chilli. Oh, God. He felt as if the air had been scorched out of the room. Napalm you can eat; that was what Dave Crosby had called red chillis. He fought the urge to put his mouth and tongue under a running tap; instead he grinned at her as if he were totally in control and put the rest of the chilli in his mouth.

The chilli-eating contest had become a set play with them very early in their relationship, a way she could assert herself when every other facet of her life was overwhelming her. When her homework was too difficult, when she was unable to find the right words to express herself in her new language, when she was defeated by cardboard milk cartons and electric can openers and VCRs and long division and English grammar, the chilli-eating duel had been a way to break the tension and a way for her to succeed.

But recently, with 'Jenny' finally victorious over her brave new world, Webb found her newfound cockiness irritating, and he cherished dreams of beating her, just once.

On the second chilli he knew it was a vain ambition.

She grinned at him, swallowed her chilli and selected another. 'Do you say uncle, Uncle?'

His eyes were streaming. He could scarcely talk. He went to the refrigerator, took out the iced water and swallowed two large glasses, one after the other. Jesus Christ. Her mouth must be lined with asbestos.

The telephone rang. He snatched it off the wall. 'Webb,' he croaked.

'Hugh?'

'Who is this?'

'It's me . . . Mickey . . .'

'Mickey?'

'Are you all right?'

'Yes . . . fine . . . just . . . just a head cold.'

Jenny grinned and wagged her finger at the lie. He turned away.

Mickey! He hadn't thought about her now for a long time. A couple of weeks. She knew just when to call, just to stir up the sediment in his life, muddy the water again.

'Is everything okay?' he asked her.

'Sure.' A beat. 'Sure.'

How long since he had heard from her? A year, perhaps more. When she and Sean first moved to Washington she had called a few times. Perhaps she felt bad about what had happened. She had occasionally left some messages on his machine, but he had not returned the calls, and he had heard no more. He thought he had closed the book on that part of his life.

'I haven't heard from you in a while,' she said. 'How have you been doing?' She sounded tired, under strain.

'Is anything wrong, Mickey?'

'No, I'm fine, really. Just called to say hi. What's new with you?'

'Not a lot.' Mickey and Sean didn't know about Jenny; he had never told them. Another good reason not to stay in touch. If he didn't think about Sean, he didn't have to trouble his conscience.

*Oh, by the way, this girl I've adopted, I'm still not entirely sure she's not your daughter.*

*Yeah, I guess I should have mentioned this before.*

*Why not? Well, at first I thought you might try to take her away and screw her up again.*

*And now I couldn't stand to lose her whether you were going to screw her up or not.*

Like they said, keep a grain of truth from someone for five minutes, an hour later you're a pathological liar.

'I saw you on the *Today* show the other week. You were talking about your book. About the refugees.'

'Yeah, I'm a big TV personality now. Like Sean. I get people stopping me in the street all the time asking for my autograph.'

Jenny made a face at him.

'Yeah?'

'Just a joke, Mickey.'

'How's the book doing?' He heard the catch in her voice. Something was very wrong. He could imagine. But he didn't want to go there right now, so he played along with the small talk.

'Good, I think. I get fan mail from Norman Mailer.'

'I got a copy at the station bookstore last week. Next time I see you, you'll have to sign it for me.'

A long silence. He did not bite at that. 'What's up, Mickey?' he asked her, finally.

Jenny dropped the spring rolls into hot oil. Suddenly he couldn't hear what Mickey was saying. He frowned at her, and she mugged back, all wide-eyed innocence.

He covered the mouthpiece. 'Take the damn things out of there!'

'It's too late. The oil will make them go soft.'

'Take them out!'

She shook her head but did as she was told.

'Sorry, the radio was on too loud,' he said into the receiver. 'What was that?'

'Me and Sean. We've split up.'

He had been expecting this. The only thing that surprised him was that it had taken so long. He had heard through the grapevine that Ryan had walked out of the job at the network. He guessed that Mickey would be next. So typical of Ryan. Other people's lives used and tossed aside like Kleenex.

'What happened, Mickey? Is it another woman?'

'Other women I can deal with. This time the other woman's a war. Her name's Afghanistan.'

'Afghanistan?'

'His buddy Dave Crosby gave him an offer he couldn't refuse. Freezing snow, rabid Islamic fundamentalists and all the bullets he could eat. You just don't pass up chances like that.'

He felt she was looking for something from him. 'You want to come and stay here for a while?'

'Maybe that's not such a good idea.'

'So what are you going to do?'

'I don't know.' She sounded contrite for having called him. 'I'm all kind of mixed up.'

'Is he coming back, Mickey?'

'He says he'll be back in three months. But he won't be. He was just saying that. You know what a coward he is.'

He had never heard anyone call Sean Ryan a coward before. Death Wish Ryan, Suicide Sean, but they had never called him a coward. But then he supposed there were many different types of courage. Men who did not shirk physical danger often ran from emotional confrontation. Ryan had never been frightened to go to the front line, but he had never had the guts to say goodbye.

'Hugh?'

'I'm still here.'

'I'm sorry.'

'What for?'

'Christ, don't make me spell it out. I've made some big fucking mistakes in my life. I have been really stupid. But the biggest mistake I made was Ryan. And maybe the second biggest was you.'

He didn't ask her to elaborate. This was a cul de sac in his life. Get this phone call finished and get back to reality. 'Are you going to be okay, Mickey?'

'Sure. Sure, I'll be okay. Keep in touch, huh?'

'Mickey?'

A long silence. For a moment he imagined himself getting on the shuttle and flying down to see her. But his pride told him no. You don't go sniffing around another man's wife as soon as he's walked out of the door. Even a complete bastard like Ryan. Besides, the thing between him and Mickey was over. She had hurt him twice. He wasn't going to let her do it to him again.

'Take care,' he said.

He hung up.

Jenny was watching him. 'You okay?'

He made a face. 'Just a date that didn't work out. You know how it is. Hey, big handsome guy like me, I'll be fine.'

She put her arms around his neck. 'You really like her, huh?'

'No, I'm over it now.'

'You got to play it cool, Uncle. You're too obvious.'

'I'll try and remember that.' He pulled away. 'You've ruined the spring rolls,' he said. 'You can't put them in the oil and take them out again before they're cooked. It makes them go soft.'

But she was not going to let him off the hook so easily. 'Got to find yourself another wife,' she said. 'You look too sad on your own.'

That was the trouble with having a fourteen-year-old around the place. They thought they knew everything. 'Well, that just goes to show how much you know. I'm just fine like I am. Now how about we forget about my love life and try and salvage dinner?'

# 60

Afterwards she imagined that it was like stepping on a landmine.

She remembered with blinding clarity the time and the place it happened, and the sudden shock of the pain. Later she could always pinpoint that moment and say that was it, I knew that I would always be crippled after that, that was the second I knew a part of myself had gone, when I knew I would never ever be quite the same again.

It was a cool, hazy evening in June. She climbed off the school bus and started the long climb up the bluff to the cottage. The wind was spiced with salt, skimmed the whitecaps in the cove, bent the branches of the pink oak beside the road. Far below her an old whaler crashed through the narrows, bucking in the swell.

Nothing happened to invoke the realisation but it hit her with sudden and unexpected force: *I can never go back again*. Until that moment, perhaps, she had been totally absorbed with her own survival in this new and alien land, too preoccupied to mourn. But now, unannounced and uninvited, the ghosts rushed back to her; she heard again the sound of rain hissing on a charcoal brazier in a Cholon alleyway, the chatter of the women selling noodles and duck eggs, the ring of the wooden bell on the cart of the old man who sold steamed sugar cane. She breathed in the fresh, wet smell of the warm tropical earth following the first rains.

Then the moment was gone, and Lincoln Cove was no longer a charmed circle, but a wasteland stirred by cold sea air, barren of the corporeal taints of life, fruit, ordure, kerosene, charcoal and diesel.

Everything I knew as a child is gone, she thought. It has been wrenched away from me, and I'll never ever get it back.

Vietnam.

It had shown her no pity and yet it was still her country. For her own survival she had been forced to cut it away like a poisoned limb, but without it she was not, and would never be, complete. She had tried to deny the Vietnamese part of her, to become all-American, but Vietnam would not deny her. She had taken root in its soil. It was as surely a part of her as the sound of her mother's voice, even though she too was long gone.

She realised how she had grown to hate this crisp, clean air that was without taint and fecundity, these unclamoured streets, without people and coffee shops and hawkers and corrupt, teeming life.

She had survived so much. But for what?

She had tried to blot out her memories of the McAdam Reef, but now they came tumbling back. She should have died there. But she had dutifully survived, like a good daughter, because her mother's last instruction to her had been: Stay alive. Don't die! Stay alive!

And for this first year in America she had stayed alive because she had thought her mother was there watching her, encouraging her, rejoicing with her in her freedom, in this America. But she wasn't with her. She was dead, consumed by the crabs, her bones bleaching somewhere on the sands of the reef. She was not here in America, she never would be. She was dead, dead, dead.

Just me here, in this strange country, in a strange town with an even stranger name, thrown up on the shore like a piece of driftwood.

The sudden emptiness hurt. It came from the pit of her stomach, a terrible ache that left her breathless and stopped her halfway up the hill. She uttered a long 'oooooooh' and took two steps back. For a moment she thought she was going to fall. It was gone, all gone. She was an outcast, an alien, and utterly alone.

The hill seemed just too high to climb.

# 61

'I can't find anything *physically* wrong with her,' Dr Clooney said. 'I'd suggest the problem might be psychosomatic.'

The blinds in Clooney's surgery in the Whaler's Reach Medical Centre were drawn against a grey afternoon shower. A fluorescent tube buzzed overhead. Clooney leaned back in his chair, his sleeves rolled to the elbow, and tapped the end of his fountain pen against his forehead, frowning. Behind him, on a shelf alongside a row of medical reference books, a wave machine pounded its gentle surf against its glass prison.

He consulted the file in front of him. 'When you first brought her to see me she was undernourished and well below the average height for her age. We treated her for lice, intestinal worms and a tropical ulcer on her left arm. Now she's five foot four inches tall and almost ninety-five pounds. She'll never play women's basketball and I doubt if she'll ever need the Scarsdale Diet, but overall she's in pretty good physical shape. I'd say you've done a good job.'

'I thought that, too, until about a month ago.'

'As I said, I can't find anything really wrong with her. She's got a bit of a head cold. I've had a head cold all week. Look at the weather for this time of year. It's not surprising.'

'She stayed in bed all last week. She said she was too sick to go to school. This week I made her go. But I don't know if it's done any good. As soon as she gets home she throws herself in front of the television and doesn't move.'

'Sounds like my daughter.'

Webb shook his head. 'I'm not the only one who's noticed a change. Her teacher rang me last week to ask me if there was something wrong. Her final assignment for last term she got an A in English, her first ever. The last assignment she handed in she got C minus. I tried to talk to her about it. She screamed at me that I was pushing her too hard, that I was ashamed of her because she was Asian, and why didn't I just get off her back?'

Clooney took off his spectacles and pinched the bridge of his nose. 'I don't know what to say to you. You've picked up a heavy load here, Hugh. You've crossed a mountain range with this kid, and now you're panicking because you've taken a couple of steps back. When you got Jenny, you had no idea what her life experience had been before she came to you.'

'I think I had a better idea than most.'

Clooney shrugged his shoulders. 'Within reason.'

'I don't understand. Everything's been going along so well. I thought she was doing really okay.'

Clooney spread his hands wide. 'I can give you a referral if you want.'

'A referral?'

'A therapist.'

Webb shook his head. 'I was hoping you'd find something physical – make it easy for me.'

'We can wait for the results of the blood tests. There might be something. But I think you've already made up your mind what the problem is. Haven't you?'

Webb nodded. Clooney was right. He had expected to have to deal with this problem thirteen months ago, when she had first come to him. But she had settled in to her new home and her new school so well, and so quickly, and he had thought it might be easy after all. But he knew in his heart it would take more than a few good meals and a private tutor to overcome this girl's past. Logic dictated that. Here was a child accustomed to squatting in open fields and sleeping on the ground, and after a month at Lincoln Cove she was washing down her vitamins with a glass of water in the mornings before running for the school bus in her new Reebok joggers; a girl who had survived alone for months on a deserted island reef was suddenly unable to run an errand to the shops without her Walkman. She had become too much like a Western teenager, too quickly. It was another survival technique, not a transformation. The very absence of problems at the beginning should have been a warning sign in itself.

'I'll take the referral and talk to Jenny about it.'

'Sure,' Clooney said. 'Good luck.'

Odile was drowning.

Jenny was in the middle of the cove, in the aluminium runabout that Webb sometimes used for fishing. She sat at the stern, one hand on the throttle of the Mercury outboard. She could see her mother over the troughs in the waves, one hand reaching skywards. She was calling out to her, but the words were carried away on the wind. She twisted the throttle as far as she could but the little boat would not go any faster and she knew she could not reach her in time. She watched her mother disappear under the grey waters of the cove.

She woke as the rain hurled another flurry of rain at the window. She sat upright in the bed, soaked in sweat, and said one word.

'Mother.'

Webb stood in the doorway. 'Time to go to school.'

'I'm sick.'

'Dr Clooney says there's nothing wrong with you. Come on. Get up.'

Jenny pulled the covers over her head and turned her face to the wall.

Webb hesitated, but he knew if he lost this battle he could forget all the ones that were to follow. He took a step into the room. 'You're going to school today.'

'Leave me alone.'

'What is it? If there's something wrong you can talk to me about it.'

'I'm sick. My head hurts.'

Webb looked around her bedroom. Over the last few weeks the posters of Michael Jackson and Bruce Springsteen had come down, replaced with pictures of Vietnam painstakingly cut from magazines, scenes of a pastoral peaceful Asia she could not remember, an idealised version of her past; peasants in straw *non la*s labouring in rice fields, water buffalo hauling wooden ploughs, incense burning at a Buddhist altar, pavement hawkers at a market, bright oranges, rambutan, a wok sizzling with noodles and shrimp. None of it had anything to do with the reality of what her life must have been like on the streets.

'You have to go to school today.'

'What's the point? So I can grow up to be a blonde homecoming queen?'

'Is that what this is about?'

No answer.

He grabbed the covers and pulled them off the bed. Jenny lay in a foetal position in her T-shirt and the woollen socks she had borrowed from his drawer to keep her feet warm even on summer nights.

'You want me to get real sick and die? Okay, I'll lie here like this till I freeze to death!'

'You're not going to freeze to death because it's summer. And you're not going to lie there because you're going to school.'

'Screw you,' she said.

Webb bit back his anger. She wanted him to react in the Western way, lose face. He would not give her the satisfaction. 'Am I supposed to be impressed by your new command of the language?'

'Screw you double.'

No good. That was it. He grabbed her by the arm and pulled her off the bed. She rolled on to the floor, screaming, covered her head with her hands. 'That's it, go on, beat me. You're just like the communists! Go on, make me do what you want!'

'You can't lie here in bed all day!'

'Why not? What difference is it going to make?'

'You survived! You didn't get through everything you've been through just to lie here and turn into a vegetable! Is that what your mother wanted for you? Is it?'

'Don't talk about my mother, okay? You didn't know my mother. Don't you talk about her!'

*But I did know her*. He nearly said the words but stopped himself.

Trembling with rage and frustration, he bent down so that his face was inches from hers. 'Okay, it's like this. It's going to be just like before, just like Vietnam, all right? You want to eat, you work for it. You go to school, I feed you. You stay at home, you starve. No food, no water, nothing.' He grabbed her by the arm and dragged her to the window. There were some jays and gulls squabbling where the ragged lawn met the rocks. 'If you get really desperate you can go back to catching seagulls. Is that what you want?'

'You're hurting my arm!'

'It's up to you, all right? You can starve in your own bedroom just as easily as on the McAdam Reef.'

He let her go and went out, slamming the door behind him.

He leaned against the wall, closed his eyes, let the anger drain out of him. He felt immediately ashamed. Oh, that was a great way to handle things. Calm, assertive, rational. Instead he had turned the confrontation into a shouting match, then a wrestling match, and had finally delivered an ultimatum that would be impossible to sustain. Brilliant.

He sat at the breakfast bar staring gloomily into his coffee. The *New York Times* lay open on the counter top in front of him. El Salvador, Afghanistan. Both superpowers tracking across the mire to the same bog. The Russians had found their own Vietnam; the generals in the Pentagon had evidently enjoyed their Saigon adventures so much they were looking to repeat the experience in Central America. He thought of the old Chinese curse: *May you live through interesting times*.

He heard movement in the hallway, and looked up. Jenny had on her windcheater, jeans and Reeboks, and her schoolbag was slung over her right shoulder.

They looked at each other.

'Want some breakfast?' he said.

She shook her head.

'You only have to starve if you don't go to school.'

'Maybe I'll have a seagull at recess.'

He took the car keys from the hook beside the refrigerator. As an afterthought he went to the pantry, found a red chilli, bit into it. He held out the other half for her.

She shook her head. 'You win,' she said.

She trailed out of the door to the jeep. He heard the passenger door slam. Yeah, he thought. You win.

A fat copper sun hung over a stand of cedars on the far side of the cove. Red and green lights were lit on the mast of a catamaran as it made its way through the neck of the channel in the hastening evening. Webb stood at the water's edge, on a large and flat piece of shale, watching the lapping of the waves, the collar of his hunting jacket turned up against the biting wind.

'You have to know for sure,' he said aloud. He wondered what he feared the most; discovering that she was after all Sean Ryan's daughter, or that she was a total stranger.

He had accepted the referral from Clooney but he had no

intention of following it up. He had grown up in a country where you didn't run off to a shrink when the dog died or you missed a bowel movement. But the fact was he probably should have sought proper counselling a long time ago. Not only for Jenny, but for himself. But it had been convenient, until now, to obscure his own motives in all of this.

Had he loved Odile? No; at least not in the way he had loved Mickey. Odile and her child had symbolised for him the pain of an entire country, and his own subsequent actions were some small measure of grace for himself.

He had leap-frogged ahead in his career by recording a country's misery. No matter in what other way he chose to cloak that fact, it was how he saw himself. He was an opportunist. His burgeoning career as an author had been founded on his experiences of Vietnam's death agony.

But what he had done for Odile, and later for Phuong – Jenny – had been his redemption.

Oh, come on now, Spider, he heard Ryan saying. Don't bullshit. Yes, you did love Odile, in *exactly* the way you loved Mickey. Didn't you?

Yes.

He had hated Ryan for taking her away, as he hated him for taking Mickey. Hated him so much it made his bones ache. Now there was Jenny, whom he had come to love like she was his own. But if she was Ryan's daughter he would not be the man he thought he was if he hid that from Sean, and hid it from her.

But he'd be damned if he was going to tell him. Damned if he was. Damned if he even wanted to know for sure himself.

So he supposed that meant he was not the man he thought he was, after all.

# 62

It was mid-morning and Webb was sitting in front of his PC, his desk cluttered with the research materials for his latest book; his old notebooks, the pages stained with dust and sweat, some dog-eared transcripts of interviews, piles of black and white glossies, half a dozen soft and hardcover books, sections marked with torn strips of paper, all the detritus of the three months he had spent in El Salvador. A pair of half-moon spectacles was perched on the end of his nose, another tactical retreat in the face of middle age.

The phone/fax rang beside him. He snatched up the receiver and cradled it to his shoulder, his attention still focused on the computer screen.

'Webb.'

'Hugh, this is Joe Norrish.' Webb felt a stab of fear. Norrish was the local police sergeant; he had met him socially a few times at summer barbecues. A big-boned and quiet-spoken man, and by all accounts a steady cop.

His mouth was suddenly dry. 'Everything okay, Joe?'

'Hugh, we got ourselves a little problem here. I'm down at the McVeigh's 7–11 on Main Street. Can you come down?'

'What's this about, Joe?'

'I don't want to talk about it on the phone, but it's your kid. Old Man McVeigh caught her shoplifting.'

McVeigh's office was at the back of the shop. The desk was cluttered with the junk of a small business – an adding machine, account books, receipts on a bill spike, hardbacked ledgers, invoice books. Phone numbers were scrawled on a whiteboard on the wall. Beside the whiteboard was a calendar emblazoned with the name of the local Shell gas station, under an aerial photograph of Lincoln Cove.

Jenny sat in a big wooden chair behind the desk, her hands

between her knees, staring at the floor. Joe and Old Man McVeigh were standing in the doorway, waiting.

As Webb walked in, Norrish gave him a neutral smile and shut the door. Jenny did not look up.

'What happened?' Webb said.

McVeigh looked uncomfortable. Webb did not know the McVeighs; he did most of his grocery shopping at the supermarket in the Whaler's Reach shopping centre. 'I was watching her from behind the counter, in the mirrors,' McVeigh said. 'I saw her putting some candy in her pocket and I just kind of thought she looked suspicious.' He did not look at Webb, kept his eyes on Norrish. 'You know, being . . . Asian and everything. No disrespect, but you know what I mean.' He let the sentence hang and his meaning was not clear at all. 'Then she just walked out the door. So I shouted at her to stop. Just then Mr Ross from out Bayview walked in and she bumped right into him. He must have heard me shouting and he just kind of grabbed her. When I asked to look in her jacket I found three packets of M&Ms, a can of Coke and five goddamn packets of Marlboro. That she hadn't paid for.'

He glared at Webb.

Webb didn't know what to say or do. 'I'm very sorry, Mr McVeigh. This kind of thing has never happened before.' He swallowed hard, trying to stay in control. 'Is she going to be charged?'

Norrish scratched his head. 'Hell, Hugh, we don't want to do that. I've spoken with Joe here and I don't think we need to go no further with this.' Webb glanced at McVeigh and realised he owned more to Norrish's good sense than the old man's. 'Mr McVeigh here got his goods back so there's no harm done. I'd like to get this sorted out between ourselves if we can.'

'I appreciate that, Mr McVeigh,' Webb said.

'I'd better get back and help Cloris in the shop,' McVeigh said, and he went out.

Jenny had still not said a word.

Webb crouched down so that he was on her level. 'Jenny. Look at me now. What's going on?'

'I don't know. I never got caught in Saigon. Guess I must be out of practice.'

He looked up at Norrish, who picked at a tooth with a thumbnail, storing away this piece of information in case it was ever needed.

'Why aren't you at school?'

'Told you I didn't want to go but you said you would starve me out if I stayed home. So I didn't have a choice, right?'

He ran a hand over his face. Great, just great.

Norrish went to the door. 'Maybe you two ought to sort this thing out at home. Now, I've made it clear to the young lady that something like this can't happen again. I'm sure you understand, Hugh. Once, well, it's kind of a trivial thing and I'd just as soon forget all about it. But if I get called to something like this again, well, we'll have to start going through due process.'

'I understand that, and I appreciate everything you've done.' He took Jenny's arm. 'Let's go. Thanks again, Joe.'

He led her through the shop to the jeep parked at the kerb outside. She got in the passenger seat, put her hands in her jeans and stared straight ahead. A refugee with attitude, Webb thought.

Just great.

They said nothing on the way home. When they got to the cottage Webb led her through the house and out on to the deck. It was a warm morning and the waters of the cove were a rich blue. He went to the kitchen to make coffee, brought it out to the deck and sat down.

'You want to tell me what all that was about?'

She shrugged her shoulders, her face a sullen mask. He wondered what had happened to the laughing young girl who had shown him how to make spring rolls in the kitchen a few weeks before.

'Please, Jenny, I'm trying to understand.'

'There's nothing to understand, okay?'

'How many times have you jumped school like this?'

'Who's counting?'

'Humour me. A rough guess.'

She pretended to think. 'Three. Four.'

'And what do you do? You spend your whole time shoplifting? If I go in your room right now, is a stack of VCRs and stolen TVs going to fall on my head?'

'No, I put them under the bed where they can't hurt nobody.' She looked away.

He was on his feet. He grabbed her shoulders and shook her. 'God damn you! What did you think you were doing?'

Her face was blank. Christ, he thought. She hates you, and you don't even know why.

He sat down again. Take it easy, he said to himself. Get angry with her and she'll just freeze over. 'What the hell's wrong with you? I got you out of that camp, I fed you, I clothed you, I gave you a place to belong, I gave you an education. Is this how you repay me?'

'I got to be grateful to you for ever? Well, fuck you!'

He had never heard her swear like that before. It took his breath away. 'No, you haven't got to be grateful to me for ever,' he said, as calmly as he could. 'Just once would be fine.'

'You're just doing this to feel good. You're a really big guy, all right, you saved the poor little gook girl, the freak who ate seagulls! That's what you want to hear, right?'

Webb shook his head, unable to believe or to understand what he was hearing. 'Okay, I get it. I should have left you on U-5.'

'Maybe.'

'Easy to say now, isn't it?'

'Just leave me alone, okay. I don't need any of this shit any more.'

Webb stood up, picked up his canvas director's chair and threw it over the rail on to the lawn. Afterwards he felt stupid. Something a child would do. But he felt better.

She was staring at him.

'God, you really are a piece of work,' he said. He took deep breaths, trying to calm down. No one had made him this angry, ever. 'Your mother would be real proud of you now, wouldn't she?'

'Don't you keep talking about my mother! You didn't know her. Don't tell me what she is thinking!'

'I know exactly what she'd think!' he shouted.

Out before he could stop it. But Jenny heard it only as a bluff. 'I bet she wasn't the kind of lady you mixed with in Saigon,' she said.

'All right, I won't tell you about your mother. Don't you tell me about me either. Because you don't know me, you don't know what I did in Saigon, you don't know a *thing* about me.' He was back in control now, but he was also tired. Tired of arguing, tired of this endless pain. This was not going to get either of them anywhere. 'I've tried really hard to love you. And you know something? I succeeded. You're not a stranger to me any more, you're not some freaky survivor. You're my daughter. That's the only way I think of you. So you go right ahead, you sleep all day for the rest of your life if you want, hold up 7–11s from here to San Francisco with sub-machine guns, I don't care. Hey, you're a refugee, right, the world owes you? But I'll tell you something else. It doesn't matter what you do, I'm still going to love you. Whatever happens. I just wish you would cut me the same deal.'

Having said his piece, he left her sitting on the deck.

Stealing M&Ms. Jesus.

She didn't even *like* M&Ms.

Yeah, you should be grateful, she thought.

Or maybe that was the problem. Everyone at school, everyone in the whole town, treats me like I should be grateful, like I should spend my whole life thanking them because they were lucky enough to be born here and they got it in their hearts to be nice to a little orphan girl. A *gook* orphan girl.

Uncle was right. When she had first seen him at Puerto Princesa, in her heart she had prayed that he would take her away from U-5, bring her to America, the golden place where her mother had told her she would find freedom.

Freedom.

But now she had this thing called freedom and she did not understand why she was not happy. She could not count the days she had spent dreaming of escaping Saigon, getting away from the soldiers, the police, the communists. Now it seemed that for the first time in her life she had a roof over her head, she had enough food, she was safe. She had survived.

But her mother, who had sacrificed so much and worked so hard for their survival, had perished. She was alive and Mother was dead.

And that was something she could not ever forgive herself for.

# 63

Webb was standing at his study window, staring out over the cove. The tide was out; on the flats the crabs would be clicking and bubbling over the mud and rocks and the seagulls would have left hundreds of arrow imprints in the mud. Peace.

He turned away, walked over to the framed photographs lining the study wall, found the one of himself, Crosby, Cochrane and Ryan standing side by side on the Tu Do. They were in their field gear and Ryan and himself had Leicas slung around their necks. They looked young and arrogant and brave. Which they were.

He heard the door open behind him. 'Uncle.'

He turned.

'Can I come in?'

'Sure.'

She had her arms crossed in front of her, and he was ready for another tirade. But when she spoke her voice was contrite. 'I guess I'm sorry, Uncle,' she said.

He did not answer straight away and she interpreted his confusion as anger.

'I guess I would be angry too if I had a daughter like me.'

He felt a flood of relief wash over him. He would have to find that referral from Clooney. 'It's okay,' he managed.

She came to stand at his side. She looked utterly different to how she had looked an hour before, her face reanimated again. He wondered at how quickly she had marshalled her emotions; sometimes she displayed a maturity way beyond her years. He guessed that should not surprise him, considering the fact that she had hardly had a childhood.

'I get lost in my head sometimes,' she said.

'Will you tell me what happened to you in Saigon?'

She did not answer him straight away. 'I don't remember very much,' she said, finally. 'It's such a long time ago. Sometimes it seems like a whole lifetime.'

'For most people it is.'

'When the communists came I remember we were living in this apartment, in Cholon, I think. My father was American.'

'Did your mother ever tell you his name?'

'No, she never did.'

'Do you remember him? Remember what he looked like?'

She shook her head. 'I just remember my mother was very frightened of the communists. But she told me it was okay, because my father was going to take us away from Saigon before the communists came. But then one night I was asleep in my bed. I remember waking up and it was very dark. My mother was shouting and pressing her weight down on me. I cried and cried. I thought I was going to suffocate. Then there was a big explosion, so loud I thought my heart had stopped, and then the whole apartment seemed to move like a giant was shaking it in his fist. I screamed and screamed and screamed to try and block out the noise. That is all I remember until I woke up in the hospital.'

'The hospital?'

'My mother told me later that the communists had fired rockets into Cholon that night. She was burned very bad, her right arm, here on her chest, this side of her face. She still thought my father would come and get us, but he never came. We had to stay there in the hospital. By the time my mother was well again the communists had been in Saigon a long time.'

Webb went to the window seat and sat down. His legs felt weak. 'Did you ever find out what happened to your father?'

'No, we never did.'

He pretended he was hearing this story for the first time.

It was her. He was sure now.

*It was her.*

'What happened after you left the hospital?'

'My mother was very badly scarred from the fire. She was never beautiful again.' She smiled and put a hand to her breast. 'But here in my heart she is always beautiful.'

A long silence, as they both reshaped the old memories before quickly replacing them on the dusty shelves in their minds. Why didn't I find her that day? Webb wondered. Why didn't I find her? He recalled the chaos of those last hours, and he reminded himself it would have been more remarkable if he had succeeded.

'So now you know all the truth about me,' she said. 'My mother is not rich, she is not beautiful, and my father does not love us. I am just a bit of dust blown around by life, worth nothing, going nowhere.'

'That's not true any more.'

'I would love to find him, my father. I would like to meet him, just once, find out what he was really like, ask him why he did not come back for my mother and me. Maybe if he really loved us, if there was just some mistake, it would be okay.'

'You can't undo the past. But you do have a future. You can do anything you want. You can have the freedom your mother wished for you.'

She gave him a bitter smile. 'Easy for you to say that. But for me it's hard to let go of the past. It's like when you walk down the street and you got chewing gum on your shoe, and you just can't get it off. No matter where you go, it's still there, tracking over other people's carpets, bugging the hell out of you. All the time you can feel it.' She walked over to him, touched his face with her fingers. 'Sorry, Uncle. I don't mean to make you mad with me. But you cannot live my life, okay? If I want to be sad, you have to let me be. I can't go round being happy all the time for everyone, I can't be saying thanks to everyone every day. Some days I don't feel like saying thanks to anyone for anything at all.'

He nodded. 'I understand.'

After she had left the room he sat for a long time, staring at the photographs on the wall. Crosby. Cochrane. Ryan.

Ryan.

It was obvious to him now what he had to do.

She went into her room and lay on the bed, stared at the pictures she had tacked to the walls. Sometimes she would close the blinds and pretend she was back in Vietnam, imagine the smell of the mud and the rain, hear again the cries of the women in the market and the roar of the Hondas on the Ham Nghi Boulevard.

She often thought about her round-eye father, and sometimes in her fantasies she imagined what she would say to him. She even wondered if there might still be some way she could trace him, here in America. She could finally find out the truth about why he had left them behind in Saigon.

And she knew what she would do then.

She would kill him.

* * *

Webb picked up the phone in his study and dialled the Washington number. He did not need to consult the teledex, even though he had never used the number before. He had memorised it without even consciously doing so.

It answered on the third ring. 'Mickey?'

'Hugh. Jesus. I never expected to hear from you.'

'How's things?'

There was a pause. She sounded much farther away than Washington. 'Okay.'

'After your call the other week, I was worried about you. Thought I'd see how you were travelling.'

'Hey, I'm okay. You know me. How about you?'

'Great.' Another silence. There was going to be no easy way to do this. 'Is Sean there?'

'He's gone, Hugh. He left for Peshawar two days ago. I haven't got an area code for the *mujahideen*. Is it important? I mean, you can get messages to him and everything. Eventually. Through the agency.'

What was it he felt? Disappointment? Or relief? 'No, I guess it can wait.'

'Are you sure?'

'Yeah, I'm sure.'

'Only you won't be able to get me on this number after next week. I won't be here.'

'Where are you going?'

'I've quit my job. I'm moving back to San Diego.'

He couldn't think of anything to say.

'I need some time to get my shit together again. I feel like a pinball, just bouncing along from one dead end to another. Jesus.'

He wanted to say: I *still think about you.* He wanted to say: *Please come out to Long Island for a few days. I'm a good listener. I'll help you heal.*

But he didn't. She had hurt him enough. Let her go to San Diego. Just let her go. 'I'm sorry things didn't work out with Sean,' he said.

'I guess you knew all along they wouldn't.'

'I hoped they would.'

'Well, you were right. Everybody was right. But desperate times call for desperate measures. I'll write.'

'Yeah, do that. Get me an address.'

'Yeah. I'll see you.'

'Take it easy, Mickey.'

When he had hung up he felt curiously light. He finally had her out of his system. Ryan was back on the blood circuit, and Mickey was going to San Diego. Let them all go now, take the same advice you gave to Jenny, leave the dead past behind and get on with your life.

In a way it was a relief it had ended like this.

He picked up his notebooks, swept them off his desk, and threw his cup at the wall. It hit exactly where it was aimed. The glass on the picture frame shattered and Cochrane, Crosby, Ryan and Webb tumbled from the wall, leaving behind a coffee-brown stain.

## Seventh Regiment Armoury

It was late and all but the diehards had drifted away. Once, Webb thought, most of these men and women would still have been standing at four in the morning. Now many of them had wives and families and golf games to play in the morning.

Crosby went to the sideboard and returned with more drinks. They would probably have to get the Marines to fling him out into the street.

'I still don't understand why she married him,' Doyle said.

'Mickey was a very complicated person in those days,' Cochrane said. 'I always got the impression she found it easier to love humanity than love people.'

Webb shook his head. 'So it was her fault?'

'No. I think she set herself up. Jesus, anyone could have told her – anyone who knew her did tell her – that marrying Ryan wasn't a good move.'

'I think she was damaged goods,' Crosby said. 'That's all.'

'And what about Ryan?' Doyle said.

Crosby threw back his port. 'Ryan was just being Ryan.'

'No, I think he really meant to turn his life around back then,' Cochrane said. 'He wanted this thing with Mickey to last. Hell, I wouldn't have given him the Washington job if I thought he was just resting up.'

'He didn't need much persuading to go to Afghanistan,' Crosby said.

'Ryan was like an alcoholic,' Webb said. 'If they want to stay dry they have to accept that sobriety is a lot more boring than being drunk. Ryan couldn't take the fact that having what other people call a normal life was going to be a lot less interesting than risking being killed or crippled day after day. Some people are frightened of dying. The only thing Ryan was scared of was being bored.'

No one spoke for a few moments. They had all, at some time, been faced with the same decision. Cochrane had opted out. Crosby was still hooked on the risks. And Webb? He had made and remade that decision several times. Only Doyle didn't yet know what they meant.

'I want to know what happened to Jenny,' she said.

Webb smiled. 'Jenny and I survived each other.'

'But did you ever tell her about Ryan?'

Crosby interrupted. 'You can't leap ahead too far. I guess if you want to find a place to end the story you have to go back to the summer of '91.'

Webb nodded. 'We were still living out on Long Island. Jenny was a grown woman by then. She'd done well at school, she could have gone on to Columbia, but she was too impatient. She persuaded a friend of mine to swing her a job in the mail room at the *New York Times*. Her naturally pushy personality took things from there. She moved up to court reporting, she even got a couple of small features well back in the paper. But nothing ever moved fast enough for her. I suppose I related to some of that ambition.'

'And that was when you told her about Ryan?'

'No, that was when Mickey came back.'

[illegible] personalities [illegible] Afghanistan [illegible]

[illegible] [illegible] they [illegible] and [illegible] more [illegible] than [illegible] [illegible] [illegible] the [illegible] leaving what [illegible] call a portrait [illegible] The only thing [illegible] [illegible] They [illegible] [illegible] And [illegible] He had [illegible] several times [illegible] [illegible]

I want to know what happened [illegible] she said.

[illegible] until [illegible] each other [illegible]

But did you ever [illegible]?

[illegible]

[illegible] Long [illegible] [illegible] but she [illegible] [illegible] She [illegible] [illegible] naturally [illegible] [illegible] a couple of [illegible] the [illegible]

[illegible] about [illegible]?

[illegible]

# VII

## New York, September 1991

'Perhaps everyone who reports on war is in part sating their own dark curiosities. I know I will return soon.'

– Askold Krushelnycky, war correspondent

# 64

## Lincoln Cove, Long Island

The sound of tinny soft rock and the charcoal smell of a barbecue drifted with the breeze from the rental next door. Webb and Jenny sat on the deck, nose to nose like gladiators, a bowl of red chillies between them on the patio table. Webb had just beaten his all-time record of five, but Jenny showed no sign of breaking under this pressure. Sweat ran down Webb's face.

'This time let's make it interesting,' she said. 'Two at once.'

Webb got up and ran inside. She saw him dash to the refrigerator for the iced water.

She laughed, delighted. '*Wimp!*'

When he came back his eyes were watering from coughing. He had a glass of water in one hand and a piece of dry bread in the other. She had told him that the bread was more effective than the water in putting out chilli fires.

'You know what I said about being pleased you came up for the weekend,' he said. 'I lied.'

She laughed again. 'No way you're ever going to win,' she said. 'Vietnamese mothers give their babies chillies instead of dummies.'

'Another lie.'

'At work they believe it.'

'How is work?'

'They give Pulitzers for court reporting?'

'Only if the court is the Supreme Court and the plaintiff is the President.'

'I might as well be invisible. How am I going to get anywhere writing about men masturbating in Central Park?'

'Philip Roth did okay out of it.'

She made a face. Very funny.

Jenny was twenty years old now, and had developed into a very beautiful young woman. Strangely, she did not remind him at all of her mother, neither physically nor in her demeanour. Her face was not as oval and she did not have her mother's pronounced cheekbones. While Odile was demure, serene and untouchable, Jenny was very much an American, her face animated with self-confidence.

She had moved out several months before, and now had an apartment of her own in Tribeca with the rest of her trendy crowd.

'Was it the same for you?' she asked him.

'I was born in England. Everyone masturbates over there. It's not newsworthy.'

'Seriously.'

'I did my apprenticeship on a provincial newspaper where the fifth anniversary of a fire at the church hall warranted a colour supplement.'

'What did you do?'

'I went to Vietnam.' He realised the implications as soon as he said it.

'Maybe I would like to go to Vietnam.'

'You can. If you want. I'll help you with the money.'

'But then I say what's the point? There's nothing there for me now.'

'I guess.' He went inside to check on lunch. Over the last eight years he had fashioned a legend for himself in local circles for his Vietnamese cooking. In honour of Jenny's weekend visit he had cooked two fillets of swordfish on the barbecue, which he was about to serve with noodles, green salad, roasted peanuts, and a sauce made from pungent *nuoc mam*, lemon and oil.

She helped him carry the plates out on to the deck.

'If you went back to Vietnam,' he asked her, 'what would you do? Discover your roots?'

'All my roots got pulled up. I don't know. Maybe it would just be good for me to see the place I was born. Through adult eyes.'

'I agree.'

'Talking of my roots . . .' She hesitated.

'Yeah?'

'I've been thinking a lot about him, lately. I was wondering how I might track him down.'

'Who?'

'My father.'

Webb went back inside, gave himself time to think. He brought the food out to the deck on a tray, laid the dishes one by one on the table, then sat down. 'What would you do – if you did find him?'

'Sometimes I think I'd like to kill him.' She saw his face. 'Only joking. Don't look like that.'

'It would be pretty hard to find him after all these years. Is it that important?'

'Maybe it is. To me.'

'Why?'

'I guess there's a few things I'd like to ask him.'

That was the trouble with a big lie, Webb thought. Once it was entrenched it grew, and kept on growing, until the roots had entangled themselves in the foundations of your life, and to tear it out meant shaking up your whole existence. How could he tell her, after all this time, that he had known – or suspected – who her father was all along?

He wondered where Ryan was these days. He had followed his progress in the newspapers and magazines through Afghanistan, Lebanon, and the Gulf War. The last dateline he had read had been in Yugoslavia.

'I'd think it would be just about impossible to find him after all this time. Where would you start?'

She selected a piece of fish with her chopsticks, held it poised between the plate and her mouth. 'Sometimes I thought you might be my father.'

He looked at her in amazement. What hint had he given her of that? 'Me? Why?'

'I don't know. A feeling. Some of the things you've said.'

'What things?'

She shrugged her shoulders, without answering, and placed a morsel of food between her teeth. She closed her eyes, savouring it. 'Not bad.'

'Would it make any difference? If I was your father?'

'Yeah. It would make every kind of difference.'

He couldn't believe she was still thinking about it. It had been so long since she had brought it up with him. He had told himself that keeping the truth hidden from her was a kindness, that it had helped her adjust. He had read somewhere that the concentration camp survivors who had coped best after liberation were the ones who had blocked out the past, pretended none of it had ever happened.

He had adopted that philosophy in his own life. He had known a few fellow correspondents, especially from his Vietnam days, who had suffered what the psychologists now called 'post-traumatic stress syndrome'. To Webb it seemed that lingering on things that had happened in the past was what had made them sick.

He had adopted an antipathetic approach: you changed what you could, forgot about what you couldn't.

'I don't know if there's much to be gained by digging up the past,' he said.

'You never had a past like mine.'

Time to change the subject. 'Are you still going out with, what was that guy's name, the one with the ring through his nose?'

'Enzo.'

'That his real name?'

'He's Italian.'

'Tell me, what does he do if he gets a head cold. I mean, how does he wipe . . . ?'

'You are so retro.'

'Is he dealing drugs?'

'Why, do you want some?'

'He looks like a substance abuser, okay?'

'Of course, you never touched drugs when you were my age.'

'That was different.'

'Of course it was.'

'We know better these days.'

'Meaning you've had *your* fun.'

'Don't you ever get sick of winning arguments?'

'Never,' she smiled. She came and sat on his lap to show there were no hard feelings. 'So what *were* you doing when you were my age?'

'I was taking photographs of church fêtes and scout jamborees.'

'You were in Vietnam reporting on a war.'

'Not until I was an old man of twenty-two.'

'Maybe that's what I should be doing. It would keep me out of trouble.'

'Don't even joke about it.'

'Another sexist remark. I can't believe you came from the same generation as Jane Fonda.'

'Please don't mention me and her in the same breath, there's a good girl.'

'Now you're being patronising. You need a woman to straighten you out.'

He grinned back at her. 'Like who?'

'What about that woman down the road, the one who always comes round here in a lycra suit pretending she's just come from aerobics classes? The one reeking of Chanel instead of sweat?'

'She tries too hard.'

'You have to stop playing so hard to get. It's about time you settled down.'

'I'm a writer. I'm supposed to be Bohemian.'

'You need someone to take care of you now I'm not around.'

'I'm forty-three years old. I think I can look after myself by now.'

'Look, I found a grey hair.'

'Don't pull it out! It makes me look distinguished.'

'You're going to need someone to wheel you about on Sundays. I can't be around for ever.'

It was a joke, and Webb laughed dutifully, but it was his first clue that Jenny was about to take her initial step away from him, and from New York.

The woman pulled the Pinto to the side of the road and parked. She could see the cottage from here, and the open redwood deck; saw a man with a young girl on his lap, a young Asian girl. She checked the mailbox again. It was the right house: *Webb*.

She studied her own reflection in the rear-vision mirror. Not bad, considering everything. She was wearing make-up, a silk blouse; her hair had been expensively styled. But she couldn't compete with a twenty-year-old.

Perhaps this isn't such a hot idea, she thought.

She had not seen him in eight, nine years. She had kept in touch, occasional letters and phone calls, but that was different to showing up on his porch unannounced wearing French perfume. What arrogance. He had his own life now, and it looked as if he was doing well at it, judging by the girl on his lap.

She turned the car around and drove away.

# 65

Webb was lunching with his editor in the Union Street café when he saw Crosby. Crosby stopped on the way to his table to shake hands. 'Hugh. Haven't seen you for years. How are things?'

Webb stood up. 'I'm fine. Good to see you, Croz.'

'Good to see you too, man.'

Webb turned to the other man at the table. 'Dave, this is Peter Crawford. He's my editor at Putnam. Peter, this is Dave Crosby. I've mentioned him a few times in my books.'

The two men shook hands. 'Right. I feel like I know you,' Peter said, and Webb could almost see his eyes glaze over. He was a good editor, and he knew what made books sell, but he thought Webb and his fellow correspondents were all certifiable, had even said so once after one too many spritzers at a book launch.

Crosby turned back to Webb. 'I've seen your stuff around. You must be doing okay.'

'I almost earned out a couple of advances. What about you?' He had noticed that Crosby was limping.

'Piece of shrapnel in my knee. Vukovar. Been covering the war in Yugoslavia for IPA. They airlifted me out for a while, so I thought while I was here I'd get myself a proper lunch. I've been hanging out for some calamari. They're all out over there.' He lowered his voice. 'That is a bad, bad scene. You imagine the Middle Ages with rocket-propelled grenades and you have some idea.'

'I'm glad I'm out of it.'

'I was with this new kid, a freelancer. He had been there one day. *One day*. I took him around, showing him the ropes, you know. He's fifty feet away from me in the street, taking a photograph, there's a thump, and that's it. Mortar round, blew the top of his head off. *His first day*.'

'Croz, I can't believe you're still doing that stuff.'

'Someone has to let the world know what's happening over there.'

He smiled, realising he was getting intense. 'Enough about me. Tell me where famous authors live these days.'

'I'm out on Long Island. Lincoln Cove.'

'Guess you're the local celebrity.'

'There's a few writers out there.'

'You're being modest. You'd better give me your address.'

'I'm in the phone book. Only one of me in Lincoln.'

'I'll give you a call. Hey, guess who I saw the other day. Remember Sean's ex? Mickey something.'

'Mickey van Himst,' Webb said, and he experienced a tight, hollow feeling in his stomach that had nothing at all to do with food.

'She's living here now. I saw her right there in the street over in the West Village. We talked for a while, you know. Seems she's nursing somewhere in some swank hospital on the Upper West Side. Looks real good.'

Webb almost asked him for her address, but stopped himself. No, that was dead now. Instead he said: 'Seen any of the other guys?'

'I saw Ryan in Zagreb last time I was there.'

'How is he?'

'You know Ryan. Still the same. Look, I'd better get back.' He indicated a table of four men on the other side of the restaurant. 'IPA people. I'm trying to persuade them to send me back to Bosnia. I think they're worried this metal in my leg will slow me down.'

'Take it easy, Croz.'

'Yeah, you too.'

He walked away through the crowded restaurant and Webb went back to the conversation with his editor, trying to forget that Mickey was probably just a couple of miles across town. No, he told himself again, that part of your life is over. You can't ever go back.

A sea breeze stirred the leaves of the crab apple tree at the bottom of the garden. Webb stared at it for a long time, his mind empty. He had barely typed a word since lunch. He was working on a new book called *Apple*, a history of and social commentary on New York, but lately there had been a lot of days like this when the words just would not come. Perhaps that was because he was just not interested in the project. He was doing it, he knew, for the money alone.

He took his coffee over to the window, sat down on the

window-seat. He set the mug down and closed his eyes, letting the sun warm his face. At first there had been so much to write. *Goodnight, Saigon* and *Voices from America* had both sold well, and his third, *Deception*, about American politics in Central America, had been a bestseller and made him something of a champion among American liberals. He had followed that with *The Fall in Spring*, about the last days of Saigon, and had written four others, about Indochina and the Middle East, using as a resource the photographs and hundreds of notebooks he had kept from his days as a correspondent for IPA. But now what he had thought was a bottomless well of experience was running dry.

He had nothing more to say.

The phone rang. A welcome distraction. He snatched the receiver off the cradle on the second ring. 'Webb.'

'Hugh?'

He felt a stab of pleasure and pain. 'Mickey?'

'How's things?'

'I'm fine.' He paused. He had looked up her number in the directory, a few times he had almost called. Keep up the pretence. 'Where are you calling from?'

'I'm back in New York.'

'Yeah?'

'I moved back a couple of weeks ago. I've got an apartment in the West Village.'

He ran a check over his own feelings, a chaos of old emotions. 'You want to do lunch?'

'Spoken like a true New Yorker. You'll be one of us one day.'

'Sorry. It's a reflex. Like "have a nice day".'

'I would like to do lunch, though. If you want to do it with me.'

'I'd like that. We can catch up.'

Her voice faltered. 'Yeah. Like old pals.'

'How about tomorrow? I'll book.'

'Okay.'

'I'll grab a cab and pick you up outside your apartment. How's that?'

'Sounds good.'

She gave him the address and he scribbled it down on a pad.

'It's good to hear your voice again, Mickey.'

'It's been too long,' she said.

After he had hung up he looked back at the PC screen. Well, so much for *Apple*. He guessed that would be about as much work as he would be able to handle for the day.

It was in the style of a number of new Manhattan restaurants that had suffixed their names with an exclamation mark. This one was called REVOLUCION! The white adobe walls were filled with poignant memorabilia collected from South and Central American countries: crudely printed leaflets of the missing that had once been handed out by the mothers of the disappeared in Buenos Aires, framed photographs of Galtieri and Romero and Allende in the attitudes of movie stars, revolutionary pamphlets collected from Peru, El Salvador, Guatemala, Nicaragua, Brazil. Revolutionary graffiti, spray-painted in Spanish, filled the empty spaces.

The waiter led them to the rear of the restaurant, to a paved courtyard where a dozen tables surrounded a fake marble fountain.

At first Webb wondered if he had made a mistake. Mickey looked around, her face grave. 'Are you making a statement here?'

'I thought it was kind of appropriate. The food's really good too.'

'If they've got tortilla on the menu I'm out of here.'

'No tortillas, but they do breed a very special kind of malarial mosquito in the fountain over there.'

She smiled at that. The years had been kind, Webb thought. They had ironed out some of the angles, and there was a poise about her that had not been there before. She was wearing an apricot-coloured loose-fitting woollen jersey over a black cotton skirt and leather pumps. Her hair was cut shorter now, and streaked with blond tips, and there was something else about her he had not seen before.

She looked relaxed.

A waiter approached with the wine list. Webb looked at her.

'I'm sticking with yuppie juice,' she said, indicating a bottle of Perrier at the next table.

'I'll do the same,' he said to the waiter.

They stared at each other.

'So.' She smiled at him, took a deep breath.

'So.'

'How have things been with you?'

'Fine.'

'Just fine?'

'I've been writing books, selling them. Doing the P.J. O'Rourke thing.'

'I saw you on the talk shows a couple of times when I was in San Diego.'

He grinned. 'Then you'll know what a big-shot I am now. Actually that's not true. I'm a little-shot with pretensions to grandeur.'

'Working on another bestseller?'

'Mostly. And working on a mid-life crisis at the same time. Busier than a one-armed paper hanger, as Sean would have said.'

The mention of Sean brought a chill to the conversation. The waiter brought their Perriers. She studied hers with the sort of passion she might once have reserved for pure vodka.

'Have you heard from him?' she asked.

'No. You?'

'We got officially divorced about five years ago. End of story.'

'Suddenly there's a draught,' he said.

She gave him a wan smile. 'He was not a part of the problem but he certainly did not prove to be part of the solution.' He watched her carefully. Nails perfectly manicured, a hint of expensive perfume, no stray ends of hair in her face. She was certainly taking better care of herself these days.

'What are you staring at?'

'You.'

'Counting the wrinkles.'

'I was just thinking how beautiful you're looking.'

She smiled with pleasure at this compliment. The old Mickey would probably have thrown an old wound dressing at him, he thought. 'How did we get on to me? We were talking about you.'

'Were we?'

'Your books.'

'There's not much else to know. I live on Long Island in a little cottage in Lincoln Cove, where I spend the days pining for lost loves.'

'Don't be sarcastic. And I'd hardly call it a cottage.'

His eyebrow arched in surprise.

She obviously hadn't meant to let that slip. She looked down at the tablecloth, flustered. 'I was out your way last weekend. I was going to look in.'

'Why didn't you?'

'You had company.'

It look a moment for Webb to realise what she meant. 'You actually got that close?'

'You can see the deck from the road. I didn't want to interrupt anything.'

'Interrupt anything?'

She gave him a look. 'You had a girl sitting on your lap.'

'Little young for me, don't you think?'

'I don't know. I wasn't that close.'

'She's twenty years old and she's a rookie journalist at the *New York Times*.'

'Lucky you.'

'I helped get her the job.'

Her eyes glittered. 'No strings attached.'

He smiled at that one. 'That's right. No strings attached. She's my daughter.'

Mickey stared. He could almost hear the gears clunk into place as she digested this piece of information. 'Your daughter. And she's twenty years old.'

'Well, I call her my daughter. She calls me her uncle. It's an unusual relationship.' He sipped his drink. 'I fostered her. A few years ago. She's a Vietnamese refugee.'

'Of course.'

'It's true.'

Mickey shook her head. 'Here I was thinking you'd become the ultimate hedonist. I should have known better.'

'Widows and divorcees are more my speed these days. I really don't believe in May-November romances.'

'Not November, surely. Remember we are about the same age.'

'July, then.'

She grinned. 'That's better.' She shook her head, surprised at his revelation. 'What's her name?'

'Her real name's Phuong but she uses Jenny. Her choice. Part of the integration process, I guess.'

'What made you . . . ?'

'What made me adopt a Vietnamese refugee? I was researching my book on the boat people and she looked like a good tax deduction.'

'Are we being serious here or what?'

'Do you have a motive for everything you do?'

'Yes, but I try not to look at my motives too closely.'

'Same here.'

'It couldn't have been easy. I mean, a bachelor. Adopting a teenage girl?'

'Easier than you'd think. Looking back from the point of view of the politically correct nineties, I guess it was a lot easier than it should have been.'

'Any regrets?'

'Lots of regrets,' he said, and held her eyes, 'but not about Jenny. Oh, she gave me my share of heartache. A brush with the law and a few other incidents I'd rather forget. She actually hit a boy at her school with a copy of Webster's unabridged dictionary after he called her a gook. She must have taken quite a swing because he had to go to the doctor's with concussion. If it had been the complete works of Shakespeare she would have killed him. But most of the problems were locked in her head, so they were harder to deal with.'

'I can imagine.'

'I guess you can. I was guru, helpline and kicking-post for the first two years. Fortunately she's very bright. She did well at school. I got her some private tuition and by the end of her final year of high school she'd not only caught up with her peers, she left them eating her dust. I wanted her to go to college, but she was in too much of a hurry for that. A friend of mine got her a job as a rookie with the *New York Times*. She's bright, she's ambitious, she's opinionated and she scares the hell out of me.'

'You sound very proud.'

'I guess I am.'

She shook her head. 'Funny.'

'What is?'

'You think you're looking so hard for something, but the problem isn't that you can't find it. The problem is you're blind.' She was leaning towards him across the table, and in her face he thought he saw something he had never thought to find.

Longing.

But just then the waiter returned with his order book and the moment was gone.

Mickey was pleased to find that the tamales and enchiladas were offered as starters only. The entrées were like nothing they had ever found at La Esperanza: green chilli with pork, grilled tuna and avocado salad.

She looked up from the menu and stole a glance at him. She noticed there was a little grey in his hair now and that he had put on a little weight. She guessed he could afford to; he had always been long and rather lean. But he still fitted well into his jeans. He was wearing a collarless grey silk shirt and an Oyster Rolex. He looked both casual and affluent.

She returned her attention to the menu, finally decided on the tuna; he chose the pasta with herbed chilli sauce.

'Why did you go back to San Diego?' he asked her.

'I had to get out of Washington. I felt a breakdown coming on.'

'Washington makes everyone feel like that.'

'This wasn't Washington. This was rampant alcoholism.'

Webb stared at her, startled by this blunt confession.

She smiled at his expression. 'You didn't know?'

He shook his head.

'It started again when I came back from El Salvador. A bottle of vodka a day, but when Ryan left I moved up another gear. When I got to San Diego I spent my first three weeks home in bed. My mother must have been worried sick. When I finally went out and got a job they found me the first day hiding under a trundle bed in the recovery room. Someone gently suggested I might like to do my own recovering before coming back to work. So I went to see this shrink for a while and he diagnosed post-traumatic stress syndrome. Vietnam disease.' She made a face. 'Hearing that made me even thirstier. Things got a little tacky for a while.'

'Why didn't you call me?'

She smiled and said not unkindly, 'And say what? I know all I've done is hurt you, but will you come and watch me break down for a while? I thought you'd had enough of me. I don't blame you.'

'So what happened?' he asked her.

'I was in and out of this place called Riverlands for a few months. I don't know why it was called that, there's no river, just a lot of trees and a big fence. Anyway, they got me straightened out to the point where I started eating again and could manage more than a couple of words at a time. When I got out I visited this therapist for a while. My mother paid for that, God bless her. We went through a lot of stuff, got a few things worked out, and I finally got to the stage where I could work again. But no more ER nursing; these days it's strictly haemorrhoids and prostates. The shrink said the trauma room was not the place for someone like me any more. Finally here I am. Forty-three years old and I'm ready to start life.'

'I had no idea things were so bad.'

'Of course you didn't. I was just this crazy broad who married the wrong guy and caused you nothing but grief.'

'So what now?'

'I nurse at a small private hospital on the Upper West Side. People of private means with private conditions. I assist in theatre and tuck them into bed at night. It's a long way from the ER at Bien Hoa but it's better for my health.'

'Any guys I should know about?'

'Why should you know about the men in my life? Assuming there are any.'

'Because I have a proposition for you.'

'We've only known each other twenty-two years. You took your time.'

'When do you next get a few days off?'

'This weekend, as a matter of fact.'

'Why don't you come over to the cottage and spend the weekend. You can have Jenny's room.'

'Can I trust you?'

'I don't know. Do you want to trust me?'

She smiled. 'I'll think it over.'

# 66

Webb grilled steaks on the barbecue and then brought out a large bowl of Caesar salad, a bottle of mineral water and two glasses. He tried to act as if mineral water was his preferred accompaniment to red meat. Mickey gave him an amused glance but said nothing.

They sat talking on the deck until the wind turned cool and forced them inside. The sun slipped below the island and Webb turned on the table lamps inside the house. Other lights glimmered on the far shore of the cove across the dark water.

While he made coffee in the kitchen, Mickey did a slow circuit of the room, examining the local scrimshaw on the stone mantelpiece, picking up and studying each framed photograph on the night tables.

Webb watched her. She was wearing a grey hooded cotton jersey and loose navy boating pants. Her feet were bare. He felt comfortable with her, as if they had been around each other all their lives. He wondered why it had taken this moment so long to arrive.

'This is Jenny?' she asked him, holding up the photograph he had taken of his adopted daughter when she was about fifteen. She was wearing braces and a goofy grin.

'The one next to it is a little more recent.'

It had been taken about six months before, on the deck of a friend's boat out in the cove. The gauche grin of the teenager had been replaced with the restrained, almost haughty smile of the confident young woman she had now become.

'She's beautiful,' Mickey said.

'Thank you. I think so too.'

'Must have been hard. Raising a Vietnamese kid, I mean.'

'It sure had its moments.'

'Why?' she asked him.

'Why . . . ?'

'Why did you do it?'

He hesitated, thinking how best to answer her. 'I'm not sure. Perhaps it was to pay back my little part of the debt. You know, I kept asking myself, was that the right place to finish it, back there in 1975? So long, folks, sorry about all the napalm? When I was writing the book about the refugees I figured I should do more than make everyone else feel guilty about it. If I wanted to help I could do something a little more constructive.'

'Ryan used to call you —'

'Jimminy Cricket. Yeah, I know.'

'You have what I think they call moral fibre.'

'Oh, and the other reason, of course, was that I thought it would help me promote the book.'

She grinned and replaced the photograph on the mantel. 'Where's all the war memorabilia?'

'Upstairs in the study.'

She gave him a questioning glance.

'I don't like to have it on show.'

'Why not?'

'I figure they would look too much like hunting trophies. The only thing I keep out is this.' He went to the coffee table and picked up what looked like a paperweight. It was a small glass case mounted on a heavy onyx base. He handed it to her.

Inside was a shiny brass .762 bullet. It had 'Hugh Webb' engraved on the casing.

'Where did you get this?' she asked him.

'Lee Cochrane gave it to me when I got back from El Salvador. It's the bullet with my name on it. He never explained quite what he meant by it.'

'If you've got the bullet that's got your name on it, you don't have to worry any more.'

'Or else it was just a friendly reminder. Did you hear what happened to him?'

She nodded. 'He was still in hospital when I left Washington.'

'Ironic. He got out of the front line because he said he wanted to die in his own bed. Then he has a heart attack at thirty-nine. I suppose if the bullet has your name on it, it doesn't matter where you are.'

'How's he doing?'

'Lost twenty pounds, gave up smoking and drinking and got into health foods. He's back with the network, only these days he chews a stick of celery while he fires people.'

She handed the paperweight back. 'Life's strange, isn't it?'

'Sure is.'

'When I first met you in Vietnam I never thought we would be standing here doing this twenty years on.'

'Nor me. First time I saw you I was sure that a few minutes later I'd just be a few bits of charcoal swept into a bag and sent out on the DOA mail. Instead here I am, a pillar of the establishment worrying about my retirement fund.'

'You ever have nightmares about that burning helicopter?'

'Not so much now. I'm down to just once a week.'

She smiled again to show she understood. She leaned her back against the mantel. 'Ever miss it?'

'No.'

'Liar.'

'Sometimes. For all the wrong reasons.'

'Would you ever go back?'

'I'm too old for all that.'

'Ryan did and he's older than you.'

'He has testosterone on his side.' He turned away, went back to the kitchen and the coffees. 'I don't know. I own the bullet with my name on it. Why worry? Right?'

'You *are* thinking about it.'

'I feel something slipping away. There's something insidious about being safe. You slip on the days like a pair of old socks. I've got enough money, I've got a nice house to live in, I know an A-37 isn't going to come screaming out of the sky and put a rocket through the window. Salvador would have settled for that. But me . . . I feel like one of those retired boxers. I'm punch drunk, but I still want to get back in the ring just once more.' He affected a nasal Brando voice. '*I coulda been a contender*.'

She went to the bookshelf, found a hardback copy of *Deception* and flicked through the pages. 'I should have brought my copy. You could have signed it for me.'

'You read it?'

'I wanted to see if I got an honourable mention. Or even a dishonourable one.'

'I didn't think that would be fair. And, to be frank, you weren't central to the issue of US foreign policy in the region.'

'I wasn't? You really know how to hurt a girl.' Her mood changed, suddenly, and the playfulness left her. 'I think I'll skip coffee. I'm tired. I think I'll have an early night.'

He showed her the spare bedroom. Jenny still used it sometimes when she came out for the weekend, so Webb had left it the way it was, with the Luke Perry and Axl Rose posters taped over the curled and torn photographs of Vietnam paddy fields, which in turn had been tacked over the Bruce Springsteen posters, the archaeology of Jenny's adolescence. On a shelf were Jenny's trophies from the debating society – Webb had always teased her that she had done all her practising on him – and there was a stuffed toy, a puppy called Woofer, on the end of the bed, which was still made up with Jenny's lace pillowslip and quilts.

'This is my room,' Webb said. 'Do you want to see where you're sleeping?'

She grinned. 'I picked you straight away for a Guns n' Roses freak.'

Webb looked around the room as if he were seeing it for the first time. 'The soft toys, the rock posters, the lace – she's actually not like this at all. When you meet her you'll know what I mean.'

'She won't mind me using her room?'

'She will, but not for the reason you think. She'll just be disappointed in me. She thinks it's *avant-garde* having a father who has to worry about safe sex more than she does.'

Mickey's mood seemed to change. She gave him a wistful look, then opened the french windows and went out on to the narrow balcony. A frog croaked in the darkness. He stood behind her, watched the lights of a boat working its way along the channel between the red marker buoys.

'It's beautiful out here,' she said. 'Peaceful.'

Webb sensed the change in her and waited, let her come to it in her own time.

'God, I've wasted so much time,' she said.

'It wasn't really wasted time. Not if it taught you something.'

'What's that, a quote from Richard Bach?'

'No, I think it might have been the Eagles. Can't remember how the tune goes.'

'Don't try and cheer me up.'

'All right, I won't. Can I ask what happened between you and Ryan?'

'What do you think happened with me and Ryan?'

'I always supposed that he found his boredom threshold about three and a half hours after getting to Washington. That he had an affair a day later and on the first rainy day that he didn't find a new Watergate to report he went off looking for a war.'

'If you could see it coming, why didn't I?'

'I suppose you were in love with him. I wasn't.'

She hugged herself. 'I guess you always wondered why him and not you, huh?'

'No, I never wondered that. I could tell myself it was because I had malaria, but that wouldn't be true. He could have caught dysentery, dengue fever and been ravaged by smallpox and he would still have got you. It's just always been the way he is. He has a deadly kind of charm. It appeals to the masochistic streak in a lot of women. I know that it isn't politically correct to say so, but it's true. All women love bastards.'

'I was just flattered, that a man like that really wanted me.'

'Okay, I can buy that. But why marry him?'

'I thought I could change him. I thought he really wanted to change. My shrink said the real reason was that he was just as damaged as I was and I'd finally found a soul mate.'

'Fascinating crap these people talk.'

'You don't think he's damaged?'

'No, but I think he's a carrier.'

'You don't think someone with a famous father who abandoned him as a baby, and later publicly drank himself to death, might have problems with that? That someone who spends almost their entire adult life taking photographs of dismembered bodies and people in extreme stages of misery might have some unresolved issues of their own to sort out?'

'You're breaking my heart. The man's an emotional vacuum.'

'He speaks well of you too.'

Webb shook his head. He didn't want to hear apologies for Sean Ryan. He was not about to forgive him for anything, because the things he had done were unforgivable.

'Do you ever have nightmares, Hugh? Was it true what you said about the helicopter? Do you still wake up with the cold sweats?'

'Not so much these days.'

'You kept your shit together. No shrinks and no booze clinics for you.'

'I guess this stuff affects people differently. I unloaded the baggage in my own way. I had my books, I had Jenny.'

'I wish I could have handled it some way that was . . . constructive. Me, I just couldn't let it go. When I got back from Vietnam everything seemed so trivial. Over there you were on the edge, the days were coloured in neon, you know? Back here every day was black and white. I couldn't get the war out of my head. People would ask you what it was like and you'd try and tell them but you knew they weren't really listening. No one was interested. You thought: there's this great human tragedy taking place over there and nobody gives a damn. I went over normal, I came back a freak.

'Anyway, this shrink straightened me out. At least, he helped me define the problem, he helped me realise that I wasn't just crazy and weak. He was a great guy, he specialised in counselling Vietnam veterans. He said you could get combat trauma even at second hand. Turns out he should have listened to his own advice. Couple of months after I stopped seeing him he committed suicide. Put a gun in his mouth and blew all those vicarious memories all over his diploma. Nice.'

Webb could think of nothing to say to that.

'Still, I may not have been good for him, but he was good for me. He told me that when I went to El Salvador what I was trying to do was recreate the same dramas and conditions I had experienced in Vietnam, that it was an attempt to recapture that phase of my life so that I could write a different ending. Except of course you can't write a different ending because women and children still die for no reason and Humpty Dumpty can't be put back together again.' She reached for his hand on the rail. 'So then there was Ryan. My doomed attempt at a normal life.'

'You didn't find any other guys after Ryan?'

'I found plenty. Most of them were vets like me. You think my shrink didn't have a good time with that?'

He waited. She was silent. 'And then?' he asked her.

'I gave up men after a while. They're like cholesterol. As you get older you have to really cut down on your intake. I gave up trauma nursing too. And the booze. Everything I enjoyed, but was killing me. Last few years I've lived quietly and peacefully, as they say.'

'So what brought you back to New York?'

'My mom died a couple of years ago. No more reason to stay in San Diego. I figured I was ready for one more crack at the world. I applied for some jobs, this one came up. I thought, sure, why not. New York's as good as anywhere else. And here I am.'

'Here you are,' he said, still not sure where all this was leading.

'I don't want to waste any more time.' She picked up his hand and placed it on her breast.

'I don't think we should do this,' Webb murmured.

'That's my line.' When he didn't smile, she added: 'I don't want to sleep downstairs with Luke Perry. I'm forty-three years old.'

He took his hand away. He wanted her, wanted her desperately, always had. When he had invited her over for the weekend, they both knew where this was going. But he had been here before, had told himself he would not let her make a fool of him again. 'Let's slow down a bit.'

She folded her arms, leaned back on the railing, close to tears. 'You're really mad at me.'

'No, it's not that.'

'Yes it is.'

He turned away and slammed his fist on the wooden balcony rail. 'Of course I'm mad at you! You broke my fucking heart!'

'Well, give it back, then,' she said gently and without irony. 'I'll see if I can mend it.'

He led her upstairs to his room. They stood facing each other in the darkness. She could hear the murmur of the waves lapping on the shale at the bottom of the garden. A full moon threw slivers of light through the blinds.

A branch rustling against the window, the green glow of a digital clock.

'I've never done it on a water bed,' she said.

'It's easy. You start with a small set of waves, build to a two-foot swell and finish with a tidal wave.'

'The two-foot swell sounds good. But you fishermen always exaggerate.'

He took her hand. 'I'm nervous.'

'Me too.'

'After all this time I'm afraid this is going to be a disappointment for you.'

'It's got to be better than the first time.'

'You fell asleep.'

'No reflection on your performance.'

'Of course. The second time was okay. Of course you were a lot younger then.'

He kissed her gently, felt the answering pressure of her body against his. This isn't going to work, he thought. After all this time, after Ryan, after everything, it just isn't going to work.

He rolled on to his back, his heart hammering in his chest, thc sweat cooling on his body. He turned towards her and their eyes locked and they both laughed.

'Wow,' she whispered. 'I guess you've got every divorcee in Lincoln Cove queuing up here during the week.'

She rolled on her side, straddled him with her knees, sat on his thighs.

'I think the water bed's leaking,' he said.

'You've got a dirty mouth.'

'I've been saving it up for twenty years.'

'It feels like it.'

'Actually, it's all just been practice for the main event.'

She smiled with genuine pleasure. He watched her, fascinated. The moon shining through the open window sculpted shadows on her body.

She held him in her fingers and stroked him. 'If only he could talk.'

'It would be a pretty short and boring conversation.'

'I don't see any signs of rust. Come on, I've been honest with you. Let's hear all your dark secrets. I can tell you haven't let this enormous talent go to waste.'

'I nearly married an editor at my publishing company a couple of years ago.'

'What happened?'

'She wanted to leave work and have children. She was too good an editor to lose.'

She laughed at that. 'And now?'

'There's a divorcee lives on Baypoint Road. She's some sort

of investment adviser. Calls by every Monday and Thursday to examine my portfolio.'

'The *National Enquirer* could do a six-week feature. Harpoons fire again at the old whaling station. There he blows!'

He groaned. 'Don't do that.'

'Do what?'

'Do what you're doing.'

'What am I doing?'

'For God's sake, woman.'

'I think he's reloading.'

'Mickey, I can't. You'll kill me.'

'It's okay. I know what I'm doing. I'm a medical professional.'

'Mickey, I'm forty-three. I have a sedentary lifestyle now.'

'I'm competing with the Monday and Thursday competition so I have to work harder. Look, I think he likes me.'

'He adores you.'

She made a sinuous movement with her hips and he felt himself slide inside her once more. He gasped. She leaned over him and he felt her hair on his face. 'No more tidal waves,' she breathed. 'Let's just surf for a while.'

He couldn't help it; he felt cheated. This was the way it should have been from the beginning, and he felt a flaring of anger at all the time that had been taken away. But then he thought: No, there is a season for everything. There is no point railing at what has gone. Perhaps back then it would have been the wrong time; there would have been too many ghosts in the way. Now they had a chance.

# 67

Webb sat behind the PC in his study, staring out of the window at the cove, whistling tunelessly between his teeth. Sunlight bounced off the windscreens of the cars crossing Southampton Bridge.

Nearly two hours' work and he had written perhaps fifty words. He couldn't get his mind off her.

The phone rang on his desk, bringing him back from his reverie. He picked it up. An international connection. 'Webb.'

'Hugh, it's me, Croz.'

'Croz. Where are you?'

'Rome. IPA made me bureau chief here.'

'Congratulations.'

'Don't bother congratulating me, they did it because my knee's fucked. I'm deskbound for a while. Look, Hugh, you've been watching TV. You've seen what's happening in Yugoslavia? It's an unbelievable story out there. Unbelievable.'

Webb steeled himself for the pitch. 'Yeah?'

'That's why I called. I thought maybe you could do some feature stuff for me. Anything we don't use, you can put in your next book. I've got authorisation to offer you some very serious money for your byline. What do you think?'

Webb almost asked him what he meant by 'very serious money' but stopped himself. As soon as people started talking about money it was taken as given that you had accepted the offer and were just quibbling over price. 'I think you're crazy.'

'Hey, you can't sit down there on Long Island for the rest of your life. You'll go insane.'

'No, going back to a war zone that's even more dangerous than Vietnam is what's insane. I don't need to do that any more.'

'You do need to do it. Maybe not for the money. But you need to do it.'

'Balls.'

'You and your quaint English expressions. What does that mean exactly?'

'It means I'm not interested.'

'Think about it, Hugh. You've got a track record on this stuff. Sarajevo's getting pounded to shit every single day and no one gives a damn. Except us. Right?'

'I've paid my dues, Croz. I'm not going back.'

'Think about it. That's all I ask. I'll leave you my number. Okay?'

Afterwards, he sat for a long time staring at the phone, as if it were an Aladdin's lamp. All he had to do was pick it up, dial a number . . .

'Still life with troubled journalist,' he said aloud. No, it was impossible. He had finished with all of that. He was not going back there. Already they had killed almost as many journalists in the Balkans as they had in the whole of the ten years of war in Vietnam. He would be crazy to go back to all of that now.

Crazy.

Webb had lunch with his new editor at a Park Avenue restaurant and then, instead of going to Penn, he took the subway to Houston. Mickey had an apartment not far away and she finished her shifts around three in the afternoon. He thought he'd surprise her. He bought roses at a florist on the corner of Houston and 67th.

A young man, dressed entirely in black, was sitting on the stoop of her West Village brownstone. He wore purple-tinted granny glasses and he had a row of gold earrings through his left ear. Webb reminded himself not to make hasty judgments; it could be one of Jenny's boyfriends.

It was meant to be a security apartment but there was someone just ahead of him and he simply followed them in before the front door clicked shut. Great security. He took the stairs to the third floor and knocked on the door of 3E.

It opened.

He found himself looking into the powder-blue eyes of Sean Ryan.

Ryan flashed him a grin. 'Well, how about that. Instant reunion.' He looked down at the roses and raised his eyebrows.

Webb looked over his shoulder. Mickey was standing in the middle of the room wearing only a white bathrobe. Nice. Cosy.

He held out the flowers and gave them to Sean. 'These are for you.'

'That's very thoughtful of you, Spider.'

'Well, I've missed you.'

Ryan lowered his voice. 'You wearing that aftershave for me as well?'

'I just had lunch with my editor. He's gay and I like to tease him.'

Mickey was still standing there, looking as guilty as hell. Well, there was no law against sleeping with your former husband. 'Well. Great to see you again. I'd better be going.'

She pushed Ryan away from the door. 'Hugh, don't go. Come in. Please. I just wasn't expecting you.'

The obvious response came to his lips unbidden but he swallowed it back.

Ryan appeared to have overcome his initial surprise. He endeavoured to appear contrite. 'Yeah, come on, Spider. I haven't see you in God knows how long. At least have a drink with me.'

Webb hesitated, then shrugged and walked in.

'I get home from work. Suddenly I have all these visitors. You guys want orange juice? I don't keep anything stronger here.'

Webb shrugged. 'Sure. Orange juice is fine.'

Ryan held out the flowers. 'Can you put these in a vase for me?'

Mickey gave him a look, took the flowers, put them on the counter top in the small galley kitchen. She went to the refrigerator, took out a pitcher of orange juice and fetched three glasses from a cupboard.

The door to the bedroom was open and the bed was a mess. 'I didn't have time to make it this morning,' she snapped, and pulled the door shut with her foot. She brought the orange juice and the glasses and put them on a coffee table. Ryan and Webb sat awkwardly side by side on the only sofa.

Mickey dragged over a chair from the dining table. 'Well,' she said, 'this is really nice.'

'Saw Crosby in London,' Ryan was saying to Webb. 'He told me how he'd met Mickey over here. I got her address from him. Thought it would be a surprise. And there you were thinking you'd surprise her too. Now look at us, mate. We're all surprised.'

Webb nodded, his stomach in turmoil, searched his mind

desperately for a little small talk. 'When did you get into New York?'

'Last night.'

'With CNN these days?'

He nodded. 'Been in Somalia, working on my tan. You still churning out bestsellers?'

Webb didn't like the emphasis on 'churning out' but he let it go. 'I'm the darling of the talk shows, didn't you know?'

'I always thought you would be,' Ryan said, with a smile.

A strained silence.

'So what brings you to New York?' Webb asked.

Mickey poured the juice and slammed the glasses on the table. She was in a bad mood. Getting caught out did that to people, Webb supposed. 'I came to see Mickey. What brings you here?'

'I came to see Mickey.'

'What a coincidence.'

'Isn't it?'

Webb felt Mickey staring at him. Her eyes were bright and angry. Well, he didn't know what she had to be pissed about. He was the one being messed around here. 'So, how's things going? I've seen you on television a few times. Hardly recognised you without your flak jacket.'

Ryan looked discomfited for the first time. 'Mate, I've tried to tell them but they won't listen. They reckon the viewers like it. Suppose it doesn't do the ratings any harm to play up the risk angle a little bit. You know how it is.'

'Sure. I know how it is.'

'You're looking well, Spider.'

'Thanks. You haven't changed a bit either.'

'Clean living.'

'I can imagine.'

Ryan tasted his orange juice and grimaced. 'Funny, I was hoping I might catch up with you while I was here. From my lips to God's ear, eh?' He was smiling and tapping his foot in time to some private tattoo. Webb could feel the anger radiating out of him. He wondered why. Because Mickey had found herself another man or because that man was Hugh Webb? Ryan would doubtless prefer it if every woman he had went to a monastery after he had finished with them. Pined after him for ever. That would suit his ego.

'Mate, I read all of your stuff,' Ryan was saying. 'It's not bad.

My favourite was *Deception*. You've got a gift, Spider. You know how to make your point in a very entertaining way.'

'It's not meant as entertainment.'

'No, but it's got to be, hasn't it? If you want to catch people's attention. It has to be either grotesque or gruesome or exciting or people just switch off. When you've got something to say you have to mesmerise them with blood stains, then creep up behind them and shout your message in their ear while they're distracted. We only have to do it for thirty, maybe sixty seconds. Doing it in a whole book is a lot harder. I admire you for that.'

Webb watched his face for signs of irony. But there were none. He meant it and Webb was flattered against his will.

'Where are you living now, Spider?'

'Lincoln Cove out on Long Island. You'll have to come out before you go back.'

'Yeah, okay. I'd like that. I can bring Mickey out with me.'

He smiled ingenuously. Webb looked at Mickey.

'We've been sleeping together,' she said to Ryan.

'I would have put it another way,' Webb said. 'I would have said I was in love with your former wife. But there you are. Different perspectives.'

Ryan seemed to be enjoying himself now. Not Mickey; she was flushed with anger and embarrassment. Which was precisely why Ryan's own mood had picked up. 'Shucks, you two,' he grinned. 'Now don't you mind me.'

'Fuck you,' Mickey said, and got up and went into the bedroom, slamming the door.

Webb stood up to leave.

Ryan looked up at him. 'Nothing happened, mate,' he said. 'I mean, before you got here. We're all finished years ago.'

'Been great catching up,' Webb said.

'Can I still come out to Lincoln Cove?'

Christ, Webb thought. He sounds like a small boy who thinks he's just missed out on a holiday treat. He supposed the way he could switch moods was part of Ryan's notorious charm. 'Mickey will tell you how to get there.' He looked at his watch. 'I'd better be going. My train leaves Penn station in half an hour.'

He walked out. Screw Sean Ryan.

And screw her as well.

* * *

Ryan knocked on the bedroom door, opened it without waiting for an answer. Mickey was changing in front of the dressing-table mirror. She had on a pair of briefs and was in the process of fixing the clasp on her bra.

'Get out of here!'

'Want a hand with that?'

'What the hell do you think you're doing? This is my apartment.'

'Nothing I haven't seen before.'

'Christ, you've got a nerve.'

'Comes with the territory.'

He sat down on the edge of the bed and watched her as she pulled on a blouse and skirt. 'You look great, Mickey. I mean, you haven't let yourself go.'

'Why would I want to do that? Because of you?'

'I didn't mean it that way. Jesus, don't be so touchy.'

She felt his eyes on her. She knew what he was doing. Here she was half naked with one of the most attractive men she had ever known and he was sitting there watching her as if she were the entertainment. She imagined he did this kind of thing deliberately, exercising his charm for the hell of it, seeing how well it still worked.

She could not believe Webb had chosen this afternoon to come calling. She knew how it must have looked.

Yet nothing had happened. Ryan had been there no more than a few minutes. The question was: would something happen? She hated herself for thinking it. She had let Ryan walk out of her life eight years ago and it should be over. Instead she heard a voice inside her whispering: stay tuned.

The last phone call had been three years ago and here he was breezing in again with his casual charm. What did he want, for Christ's sake?

'You look like you've really got things together,' he said. 'That's good.'

She finished dressing. She brushed past him, took a comb from the dresser and dragged it through her hair. She was painfully aware of how close he was. She could feel the heat of him. 'What do you want?' she said.

'I just wanted to see that you were okay,' he said, and it sounded as if he genuinely meant it. But that would be in character, she thought. He meant well for everyone, as long as he didn't have to be responsible for their welfare. There wasn't a mean bone in his body. Or a considerate one.

He put his hands on her hips. 'How about we grab some dinner someplace?' he said.

She moved out of reach. 'What is it, Sean? You're in town and at a loose end so you want some company for the evening and a guarantee you'll get laid at the end of the night? You've come to the wrong house.'

'I came to New York to make sure you were okay,' he repeated.

'And if I hadn't been?'

He shrugged. 'Croz said you had your shit together. I just wanted to be sure. I've always felt bad . . .' He let the sentence hang.

'So you should.' Then the significance of what he had said hit her. Crosby had told him she was okay. So he had known that it was safe, had been guaranteed before he got to New York that there would be no demands on him. He could assuage his conscience – if he had one – knowing he could walk away afterwards without feeling bad. Perhaps even feeling vindicated.

Oh, the hell with it. He was what he was, and the faults in their marriage had been as much hers as his. 'There's a little Italian place round the corner,' she said. 'They do great tortellini.'

He grinned. 'I love it when you talk dirty,' he said.

# 68

Ryan appeared in Lincoln Cove with Mickey in the back of a stretch limousine. Webb stood on the porch with his hands in his pockets, shaking his head. A typically restrained gesture, he thought. The only wonder was that he had not hired a helicopter and landed on the back lawn.

Mickey came up the path first, threw her overnight bag on the steps. They looked at each other.

'Hi, Mickey.'

'Hi.'

'Did you have a swim on the drive up?'

'It's only the standard model. It hasn't got a pool, just a sauna.'

'Shame.'

Ryan tipped the driver and followed Mickey up the path. He was wearing a camouflage utility with cutaway sleeves, faded jeans and Fabiano leather boots. Webb guessed he was making some kind of statement. The combat photographer on holiday.

'Nice ride,' Webb said.

'Live for today. You never know what's going to happen tomorrow.'

'I suppose you've hired the *Queen Elizabeth* to go home in.'

'Peter Arnett's already booked it.'

Webb wondered if this was really such a good idea. 'Come on in,' he said. 'I'll make you a nice English cup of tea.'

'Nice place,' Ryan said.

'Thanks.'

He strolled to the french windows overlooking the deck. It was early evening and the Japanese lanterns were alight in the neighbour's garden. The evening breeze was scented with charcoal and sea salt. The crickets chirped from somewhere across the darkening lawn. 'Great spot for seduction,' Ryan said. 'Isolated.

Dark. In Lincoln Cove no one can hear you scream.' He grinned at Mickey, then turned back to Webb. 'Where are you working on the Pulitzer Prize?'

'My study's upstairs.'

'Mind if I see? I've never been in a real writer's place before.'

Webb could see this was going to be a very long weekend. 'If you agree to tone it down a bit,' he said, and led the way upstairs.

Ryan stood in the middle of the room, looking around. Webb leaned against the door lintel watching him. 'I can just see you here, mate,' Ryan said. 'Sucking on a pencil, ruminating on the meaning of life.'

Webb knew he was being baited. He said nothing.

He hasn't changed, he thought. Ryan's self-discipline had helped him overcome bullet and frag wounds and bouts of tropical illness, and he was still fit and hard, carrying no spare. His genes had helped too, he supposed. While his contemporaries got greyer and fatter, Dorian Gray was still in the front line chasing women and ambulances, the *Boy's Own* fantasy with the body of a thirty-year-old.

'I envy you,' Ryan said for no apparent reason.

'Envy me?'

'You've got your life in order. I never seemed able to do that.'

'Don't give me that bullshit, Ryan. You're as happy as a pig in shit, you always have been.'

'I'm okay when I'm doing stuff. It's only when I stop it scares me.' They stood for a long time in contemplative silence. The room grew darker and the shadows lengthened. 'I never thanked you for saving my life at Que Trang.'

'No, you didn't.'

'I'm not going to either. It was the least you could do for a mate. But I still don't understand why you did it. If I were you I would have let them bloody shoot me.'

'No, you wouldn't.'

'I might have, mate. If there was a woman involved.'

'Well, that's where you and I are different.'

'I'm trying to think of one way you and I are the same.' He switched on the desk lamp, studied the photographs on the wall. 'God, we looked young.'

'You still don't look any older, you lucky bastard.'

'Some would say it's because I never grew up.'

'I saw Croz when he was in town.'

'Yeah, he told me.'

'He had some shrapnel in his knee.'

'I told him it was lucky he forgot to duck. Or it would have got him in the head.'

'He said he saw you in Zagreb. I still can't believe it's twenty years on and you two are still at it.'

'It's in the blood. Anyway, what else would I do?'

'Aren't you bored shitless with it all?'

'Mate, I can't live without it now. I'm hooked. A real war junkie, right? If I'm not out there on the edge I can't feel anything any more. Which is probably just as well, because if blokes like me and Croz aren't there to document what goes on, who's ever going to know what happens to the poor bloody victims?'

'I don't know if people really care that much any more. It's getting harder to shock people. El Salvador cured me of just causes.'

'I think we still do make some difference. That's one thing I learned from you.'

'From me?'

'I accused you of being Jimminy Cricket. Well, that's me, these days. When you retired I decided to take over your job. I sit on the world's shoulder and just keep yabbering away. I'm going to keep yabbering till they put me in a box.'

'And probably after, knowing you,' Webb said.

Ryan grinned.

'You're not going to change anything, Sean. You can risk your life getting pictures to a television set, but people are immune to it now. Maybe even a bit punch drunk. They see so much violence on TV they're shock-proofed. Or maybe they can't tell the difference between the entertainment and the news.'

'Maybe you're right. But that's not why you gave it up. You did that because of you.'

'Me?'

'You expected too much from the job. You didn't want to stop one war, you wanted to stop people going to war. You're an idealist, that's your trouble.'

'There's nothing wrong with that.'

'All idealists are also unrealists.'

'Great. You make up that word or did you go to one too many military briefings?'

Ryan ignored him. 'Blokes like you run around saying war is hell. That's bullshit. War depends on where you're standing. If you're the poor fucker running for his life over a bridge or the rice farmer getting chased through a paddy by a gunship then, yeah, war really is hell. If you're cold and hungry and you've just lost your family in a mortar attack it's a real bitch. But if you've got a bloody big gun and the other bloke hasn't, war isn't hell any more. It's fun. It's like a big video game. You've seen it yourself. The door gunner blasting away at some piss-poor Vietnamese rice farmer with an M-60 doesn't think war's hell. He's having a fucking ball. Like the Serbs blasting the living shit out of Vukovar. Tell them war's hell. They're having the time of their fucking lives. They've never felt so sexy. I'll tell you something, Spider, I've seen wars of liberation, wars of attrition, wars of atonement, every kind of damned war. But you know why people really go to war? It's not to liberate, it's not to atone. They do it because they fucking well enjoy it! So don't think you failed because you didn't make Vietnam the war to end all wars. Getting men to stop fighting is like trying to make them stop fucking. All we can do is try and regulate where and when.' He turned away, smiled self-consciously. 'Listen to me. So intense. I sound like John Pilger.'

'You could have a point, though,' Webb conceded.

'Maybe. But that wasn't what I came up here to talk to you about.'

'Mickey.'

'Yeah.'

'None of your business, Sean.'

'Well, if you're dipping your wick in my wife, I think it is.'

Webb shook his head. He supposed he should have expected this. It amazed him how quickly Ryan could switch from high moral debate to crass outbursts aimed solely at protecting his own ego. 'Your ex-wife.'

'That's playing semantics a bit.'

'Semantics? The divorce did go through, right?'

'It's still hard not to take this personally.'

'You mean that?'

'My oath I mean it. Jesus. I thought you were a mate.'

'Well, you thought wrong. And don't go preaching to me about sexual morals. Me least of all.'

'Why you least of all?'

Webb raised an eyebrow.

'We're back to Saigon. I knew it. You're never going to let that rest, are you? Christ Almighty, how many times do we have to go through it? It wasn't my fault. I didn't arrange to get myself blown up.'

'You should have foreseen it.'

'What am I, a fucking gypsy? And how does that make what you're doing okay?'

'You've been divorced for five years!' Webb realised he was shouting and lowered his voice. 'What the hell's wrong with you?'

'I still love her, Spider. I didn't divorce her because I didn't love her.'

'You don't know the meaning of the word.'

'I don't like the idea of one of my mates sleeping with my ex-wife.'

'What ever gave you the idea that I was your mate?'

He looked at Ryan and watched his face undergo a transformation. He realised that this perspective had never occurred to him, despite everything he had said to him in the past. It was a given with him that everyone would like him no matter what he did.

'Well, I always liked you.'

'To coin a phrase, so you should.'

Ryan turned around slowly and took a deep breath. He peered more closely at the framed photograph on the wall: himself, Webb, Crosby and Cochrane on the Saigon street. Webb had had it reframed, but there was still a brown stain in one corner where the coffee had splashed. 'They were good days back then. We'll never ever get another war like that one.'

'They're all like that one, aren't they?' Webb said.

'If you say so.'

They went back downstairs. Mickey had changed into a tracksuit, and her hair was tied back with a rubber band. She had made the tea and was carrying a tray with three cups and a teapot to the coffee table by the window. 'I took Jenny's room. I hope that's all right.'

'Where do I sleep?' Ryan said.

'Why don't you two sleep together,' Mickey said, 'then we'll all be even.'

'Only if Spider's on the bottom. *Then* we'll be even.' He grinned, but his eyes weren't smiling.

# 69

Ryan was up early, the habit of a lifetime. He was disappointed to find Mickey and Webb were already up and gone. He padded into the kitchen and was making coffee when he heard the throaty exhaust of an old car. He looked out of the window and saw a canary-yellow Volkswagen pull up in front of the gate. A young Asian woman got out and strode up the path in a Mets windcheater, jeans and Reeboks. She unlocked the door.

She stared at him, open-mouthed. He looked down. He was wearing jockey shorts at least.

'G'day,' he said.

'Hi.'

'You must be Jenny.'

'You're Ryan.'

'That's right.'

'I've seen you on the news. Uncle's got your photograph upstairs in his study.' She looked him up and down. 'Nice bod.'

'Thanks.'

'It's okay.'

Apart from the obvious physical features there was nothing Asian about her at all, not in her voice nor in her expressions or manner. She had assumed the brash exterior of a young American.

She threw her daypack on the floor and shut the door. 'You're the last person I expected to find out here. Uncle thinks you're a jerk.'

'He doesn't think that?'

'Yes, he does. I heard him say so.'

He smiled. He liked this girl. Apparently she always said exactly what she thought. 'I'm sure he didn't mean it.'

She went to the refrigerator, took out an apple, sat down at a bar stool and started chewing. 'I don't think he was joking.'

'Must have been. Me and Spider are like that.' He held up his index and second fingers and interlocked them.

'Spider?'

'Your father. Spider.'

'Is that what you call him? Spider?'

'Webb. Spider. It's what I call your dad. It's traditional in Australia. Like calling blokes with red hair Blue.'

'I don't call him Dad. He's not my father. I call him Uncle.'

'Okay. Right.'

'It's a little more correct and it shows respect.'

'Whatever. Anyhow, I was hoping I'd meet you. He didn't stop talking about you all last night over dinner.'

She raised her eyes. 'Sorry. He's a major embarrassment. I think when you foster a kid it makes it worse. You're always over-compensating.'

'I guess. I wouldn't know.'

She bit into the apple and studied his body with frank and unnerving interest. A long time since a woman had taken him off guard. 'An impressive collection of scars. You look like a quilt.'

He looked up at her. She was smiling. 'Want a coffee?' he said.

'I don't drink coffee.'

'Why not?'

'The caffeine isn't good for you.' She took another bite of the apple. 'You've got quite a reputation.'

'For combat photography?'

'No.'

'Then for what?'

'Women.'

'Jesus. That was a long time ago.'

'Yeah, I guess it was.'

'Well, not that long,' he said, and she gave him a mocking smile. 'Spider says you're working for the *Times*?'

'That's right. You have a Bible club meeting you'd like me to write up or you've had your basketball stolen, be sure to give me a call.'

'He showed me a piece you did on the homeless. That was great writing. Spending a whole night on the streets of New York took a lot of guts. I'm not sure I would have done it.'

'Uncle had a fit.'

'Well, if I was your father . . . uncle, whatever . . . I would have had a fit too.'

'It was okay. I was made up like a bag lady. I had a friend in the theatre, and she did the make-up. I looked so horrible any rapist with self-respect would have jumped a dog before me. I had three pillows under my dress and one under my back. You never saw any derelict this ugly.'

'It still took a lot of guts.'

'Yeah, well, next day I was back at the criminal courts writing up the crack dealers.' She took a cup down from one of the shelves, put a spoonful of instant coffee in it, and poured in some hot water.

'I thought you didn't drink coffee,' Ryan said.

'This is for Uncle. I'd better let him know I'm here.'

'Too late. He was up and out before I got up.'

'Where is he?'

He nodded towards the beach. Two figures were walking side by side along the rocks from the bluff. 'Here he comes now.'

It was chilly at the water's edge and Mickey pulled her jacket tighter around her shoulders. The dawn was a burned orange stain in the sky over Southampton Bridge.

'Nothing happened between me and Ryan,' Mickey said.

'Okay.'

'I don't know why I'm doing this. I don't have to justify myself to you. Did I ask you if the investment adviser was round this week to update your portfolio?'

'I just want to know where I stand with you.'

She stopped, looked up at him. 'Where exactly is it that you want to stand?'

'I want to marry you.'

She suddenly looked scared and confused, as she had done at Bien Hoa. 'We're going to have to give it some time.'

'The last thing anyone can say is we rushed into this.'

'We really haven't known each other that long. It's about a couple of months maybe, if you don't count the gaps.'

'But I do count the gaps. I count them every day. They're bloody long gaps.'

'Let's just take this one day at a time.'

'You knew Ryan for about three weeks and you went straight back to Washington and married him.'

'And look what happened. Anyway, what's the rush?'

He searched for the right words. 'I love you. I've always loved you, from the moment I first saw you. I don't need time to think about it, to test the water. I didn't need it then, I don't need it now. There are no more fish in the sea for me. I've got one ocean and it's all for you.'

'You should have been a writer.'

'Mickey, don't do this to me again. Please.'

She looked back at him. 'It's not you I don't trust. It's me. I don't want me to hurt you any more.'

They heard shouts from the house. He saw Jenny running across the lawn towards them. 'To be continued,' he said.

After breakfast Ryan and Mickey climbed in the jeep and Webb drove them into town, the perfect host. He showed them the whaling museum and the Civil War monument and the old Customs House on Lower Main Street, a narrow thoroughfare that was lined with eighteenth-century houses of white clapboard and grey shingle. The tourists were already out, crowding the wharves and the cafés. Ryan went into a souvenir shop and bought them all T-shirts bearing the cartoon whale logo of Lincoln Cove. It was a typically grand gesture and Webb was irritated by it. Mickey took her shirt back into the shop and asked for a refund.

When they got back to the cottage the morning was appreciably warmer and Jenny was already sunbathing on the deck. She lay on a sunchair reading P. J. O'Rourke's *Holidays in Hell*, wearing Raybans, a gold bracelet and a black string bikini. Mickey studied her through the french windows; snake-hipped, raven-haired, her body gleaming with coconut oil. When she was her age she would have killed for skin like that.

Ryan joined her, sat himself down on one of the cane rockers, and made small talk. Mickey looked around for Webb. He was watching them too, from the breakfast bar, his jaw muscles working in his cheek. She wanted to say something to reassure him, but she couldn't think of a thing.

Webb watched them on the deck together as he made the coffees. Shit. He looked down at the bench, realised he had poured boiling water all over the counter.

*Christ!*

Surely she knew. Perhaps she had not recognised him in the photographs, but in the flesh . . . after all, he had not changed that much. Hardly at all. Was it possible that a five-year-old girl did not carry some residual memory of her father?

And yet, and yet, he reminded himself, it had been fifteen years ago, and Ryan had hardly ever been there. So much had happened to this girl since then. He remembered Jenny had once told him that she looked at every American male over thirty-five she ever met and wondered if he was her father. Perhaps her own imagination had muddied the waters of her recollections to such an extent that she would not even trust her own memories and instincts any more.

And he didn't want her to know. Not ever. He wanted everything to stay as it was. Now, seeing Ryan flirting with her, he just wanted to put his fingers around the bastard's throat and squeeze.

He finished making the coffees. Shit, his hands were shaking. Get a grip. He took a breath and went out on to the deck holding a tray. Jenny and Ryan looked up at him as if he were interrupting a private conversation.

He forced a smile. 'Looks like a good day for sailing,' he said.

The *China Sea* rolled as another deep swell passed under the hull. They were four kilometres from shore in Gardiners Bay, two lines drifting from the stern. Webb emerged from the cabin and threw a can of Budweiser at Ryan. Then he opened a beer for himself and sat down behind the wheel in the cabin.

There were just the two of them. Mickey had decided to stay behind at the cottage with Jenny. 'You two go bond,' she had said.

'Nice boat, mate,' Ryan said.

'Thanks.'

'You've done all right. Really dug in, aren't you?'

'I guess.'

Ryan sipped his beer. A gust of wind shook the boat and whipped the pennants on the flying bridge. 'Don't you ever miss it, but?'

'Miss what?'

The sky was overcast. Webb watched the horizon. An ink-black border of cloud was climbing the sky. They would have to head back to Lincoln Cove soon and beat the weather.

'Miss being in the front line, mate.'

'Why the hell would I miss that?'

Ryan shrugged, as if the answer were obvious.

'It's a simple choice. Would I rather be shot at or would I rather go fishing?'

Ryan seemed disappointed with the answer. 'You did well enough out of it. It was worth a few books.'

Webb didn't like the criticism implicit in the remark but he let it pass. Instead he said, 'Remember Odile? And the little girl?'

'Christ, Spider, not again!'

'I just wonder if you ever stop and wonder what happened to them.'

'I know what happened to them. You always bring this up. I can't change the past.'

A sudden squall of rain spattered against the windshield. 'Let's get the lines in,' Webb said.

Ryan didn't move. 'I said I can't change the past.'

'I'd forgotten how much you piss me off, Sean. You go out there and take food parcels to all the orphanages and steal medicines for them from the PX but when you had a chance to do something for someone you actually knew, for someone who loved you, you screwed up. And what really makes me angry is that I know, I just know, that if you had the chance over again you'd do the same bloody thing.'

'I know what I am. I don't need you to remind me. Christ, you haven't changed a bit, have you?'

'Nobody changes, they just get older.' Webb finished his beer, crushed the can in his fist and threw it on the deck. He went to the stern and started reeling in the lines.

Ryan brooded, sitting on the gunnel. Another gust shook the boat. 'You'll go back, mate. One day someone will ask you if you want to do a job in Afghanistan or the Balkans or somewhere and you'll go back.'

'Not me.'

'Yeah, you will.'

Webb laid the rods in the fibreglass compartment below the gunnels. 'Don't you ever think about taking it all, Sean? Three score years and ten they promise us in the Bible. Don't you ever think it might be all right to take that and not end up with a bullet in your head in some godforsaken little country while you're still only halfway through?'

The wind whipped Ryan's hair. 'When I was twelve I had a fight with this red-haired kid in my class. Delaney, his name was. His old man was the publican at the hotel. I beat the living shit out of him. This was a Friday afternoon. Well, Friday night some of my mates came round and told me Delaney's big brother was looking for me. This kid was sixteen and built like a brick shithouse. Well, at first I thought, okay, I'll pretend to be sick. Take a few days off school. Or maybe if I get to school late and run home early I can avoid him. But then I thought, what's the point? He's going to find me sooner or later. So instead of hiding I went round the pub first thing on the Saturday morning and fronted him. I remember he was round the back carting beer kegs, and his sleeves were rolled up past his elbow and he had muscles like bags of potatoes. I knew I never had a chance. But I know I scared the shit out of him when I showed up, and the hiding he gave me wasn't nearly as bad as I thought it was going to be. I won his respect, I suppose. And you know something else? I nearly beat the big bastard. That's how it is with me and dying, Spider. I'll front him on his own turf so I don't have to spend the rest of my life hiding and worrying about it. Does that make sense to you?'

There were whitecaps on the ocean now, long black clouds scudding towards them. 'Then again, if you'd taken a few days off, Delaney's brother might have forgotten all about you,' Webb said, and he went up to the flying bridge and hit the motor to pull in the anchor.

'So Sean's your ex,' Jenny said.

'Yeah, he's my ex. Hard to imagine, isn't it?'

A flurry of rain spattered against the windows. A mist had drifted down the channel, obscuring the far side of the cove. Jenny had pulled on a woollen jersey and jeans against the sudden chill and now lay sprawled on the sofa, P. J. O'Rourke discarded beside her on the Chinese carpet. Her face was framed by a long tapered finger held against her cheek; the other hand held a glass of white wine. Mickey was curled on a lounge chair beside her, her feet tucked underneath her, cradling a steaming cup of black coffee.

'What a cosy weekend,' Jenny said.

'Well your father . . . uncle . . . whatever you call him . . . he and Sean were friends long before I knew either of them. We met in Vietnam.'

'Uncle likes you very much.'

'Does he?'

'He talks about you all the time.'

Mickey wondered what Jenny was trying to tell her, whether this was meant as a warning or as encouragement. 'I like him too.' The silence hung suspended, so she added: 'There haven't been many men in my life recently. I gave them up for Lent a few years ago.'

Jenny grinned. 'Why did you do that?'

Jenny made her uncomfortable. She felt as if she were being interrogated by the thought police. Such an intense young woman. 'I'd just split up with Sean. Divorce is pretty tough on your confidence. I came away feeling like a failure, even though I blamed him for everything, of course. And then after a while I started to wonder if the penis, and its ancillary attachment, wasn't a little overrated.'

'I can't comment. The jury's still out on that one for me.'

Mickey smiled, feeling some of the frost between them thaw. 'I think Hugh just dragged the decision back to the appeals court for me, too. I'm listening to arguments.'

'How did you meet?'

'When I was a nurse at Bien Hoa in 1970. It wasn't easy. I worked long hours and he spent a lot of time out in the field.'

'I hate to use the word, but it sounds romantic.'

'Oh, Bien Hoa wasn't romantic. Nothing in Vietnam was romantic. Was it?'

Jenny stared into her wine glass. 'It's a long time to know someone and not do something about it.'

Mickey wondered how to answer that. Finally she said: 'We lost touch after I got back. Well, it was deliberate. He was still there, was going to be in Saigon for years and I was . . . here. He hasn't told you the story?'

Jenny shook her head.

'I suppose there's not much to tell. When I came back from Nam – Vietnam – my head was a little messed up.'

She waited for Jenny to get her off the hook, as most people did, make some joke that would break the mood. But she didn't. Instead she asked her, 'How did it mess you up?'

'I lost my faith.'

'Your religion?'

'I didn't have a religion. My parents were Baptist, for all that means. What I lost was my faith in people and in some sort of kind, beneficent God. I found I couldn't carry on a normal life without all those things as a given. Try it some time as an exercise in your head. After a while everything seems futile and demeaning and meaningless.'

'Did you try and kill yourself?'

Mickey felt her guard come up again. Perhaps it was the way Jenny was looking at her, as if she were a particularly interesting specimen in a jar. 'That's a hell of a question.'

'It seems logical.'

'Well, Dr Spock, we Vulcans are a little more tenacious than that. I opted out of suicide and did alcoholism and promiscuity instead. It's the same thing only it can be a little more fun. For about five minutes.'

'And you got better?'

'Yeah, I got better.' Jenny was still staring at her with the same candid intensity. 'I didn't quite give up. I just tried to cut my intake down to a healthier level. But I still miss the old me sometimes. You can get back a lot of things but never innocence.'

'Is that why you gave up guys?'

'Maybe.'

'And drinking?'

Mickey held up her coffee. 'It's killing me watching you drink that. But that's the way it is. Once a lush always a lush.'

'Don't be angry,' Jenny said. 'I really admire you. You must be very strong inside.'

'I'm not angry. I'm just being open, okay?' But she was angry. She felt as if her defences had been trampled down, and yet Jenny had not forced her to reveal anything she did not want her to know. Perhaps it was just that she had been private for so long that whenever she revealed anything of herself it was like bleeding.

'I was going to kill myself once,' Jenny said.

Mickey met her eyes but did not know how to respond to this revelation.

'It was the first year I was here. I thought I would just walk down the garden over the rocks and into the water. And just keep walking.'

'What stopped you?'

Jenny seemed to shiver. The room became very still. 'My mother told me not to.'

'Your . . . mother?'

'In those days I heard her talking to me all the time. Like a voice in my head. I guess I was a little crazy.'

'No,' Mickey said, 'I was the same, I heard voices all the time. My head was like a bar room, loads of people all shouting for another drink.'

'What were they saying?'

'Different stuff. About the war.' Mickey reached out her hand, touched Jenny's fingers. 'Did you ever talk to Hugh about this?'

'Uncle would not understand.'

'He might.'

'Well, it doesn't matter now. I obeyed my mother's voice so now I guess everything is okay.'

Mickey wondered what her old therapist in San Diego would have said about this sort of radical treatment. 'I guess so.'

Jenny ran her fingers through her long black hair and pushed it back over her shoulder. 'I just wish I had a last time to show my mother how much I loved her,' she said.

'I'm sure she always knew that.'

'Yes, I suppose she did. But this is not for her, this would be for me.' She shrugged her shoulders, finished the wine. 'I must have come through it for a reason.'

'It depends, I guess, on whether you believe in destiny.'

'I can't think of any other reason. I don't think anyone survives just by luck.'

Mickey thought about Ryan and that night in the mountains of Suchitoto. Ryan had always been lucky. It seemed to her that luck was the only way of explaining it, but she heard herself say: 'I'm sure everyone has a destiny.'

They heard the jeep pull into the drive. Both women jumped up, watched Webb and Ryan scramble out and run up the path. They were immediately soaked through, but Ryan was laughing about it, enjoying himself

'You know, for an attachment to a penis,' Jenny said, 'he is very charming.'

Mickey shook her head. 'You're very smart for twenty. But you've still got a lot to learn.'

# 70

I have to tell her, Webb thought.

I have to tell her about Ryan. I don't know if it's going to make any difference now, and I don't know what she'll do about it. But it had been weighing heavy on him all weekend; seeing them together on the deck and watching Ryan flirting with her had made him feel physically sick. He could not let it go on. He had convinced himself for the last ten years that Jenny's future was best served by his silence, but that was easier to believe when Ryan was not around. Now his presence that weekend had convinced him to tell her the truth.

He had almost told Ryan that afternoon, on the *China Sea*. Perhaps if the storm had not blown in he might have given him the whole story. He was relieved now that he had kept his silence. Somehow it still seemed like giving Ryan the easy option. It left him in control; the ball was in his half of the park.

But if he told Jenny, she would have the advantage. For once.

Of course, he would have to face the fact that Jenny might never forgive him for keeping the truth from her for so long. How could he explain and excuse that? If he were honest, he would also have to say that he had done it not only to protect her, but also to protect himself. Jenny was the one woman he had cared about that Ryan had not taken away from him.

And now, after witnessing the little scene on the deck, he guessed it was time to protect his family for once and for all.

He had not expected her to stick around on the Sunday evening after Ryan and Mickey had left. He gave them a ride down to the train station, and when he got back to the cottage Jenny was still there, in the kitchen, preparing dinner.

She was chopping shallots, with rapid, nervous movements of the knife. Something was wrong. Whenever she needed to talk she always went into the kitchen, started preparing food. This seemed to her a natural adjunct to important conversation.

'Don't you have to be at work tomorrow?' he asked her.

'I've got the day off.'

That seemed unusual. He stared at her, as if mentally saying goodbye, remembering how she looked, wondering if she would ever speak kindly to him again after what he had to tell her.

'Fun weekend?' she asked him.

'Not really.'

She separated some cloves of garlic and mashed them with the blade of the knife. 'I like this Mickey. She's okay.'

'I didn't think you noticed her much.'

She spilled one of the cloves on the floor. Her hands were shaking. 'We had a good talk this afternoon.'

'I meant you seemed to have your eyes elsewhere.'

'You mean your friend Sean? It's all right. I saw how he was looking at me. But you don't have to worry. He's old enough to be my father.'

She knew. She had to.

He stared at her. She held his eyes. *What's wrong?* 'There's something I have to talk to you about,' he said.

She dropped the knife on the counter top. 'No. Me first. You probably want to know why I've got the day off tomorrow.'

He shrugged his shoulders.

She took a deep breath. 'I've got every day off.'

He felt a sickening lurch. 'You lost your job?'

'I quit.'

'Quit? Why?'

'Because I'm sick of writing up court reports and traffic accidents. I want to do proper journalism, not that crap they're feeding me.'

'Wait a minute. The *New York Times* is one of the country's – the world's – leading newspapers. There's kids would give their right arm to get a break there. You're only twenty years old, for God's sake!'

'What were you doing when you were twenty?'

'I was working on a provincial newspaper in Surrey.'

'While you figured out some way to get to Vietnam! If you want to get out of the herd you don't follow the rest. You taught me that!'

'Well, you really got out of the herd, didn't you?' He tried to swallow down his anger, knowing it wasn't going to do him a bit of good. She was a grown woman now, and she had a right to make her own mistakes with her own life. 'So what's the lost little calf going to do now?'

'I'm going to freelance.'

'At your age that means you're going to starve.'

'You didn't starve.'

'Things were a lot different then.'

'Well, where I'm going, everyone starves, so it's not going to make any difference.'

'What are you talking about?'

'Yugoslavia.'

He felt as if his heart had stopped. 'You're not serious.'

'It's my Vietnam.'

'It's dangerous!' he shouted at her, and hammered both fists on the counter top. He suddenly realised how ridiculous that sounded. He searched desperately for some strategy to talk her out of this. 'I want you to stop and think about this.'

'I've made up my mind.'

'Have you? Have you really thought about it? Maybe you don't realise this, but war zones cost money.'

'I know. Ryan told me how expensive it is to survive.'

'You told a total stranger about this before you told me?'

'I didn't tell him I was going myself. I just asked him about it.'

'And what else did he tell you?'

'He told me to get myself a camera, like you did. That I had more chance of selling my stories as a freelancer if I could provide the pictures as well.'

'All right, did he also tell you that this little war in Yugoslavia is one of the most dangerous journalists have ever worked in, that attrition rates among the correspondents there are far higher than they were even in Vietnam?'

'I'm prepared to take the risk.'

His heart felt like lead. Yes, she was prepared to take the risk. Never mind that she was going to break his heart. But it's her life, he reminded himself. You can't hold her back, no matter that you love her like she's your own. This is what real fathers have to come to terms with one day. You gave her a chance at a better life, and now she's taken up the challenge you handed to her. You can't blame her for that, and if you try to block her she'll remember it and hate you for it.

'You have hardly any experience and you think you can go there and make your fame and fortune overnight?' he asked her.

'You did.'

Ah, but that was different, he wanted to say. But it wasn't, not really. He had found the right contacts, he had got lucky, and he had survived. And he had lived off that one risk for the rest of his life. Just as she intended to do.

'It's not as much fun as it sounds. You'll find yourself throwing your credit card on Hertz counters and at hotel clerks and every month your statement is going to come in and you still can't be sure if any newspaper really will pay you your forty bucks for the photograph of the burning tank. Which is not going to cover even one night's accommodation anyway.'

She stared back at him, unmoved.

'Is this a done deal?' he asked her, dreading the answer.

'I've given notice on my apartment. I've saved a bit of money over the last twelve months and I've got the car to sell.'

'This isn't a spur-of-the-moment decision, is it?'

'No, it's not.'

He couldn't believe it. He hadn't even suspected that she had been thinking about this.

'The features editor was real nice to me,' she said. 'He gave me a letter saying they'll consider any material I send them. And I have a friend who works at *Rolling Stone* and he got me another letter from them. I'll fly to Zagreb and get accredited with UNPROFOR. And the rest, as they say, is up to me.'

She had it all worked out. 'It's over a hundred dollars a night to stay at the Intercontinental in Zagreb. Then you have to hire yourself an interpreter.'

'I'll have two thousand bucks after the plane ticket. I guess I'll just have to sell some photos to one of the agencies as soon as I can.'

He could imagine the sort of risks she would be tempted to take to do that. But he knew it would be useless to argue. Her mind was obviously made up.

He went to the window. The storm had passed and a few stars appeared between the inky black clouds.

'It's your decision.'

'I thought . . . I hoped you'd be supportive.'

'Supportive. I hate that word. Don't be so damned politically correct. I'm . . . I'm not your uncle, for God's sake. You can call me that, but the fact is, for the last eight years I've been your father. I love you like a father. If you go and do this insane thing I will die a thousand times a day until you're back again.'

'I can't let that stop me.'

He had to agree with that. No, she couldn't let that stop her. If youth ever waited for its freedoms to be handed over, no child would ever grow up. He often forgot that he had taken into his home one of the great survivors. This was a girl who had once taught herself to catch and eat seagulls in order to stay alive. She very possibly had more of the resources needed to be a good combat photographer and journalist than he had ever had. His own career had grown, after all, in relation to the time he had stayed away from the war zones.

He sighed, conceding defeat. 'Do what you have to do,' he said. 'I'll try not to embarrass you at the airport.'

'I'm sorry,' she said. For you, she meant. He knew it was not intended as an apology.

There was a long silence.

'What was it you wanted to tell me?' she asked him finally.

He shook his head. 'It doesn't matter,' he said. They faced each other from opposite sides of the room, the distance complete.

Ryan's room in the UN Plaza Hotel was a model of opulence, furnished in ochre and gold. From the window he looked out at the stainless-steel spire of the Chrysler building and over the East River towards Queens. Perhaps this was how it felt to live in heaven, he thought. A kind of gilt luxury, detached from the mortals below, far above the noise and smog. It was just a theory, of course. With his track record he supposed he'd never get the chance to test it for himself.

This feeling of detachment and dislocation had been reinforced by experience since he had arrived in New York. He felt as if he had been trapped in some aberration of time and space; he had stayed the same but everyone else had grown older. He found no satisfaction in it. It actually woke in him an even more urgent desire to work harder, an irrational fear that as soon as he stepped off the treadmill the world would catch up with him, the spell would somehow be removed, and he would crumble away to dust.

They envied him, he knew, all his old mates; yet he in turn felt that they had something that he had missed. The grey hair and the lines on their faces had been well earned. They had learned and had grown while he had simply repeated the same experiences. Even the edge can lose its ability to enthrall when you have balanced there all your life, he thought.

He picked up the phone and dialled Mickey's number. She answered it on the third ring.

'Mickey. It's Sean.'

'Hi, Sean.' She sounded very cool, or perhaps she was just tired.

'Did you enjoy the weekend?'

'Look, Sean, is this a social call? I'm just on my way to work. I've got a late shift.'

'I was wondering if I could see you for lunch tomorrow.'

'I'll be getting in some cot time,' she said, using an old army phrase that she had somehow neglected to expunge from her vocabulary.

'What about breakfast?'

'Sean, I don't think it would be a good idea.'

'It's just I don't know how much longer I'll be in town. It would be good to catch up again before I go.'

There was a long and uncomfortable silence.

'You still there, Mickey?'

'What do you really want, Sean?'

Good question. A difficult one to answer. 'I'm not trying to move in again or anything.'

'As if you could.'

'Hey, we're still friends, right?'

'Yes, but not close friends.'

If I were on stage, he thought, I would be dying. Better not to embarrass myself further. 'Okay, sorry. I'll call you before I go. All right?'

'Sure.'

'Catch you, Mickey.' He hung up. Well. The silver-tongued devil had finally deserted him. Perhaps she was right. If she had said yes, I will come to lunch tomorrow, would he have tried to make room for her again in his life? Or was that just another mind game? Wouldn't it just be Washington all over again? In a year, two at the most, he would be staring at some television screen, listening to the sounds of automatic gunfire and watching the explosions in some damned and ravaged city, and he would feel the urge to go and face Delaney again. To get back to the edge, to feel the wonderful rush of fear and adrenalin. He was addicted. He couldn't go cold turkey as Webb had done.

To hell with it. He would call Cochrane instead and tonight they would go to the Oak Room or the Blue Note or Nell's; and whatever else happened, he promised himself he would not sleep alone in that massive bed tonight.

But something still haunted him, a feeling he had had ever since the weekend at Lincoln Cove, made more poignant since he had spoken to Mickey a few moments ago. He finally recognised it for what it was.

He was lonely.

# 71

I wonder if my parents felt this way, Webb thought. I wonder how they felt when I was leaving for Vietnam. They must have experienced this same tide of emotion, the same grief and dread and helplessness. He could not ask them now. They were both dead, their unmarried, vagabond only son perhaps their greatest disappointment.

As he thought of his mother and father, his gaze moved along the study wall until it found a framed black and white photograph, a little out of place alongside the combat souvenirs. A young boy with a crooked school tie, matchstick legs protruding from his school shorts, grinned self-consciously at the camera. Hugh Webb, the prototype version, he thought with a wry smile. Hard to imagine he was once that person.

The resemblance to that long-ago schoolboy might have been closer if he had not gone to Vietnam. It was a risk he had taken, a monumental risk, but it had paid off. Surrey to Saigon was about as far as you could travel in those days without actually stepping off the planet. His mother had not even known where Vietnam was; she had believed it was in South America. Neither of his parents could understand his ambition and what it was that he wanted from his life. His father had thought him a man of influence because he had twice got him into Chelsea games for free when he was on photographic assignments. And then one day he had announced that he had resigned his job to take photographs of a war whose gory images were already regularly featured on the BBC News and ITN's *News at Ten*. They must have thought he was mad, and that they would never see him again.

They were right on the first count, only a little wrong on the second. It was not the war that took him away from them, it was his career. Vietnam eventually led him to the United States, then to further assignments in Angola and the Middle East and Central America. Now he was as far from that tousle-haired schoolboy as it was possible to be. Hugh Geoffrey Webb, only ever an average student, once almost expelled from grammar school for smoking in the boys' toilets, was now a minor celebrity, his English accent corrupted with a New York twang, as much at home on daytime television chat shows as he was on his cabin cruiser in the cove. He had come a long way because of the risks he had been willing to take. Why could he not encourage his adopted daughter in her own adventure?

A flurry of rain slapped against the windows. The mournful sound of a foghorn came from somewhere on the other side of the cove as a fishing boat made its way through the mist. A grey winter had descended on Long Island.

He went to the bookshelf and took out a leather-bound photograph album. He opened it at random and stared at the images, both stark and fond, of a place called Vietnam; a place that no longer existed. This Vietnam was permanently at war, was peopled and governed largely by Americans. The main form of transport was the helicopter and the favourite form of dress was camouflage gear or a body bag. A long time ago.

He took out a photograph of himself and Ryan arm in arm outside the Continental Hotel. He should never have kept the secret for so long, he supposed. But there it was. He had thought the truth was best left buried and perhaps it was. He was still not sure if he was about to do the right thing.

Jenny was downstairs, her luggage open on the floor. She was sorting through it yet again to find items she could safely leave behind. Travel light, he had told her, and she had taken him at his word. Everything for God knows how long – three weeks, perhaps three years – in a backpack and a green canvas ex-US Army-issue holdall.

She had moved out of her Tribeca apartment and was now spending her last two nights here in Lincoln Cove before the flight to Zagreb in the morning. He had promised to drive her down to JFK himself in time for her early morning flight.

He watched her for a long time. He felt a sudden surge of pride; she might as well have been his own flesh and blood. If he had been a religious man he would have prayed then for her safety, but he wasn't; all he believed in was luck. Like Ryan. You were either lucky, like him, or you weren't, like Prescott.

And you were lucky until the day your luck ran out.

He held out the black and white photograph he had taken from the photograph album. He handed it to her.

'What's this?' she said, surprised.

'Take it with you.'

She gave him an uncertain grin. 'You had a lot more hair then. Hippy. Haven't you got a more recent photograph?'

It would be so easy to back off, make a joke of it, but this time he would press on. He had made up his mind. She had to know. 'You always asked me about your father,' he said.

She stared at him.

'The one on the left.'

She looked down at the picture and the blood drained from her face. 'That's Sean Ryan.'

He said nothing.

'He was here in the house. A whole weekend.'

He could not look her in the eyes. This was going to be every bit as bad as he had imagined.

'You never told me.'

'I had . . .' He was going to tell her he had his reasons, but his reasons would sound lame now.

'You never told me,' she repeated.

'No, I never told you.'

She sat down heavily on the sofa. 'Why?'

'Does it make any difference?'

'Of course it makes a difference!' She stared at the photograph. 'I can't believe this. I can't believe you didn't tell me.'

Well, I can't believe I *did*, he thought. Perhaps it was watching him flirt with you that day. Perhaps knowing that you two will almost certainly see each other again in Zagreb. 'I knew your mother,' he said. 'Through Ryan.' He had thought of telling her a little about his role in that sad episode, but changed his mind. It would sound as if he were trying to make himself appear heroic. If she was going to hate him, let her. He continued, his voice a monotone. 'It wasn't his fault. I'm sure he planned to get you and your mother out with him. But there was a rocket attack a couple of nights before Saigon fell. That was when your mother was wounded. Ryan had been hit in the head by shrapnel a few hours before at Newport Bridge. He was medevacked out of Saigon. Me and Dave Crosby went looking for you, but we couldn't find you. You have to realise what the city was like then. Anyway . . . That's what happened. He didn't abandon you.'

He was giving Ryan a little more credit than he deserved, but what the hell.

'Did he ever come looking for us?'

'We all thought you were dead.'

She just stared at the photograph, rocking backwards and forwards, her arms crossed across her stomach, as if she were winded.

'You really don't remember him?' On the weekend Ryan was at the cottage, Webb had thought that seeing him again would jog her memory, but there had been no sign of recognition – from either Jenny or Ryan.

'I remember a man who came to our apartment when I was a child. But I don't remember what he looked like. So much of that time is just shadows.'

'I think he was in Cambodia a lot of that time. Vietnam had stopped being news by the early seventies.'

'Why did he wait so long?' she said. 'Why did he wait so long to get us out?'

Webb said nothing.

Jenny pushed the photograph into the breast pocket of her shirt. She stood up slowly, her eyes unfocused, like a sleepwalker. 'I just can't believe you didn't tell me before. How long have you known? Did you always know?'

He nodded.

'Then perhaps it's best I'm going away,' she said, and she went into her bedroom and closed the door.

# 72

When he got back from the airport the front door was open and there was a woman sitting on the deck.

He parked the jeep and walked inside. He went first to the liquor cabinet, then changed his mind. He walked across the room, leaned against the french window. It was cool but pleasant outside. The sky was a washed blue and a pale, watery sun was chasing the shadows across the deck.

'Mickey,' he said.

'I took the day off. I figured you could do with some moral support.'

'Thanks.'

She was sitting in one of the director's chairs, her legs up on the rail, staring at the cold harbour. She was wearing a hooded jersey, her hands thrust deep into the pockets. The wind had raised a flush of colour to her cheeks. 'You okay?' she asked him.

He sat beside her. His body felt like lead. 'Not really.'

'Jenny's a survivor. One of the best. She'll be okay.'

'I hope so.'

She reached out, took his hand. They sat for a while in companionable silence, watching the waves lap against the flat shale rocks at the foot of the garden.

'I don't know if this is a good time to say this,' she started, 'but . . . I've been thinking a lot about us lately. I've been making a decision. Want to hear it?'

A seagull landed on the lawn, summoning painful memories. It seemed he had reached a nexus; today had apparently been chosen as the day he must wipe the slate clean and try again, without secrets. He took a deep breath. 'Before you say anything, there's something I think you ought to know.'

'Does it affect us?'

'It might. It might affect the way you feel about me.'

'Oh.' She took her hand away. 'Then perhaps I don't want to hear it.'

'It also has to do with Jenny, and it has to do with Ryan.'

She took her feet off the rail and sat up, as if bracing herself for a physical blow. 'Okay. Then I guess you'd better tell all.'

## McSorley's Old Alehouse, New York

It was reckoned by some to be New York's best bar, and was packed to the rafters this particular Saturday night. It was decorated in the style of a turn-of-the-century alehouse, with timber panelling and antique chairs and tables, sepia photographs and cartoons crowding the walls. Halfway along one wall was a wrought-iron stove with a flue that arched over the drinkers' heads.

It was also known as McSurly's because of the attitude of some of the bar staff.

Webb, Crosby, Cochrane and Doyle had made their way there in a taxi after leaving the Seventh Regiment Armoury. None of them wanted the evening to end. And there was still the rest of the story to be told.

'I don't believe you left it at that,' Cochrane was saying. 'I know you. You would have tried something else to stop Jenny leaving.'

'She'd made up her mind.'

'I've met her,' Wendy Doyle said. 'In Sarajevo. An extraordinary person.'

Crosby was getting boozy, Webb noticed, the state of drunkenness people take on when their brains are already addled by a lifetime of abuse. This was more like the Crosby he knew; the debonair adventurer of earlier had disappeared. 'Ah, Bosnia. Perhaps in twenty years' time we'll be having a Sarajevo reunion. Maybe there'll be a television series and compilation album. Music from the Bosnia era.'

Webb shook his head. 'I doubt it.'

'And so off she went to war,' Cochrane said. 'Your little war baby. What happened to her?'

'I don't really know all the details about the first part of the story,' Webb said. 'I didn't go to Bosnia until much later. Perhaps Wendy here can tell it.'

Doyle smiled. 'Not really. I didn't know her then. Besides, I wasn't in Zagreb long enough. I was trying to get through to Sarajevo. I only spoke to Ryan for a couple of minutes. I just remember seeing this Eurasian girl standing in the foyer of the Intercon looking completely lost. My God, she looked like a kid. It was hard to imagine how she was ever going to survive.'

'And that was where she met Ryan?' Crosby asked Webb.

'Well, that part of it was inevitable, I suppose. And I imagine if he hadn't been there, I'm sure she would have gone looking for him.'

'Well, come on,' Cochrane said to him. 'Don't keep us in suspense. I've always wanted to know what happened there.'

Webb shrugged and smiled. 'I only got the story second hand, of course. But I'll tell you what I know.'

# VIII

## Croatia,
## December 1991

'Most wars literally, not merely photographically, go through people's living rooms.'

– Charles Mohr, war correspondent

'Nothing makes an easier lead sentence
than a stray mortar round hitting a starving baby
in a typhus hospital.'

– P. J. O'Rourke, *Holidays in Hell*

# 73

## Zagreb

Jelacic Square had been, before the war, one of the city's most pleasant squares, closed to traffic and surrounded by stately cream and grey Habsburg buildings. It echoed to the sound of tram bells and the cries of the balloon sellers; skateboarders with fluorescent watches weaved their way through the crowds, money changers plied their trade, constantly on the lookout for tourists with hard currency to exchange.

But now the peaceful Croatian city was marching to the sound of another drum. The Ustashas had taken over the square, all wearing their Ante Pavelic T-shirts, clustering around the granite tiers at the base of the lampposts to hawk the Croat-language newspapers that enshrined their fascist philosophies while their radios blared '*Ostaski Becarac*', the nationalists' street fighting song.

The statues in the nearby cathedral had been winched down from the walls and transferred to storage in anticipation of air strikes. Refugees stood in long queues ouside the Caritas office. All the shops in the centre of the city had *God Protect Croatia* plastered across their windows in stick-on white letters.

Meanwhile, the people of Zagreb seemed to do little but read the newspapers for the latest news; *Vjesnik* or the tabloid *Vecernji List*. Zagreb TV broadcast war news all day, the bulletins interspersed with patriotic music videos, images of Croat soldiers running through fields of grain in slow motion firing AK-47s, the empty cartridge casings somersaulting out of the magazines to the music of *Brothers in Arms*. The main item of news was the siege of Vukovar, a town in eastern Slavonia that had become Croatia's Stalingrad. Now it was just a pile of rubble.

The war was creeping closer.

* * *

There was a bizarre festive atmosphere in the Press Centre in Zagreb's Intercontinental Hotel. Correspondents, photographers and television news crews were planning their days at the front with all the enthusiasm of children going on an outing. Every major news organisation was represented: the *Guardian*, Reuters, the BBC, the *Washington Post, Newsweek*, AP, UPI, IPA, CNN, *El Mundo*. Guides and interpreters were hastily arranged. Other journalists were occupied at one of the two press conferences currently under way. Those with a greater sense of self-preservation were spending their war in the bar, taking their information from the eavesdropped conversations around them and the thrice-daily English-language news bulletins on Croatian radio.

Ryan was in the foyer, planning his day's itinerary, when he saw her. She was wearing a fur-lined bomber jacket, olive-green fatigue pants and hiking boots. She looked utterly lost, he thought, like a kid on her first day at a new school. No friends to talk to and no idea where to go for her first class.

After he had overcome his initial surprise he got up and walked over. 'Jenny,' he said.

He thought she would be both relieved and delighted to see him, to find at last an ally among the chaos. But when she saw him her expression was somehow indecipherable. The smile of recognition came almost reluctantly.

'Sean,' she said.

A stiff embrace. 'What are you doing here?' he said.

She indicated the UNPROFOR press accreditation on her jacket.

'The *Times* send you?' he asked, knowing that was impossible.

'I've gone freelance.'

'Here? It's not the best bloody place to start.'

'It's a war and it's on the front page.'

'Hugh let you go?'

'I'm twenty years old.'

He put her belligerence down to fear. But there was something else about her attitude, something he could not fathom at all. It was the demeanour of a spurned former lover. Strange.

'How long have you been in Zagreb?'

'A couple of days. I'm still getting myself organised.'

'Let me buy you breakfast,' he said. 'Perhaps I can help you out.'

* * *

'The first thing you have to remember,' Ryan told her, 'is that twenty-one journalists have already died covering this war. The Vietnam war cost sixty-three lives, but that was over about twenty-five years. This place has chalked up a third of that total in about six months. I've been to Vietnam, Cambodia, Lebanon, Angola, El Salvador, the Gulf War – I reckon this is the most dangerous assignment I've had. The Serbs are deliberately targeting us. Go out there in a car with a press sticker on it and you might as well draw a bullseye on the side. Have you got yourself a flak jacket?'

Jenny shook her head. 'I don't have the money.'

'I'll get you one.' She started to protest but he held up his hand. 'You can pay me back later. Or I'll work it into my swindle sheet somehow. I'll say mine got flogged. It happens all the time. The baggage handlers at the airport steal them and sell them on the black market. The bloody things weigh about twenty kilos, probably more than you do dripping wet, but it could save your life.'

'You don't have to do this.'

'It's just the kind of bloke I am. Look, I've known Spider a long time. I owe him a couple.'

She put her spoon in her coffee cup, toyed with it. It had gone cold.

'You need a few basic items,' he said. 'Are you planning to take snaps?'

'I'm not an expert. But I've got a camera.'

'Got condoms?'

She stared at him. 'We're in a war zone. Safe sex wasn't my first priority.'

'You put your used films in them to stop them getting wet. I suppose Spider's made sure you've got the rest of it. Flashlight, Swiss army knife, that sort of thing?'

She nodded.

'What about morphine?'

'Drug parties?'

'You get yourself shot up, you won't think it's a joke.'

'I have a basic first aid kit. Field dressings, rubber tubing for tourniquets.'

'You'll need cash in German marks, British pounds and Croatian dinars. I hope you brought plenty of spare film. One roll costs two hundred American in the lobby.'

'Uncle even gave me a spare camera. An old Leica 3-C.'

'Good.' He shook his head. 'What did he think about you coming here?'

'He was against it.'

'I bet he was. You must be out of your mind.'

'Fast track to the top.'

'I'll give you another cliché. Easy way to get killed.'

'Uncle always said he was one of the few people the Vietnam war was good to. He always said it was a simple equation. You have to be in the right place, at the right time, and not die.'

'Yes, you too can be Sydney Schanberg. Is that what you want?'

'I don't want to be doing court reports the rest of my life.'

'Let me tell you a story. Last week I met this Pommy bloke. He drove out from England in a clapped-out twenty-year-old Vauxhall Viva. A Photographer of Fortune, he called himself. He was here three days, sold two photographs to the AP for about forty bucks each, and on the third day me and a photographer from Sigma loaded him into a box. Or the bits of him that were left, anyway. He couldn't afford a flak jacket either.'

'You're not going to frighten me away.'

'No, I'll leave that to the Serbs. Have you got yourself an interpreter?'

She shook her head.

'Well, how about I save you some money. You come with us today. Be the sorcerer's apprentice.'

'I don't want to be anybody's apprentice.'

'Believe me, when you're as green as you are, you need all the help you can get. Put your pride under your flak jacket. It's the first thing that gets blown away.'

She looked frightened all right, he thought. Fear is something you can smell. But she was a survivor. Webb had told him her story. There had to be some tempered steel in there somewhere.

'Why are you doing this?'

'You're my mate's kid, for Christ's sakes. What would Spider say to me if I let his little girl get hurt? He'd never forgive me.'

'I'm not his little girl.'

Ryan shrugged and laughed. 'Well, you're somebody's little girl,' he said easily.

But Jenny didn't even smile.

* * *

He had crewcut blond hair and large, horsey front teeth. He was a big man, with ruddy cheeks, always grinning. 'German,' Ryan told her. 'His name's Helmut. Now there's a man who was born to work in a war zone. No matter where we go, we've always got a Helmut. Also the best cameraman I've ever seen. No nerves at all.'

In contrast, Ryan's soundman was shy and soft-spoken, a small, wiry man with large ears that stuck out from his head at crazy angles. Jenny never discovered his real name. The others called him Radar.

Ryan himself was resplendent in a fisherman's body warmer worn over an ex-Gulf War kevlar flak jacket. His army boots were caked with mud. He led the way to the transport, a red Lada Niva. As she got in, Jenny noted the holes in the rear passenger side door. 'What are these?' she said.

'Bullet holes,' Ryan said. 'Still want to come?'

They headed out of Zagreb on the deserted Zagreb-Belgrade motorway. There were reports of heavy fighting around western Slavonia, and Ryan hoped to get some combat footage from the front lines. A heavy mist blanketed the highway as they drove south-east, and their driver-interpreter, a taciturn Croat by the name of Dragan, had to drive cautiously because of the stray cattle that had wandered on to the road.

There was hardly room to breathe in the tiny Niva. Jenny was crammed in the back between Radar and Helmut, the sound equipment and camera and battery packs and leads strewn around her lap and on the floor. Ryan sat in the front, tapping impatiently on the dashboard, making desultory conversation with Dragan.

As they drove, Helmut told her his life story in his idiosyncratic English. Apparently he had once taken pictures of models before making the transition to television work. 'I am fashion photographer,' he said. '*Vogue*, yes. *Elle*. *Cosmopolitan*. Now I go from bum-bum to boom-boom, yes?' He laughed at his own joke.

Once they passed a column of white armoured vehicles moving slowly in the opposite direction, flying the blue flag of the UN. The officer sitting in the turret of the lead vehicle sported huge goggles and canary-yellow gloves.

'UNPROFOR,' Ryan said. 'Also known as the Unprotection Force by the locals.' He leaned out of the window and waved.

'About as much use as tits on a bull. The idea is to put these blokes in the middle of two armies who are slavering at the mouth and armed to the teeth and then hope neither side shoots at them. Great idea. Still, that's what makes the United Nations the dynamic institution it is.'

They turned off the motorway and headed north towards Pakrac.

The villages showed signs of the recent fighting. Wrecked cars littered the streets; many of the houses had gaping shellholes in the roofs and walls. Jenny saw handbills pasted on every available space: *Hrvatska Vas Zove!* Croatia needs you now!

'It's like a cake,' Ryan was saying. 'You mix all the ingredients together, and then, after you've baked the damn thing, all the ingredients decide to go back the way they were before. That's what's happened here. You've got Croats, Serbs, some Jews, Slovenians, Moslems, Albanians, Montenegrans all living together for the last fifty years, the way Tito wanted. Now he's dead and they're trying to unbake the cake.'

But Jenny was only half listening to what he was saying.

This was him, she kept telling herself. This was the man she had wanted to find all her life. Where was her rage when she needed it? Where was the hatred? She could not summon her venom now and she felt ashamed. She had been searching for a monster, and the monster had turned out to be a brave man with a big heart who had not hesitated to help her when she needed it.

'The really amazing part,' Ryan was saying, 'is that there ever was such a thing as Yugoslavia. Tito must have been quite a bloke. His father was Montenegran and his mother was Slovenian yet he cobbled this whole state together and kept the Croats and the Serbs living side by side in the republic for almost fifty years. Incredible.'

Dragan turned off the road and down a dirt track. The Lada bounced over the wheel ruts in the frozen mud. 'Where are we going?' Jenny asked.

'I've got some deliveries to make,' Ryan said.

A road sign, pockmarked with bullet holes, identified the village as Otovac. It appeared to be deserted. Many of the houses were boarded up and Dragan had to manoeuvre the Lada around shell craters in the road. Pieces of bitumen lay in huge lumps in the street and the shellholes were rapidly filling with black and icy water from the melting snow. A modern Pik supermarket had been looted and its entire front window lay shattered on the footpath. All the shelves inside were empty.

A dog nuzzled the spilled innards of a dead cow outside a petrol station.

Dragan turned into an alley, parked the Lada outside a large and desolate brick building. Ryan went to the boot and unloaded two large cardboard boxes from behind the back seat. They were marked with the names of Swiss and German medical companies. Helmut lifted two other cartons, one of concentrated milk powder, the other tinned fruit.

'Come and have a look,' Ryan said to Jenny.

A woman appeared at the doorway of the building. She was tiny, with mousy brown hair, and she wore a white coat. She shouted a greeting to Ryan in Serbo-Croat and he answered her in her own language. She led the way inside.

There appeared to be no light or heating and the building's interior was gloomy, and cold as a tomb. There was an overpowering smell of urine, damp, and sour boiled food. The woman in the white coat led the way into what appeared to be the kitchen. It was a sizeable room, with several sinks and ovens, large enough to accommodate the preparation of a meal for a small army. There was a huge pantry with rows and rows of wooden shelves, but they were mostly empty. Jenny counted just a few packets of rice and a tin of strawberry yoghurt powder.

Helmut and Radar tore open the cardboard boxes and started to unload the contents. The woman threw her arms around Ryan's neck and embraced him.

'What is this place?' Jenny said.

Ryan disengaged himself from the woman in the white coat. 'Come and see for yourself.'

He led the way into a long dormitory. The windows had been blown in by shellfire and were open to the freezing rain. Fifty or sixty children lay on cots and metal frame beds, staring at the ceilings and walls in morose silence. When they saw Ryan and Jenny there was a general stampede. Jenny took a step back.

They stank and most of them wore no more than ragged T-shirts, even in the Dickensian cold of the dormitory. Jenny recoiled from the matted hair, wild-eyed faces smeared with dirt and mucus, bare legs crusted with dried excrement.

The children pulled at her arms and tugged her hair, thrust their hands into her pockets, pawed at her, swarming around her like ants on the carcass of a beetle. 'Fuck you, bitch! . . . you give me cigarette . . . fuck you, bitch! fuck you! . . . you give me food, you give me money, bitch, fuck you!'

Jenny backed towards the door. Ryan caught her arm and held her. 'Hard to feel sorry for orphans when it's like this, right?'

He pulled her away, down the corridor to the next room. 'This is the hospital,' he said. It was scarcely different from the dormitory from which they'd just come, except perhaps for the tattered posters tacked to the walls: the Pink Panther, Asterix the Gaul, Donald Duck.

The woman in the white coat was sitting on one of the beds. She was holding a basin of near-freezing water with which she was bathing the stumps of a young girl's legs. 'That's Dr Pavlovic,' Ryan said. 'She's in charge of the orphanage here. A lot of the kids here are Serbs. Some of them had their parents murdered by the Croats, or got separated from their families when the fighting started.'

There was a large iron bedstead pushed against the wall. A young girl, perhaps no more than four or five years old, lay there staring at the ceiling. Her ankle was chained to the rail of the bed. 'That one's a Croat,' Ryan said. 'The Chetniks came and raped her mother right in front of her eyes, cut her throat. For some reason they let the kid be. Perhaps they were feeling kind that day. Anyhow, any man comes close to her now she goes berserk.'

'Why is she chained up?'

'They do it for her own good. If they don't she'll go over to the wall and bang her head against the bricks until she's unconscious.'

Jenny stared at him.

'I suppose you understand this better than I do,' he said. 'You came through something like this and survived.'

'I don't know if I do understand. I'll never comprehend how human beings can do this sort of thing.'

'The blokes who did this to her mother haven't got two heads or anything. They're probably kind to their own mother, and I dare say they go to church every week and say their prayers.'

He pointed to one of the other cots. A four-year-old boy was watching them. He was holding a toy gun, a Kalashnikov made of black plastic.

'I brought him a teddy bear last time I was here,' Ryan said. 'He didn't want to know, threw it on the floor.'

The boy kept pointing the weapon at her, imitating the barking cough of a machine gun. *Ah-ah-ah-ah-ah-ah-ah-ah* . . .

'Why don't they take that thing away?' she said.

'They did a couple of times. He practically fits, throws himself around, does himself damage. So they had to give it back.'

Jenny turned away but she could still hear him, he was still doing it. *Ah-ah-ah-ah-ah-ah-ah* . . . 'What happened to him?'

'Who knows? Come on, get your camera out. You should be able to sell that one to AP. Make sure he's looking right at the camera. It's the face that's important, every single time.'

Jenny self-consciously raised the Canon and shuttered off a few frames. The plastic Kalashnikov, the child's blank expression, the heart shaped mouth, the frigid blue eyes.

'Come and see the babies,' Ryan said.

The babies . . .

The babies stank. There was not enough water to wash them and too few staff to change their nappies. Jenny bent over one of the cots. With none of the plumpness of an infant, the child that lay there was painfully thin, its skin grey, eyes huge and lifeless, like a fish on a stone slab.

She bent to pick him up.

Ryan stopped her. 'Don't do that.'

'I don't care if I get shit on me.'

'Neither do I. But Pavlovic doesn't like it. She says they cry for hours afterwards. It's better you don't touch them at all.'

She wanted to get out of this place. Too many memories coming back now, too many hellish images of her own that she had sought to bury. She fought to control her breathing, her body's urge to hyperventilate. Hard to accept that the man she had blamed for her misery, for her mother's misery, was right there beside her. Once she had imagined in her fantasies of revenge that she would have to force him to see the harm he had done; and yet he knew, he knew better than anyone.

'How often do you visit here?' she asked him.

'When I can. I try to organise some food and some medicine from as many different places as I can. I've got some contacts inside UNPROFOR. I get some of the medicines sent out from the States. Sometimes it gets flogged at the airport, but you can't win 'em all.'

'Why? Why do you do it?'

He grinned. 'Every little bit helps, as the old woman said as she pissed in the sea.'

*And there was her mother's face. Not beautiful any more, not as she was in her childhood memory, serene and lovely. Her skin had been dried to the colour and texture of old leather by long years of work in the fields in the Zones. The long tapered fingers that had once joined in prayer were gnarled by disease and work and poverty. A tooth in the top of her mouth was missing. She was passing her a bowl with a little rice, all they had to eat, and whispering: 'I am not hungry, little bird, you have it.'*

*She remembered her on the stinking, wallowing boat, handing her the meagre ration of water in the tin cup: 'I have had enough now, little bird, you drink it.' She remembered with burning shame how she had gulped it down.*

*Now she looked again into that tender, tormented face. And she heard that same voice say to her: 'This is the man who did this to me. I cannot do it, little bird. You kill him.'*

They heard shouting from the hospital ward. It was Dr Pavlovic's voice. Ryan ran outside and Jenny followed him.

Pavlovic had Helmut backed against the wall. She was poking him in the chest with her finger; he had his television camera raised above his head with both hands, as if her index finger were a Kalashnikov. The doctor was trembling with fury, the frenetic anger of exhaustion.

Ryan asked Radar what was going on.

Radar nodded to one of the children. The top half of his head was swathed in bandages. 'It's the blind kid,' he said. 'Pavlovic told us she'd found out that both his parents had been killed at Pakrac. Helmut asked her if she could tell him the news right now so we could film it. She just went crazy.' Radar shrugged. 'Jesus, he's got to find out some time. It's not like he'll see us or anything.'

'Cretin,' Jenny said.

'Reserve your judgments,' Ryan said. 'If you survive three months of this, you won't believe some of the things you'll be tempted to do.'

'I'm not here to trade on other's misfortunes.'

'Yes, you are. Even if you don't mean to.'

Pavlovic was still screaming at Helmut. He just stood there, pinned against the wall, grinning. 'I am just asking a question,' he said to Ryan. 'Crazy woman!'

Ryan put himself between Pavlovic and Helmut, grabbed the big German and pulled him towards the door. But Pavlovic had spent her anger. She turned and ran out of the ward.

The skeletal branches of the trees were silhouetted against a grey sky. All the colours seemed to have been leeched from the landscape, an amorphous panorama of mud, frost, ice and mist. In the distance the hollow boom of shellfire. Jenny felt the first liquid thrill of fear. She wondered if her nerves would hold. Or would she make a complete fool of herself?

Pavlovic was leaning against the wall, her eyes closed. Then she heard Jenny's footsteps and spun around. 'No photograph,' she said.

Jenny realised she still had the Canon in her hands. She replaced the lens cap and slung the camera around her neck. She reached into her pocket and took out a packet of Marlboro.

Pavlovic took one gratefully. Her hands were shaking. 'Thanks,' she said.

Jenny put the Marlboro back in her pocket.

'You don't smoke?' the doctor asked.

Jenny shook her head, then, realising what she had meant by the remark, retrieved the pack and held them out. Pavlovic took them with a rueful smile. 'Thanks. Good for nerves, yes?'

'They say.' She fumbled for her matches, lit her cigarette for her.

'It is very bad to lose the temper this way. But this man makes me very angry. Very angry.'

'He used to be a fashion photographer,' Jenny said, apropos of nothing, embarrassed.

'Fashion,' Pavlovic repeated. 'Now Croatia is fashion. Now war is fashion. Yes?'

Jenny did not know how to answer that. The doctor's hollow-eyed accusation hung in the air between them.

*I'm not here to trade on others' misfortunes.*

*Yes, you are. Even if you don't mean to.*

'So, you are a fashion photographer also?'

'I'm a journalist.'

'Croatia has so many journalist now. Maybe one day United

Nations will give journalist their own republic. Why not? They give the Serb, they give the Croat, why not the journalist?' Her hands were still shaking. 'I am sorry. Not your fault.' She rubbed her eyes. 'How can he ask to take picture of this boy so all the world can watch him suffer? Will the whole world then help him escape this war? Whole world going to find him new father, new mother?'

'If the world knows what is happening here, perhaps it will make the governments do something.'

The doctor's mouth creased into a tight, bitter smile. 'You are very young. You will learn.' She stubbed out the cigarette on the ground with her heel. 'Not good to smoke cigarettes. My husband always tells me this.'

Jenny nodded. 'Where is your husband?'

Pavlovic ignored the question. 'But it is not a good time for me to give up the smoking. You are a friend of Mr Ryan?'

Jenny hesitated. 'We go way back.'

'This is very good man, I think.'

A very good man. The words echoed inside her head. 'Why do you stay here, Dr Pavlovic? Surely you're in danger.'

Ryan appeared in the doorway. 'Time to go,' he said.

Jenny turned to Pavlovic, tried to find the right words, but there were none. 'Goodbye,' she said.

'Stay alive,' Pavlovic said to her, and went back inside.

'What happened to her husband?' Jenny asked Ryan as they drove away.

'He's dead.'

'What happened to him?'

'He was fighting with the Croat army at Osijek. He went out on night patrol with three others. They found their bodies the next morning.' Ryan hesitated, imparting the last piece of information with something like embarrassment. 'There were signs they had been tortured before they were killed.'

There was silence in the car.

'That's what the Serbs did to her husband.'

'She must really hate them,' Jenny said.

'Not really. Dr Pavlovic is a Serb herself.'

# 74

'Pull over here,' Ryan said.

They were in a small village called Vojnovar, had just passed through a roadblock manned by Croatian militia sporting a variety of weapons.

'What are we doing?' Jenny asked.

'Easy to cross the front line without even knowing it. Sean Ryan's golden rule: If you're going to take a risk, know what the risk is. I'm going to sweet-talk the local constabulary. See if this place has a McDonald's.'

The police headquarters was a sad and grey building opposite the post office; but unlike the post office it had not received a Serb shell through its roof.

A uniformed policeman sitting behind a grey steel desk looked up suspiciously from his paperwork. Ryan noticed that the old red star on the cap and shoulder flashes had been replaced by the *sahovnica*, an armorial shield with a red and white chessboard pattern, the medieval coat of arms of Croatia, the symbol used by the dreaded Ustashas during World War II. Its use had been banned for forty-five years and now it was everywhere.

Ryan took out his passport, his UNPROFOR accreditation, his Australian driving licence, his international driving licence, a library ticket for the Mosman Park library in Sydney which had expired in 1963, as well as a laminated membership card from a video library in Kensington in London, and laid them all on the desktop.

'CNN,' Ryan said.

The policeman shook his head, bemused.

'CNN, New York!'

Nothing.

Ryan decided to try another tack. 'BBC!'

'BBC Lonn-donn!'

'Yeah, BBC, Lonn-donn,' Ryan repeated. He didn't know why none of the big American networks had the same clout. And his own network might as well be the Venezuela Radio Service for all the weight it carried here.

'Lonn-don,' the man repeated. 'Liver-pool. Manch-est-er.'

'Yeah, Manchester,' Ryan said, leaping at the opportunity to find common ground. 'Manchester United.'

'Manch-est-er! Bobby Charl-tonn!'

That ages you, Ryan thought. 'Bobby Charlton!' he agreed.

The man beamed, the conversation now going well. 'Bobby Charl-tonn!'

'George Best.'

This time Ryan really hit the jackpot. The man hooted with laughter and, forming a ring with the finger and thumb of his left hand, moved the index finger of the other in and out in the universal symbol for fornication. 'George Best!'

Ryan tried desperately to think of some Yugoslav soccer teams but the only one that came to mind was Partizan Belgrade, and he thought it might not be a good tactical move to mention them. But with a rapport now established, he produced a map of the area from his jacket pocket and laid it on the counter. 'Chetnik?' he enquired.

'George Best – Chetnik?'

'No, forget about George Best, for Christ's sake. Just Chetnik.'

The policeman frowned. He took a biro from his uniform jacket and started to write on the map.

There was an etiquette to be observed at roadblocks.

As Dragan slowed the car, Ryan wound down his window, put his passport on the dashboard with his hands either side of it. 'Don't try and get out of the car until they ask you to,' he said to Jenny. 'Keep your hands where they can see them and don't make any sudden moves. We entered the Middle Ages three roadblocks back.'

The militia who waved them down was dressed in camouflage fatigues and a black bowler hat, and had an ancient Mauser hunting rifle slung from his shoulder. He kept the barrel of the weapon pointed through the window at Dragan as he leaned in, his face contorted into a scowl of contempt. There was several days' growth of beard on his face, and Jenny could smell his breath from the back seat. *Sjlivovica*, plum brandy.

There was a hurried exchange between the man and the driver.

Jenny looked out of the window. The checkpoint was actually just a few sandbags decorated with a looted shopfront mannequin dressed in Croat uniform. Several other soldiers lounged around, ostentatiously flicking the safeties on their weapons on and off.

Ryan took the Marlboro from the dashboard and offered the packet to the militia. He accepted one with bad grace while he examined their passports.

'He's reading it upside down,' Jenny whispered.

'He's so drunk he can't even focus on the photographs,' Ryan said, still smiling at the man, offering some of their chocolate.

The man barked another question in Serbo-Croat. Dragan translated this and Ryan shrugged and grinned. 'What did he say?' Jenny asked.

'He wants to know if we've got any money,' Ryan answered.

Dragan leaned out of the window and there was another sharp exchange.

'Now what's going on?'

Dragan turned around. 'I told him you were just three stupid Belgians and an idiot Chinese. If I told them you were from an American television company they would think you were rich and we'd be here for hours.'

The militia kept the Mauser pointing at the car while he discussed the dilemma with his friends. Ryan swore under his breath. 'He's probably had a big fight with Mrs Bogtrottervic, or he's bored, or he's looking for an easy way to make some fast dollars. So he's dug the old man's Second World War rifle out of the barn and come down the road with his mates to entertain himself for a few hours.'

The militia returned and contemptuously tossed the passports though the open window.

Dragan was white. He seemed relieved that it was over. Only Ryan did not appear concerned. 'Ask him if the road ahead is safe,' he asked Dragan.

Dragan seemed amazed by the naïveté of the question but he repeated it. '*Dali put seguran napred?*'

The guard grinned, revealing bad teeth, and his mates laughed uproariously.

'What does he say?' Helmut asked Dragan.

'He says sure it's safe. And who's going to miss a few Belgians and a Chink if it isn't?'

Ryan shrugged and checked his map. 'Keep going,' he said. 'According to the local cops we're still five miles from the front lines.'

# 75

The road had deteriorated to a mud track. The woods seemed to close in around them; thick mist drifted through pines dusted with snow. The sound of shellfire was ominously close. They had not passed another car since they had left Vojnovar.

Ryan consulted the map. 'Where are we, Dragan?'

Dragan pulled the car over to the side of the road. He stared at the map, and shook his head. 'I do not know this road,' he said.

'We should have reached this village by now.' Ryan pointed to his map. 'Gravina.'

'Are we lost?' Jenny said.

'No, we're not lost. We just haven't got a fucking clue where we are.'

'Should we go back?' Jenny said.

'Shit, no,' Ryan said. 'Not until we've got some film I can use.'

He was still apparently relaxed but Jenny felt the tension among the others. She clenched her fists in her lap, trying to control her own fear. Old friends returned, voices she had not heard since her childhood, the voices that had sustained her in the Zones and on the streets of Saigon and, most of all, during the nightmare voyage to the McAdam Reef. *Be still, be calm. You will see this through.*

They drove on another two kilometres. There was a sense of unreality to all this, she thought. The craters in the road and the shellholes in the buildings and the soldiers at the roadblocks could all have been theatre.

'Here we go,' Ryan said. He read the sign beside the road. 'Zenac. Zenac? It's not even marked on here.'

A few red roofs appeared through the mist. They drove through the main street and Dragan avoided a dead pig that was lying in the middle of the road. They passed a house that had its whole front wall blasted away, leaving the interior exposed like some giant doll's house.

The village appeared deserted, but then Ryan spotted a woman pegging out her washing in the garden of a neat detached house at the end of the street. An old man was washing his car in the driveway.

In the distance they heard the sharp crack-crack of sniper fire.

Ryan got out of the car with Dragan and went over to the old man. He was wearing an old woollen jacket over a threadbare brown jersey, and the teeth he had left were brown and crooked like old tombstones. He looked up when they approached, but the old woman ignored them completely, and continued with her chores.

Dragan introduced them and bid the man good day. The man returned the greeting with the same air of casual politeness.

'Ask him if there are Croat soldiers up ahead,' Ryan said.

There was a long exchange in Serbo-Croat. Dragan turned away. 'He says he doesn't know anything about soldiers. He says yesterday some bastard shelled the village and everyone left. He says he lived right through the Second World War and he can't be bothered with this little gang war. He just wishes everyone would fuck off.'

'That was what he said?'

'His words.'

They went back to the car.

'What are we going to do?' Jenny asked.

'I don't get a good feeling,' Dragan said. 'I think we should go back.'

Ryan nodded. 'This time I think you may be right.'

Helmut grunted. '*Scheiss!* No balls!'

Ryan rounded on him, and for the first time that day he looked angry. 'I was taking pictures of this shit when you were still standing around catwalks with a Kodak Brownie, trying to see up Claudia Schiffer's skirt. One thing I learned was to listen to my instincts. It's why I'm still around to take crap from people like you.'

Helmut stopped smiling for the first time that day. 'Okay,' he said. 'But first I take the pictures.'

'Want to do a stand-up?' Radar asked.

'Not here.'

'Go on and get whatever you want. Don't be long,' Ryan said to him.

Helmut jumped out of the car. Radar followed him down the street, slipping on his headphones, the radio gear suspended on a strap over his shoulder.

Jenny climbed out of the Lada and looked at Ryan. 'Are we in danger here?'

'No, we're not, but that fat German bastard's in danger if he pushes me any more.'

Jenny hesitated, then grabbed her camera from the front seat. 'While I'm here, I suppose.'

She crossed the street. The sniper fire had stopped and the silence was terrifying. She walked slowly down the street, spooked by the sound of her own breathing. She stopped outside a house with a gaping hole in its front wall. The room inside appeared to be hardly damaged; there was a framed picture of Tito on a wall, and a cup of tea frozen solid in the middle of the dining table. A pin-up photograph of Tom Cruise lay soggy in the mud at her feet.

She brought the camera up to her eye and clicked the shutter. She crept further along the street, running off frames of the dead pig, a looted shop. Ryan followed her.

'Helmut's taken a lot of film,' she said.

Ryan shrugged.

'You don't think this is newsworthy?'

'People being driven from their homes by war? I think it's an outrage, but no, I don't think it's going to excite the editors back home. To make film really interesting you have to have people in it.'

She put down her camera. 'If you were me, what would you do?'

'You're supposed to be a journalist, not a photographer.'

'Maybe I'd like to be both.'

'Well, I would have got that one of Tito through the hole in the bricks, just like you did. I would have made sure I had his pompous expression right in the centre of the frame. But you missed the broken wedding photograph lying in the rubble. I would have taken it close enough so you could see their faces through the splintered glass. And I wouldn't have wasted film on the pig.'

'Why not?'

'I didn't like its expression.'

Jenny searched his face. 'Was that a joke?'

'It could have been. But you didn't laugh.'

She shook her head. 'I can't work you out.'

'I'm a shit with a compassionate streak. If you don't try and twist me to make me the other way round, I'm easy to figure out.'

'Why does Uncle hate you so much?'

'Spider? Has he ever told you he hated me?'

'Not in those words.'

'There you are, then. Now where's my Teutonic mate?'

They both heard the sound at the same time; even Jenny recognised it for what it was, perhaps from the war movies she had seen on television, or from the evening news. She had never seen a tank at close quarters but the sound of the tracks in the mud in that cold and deathly silence was terrifying.

Ryan grabbed her. 'The Croats don't have tanks yet, if that answers your question.'

He pulled her towards one of the houses and they both crouched down behind a wall. The squeal and rumble of the tracks was getting louder, but as yet they could not see the tank. Ryan looked back. He could see Dragan standing next to the Lada.

'Come on, sport, get off the street, for Christ's sake,' he said under his breath.

Dragan hesitated a moment, then ran down a laneway between two of the bombed-out buildings.

A few moments later the huge metal monster rounded the corner, the double-headed Serbian eagle emblazoned in a crest on the turret. The cannon swivelled, looking for a target. They were close enough to hear the whirr of the machinery.

'A Russian T-72,' Ryan whispered.

It stopped, turned and clanked down the street towards them. The abandoned Lada was directly in its path.

'What should we do?' she said. To her surprise she felt absolutely calm.

'Nothing for the moment. They may be looking for targets. It's important we don't give them one.'

The tank driver must have seen the car in his path; perhaps he was just looking for a little fun. He did not deviate, sent the tank clanking and screaming right over the top of the Lada, leaving it a crumpled and twisted wreck.

Ryan peered over the wall. 'There goes Dragan's no-claim bonus. Time we shot through.'

They ran across the rubble of bricks and blackened timbers and out through the back of the house.

They found Helmut and Radar sheltering behind a broken wall. Helmut's eyes were like soup plates.

'The car is fucked!'

Ryan pulled Jenny down beside him. She was panting, and he recognised the panic in her face. Her first time. He felt the adrenalin charge through his own body, a familiar, welcome sensation, almost soothing, like a drug.

'What are we going to do?' Radar said.

Ryan didn't answer him. It struck him as curious that people wanted to do things on battlefields. Sometimes all you could do was eat dirt and stay out of harm's way. That was common sense, but often the body's instincts for fight or flight took over, and it was an effort of will to stay still and calm.

They were a hundred, perhaps two hundred, yards from the tank, which was still only halfway down the village's main street. Occasionally they saw the turret through a broken wall, through the shelled-out hollow of a house.

'Will there be soldiers following behind?' Jenny asked.

'Possibly,' Ryan said.

Helmut grabbed Radar and started to drag him back the way they had come. It was difficult, for they were weighed down with the heavy equipment and attached to each other by black cable like an umbilicus. Helmut shambled ahead like a bear, Radar trotting behind him, dragged along by Helmut's force of personality and his own instinctive response to go for the film.

'Radar!' Ryan shouted. 'Get that silly bastard back here!'

But Helmut was not listening. He stumbled twice on fallen masonry, limped the last few yards, and took up a position at the end of the street. He waited a moment while Radar checked the sound levels, then darted out into the middle of the street, got down on one knee, and brought the lens up to his eye. Almost immediately there was a burst of machine-gun fire, the rounds so close together that it sounded like one loud *crack!*

Jenny ducked her head instinctively. When she looked back, Helmut lay on his back in the street, Radar sprawled a few feet away.

The tank passed fifty metres away, tracks clanking on the fallen masonry, the motor a deafening roar. Ryan looked down at Jenny. 'Stay here,' he whispered.

She caught his arm. 'They're dead. You can't help them.'

The tank was past them, moving away. 'I want the film,' Ryan said. He jumped up, and headed towards the bodies in a low, crouching run.

Jenny followed Ryan along the lane. The carcass of a horse lay in the middle of the road, the purple-green mess of its intestines spilling in the dirt. Ryan vaulted it easily, and she followed him.

The houses backed on to a bare field, the brown earth covered with a dusting of frost. Ryan stopped, crouched down, his breath coming fast and crystallising on the chill afternoon air.

'Listen,' he said.

Jenny tried to hear the sound of her own breathing, her blood pounding in her ears.

'I can't hear the tank,' he said.

She looked back the way they had come. The laneway was empty.

She felt eerily calm. I'm a survivor, she reminded herself. I've always been a survivor. Hard to accept that Helmut and Radar were really dead. It was like a game, another piece of theatre.

Ryan seemed unaffected by the tragedy. Of course, he had been through all this a hundred times before, she reminded herself. Still, she had expected something from him, some reaction. The two men had been friends and colleagues, were part of his own crew. She thought there would have been something more on his mind than just the film.

'You checked the bodies?' she said.

Ryan looked at her. What was it in his face? Scorn? Amusement? 'They were dead. Okay?'

She nodded and stared across the field. Perhaps a hundred metres of open ground to where a line of skeletal horse chestnuts marked the road. As they watched, a black VW Golf drove fast down the road, braking suddenly and stopping almost directly opposite where they lay.

Some armed men jumped out and stood by the car. One of them focused a pair of binoculars on the village. 'Croat volunteers,' Ryan murmured.

'Will they help us?'

'They might. Are you ready?'

'What are we going to do?'

'We're going to leg it across that field.'

'What about the tank?'

'What about it?'

His face was close to hers. Yes, stupid question, she thought. If they see us they'll shoot us. But we can't stay here. 'Okay, let's go,' she said.

He grabbed her hand to help her, but she pulled away. All she had to do was get up and run. She could do that on her own.

'Now!' Ryan hissed at her.

But she couldn't move. Fear had immobilised her, she realised. All the while she was congratulating herself on how calm she felt, the poison was spreading through her muscles, paralysing her.

I'm a survivor, she thought. I can't die here, I'm a survivor.

Ryan was already halfway across the field.

Finally, with an effort of will, she pushed herself to her feet and ran faster than she had ever run in her life.

# 76

The Croats thought it was funny.

They stood beside their Golf, following Ryan and Jenny's slow progress across the field. There were three of them: one had a pair of Zeiss binoculars trained on the village; the second was holding the car mike, talking animatedly to his headquarters through the car radio; the third was cradling a Kalashnikov in his arms like a baby, crouched down against the radiator. He shouted something in Serbo-Croat and the others laughed.

They were all volunteers. They wore East German padded winter suits with the *sahovnica* flash sewn on the shoulders, and camouflage forage caps.

Ryan reached them first, hands in the air. 'CNN!' he shouted. 'BBC!'

'*Presna*!' one of them shouted to the others. 'Journalists!'

Ryan threw himself over the ditch and scrambled up the bank to the car. The man with the Kalashnikov nodded at Ryan's jacket. He was wearing some of Helmut's blood. 'You fucking crazy,' he said.

Ryan was breathing hard. It was apparent that these men did not present a threat and he began to relax. He looked back, expecting to see Jenny just behind him, but she was still fifty metres across the field, stumbling through the frozen mud.

The man with the Kalashnikov realised that Ryan's companion was a girl and he made a joke in his own language and again the other two men laughed. Just what we need right now, Ryan thought. A probable psychopath with a sense of humour.

'Hey, *presna*,' the man said. 'Chetniks in that village?'

'No Chetniks. Just a tank.'

The man stopped smiling, and translated this information for his companions. There was an awed silence.

Jenny reached the edge of the field, crawled the last few yards to the ditch on her hands and knees. Amazing what fear can do to a healthy young body, Ryan thought. He helped her up the embankment to the road. The three Croats were having a heated discussion by the side of the Golf.

Jenny leaned against Ryan, her cheeks flushed with exertion. 'You went without me.'

'I thought you were right there. Anyway, I'm not your mother.'

She sat gasping for breath on the ground. 'What's happening?'

'I've just told our three new friends about the tank.'

'What are they saying?'

'I don't know. What's *Let's get the fuck out of here* in Croat?'

They all heard a roar like a bulldozer scooping metal from a road. The T-72 was on the move. The turret and the barrel of the cannon appeared at the edge of the village, glimpsed for a moment through the ruins of a house.

The man with the Kalashnikov left his two companions, turned back to Ryan. He looked down at Jenny on all fours in the slush beside the road. 'Get in the car. Hurry,' he said. 'Your friend, too.'

They did as they were told. The driver executed a quick three-point turn and they sped back up the road towards Pakrac.

The Croat irregulars had commandeered a farmhouse and a barn three kilometres up the road. When they arrived there were several groups dressed in paramilitary fatigues sitting or standing around fires drinking *sjlivovica* and oiling their guns. A cassette player blared out banal disco music. Ryan thought he recognised the Bee Gees. 'Saturday Night Fever'.

Many of the men were wearing black berets, the hated trademark of the Ustase, some wore Nazi Iron Crosses or SS caps and other Second World War memorabilia. They stared at them as they got out of the car; when they saw Jenny there were raucous shouts and laughter.

It seemed that the one with the Kalashnikov had decided to take them under his wing. He identified himself as Milan. He was handsome, Jenny noted, with cropped Slavic blond hair, greased back, and a quirky, lopsided smile. His eyes were hidden by a pair of Raybans. But she knew he was looking at her, and she guessed what he was thinking. She supposed an Asian-American journalist was a little exotic, even here, where eccentricities seemed to be commonplace.

He was grinning as if the whole thing were some crazy game. He led them inside the barn, where a group of HVO regulars were standing around a ham radio set. Jenny stared in amazement at the corner of the barn. A plastic Christmas tree had been erected, complete with decorations.

'You'll be safe here,' Milan said.

'Can you get us back to Zagreb, mate?' Ryan asked him.

Milan shrugged his shoulders. 'Perhaps tomorrow,' he said.

The HVO soldiers were passing the *sjlivovica* from mouth to mouth. One of the men was seated at the radio with a hand mike, and every time he said something into the microphone his comrades laughed and cheered.

'Who is he talking to?' Jenny asked.

'He's talking to some guy he used to work with in the brick factory before the war. Vlado.'

'He's with another unit?'

Milan liked this. 'Yes, he's with another unit, all right. He's with the Chetniks who tried to blow your ass off this afternoon.'

'What's he saying?' Ryan asked.

'He's asking the useless Chetnik scumbag when he last had a bath. Vlado's just told him he screwed his sister. You know, they're just fucking with each other.'

The man, Danko, shouted a warning and dropped the mike. Milan laughed again. 'Shit, now he's really made him crazy.' He grabbed Jenny and pulled her under the table. Ryan scrambled down beside them.

There was a hollow thud fifty metres away as the mortar round landed. Danko grabbed the mike again and began screaming more abuse into the radio. Milan looked at Ryan and shrugged, grinning, as if to say: They're all crazy, but what can you do?

'Can you believe it?' he said. 'They used to be friends before the war. They played in the factory soccer team together. Vlad was the winger, Danko was striker. They were one hell of a partnership. Vlad was always lobbing the ball on to Danko's head. Now he wants to lob mortars on it.'

He seemed to think this was hilarious. Jenny looked at Ryan. Crazy, all of them. This wasn't a war, this was a circus.

And about three kilometres away, two of the spectators at the circus were lying dead in the street at Zenac.

* * *

It was late in the afternoon. A heavy curtain of mist fell over the valley, precluding further mortar attacks. Danko sat by the window, lounging in an armchair that had been hauled over from the farmhouse. He had a box of dum-dum ammunition and a bottle of warm *sjlivovica* next to the chair.

'If the tank comes along this road, we're ready,' Milan was saying. 'We have three Armbrust rocket launchers. German-made, very good. That will give those bastard Chetniks something to think about.'

Danko passed them the *sjlivovica*. Ryan took a swig and winced. He passed it to Jenny. She gulped down a mouthful without a murmur.

Milan raised his eyebrows in admiration. 'How is it you *Americanski* were in Zenac?'

Ryan told him the story. Milan passed on the tale to his compatriots. Danko swigged from the bottle and shouted something they all thought very amusing.

'What did he say?' Ryan asked him.

'He said he would like to see your driver's insurance claim.'

Ryan took out his Malboros and handed them around. 'You people are crazy,' Milan said.

'It's our job.'

'No, you're crazy, but it's good you are here. Somebody has to tell the world the truth, how the Serbs are attacking us here in our own country. Perhaps finally Mr Bush will do something. This Milosevic is like Saddam, you know? You think?'

Ryan shrugged. 'Sure,' he said. He had made it a lifetime rule never to debate politics with his hosts.

'You think Mr Bush will help us?'

'Perhaps.' Never in a million years, Ryan thought. 'Trouble is, you don't own any oilfields.'

'But we have justice on our side.'

'So does everyone,' Ryan murmured.

'This is your friend?' Milan pointed to Jenny. Ryan realised he was trying to establish ownership of the only available woman within miles.

Ryan nodded. '*My* friend.'

Milan made an obscene gesture which Jenny was not supposed to see. He pointed at Ryan.

Ryan nodded again.

But Jenny did see. She glared at him.

He leaned towards her. 'It looks like we'll be here overnight,' he whispered. 'You want me to tell all these young boys that you're unattached and looking for a boyfriend?'

Darkness had fallen quickly. She looked around the room. Men's eyes glittered in the candlelight. The *sjlivovica* was starting to take effect.

She put her arm through Ryan's and held on tight.

Milan led them to a tiny room at the back of the farmhouse. The walls were bare brick, running with damp. There was a single wooden bed, the mattress stained and mildewed, and an ancient wardrobe in the corner. She looked inside. It was empty and smelled of rot.

After Milan left them Ryan gave her the candle and manoeuvred the wardrobe in front of the door.

'For your protection,' he grunted.

Then he put the candle on the windowsill, and let it bleed into its own wax.

Jenny took off the heavy flak jacket, dropped it on the floor and massaged her aching shoulder muscles. Then she stood in the middle of the room, shivering.

'Well, I've seen worse places,' Ryan said.

'Really?'

'They wanted to check us into a standard room but I did some fast talking and they upgraded us to the honeymoon suite.'

'Not funny.'

'Just putting a brave face on things.'

She sat down on the bed. She was cold, despite the Gortex jacket and pants she wore under the flak jacket. Ryan sat down next to her on the bed and put an arm around her shoulders.

'Been a rough day,' he said.

'I'm all right,' she said, and shrugged his arm away.

But it was not all right. She could not stop thinking about Helmut and Radar. She didn't even know Radar's real name. The trembling got worse, and now it had nothing to do with the cold. She suddenly wanted Ryan to hold her again.

He must have read her thoughts. He knelt behind her on the bed and put both his arms around her shoulders. 'It's normal to feel this way,' he said. 'It's a delayed shock.'

I can't believe they're dead, she thought, and then heard herself saying it aloud.

'It's all right,' he said. 'It's better to talk about it.'

'I didn't feel scared. But when you started running across the field, I couldn't move my legs. I just sat there.'

'Everything you're feeling is normal. It happened to me the first time, too.'

She stared at the candle, trying to slam the door on the other memories that now swarmed through. She saw the bodies floating in the lagoon after the wreck on the McAdam Reef, bloating in the sun and being taken one by one by sharks. She remembered the former ARVN colonel who had befriended her mother at Rach Gia SEZ. Because he was a former officer he had been treated even worse than the rest of them, and one night he had tried to escape. He was caught the following morning, and the political cadre had paraded him in front of the whole camp before casually shooting him through the head with his pistol. She recalled how the blood had spurted from his head in a little fountain, before he kicked and was still.

Perhaps it was this and not her ambition that had brought her here. Perhaps she was in the thrall of her own past, was still trying to exorcise those demons, understand what had happened to her country, to her mother, to herself.

'I remember the first time I was shot at,' he was saying. 'I just couldn't believe anyone would really want to kill me. It seemed like a game until the bloke in front of me fell backwards and died right in front of my face with blood coming out of his neck. That's when I swore if I could just get out of this, I'd never put my life in danger again. I even prayed. I said, God, listen to me just this once, get me out of here alive and this is the last time I ever gamble with my life.'

'And?'

'And you can do two things after you come back. One, you can keep your promise and tell your children and your grandchildren the story. Or two, you can do what I did, figure you're something special, like you've just passed some murderous initiation. You tell yourself you're lucky and if you did it once, you can do it again. Also, I suppose it's like a challenge. Okay, I was frightened that time, so I have to do it again to prove I've really got some bottle. And so you go back and it starts all over again.'

She remembered how she had made that same bargain out there today. God, just get me out of this . . . But unlike Ryan she could not imagine ever coming back. She had not survived all those years in Vietnam and the wreck on the McAdam Reef to throw it all away in some stupid Balkan feud.

'I didn't think you were the kind who prayed,' she said.

'Like the old saying, there're no atheists in foxholes.'

'You believe in God?'

'Which one?'

'God is God, surely. My mother believed. She was a good Catholic, my mother.'

'Well, I suppose everyone believes in something.'

'I thought I did. But this morning I wondered . . . if there is a God how can He let children suffer like those children in the orphanage?'

'It depends on how you look at things. My view, this is hell. Devil rules here, not God. He doesn't have any say in the way it's run. You can pray all you like but there's bugger all God could do for you down here, if He exists. And if there is some place called Heaven, maybe it's like the Buddhists say, you have to give up everything to find it. If you ask me, I don't suppose God would be seen dead down here.'

She thought he was making fun of her. But when she turned around his expression was deadly serious. 'You have a very strange philosophy.'

'Well, yours doesn't sound any better to me. You remind me of Spider. He wanted to save the world and when he couldn't, he got sour about it. He really thought a few journalists and photographers could stop a war. He's a dreamer. War has everything a young man could possibly want. Companionship, an outlet for aggression, fresh air, and sometimes, if you're real lucky, a little illicit sex thrown in. It's a game with no laws, and no rules. You'll never stop it. I spent one whole afternoon with a Serb sniper outside Vukovar. He was just sitting there, on a wooden chair, the barrel of his Kalashnikov resting on the wall. He was killing people half a kilometre, sometimes a kilometre away. It was like a video game. He couldn't see their faces, couldn't see the blood, couldn't even hear them scream when he hit them. He was having lots of fun. It was like a Sega game with real bullets.'

'But that guy, Danko, this afternoon. You heard what Milan

said. His friend is in the front lines a couple of kilometres away. He fired a mortar on Danko's position.'

'What would they do if they really hated each other, right?'

'It doesn't make sense.'

'Sure it does. Look at what husbands and wives do to each other when they get a divorce. If people think they can justify it, they'll do anything, absolutely anything. Remember Cambodia? Once people start repeating versions of 'the end justifies the means', anything is likely to happen. Anyway, you heard what Milan was saying. *It's good you are here to tell the truth.* As if there's only one truth. Everyone thinks they have a monopoly on the truth. No one even suspects they might be wrong. In the last war the Croats sided with the Germans and the Chetniks were on our side. The Ustashi committed some unbelievable atrocities. Ante Pavelic supposedly kept a box in his desk that was full of Serb eyeballs. It's because of blokes like Pavelic that the Serbs are justifying what's going on today. It's insane. It's not ever going to stop.'

'So why do you do this? If you don't think it's going to change anything.'

'Why do you?'

She didn't answer.

'Now you're giving yourself a bad time because you came here to try and become famous. Well, don't feel too bad. Spider started off like you and look at him now. He ended up championing the Common Man.'

'Don't make fun of him. It's not wrong to want to make a difference.'

'Wanting to make a difference is what drove him out of the job. He carried the flag for the underdog, the poor fucker who'd lost his home and his family and his cow because some bastard just drove their battalion through his back yard. In the end he thought it was his fault that the world didn't care about things as much as he did. But you can't take the blame for that.'

'What about you? Do you have a higher motive?'

He laughed, deep in his chest. 'No one could ever accuse me of that.'

'I don't believe you.'

He stroked her hair. 'I suppose I'm obsessed with evil. I document it. Not just really big evil, like Pol Pot. The evil in all of us. It's in me too, only I keep it in check. I'm more a voyeur, I get my kicks out of watching. But then I guess I've never lost my home or my family. I've never had a stake in the game, so I don't know what I'm capable of.'

She was shivering uncontrollably now. He took four space blankets from the pockets of his fisherman's warmer and started to unfold them. 'Always come prepared,' he said. 'I was a Boy Scout.' He wrapped one of the blankets around her. 'Now you're a classic case in point,' he said.

'Me?'

'You did lose your home, your family, everything. You have just cause for a war, don't you?'

'You think I should open hostilities with Vietnam?'

He laughed. 'Not on your own. But do you blame anyone for what happened to you?'

'Perhaps.'

'Then you probably have fantasies about getting even.'

Jenny took a deep breath. She could hear her blood pounding in her ears. 'My mother did not believe in revenge.'

'She must have been a remarkable woman. It couldn't have been easy surviving that long after the communists took over with a round-eye kid.'

Was it possible that he knew? Had Webb told him? Was he just playing with her? She wrapped the blanket more tightly around her body. She could hear the soldiers shouting and laughing outside. They were drunk. The candle flickered in the draught, shadows loomed on the walls.

She looked into the flame. Odile was there in the room. The soft, tired face was contorted now into a scowl of rage. *'It couldn't have been easy surviving that long.' Is that what he says? Only you can tell him how difficult it was! This is the man who destroyed me! What are you going to do?*

'No, it wasn't easy.'

'You must be a very special woman to go through everything you have. Even more special to do what you're doing now.'

He turned her face towards him. His own face was half in shadow. There was stubble on his chin and grease from Milan's Kalashnikov had somehow been smeared across his forehead. 'You have the most beautiful eyes,' he whispered. 'It's like looking into the ocean.'

What a ludicrous position, she thought. Alone in a room with the man she hated most in the world. She heard the sound of heavy boots in the corridor outside, the sound of drunken singing.

The door handle turned.

# 77

The door opened, then jammed against the heavy wardrobe.

'It's all right,' Ryan whispered. 'The drunken bastards can't get in.'

She held on to him, frightened, and also ashamed of her fear.

'I'll keep you warm,' he said. He took her hands and cupped them in his own, blew on them, kissed them.

She felt the heat of his body pressing against her. She welcomed its warmth for the moment, the comfort of it. Then she pulled away.

'It's all right,' he said.

He was strong. He tried to kiss her.

'No.'

'Jenny . . .'

The candle guttered and died, betraying her.

'You're so beautiful, Jenny. I've never known anyone like you.'

'Don't.'

He kissed her neck. She felt his hands cup her breasts through her jersey. Somewhere her mother was crying.

She fought him off, used her nails, her fists, her knees.

He yelled and retreated to the far end of the bed. 'Christ, okay! What's wrong with you?'

'I said no!'

'Okay, okay. Jesus. You nearly had my bloody eyes out, you minx! What the hell's wrong?'

'There's something you should know. It's about my mother.'

She could not see him in the darkness but she could hear his breathing.

'Do you remember, years and years ago, there was a woman, a novice in the Carmelite order in Saigon? Her name was Odile.'

He didn't answer her. For a long time.

Then she heard a long-drawn-out 'Oh, Jesus wept.'

He swung his legs off the bed. She heard him fumbling for his cigarettes. He struck a match, and his face was silhouetted for a moment by the flame. He found another candle in his pocket, lit it, stood it in the melted wax of the first candle on the windowsill.

'I don't even remember your name,' he said at last.

The wheel turns, he thought.

He wondered what he should feel. Shame? Disgust? Guilt? But he felt none of those things. The emotion he was struggling with was sadness; he was sad for her, and for Odile. Sad also that it should come to this, trying to seduce his own daughter.

He had never denied that he was both selfish and self-obsessed. But he had never meant to hurt anyone, had never been intentionally cruel. But here were the ghosts from the past, come to accuse him.

'When did you know?' he said.

'Before I left to come to Zagreb. Uncle told me.'

Typical of Spider to twist everyone on the screw long before administering the coup. The *shit*. He had never even hinted at his little secret the last time he had seen him, when they were all there in his house; like some mad fucking scientist he just kept his little specimens under his microscope, watching what they would do. His grand experiment in conscience. His own personal morality play using real people.

'You must have been bloody pleased to see me, then, at the Intercon.'

'I don't remember how I felt.'

'Quite a coincidence.'

'That Uncle found me in the Philippines was the miracle. When you think about it, everything else was inevitable.'

Ryan stubbed out his cigarette, lit another. 'When were you going to tell me?'

'I don't know.'

'You must have thought about it.'

'Nothing ever works out quite the way you plan it.'

'Well, isn't that a fact.'

The sadness had evaporated. Now he felt angry, even bitter. Hardly justifiable in the circumstances, he decided, but there it was. He looked at Jenny, but he could not see her face clearly in the candle-light. But even in broad daylight he did not think he could conjure any likeness to her mother. Odile's face was oval, her nose less European, her cheekbones more pronounced. Also, this Jenny was the product of an adolescence spent in America, a non-culture of rap songs and hamburger chains that had made her brash and sexually confident. Odile had been the product of another place and another era. Her whole demeanour and tone of voice had been different; he remembered her as shy, modest, softly spoken.

'So what now?' he said.

'I don't understand.'

'Isn't this where you castigate me for all my sins? Am I supposed to break down and cry for your forgiveness?'

'Is that what you want to do?'

'Not really.' He looked at her, lying stiffly under the silver blanket. He thought she should be angry, but she just looked cold and frightened. 'I didn't mean to leave you or Odile behind. I got hit out at Newport Bridge. It just happened. After the fall I couldn't get back in. End of story.'

'You have no idea how we suffered.'

'No, and I suppose I never will. And even if I did, it wouldn't matter stuff all because I can't change the past. It's done, it's happened, and there you are.' He finished his cigarette. 'You must have been rapt when Spider told you he knew who your father was.'

'I couldn't believe he kept it from me for so long.'

'Wouldn't forgive him for it if I was you,' he said. 'Bugger him as well. He should have told me first, or just kept his mouth shut. But the way he played it, I reckon he deserves to suffer too.'

He looked at her again. My daughter. Am I supposed to feel something?

You dirty miserable bastard, Ryan. So much for Dorian Gray. Time gets you one way or the other.

'So now what do we do?' she said to him.

'Now we just go to sleep.'

But he couldn't sleep. Instead he stayed up all night staring into the candle. He had to think this one through.

# 78

She woke while it was still dark, her insides in revolt. Probably a delayed reaction to the events of the previous day, she decided. It was completely dark in the room, and despite the space blankets her face, her fingers, even her feet inside her boots were numb with cold. Slowly her eyes grew accustomed to the dark and she made out Ryan's silhouette, curled up on the end of the bed, his knees drawn up to his chest.

She fought her own body's needs. She could not imagine venturing into the cold and dark to pick her way over the bodies of the sleeping soldiers, risk one of the sentries pawing at her. And then do what? Squat in the field, knowing that the Serbian snipers had infrared scopes on their rifles. Where was safe? She realised that if she got up she would have to wake Ryan and ask him to stand guard while she performed this most basic of bodily functions, and that would be just too embarrassing and humiliating. Besides, she no longer wanted to be in his debt for anything.

She tried to sleep, but it was impossible. She looked at the luminous dial of her watch. Five a.m.

Dumb, she told herself. Dumb, dumb, dumb to think she could go green into a war zone and survive. But she had survived, hadn't she? the voice in her head reminded her.

The last twenty-four hours was a kaleidoscope of images and emotions: the orphanage; Helmut and Radar lying dead in the streets of Zenac; the final confrontation with Ryan. This last was an anticlimax somehow. She had found in him neither the contrition nor the shame she had hoped for. It had achieved nothing, won her nothing.

Her stomach growled again.

She would have to get up . . .

But then the decision was made for her. A heart-stopping bang, as if a truck had driven straight through the wall by their heads.

Mortar attack.

The Serbs were coming through.

Ryan was awake immediately. He grabbed her and dragged her on to the floor. Somewhere in the farmhouse someone was screaming.

She fumbled in her pockets for her pencil torch, flicked it on. Ryan crawled across the floor to the door, heaved the wardrobe out of the way with his shoulder. They ran outside into the passageway.

Green tracer bullets arced through the night. The barn had been hit by mortars and was on fire. One wall of the farmhouse had been blown in by a rocket. A Croat soldier lay on his back screaming; one of his comrades bent beside him trying to stop the bleeding from his shattered leg. Other soldiers rushed around them in the darkness. Jenny saw the bright muzzle flashes of small-arms fire from the dark fields, and then the Croats returned fire. The deafening concussion of sound seemed to numb all her other senses.

In a lull in the fighting she saw a figure run, crouching, from the barn. '*Americanski*! Where are you?'

'Milan!' Ryan shouted. 'What's happening?'

'The Chetniks are attacking. We have to get you out of here!'

The soldier with the shattered leg had stopped screaming, was only half conscious of what was happening to him now. His friend was trying to fashion a tourniquet around his thigh with his belt. The fire in the barn illuminated the wounded man's face for a moment. It was Danko.

'He won't be scoring any more goals,' Ryan said.

'Chetnik bastards!' Milan grabbed his shoulder. 'This way!'

Ryan and Jenny followed him out of the back door. In the flicker of the burning barn they could see the black Golf in the farmhouse courtyard. Milan, his Kalashnikov over one shoulder, headed towards it. Ryan set off after him.

They were halfway there when Milan seemed to lurch to one side and fall. Ryan immediately threw himself on his face and Jenny did the same. The sound of the automatic weapons fire echoed around the courtyard fractions of a second later.

She remembered what Ryan had told her the previous evening about his first time under fire. The unreality of it. *Someone is actually trying to kill me*.

But all she could think was: *I need to find a toilet*.

She heard Milan gasp and instinctively she started to crawl towards him.

He lay on his side in the cold mud. He did not appear to be in pain. He stared in dull surprise at the dark, glutinous mess of his intestines in his hands, tried to stuff them back into his body. He looked up at her and seemed embarrassed at being caught naked in this way. He gave a short barking laugh, and then lay still. It took Jenny a few moments to realise that he had died.

Ryan had reached the Golf. 'Jenny! Jenny, where are you?'

Her hand found Milan's Kalashnikov lying in the frozen mud.

I always said I would kill him one day if I ever found him, she thought.

He was invisible to the naked eye in the darkness but was captured perfectly in the cross-hairs of the Kalashnikov's night sight. He was coming back for her, crawling on his belly across the courtyard. The perfect revenge. No one would ever know it was her bullet that finally paid him back for all the misery he had caused her mother.

# IX

## Bosnia,
## October 1992

'Working as a war correspondent is almost the only classic male endeavour left that provides physical danger and personal risk without public disapproval and the awful truth is that for correspondents war is not hell. It is fun.'

– Nora Ephron

'It is not the bullet with my name on that worries me.
It's the one that says: "To whom it may concern."'

– resident of Belfast

# 79

A late afternoon sun glinted on the minarets of the ancient Ottoman town. Travnik had once been the capital of Bosnia in the days when the province had been a possession of the ancient Ottoman empire. Now, with the Croatian border closed, it had become the lifeline to the beleaguered Moslem outposts of northern Bosnia.

The Moslems would have been swamped by the Serbs if it had not been for the intervention of the Croatian army. Even so, the Serbs had managed to acquire two-thirds of the province and the Moslems had been trapped in enclaves around Sarajevo, Gorazde, Bihac and Travnik.

Travnik serviced the besieged towns of Jajce and Maglaj through narrow and perilous corridors that bulged through the front lines into Serb-held territory. The town of Jajce, twenty-five miles to the north of Travnik, had been under siege for five months. Reinforcements hiked in through the woods; ambulances and ammunition trucks made their way in by night, under almost constant fire from Serb mortars and snipers.

Every day more refugees poured down from the mountains after journeying for days on horse-drawn carts or marching on foot, with their families, their dogs and their farm equipment, bringing tales of rape, looting and murder.

Webb arrived in Travnik on the back of a United Nations truck. The town was overflowing with soldiers: Croat soldiers in camouflage fatigues with the red and white chessboard shoulder flashes, black-shirted HOS militia, Moslem *armija* in ragtag uniforms, leather jackets, baseball caps, jeans, running shoes. He saw a smoke-blackened wall scrawled with graffiti, in English, for the benefit of the Western journalists: *Please Help Bosnia Now*!

Then there were the refugees; the blank stares in the faces of the old men, terrified old women, the gaunt, bewildered faces of the children.

It was like he had never been away.

He had once promised himself that he was finished with it all. But a part of him had always known that one day he'd come back, find another war, another outrage. He was not sure what it was that had finally made him do it. Perhaps he needed to satisfy himself that he had not lost his courage, to prove to himself he could still do it, that he had not gone soft; perhaps also he still felt that this was the highest calling in his profession, and he wanted once more to belong. Most of all, after so many years away from the front lines, he knew he had gone stale and had nothing new to write about. He was returning to the sharp end to rescue his career.

And it had to be this war because what was happening in Yugoslavia represented the moral dilemmas of the world of the nineties. He told himself that it was only incidental that Jenny was also here. Against all odds she had survived in Croatia and Bosnia for almost a year as a freelancer, had even achieved a limited fame, at least within her own profession. She had sold photographs and feature pieces to a number of British and US newspapers and magazines, and the previous month her byline had even appeared in the *New York Times*.

Her letters to him had been less prolific; a few scribbled notes from Zagreb or Dubrovnik or Sarajevo to say she was still alive, nothing more. She had not mentioned Ryan.

He had also noted that she no longer used the name Jenny Webb for her work; she had reverted to her mother's name, Jenny Ngai. He told himself it wasn't personal, that it was just a need to establish her own professional identity.

But it had hurt.

When Crosby had approached him again he had delayed only a day or so before accepting. It was a lucrative offer, although the money was now not that relevant. He would probably have come anyway.

Most of the Western media were concentrated in Sarajevo, which had now been under siege for over six months, but Webb had instead chosen to head for Travnik. He had heard, through Crosby, that Jenny was here, trying to get inside Jajce. He was determined to find her. Too many things had been left unsaid and life was too tenuous to leave it be any longer.

Samir Music was shouting orders at the ring of men surrounding his desk. His skin was grey with exhaustion and there were plum-coloured rings under his eyes. The last few months had taken a heavy toll. As commander of the *armija* forces controlling the corridor in and out of Jajce, Music carried a heavy burden of responsibility.

He was twenty years old.

His headquarters was in a former restaurant called the Blue Water. A stream rushed under a bridge right outside the front door, and Webb tried to imagine how it had been in more peaceful times. Now the surrounding buildings had been requisitioned as a barracks and the courtyard was a chaos of wounded men and field gear, the stench from the latrines overpowering.

Music's office was thick with cigarette smoke, his wooden desk littered with cigarette butts and *sjlivovica* bottles and a single battered black field telephone. The tattered map tacked on the wall behind him was covered with red stencil marks.

He turned away from the shouting match going on around him and looked up at Webb. His face told the story: another problem he could do without. But his innate Moslem hospitality overcame his fatigue. 'Journalist?' he said, studying the UNPROFOR badge on Webb's lapel.

'Hugh Webb. I'm with IPA.'

'Sit down, sit down. Drink?' He picked up a bottle of *sjlivovica* and splashed two fingers into a glass. His attention immediately returned to the bedlam around him. Half a dozen of his junior officers were shouting and vying for his attention. Finally Samir got to his feet and issued his orders. The men trooped out in sullen compliance.

He looked back at Webb. 'One of the Croat HVO soldiers tried to rape a Moslem refugee girl last night.'

'The HVO? They're the ones I saw in black uniforms?'

'Fascists, of course. But in a war you cannot choose your comrades.'

'What happened to him?'

'Two of my *armija* caught him and now my officers want to shoot him. I told them they have to hand him over to his own commander for justice. It's not good for morale to go shooting your allies. You agree?' He poured himself some of the plum brandy and raised his glass. '*Jivili*. To life.'

'*Jivili*,' Webb agreed. The *sjlivovica* had a kick like a horse.

'What can I do for you, Mister IPA?'

'Your English is very good,' Webb said.

'Before this war I was an English student in Zagreb. I wanted to be travel guide, you know? But this year Thomas Cook does not want to go to Jajce.'

'I do.'

Samir looked weary, as if he had feared this all along. 'Why do you want to go there? It is just people living in holes and dying in their own shit. Even if I can get you in, maybe I cannot get you out.'

'I'm a journalist. I get paid to take risks.'

'How much do they pay you for your life? One million US? Two million?'

'If I told you, you'd get depressed.'

He lit a cigarette. 'So what will you do if I can get you inside Jajce?'

'I want to take photographs, write about it. It is important the world knows what is happening here.'

'The world? The world sees what is happening inside Sarajevo, yes? And what good does it do? The world does not care about us, Mister IPA.'

'Someone has to listen.'

Samir leaned forward. 'Then you tell them. You tell them what we need is not their sympathy, we want more boom-boom. The Chetniks have plenty of boom-boom. They have big arms factories, they have the Russians and Greeks to help them, they have the old Yugoslav army that our taxes helped pay for. If it is not for the HVO, that bunch of fascists pigs, we will all be dead long ago. Zagreb has Germany and the *mafiosi* in Italy to help. So who does this arms embargo hurt, yes? Only Bosnia. We have no one to help, we have no coast to smuggle in what we want, what we need. Tell them in your newspaper we do not want the world and Mister Bush to cry for us. We just want them to give us some way to defend ourselves.'

'That's why I want to tell people what it's really like in Jajce.'

'Crazy.' Samir lit another cigarette from the remains of his first. 'Every night I send in ambulances and lorries with medicines and supplies. The last two nights they have had to turn back. But we will try again tonight. If you want to go, you can go. With the other crazy journalist.'

Webb swallowed hard. 'The other journalist?'

'Some girl. Very young, very beautiful. Maybe Russian, maybe Chinese, but she has this American accent. She is crazy too. She should be home making babies.'

'Where is she?'

'She has a room in the barracks on the other side of the courtyard. Go and talk to her if you want.' As Webb got up to leave, Samir shouted after him: 'You can talk to her about how you will both die in Jajce.'

Jenny stopped to fill her water bottle from the Ottoman freshwater tap in the main street. They said Suleiman the Magnificent had once passed this way. How many other armies had travelled over this ground? she wondered. The Serbs, Croats and Moslems had been fighting over this land for centuries. As in Palestine, its savage tribes would always find a new season in which to fertilise its soil with blood.

When she looked up he was standing on the other side of the square.

Less of a surprise than it might have been; she had received a fax from him two weeks ago at the Intercon in Zagreb, telling her he had taken the contract with IPA. He was wearing the old Vietnam utility she had seen in his drawer at home, camou pants, and a new UN flak jacket. He looked ill at ease in it; he had been away from the action for too long.

She was still not sure how she felt about seeing him again. Bitterness had become a redundant emotion in her life, she had decided; there had been too much of it, secretly harboured, and the taste of it had turned rank. The sight of him touched her in some way. She remembered that he had always been there for her and now here he was again, her guardian angel, in the shape of the old veteran in a young man's game.

Refugee children shouted and played in the glow of the bonfires. Looted cars and *armija* patrols just back from the front were silhouetted by the flames.

Webb and Jenny sat around their own campfire in the barracks courtyard, drinking coffee. In the firelight she looked thinner, tired, and much older. Her long black hair had been lopped to shoulder length and was kept out of her eyes with a red bandanna. She wore loose fatigues under a kevlar jacket, and had a blue NATO helmet hooked on to her belt. Her fingernails, which at home were always polished and carefully manicured, were broken and dirty.

He was shocked at her appearance, but not surprised. He knew the physical cost of endless months in the front line. But she was different in other, more subtle, ways. She was no longer the brash and sometimes grating young woman she had been; she seemed less eager to prove herself, and more tolerant perhaps.

It seemed that in the last year his little girl – for he still could not think of her any other way – had grown up.

He had missed her so much, worried about her endlessly. And now she was here, sitting next to him, and he found he couldn't tell her any of it. It was as if she wanted to pretend that they had never been apart, and that their last conversation had never taken place.

He did not know where to begin to repair the damage.

Despite the current privations she had learned to make coffee in the Bosnian manner and insisted on drinking it no other way, double-boiled in a *dzezva*, and so thick it slithered into the cup like oozing mud. Bosnian tradition then required that you dip a sugar cube into the brew and suck on it slowly before drinking the coffee black and bitter.

They talked about the war, and she told him about some of the battlefields she had seen: Osijek, Vinkovci, Sarajevo, Srebenica, Gorazde. She was as delighted as a child to hear that he had seen and read some of her features in major newspapers, proudest of all of the photograph she had taken of a Bosnian Serb pressing the barrel of his Kalashnikov into the neck of an old Moslem as he lay cowering on the ground in Mostar. That had appeared as a full-page colour photograph in *Time*.

As she talked she glossed over the dangers and the close calls; Webb remembered how he had always done that. You didn't want to think about it, and talking about it just made it worse next time.

There was a stiffness and a formality between them. She appeared distracted. They both were, he supposed; both had their minds on the convoy that would be leaving in an hour for Jajce. There were long silences that they spent alone with their thoughts, desultorily picking up threads of conversation from a few minutes before, turning their attention back to the convoy's preparations, mentally checking their own baggage, physical and emotional.

Finally Jenny said, 'You haven't asked me about Ryan.'

'Haven't I?'

'Don't you want to know?'

He shrugged. 'Are you going to tell me?'

A beat. 'He got into Jajce a week ago. No one's heard from him since.'

Webb nodded but said nothing.

'He helped me a lot the first few weeks.' She stirred the embers of the fire with a stick. 'He quit the network.'

'I heard.'

'He's back working for *Time*.'

Another long and uncomfortable silence.

'Did you tell him?' His voice sounded hoarse, not his own.

She nodded.

They both waited for the other to speak.

'I wanted to kill him,' she said, at last.

'I guess I can understand that.'

'And if you'd been standing next to him . . .' She left the sentence unfinished.

He took a deep breath. 'I never forgave him for what he did to you. I decided not to tell you because I thought it would only hurt you. I was right, wasn't I?'

She shook her head. 'No.'

He nodded. He had suspected this from the beginning. 'No.'

'I saw my mother a few days after I got here,' Jenny said.

Webb felt the hairs on the back of his neck prickle, hearing Odile invoked on this other battlefield. Oh, Jesus.

'Just my imagination, of course,' she said, quickly, as if she knew what he was thinking. 'I often imagined her when I was in Lincoln Cove, asked her what she thought of the house, this boyfriend, that new date. And when you told me about Ryan I imagined she still hated him. But that was just me. Odile was never like that, was she?'

Webb shook his head.

'I think perhaps I've stopped wishing her back from the other world. Ryan talked to me a lot about her, told me all the things I never knew. I can let her rest now. Make up my own mind about things.'

'That's good, Jenny.'

'Yes,' she said. 'That is good, isn't it?'

Webb experienced that same old terror again, turning his guts liquid. He was afraid of being afraid, too preoccupied with the vivid reality of just being alive to feel anything else but the fear. But it was too late to back out now. Once more into the lion's mouth.

Samir was there to see them off when the convoy left for Jajce, a cigarette between his fingers. 'Once you're in,' he said, 'stay in the command post and don't try and move around.'

Webb looked at Jenny. They had not come all this way to sit in a bunker.

He led the way to an ancient and battered Citroën at the rear of the convoy. Webb volunteered to sit in the back; they both knew that was the worst place because you couldn't get out as fast.

'We'll try and get you out again,' Samir said. 'But I can guarantee nothing.'

'We'll take our chances,' Webb told him.

'Of course.'

They climbed in. Their driver started the engine, touched the prayer beads that hung from the rear-vision mirror, for luck.

'Stay alive,' Music shouted as they drove off.

'*Inshallah*,' Webb whispered under his breath.

# 80

Their driver's name was Hajruhdin Hosic. He conformed to the dress code of all non-observant Moslems: blue jeans, denim jacket, white socks and loafers. His hair was long on top and cut short at the sides. He might have looked like any fashion-conscious Levantine Arab except for the blood-soaked wound dressing on his forehead.

They followed the convoy of ambulances and trucks in the darkness down the road towards Jajce. Webb and Jenny both put on their flak jackets and blue UN helmets.

As they passed the last checkpoint a Bosnian soldier waved to them. 'Stay alive!'

'That's wearing a bit thin,' Jenny said.

Webb shrugged. 'I think they mean well.'

Hosic turned off the lights and the pace of the convoy slowed to a crawl.

'This help just a little,' he said. 'Sniper has night sight, yes? Also they hear us on road, they send mortar and rocket. Boom-boom!'

Webb looked out of the windows, saw the silhouettes of wrecked and burned-out vehicles by the side of the road.

They drove on in morose silence, waiting for the cataclysm.

Time contains its own paradox, something Webb had never been able satisfactorily to explain to himself. He sometimes thought that if someone really wanted to live longer, they should spend their whole life in a war zone. In his life he had known minutes of terror that seemed to last an hour, while back in the tranquillity of Lincoln Cove a weekend could pass in a few minutes.

Inside the car the tension was palpable. On an impulse he reached forward and took Jenny's hand. He felt the answering pressure.

There, that was it.

Redemption.

'How much further?' he asked.

It was too dark in the car to see the odometer; there was no way of knowing where they were. Pitch black outside, no moon. On the bends Jenny had to put her head out of the passenger window to tell Hosic how far they were from the edge of the road. Webb's hands felt as if they were lathered in cold grease.

'How much further?' he repeated.

'*Nema problema*,' Hosic said.

No problem.

# 81

The mortar round hit the truck directly in front of them. There was an orange rush of flame as the petrol tank exploded, flaring briefly in the darkness, and the dull thud of the explosion. Hosic yelled out in alarm, braked hard. The fireball illuminated a dirt track leading off to the right. He spun the wheel hard towards it, and gunned the engine. The Citroën's motor screamed in protest as it climbed the gravel path up through the trees.

Stones and metal pinged against the thin metal skin of the car. Shrapnel. Webb twisted around and looked out of the back window. The truck was still in flames; he could see silhouettes moving in the darkness as the survivors scrambled clear.

Another fireball further along the road. The Serbians had found the range.

The Citroën bounced over the track. Webb was thrown on to the floor, jarring his spine, and he cried out. Jenny spun around, thinking he was hurt. She shouted something at him, but he could not hear her over the scream of the car's engine.

Hosic changed down into first gear and pushed his foot harder down on the accelerator. '*Nema problema*,' he shouted.

Right. No problem.

Ten minutes by Webb's watch, ten long minutes of jarring pain in his spine, waiting for sniper fire or mortar fragments to blast through the windows, braced against every jolt and roll of the Citroën. Tree branches cracked against the windows as they careered along the track. Suddenly they were out of the forest and on to a tarmac road. Webb groaned with relief.

The black shells of bombed-out houses loomed from the darkness. No lights, no sign of life at all.

'Jajce,' Hosic said.

They rattled across a bridge and Hosic made two more hard

turns. Then he slammed on the brakes and immediately jumped out of the car and threw open the doors.

'Hurry, please hurry,' he said.

'*Nema problema*,' Jenny said. Webb, if his back had not been causing him so much pain, would have laughed at that. He admired her nerve; it took a special kind of cool to make jokes under pressure. Then he realised who that reminded him of. Sean Ryan.

Hosic grabbed Jenny's arm, dragged her out of the car and into the shadows. Webb hobbled after them.

Jajce's Command HQ was situated in the basement of a pizzeria, or what was left of it. The old shop above had been completely destroyed by shellfire. It was cold and dank in the cellar and crowded with refugees who were all huddled together, shivering in their wet clothes. Soldiers were propped against the walls, glassy-eyed with fatigue, smoking cigarettes, rifles cradled in their arms, staring listlessly at the walls.

The commander's name was Gerovic. He looked up in amazement as they entered. He and Hosic had a hurried and whispered conversation and then he turned back to Webb and Jenny.

'*Presna*?' he asked them. 'You must be crazy.'

'Hugh Webb, IPA,' Webb said. 'This is Jenny Ngai, she's a freelancer.'

'Crazy,' he repeated. 'Why would anyone wish to come here?'

'We want to tell the world your story,' Jenny said.

'Our story? The story is simple. We are dying.' He shook his head, reached for the cigarettes on the desktop and lit one. 'You were lucky to get through. Two of the trucks and an ambulance were destroyed. But you are here. Please make yourself welcome.' He made a sardonic gesture that embraced the huddled and miserable humans crouched in the basement. 'Enjoy our hospitality.'

The muscles in Webb's back went into spasm. He winced and eased himself down on to the cold floor.

'Are you hurt?' Gerovic asked.

'Jarred my back,' Webb said. 'I'll be okay.'

Gerovic laughed, a short, humourless bark. 'How can you be okay,' he said, 'when you have just fought your way into hell?'

# 82

Webb lay in the darkness, listening to the shelling. They had thrown their sleeping bags on to the cold cement floor and were curled up inside, trying to stay warm. A few feet away, the Moslem commander pored over ancient maps of the city by the light of a candle, occasionally shouting orders into a telephone. After his initial chilly greeting he completely ignored them. He had too many other problems to worry about a couple of crazy journalists.

Webb felt Jenny curl her body against him, for warmth. 'How's Mickey?' she whispered.

'She's fine.'

'Are you still seeing each other?'

'I'm too young to settle down.'

'She'd be good for you.'

He didn't answer her. She was quiet for a long time and he thought she had gone to sleep. But then she whispered: 'Have you been worried about me?'

'An understatement.'

'Is that why you're here?'

'No. Yes. Partly.'

'Well, that's clear.'

'Let's say I'm mixing business with . . . worry.'

She patted his shoulder. Infuriating girl. And yet, he was proud of her. Prouder than he would ever care to admit. If there was one thing he had really got right in his life, she was it. She had turned out all right, because of and despite of his best efforts.

A massive explosion, very close, and the cellar floor seemed to leap like a bucking horse. Women screamed. Webb felt dust and plaster fall on his face. One of the soldiers said something, and his companions laughed. It had been close, but not too close. They were alive.

'I never ever thanked you, did I?' she said.

'What for?'

'For everything. For the last ten years.'

It was the last thing he had expected to hear from her. He didn't know what to say. Before she left the States, the old Jenny would never have dreamed of saying that.

'It's okay,' he mumbled.

'You've been a good father.'

A while later she was asleep. There was a time when he too was able to sleep with the sound of shells exploding nearby, but not any more. Perhaps that was the reason he stayed awake most of the night. Perhaps.

He slept for no more than an hour, woke with a start just before dawn. Something was wrong. It took him a few moments to realise what it was. The shelling had stopped.

He sat up. The pain in his back had eased. Good. He shook Jenny's shoulder. Her eyes blinked open and she was instantly awake. 'What is it?'

'It's stopped. Come on.'

They slipped out of their sleeping bags. A few feet away, Gerovic had his head on the table, asleep. The candle had burned down and the wax had leaked across one of the maps. They picked their way over the sleeping bodies of the soldiers and refugees. Only one of them was awake, an old man in a dressing gown and slippers, who was listening to Bach on a Walkman.

They moved silently up to the street, adjusting their helmets.

Jajce is an ancient fortress town at the confluence of the Urbas and Pliva rivers. The imposing ruins of the old castle loom over the shingle roofs and the white and green stucco dome of the Esme Sultanija mosque. It was in Jajce that Tito and the leaders of the Partisans had proclaimed themselves the legitimate government at the end of 1943, and thus brought Yugoslavia into being.

The new republic had demanded a high price. In most recent years the fumes billowing night and day from the nearby ferro-silicon factory had left a creeping chlorine haze over the town, obscuring the rose gardens and the whitewashed houses. Some of the oaks and beeches on the surrounding hills had been felled, the cleared ground spelling out the name *Tito* in letters climbing three hundred feet up the mountain.

But *Tito* had become obscured by new bushes and saplings since his death, and now the Serb artillery and snipers had found cover in the regrowth.

Webb and Jenny crouched behind a wall, straining their ears to the icy silence of the October morning. There was hardly a sound in the town itself because almost everyone was living underground.

Light seeped into the eastern sky, and the mountains and the ancient castle loomed, forbidding, through the grey autumn haze.

Webb looked around. Much of the town had been levelled; the street he was in was strewn with bricks and broken glass and empty shell casings. A tree lay across the road, splintered halfway up the trunk as though it had been struck by lightning. Pieces of bitumen had been ripped out of the road by mortars, and a broken television set lay upside down on the footpath. Most buildings had been gutted to shells, and remained pockmarked by shrapnel and blackened by fire. The stench of the city permeated everything, the smell of refuse and human waste.

'Christ, look at that.'

It was a dog, the only thing moving on the street. It had something in its mouth. Webb wasn't immediately sure what it was, but as the wretched creature came closer it gave a cough and dropped its precious cargo on the ground. It was a human foot.

Jenny immediately scrabbled for her camera and ran off half a dozen quick frames. He watched her, with a feeling of both nostalgia and revulsion. He had been like that once, looking for the one great photograph that would explain the world to itself, something that would make those at home rebel and throw up their hands and cry 'Enough!' But that was before he was old enough to realise that such images were the ones that people secretly enjoyed, and that they would never cry 'Enough' because there was never the supply to meet an insatiable demand.

Nothing sold newspapers or achieved ratings like other people's misery.

He fumbled for his own camera and dutifully took the shot. IPA might want it, and, after all, they were paying.

There was an old woman adjusting sandbags in front of the shattered windows of her house. The garden was still flowering with the last of the summer roses, and a child's three-wheeler lay on its side in the front yard, a neglected memory of a more peaceful time in Jajce. Webb photographed the old woman from across the street. Then she heard or sensed something that he could not, and ran inside.

The early morning fog had protected them from snipers and precluded accurate artillery fire. But as a yellow-white sun rose over the mountains, the mist began to burn off and the tormentors on the hillside lobbed the first of the day's ordnance on to the town.

Webb heard the sound of the shell leaving the barrel. A few seconds later there was an explosion on the other side of the town and a plume of smoke rose behind the pockmarked silhouette of the mosque's minaret.

The next mortar landed a hundred metres away in the street. Sixty-millimetre, Webb guessed. There was a thud and a puff of white smoke.

They threw themselves on to the ground. 'Where to?' he shouted, desperately looking for shelter.

'Over there,' she shouted.

He looked up, saw someone in a green gown scuttling down some basement steps on the other side of the street. They stood up and ran, crouched over, braced against the next shell burst. As he ran Webb glimpsed a skip full of bloody bandages, a swarm of black flies, a dog toying with a long strip of darkly stained gauze.

A hospital.

Another mortar landed, closer this time. Shrapnel zipped over their heads. They ran down some stone steps and into the subterranean ward of Jajce's hospital.

It took Webb a moment for his eyes to adjust to the gloom.

'Well, bugger me,' he heard a voice say. 'The Spiderman returns.'

Webb would have known that voice anywhere.

It was Ryan.

# 83

There were two rooms with bare cement floors and walls, perhaps fifty or sixty soldiers and civilians crammed together side by side in cots in the wards and the hallways. There appeared to be no heating and no power. Webb stared. A few feet away a surgeon in a blood-spattered green gown was operating on the leg of a screaming child while a nurse held a torch; on the next cot a young woman with a chalk-white face stared vacant-eyed at the ceiling, two bloodied stumps where her legs should have been.

Somewhere, a man was screaming. The stink of antiseptic and blood. Numbing cold. A shell landed very close, and the walls shook. No one seemed to pay any attention.

Ryan was sitting on the floor, his back propped against the wall, shivering. He had just a thin woollen blanket gripped around his shoulders, but, as always, he was grinning.

Jenny knelt down beside him, immediately solicitous. Webb felt a stab of – what? Jealousy?

'I'm all right,' Ryan said. Webb had never doubted it for a moment. 'Got some mortar frags in my shoulder.'

Jenny pulled back the blanket. There were bloody dressings on his shoulder and on his arm just above the elbow. His face was grey in the candlelit gloom. Webb guessed he was in considerable pain.

Another wound, another chapter in the legend.

'Can't believe it,' Ryan was saying to Jenny. 'Ever since I lost my lucky green towel that time in El Salvador I haven't had a scratch.'

There was a sudden commotion on the stairs, and a soldier ran down the steps, clearing the way for two stretchers. Webb glimpsed what looked like a piece of raw steak from a butcher's shop window lying on one of the stretchers. On the second he saw a chalk-white face and a hand hanging limply over the edge.

He had been away too long. He had almost forgotten what it was like.

He knelt down and peered under the dressings on Ryan's arm. 'Has this been cleaned?'

'Doctors are busy, mate. I told them not to worry about me until all the bullshit dies down a bit.'

'How long have you been sitting here?'

'Since last night. How long have you been here?'

'Since last night.'

'I mean in Bosnia.'

'I flew into Zagreb about a week ago.'

'New chum, eh?' Ryan looked at Jenny. 'Been showing him the ropes?'

Jenny looked at Webb, apparently amused, but to her credit, he thought, she said nothing.

'You need to get these wounds debrided,' Webb told him.

'I know that, Spider, but this isn't Walter Reed. Got a gasper?'

Webb searched his pockets, brought out a packet of Marlboro and put one between Ryan's lips. He lit it for him and he dragged in the smoke gratefully. 'Some of these blokes have been drying out tea bags – after they've used them for cha ten times – and then wrapping them in bits of newspaper and trying to smoke the bastards. I keep telling them it's bad for their health but they won't listen.'

'These days they make tea bags with filters for just that reason.'

Ryan smiled. 'I had a bet with Croz you wouldn't be able to stay out of this one. One way or another he'll come over, I said. Probably spend a day holed up in the Holiday Inn in Sarajevo, then he'll write a book and get on the Letterman show in his UN flak jacket and lecture America about Bosnia.'

'I've never jammed my fist into a frag wound before but you're starting to tempt me.'

'Mate, if we could get some grass and some grog and a couple of tea girls it would be just like the old days.'

'How have you been? How's Mickey?'

'She's all right.'

He turned to Jenny. 'You look buggered.'

'So do you.'

She took off her helmet. Her hair and her bandanna were soaked with perspiration. She wiped the sweat from her eyes with the back of her sleeve, then reached for Ryan's hand, squeezed it. Webb noted the unspoken intimacy between them and felt another stab of bitterness.

Two orderlies went past them, hefting bins overflowing with bandages saturated with bright red blood. In the corner a baby was being born. A nurse held a candle for the doctor above the woman's thighs. The woman's screams drowned out every other sound for a few minutes.

'Even in the midst of death we are in life,' Ryan said.

When it was over he turned back to Webb. 'Remember that night in the Central Highlands? Those Special Forces blokes were up there with the Yards, they'd been under siege for three months. Can't even remember the name of the place.'

'Que Trang.'

'Right. Que Trang. Jesus. We spent the whole night getting creamed by Charles but the next morning they sent a chopper for us and two hours later I was lying in a nice clean bed in the 71st Evac at Pleiku wondering what was for breakfast. Now that was the way to run a war. It was almost civilised. Not like this bullshit.'

'I heard you'd left the network.'

'Yeah. After the bread queue massacre in Vase Miskin Street. The bastards wouldn't show the pictures. They edited it back to the sound bites and a map of Bosnia with a fucking little yellow star over Sarajevo. The network said it was too distressing for their viewers to watch. Too distressing! Of course war's fucking distressing. How distressing do they think it is to have your wife or your son end up without their legs or their face because some bastard on Trebevic decides to lob a mortar on you? That's when I first decided to quit. I thought, it's just like Vietnam. We show a sanitised version of the war, the soldiers going off to fight, we don't show them coming back without their legs or their eyes.'

The shelling had begun in earnest above them, a tattoo of incoming mortar and artillery rounds, setting the floor and walls shaking, a steady attrition of noise that left the mind and nerves ragged. You'll have to get used to this, Webb thought. Tune it out.

'Anyway, welcome to Jajce, mate,' Ryan was saying. 'It looks like the three of us are the only representatives of the foreign media at this time. Let me point out a few of the sights. See that bloke over there, the one lying on his back, staring at the ceiling? He's not really as bored as he looks. The doctors say he's brain dead but the bastard won't die. He went out about a week ago to bury his two sons who'd been killed in the shelling the day before and a sniper picked him off as he was kneeling next to the graves. Right through the head. It's a real bugger how that sort of thing can stuff up the wiring.

'And if you look to your left you'll see an old girl without any legs. She's more embarrassed than anything because she's a good Moslem and the doctors keep peering at her thighs. What's left of them, anyway.

'The bloke on the floor asleep next to her is her son. He's doing all right except for the fact that his mother's the last one of his family left alive.

'Directly in front of us that twelve-year-old boy has lost his right leg. But the real bummer, from his point of view, is that most of his balls went with it. He won't even get in the Sistine Choir because he's a Moslem. Just wasn't his day.'

'Stop it, Sean,' Jenny said, gently.

Ryan nodded. 'You're right, I talk too much, don't I? Sometimes you can spend too bloody long in a place, right?'

Webb had been watching Jenny all the time Ryan had been talking. Several times she had raised her camera to take photographs, had changed her mind, lowered it again. She saw him watching her, and their eyes met. He knew what she was thinking. He remembered having those same doubts.

A man in a soiled green surgical gown and plastic overshoes saw them and came over. His face was etched with exhaustion, and there were deep black lines carved into it like charcoal strokes. Webb noticed that his hands were stained with blood.

'Journalists?' he said.

'Two of my mates from the democratic West,' Ryan said.

'Perhaps they can help us,' the doctor said. 'How is your arm?' he asked Ryan.

'It'll keep.' He introduced Webb and Jenny. 'This is Dr Grzic. He's responsible for putting Humpty Dumpty back together again.' He nudged Jenny with his foot. 'You're not here to gawk. Go and do some work.'

She hesitated.

'Mate, can you show this young lady what life is like on the workshop floor?' he said to Grzic.

'Of course. I take it she has a strong stomach.'

'See if you can get him on the front cover of *Time*,' Ryan

said to her. 'Maybe then they'll send him some anaesthetic and IV fluids.'

Jenny got up and went with Grzic. Ryan finished his cigarette and asked for another. As Webb lit it for him, he whispered: 'Well, a nice bastard you turned out to be, mate.'

'You're going to lecture me about ethics?'

'You should have told me.'

'Why?'

Ryan made a sound, something between a broken laugh and a cough. 'You would have loved it. Did she tell you?'

'Tell me what?'

'I tried to seduce my own daughter. Shit.'

Webb almost felt sorry for him. He realised then that he did not hate this man, that his feelings for Sean Ryan were complex, made of many intertwining strands: comradeship, shared history, contempt, pity, jealousy, admiration, all making up a thick twine that had formed an inseparable bond between them.

'We're getting old, Spider.'

'That's not so bad if you consider the alternative.'

'Depends on your point of view. I think I've had a gutful. I'm pissed off with getting shot at, and I'm bored when I'm not. Also the women I fancy are all old enough to be my daughters.'

'Not funny.'

'I'm not joking, mate. That time I was in New York it felt like I was in a time warp. I'd stayed the same and everyone else had moved on. So what do I do? I scuttle back here and spend my life living in holes in the ground, like this one. Like a fucking cockroach. Only place I feel at home these days.'

'She's forgiven you,' Webb said, his own mind heading down an entirely different path.

Ryan frowned, took a moment to follow this *non sequitur*. 'It hasn't done her any harm.' He paused, then said: 'You look disappointed, mate.'

'I suppose I am.'

'Christ, you carry a grudge a long time. I'm glad it wasn't you I left behind in Saigon. I'd hate to see you really annoyed.'

'You're right,' Webb said, and the sadness hit him like a wave, rising out of an ocean of feeling with sudden violence. 'You're right, I set you up.'

'Mate, it was Odile I scorched, not Jenny. If it's any consolation to you, I'm sure Odile is waiting for me down there in the hot place with the whips and the burning oil. But that's between us.'

'You know what amoral means?'

'For Christ's sake. What do you want?'

'I don't know.'

'Jenny's turned out all right, thanks to a nice twist of fate, and thanks to you. Of course.'

'I appreciate the credit.'

'She's a nice kid. She's one of us now. Like Croz, or Cochrane.'

'That's it? "She's a nice kid." Is that all she gets from you?'

'What am I meant to feel? It's just biology, Spider.'

Webb was silent.

'It's over now, you haven't got any more rabbits in the hat. At least I fucking hope not. So let it go. She has.'

Webb slid down the wall on to his haunches. He felt suddenly mean and dirty.

'The fact is,' Ryan was saying, 'if I had another shot at it, I'd probably do it the same way again. I couldn't miss the biggest story of my life. My one real bloody regret is I wasn't Neal Davis, standing there in the palace grounds in Saigon when that North Vietnamese tank knocked the gates down. That's what I really wanted. I'm not good at people. I'm good at photographs.'

Webb watched Jenny follow Grzic along the ward, taking notes, camera over her arm, shooting off flash-frame after flash-frame, her almond face tight with concentration. 'And is it what she's good at?'

'I guess. She's a lot like me, Spider. She'd do anything for a good story.'

The bodies had been well preserved because it was cold in the mountains at night, even so early in the winter. They had been missing since going out on patrol two nights before. They had been found by their comrades that morning and brought to the morgue at the back of the hospital.

They lay on the white-tiled floor. Their green camouflage uniforms had been stripped off and they lay in rigor, their skin taking on a translucent pallor, like waxworks. Every single one had been mutilated: ears and noses cut off, skulls fractured, teeth pulled out.

'I have to tell myself they were dead when this was done to

them,' Grzic was saying, 'but there are signs that they were still very much alive. I don't know, young lady, perhaps you are more accustomed to this than I am. Before this war I took out tonsils and delivered babies. So can you tell me what sort of man could do such a thing?'

Jenny stared at the three bodies, remembered what Ryan had once told her at the orphanage in Otovac. 'All I can tell you,' she said, 'is that they're probably kind to their mothers and they go to church every week.'

# 84

The population of Jajce had lived in cellars for months on end, under shellfire day and night. All they had to eat was rice and pasta. When Samir's lorries arrived from Travnik people ran from the basements to meet them, and this was how many were killed or wounded.

Just to venture above ground was to play cat and mouse with the watching snipers. Webb and Jenny spent their time crawling on their hands and knees through gardens, running between buildings, waiting to catch their breath before the next sprint, always aware that somewhere in the surrounding hills a Serb sniper might have them in the cross-hairs of his Kalashnikov.

It was on their third day in Jajce that it happened. They were making their way from the hospital back to the command post. Jenny pointed to something that had been scrawled in black paint on the whitewashed wall on the far side of the street: *Pazi snajper*. Beware sniper.

The warning only reinforced what they could see for themselves: the cross-section in front of them was directly exposed to sniper fire from the surrounding mountains. 'Ready?' she asked him.

'I was doing this before you were born, young lady.'

She grinned. 'That's what worries me.'

It infuriated him to think that *she* was looking out for *him*. 'You first,' he said. If there was a sniper watching the intersection, he would be alerted by the first runner; the second would lose the advantage of surprise. She knew what he was doing and she hesitated.

He pushed her in front of him. 'Go!'

He winced at the pain in his back where he had jarred it on the wild drive into the city. Difficult to run. He heard a sharp crack-crack echo around the street, and he saw Jenny go down. At first he thought she had been hit, but then he saw her scramble for cover behind a pebbledash wall.

He had no idea from which direction the sniper fire was coming. Should he run to the right or the left? He felt something sting him in the buttock, close to his hip, but he kept running. He saw Jenny's face, her eyes wide with terror, urging him on. He suddenly felt light-headed, knew he could not run much further. He threw himself forward like a sprinter heading for the finish tape.

He tumbled on to the footpath behind the wall, bruising his knee. He leaned on one elbow, grinned at her. 'Made it,' he said.

'Are you all right?'

'Of course I'm all right,' he snapped. There was something wet soaking into his fatigue pants. At first he was embarrassed, thought he had actually wet himself. Oh God, not in front of Jenny, he thought. He casually put a hand down to his side. When he brought it up, it was wet with blood. He couldn't believe it. He'd been shot.

'Look at this,' he said in wonderment, and passed out.

The candle on Gerovic's desk was a thick strip of wick floating in a cup of oil. They sat around it, watching the flame grow fainter, sharing a bottle of Lorza brandy. 'You have to get out tonight,' Gerovic was saying. 'Our front lines are crumbling and there are rumours that the HVO may pull out and abandon us.'

Jenny fought to control her own sense of panic. She had been in the war for almost a year now, had been frightened many times, but never like this. Webb's wound had shaken her badly. She just wanted to get out of this wretched place. She needed no encouragement from Gerovic.

She looked over at Ryan. The doctors had dressed his shoulder wound and put his arm in a sling, but he had thrown the sling away. 'You need two hands in this bloody place,' he had said. The constant pain of the wound had aged him. He sat slumped in the chair across the desk from Gerovic, massaging his aching shoulder, his eyes rimmed with the dark lines of exhaustion.

'How is your friend?' Gerovic asked.

'I think they call it a flesh wound,' Ryan murmured, and he looked up at Jenny and gave her an unexpected grin.

'He can't walk,' Jenny said. 'The doctors think it may have splintered his hip.'

'He's still lucky,' Gerovic said. 'He wanted to come here yet he will probably live. Look at these men.' He nodded to the soldiers sitting around the basement floor; one wore a black headband, another had on bright red sneakers, yet another had a silver medallion fashioned in the shape of a peace sign nestling between curly black chest hairs and a sleeve rolled up to reveal a tattoo of the Bosnian lily emblem. They were listening to U2 on a small tape recorder. 'Unforgettable Fire'. 'These men did not wish to be here yet they are all going to die.'

Ryan and Jenny stared at the floor.

'Don't leave your friend in our hospital,' Gerovic said. 'You must leave and take him with you. We are evacuating the town tonight. After sunset I absolve myself of responsibility for all of you.' He reached across the desk and shook their hands. '*Zivi u Miru*,' he said.

Live in peace.

The evacuation started after nightfall. Almost the entire population of the town emerged from the basements and cellars to begin the exodus through the mountains towards Travnik. Suitcases, children's plastic toys, bicycles, tables, old armchairs, wooden chairs, even wardrobes, were dragged on to the streets and loaded on to the procession of cars, trucks, tractor trailers and horse carts that were gathered for the journey through the passes, past the Serbian guns.

A man called Irfan agreed to let them travel with him and his family on the back of his wooden horse cart. Ryan and Jenny loaded Webb's stretcher and then clambered on beside him. They set off in the darkness, back towards Travnik, along the perilous lifeline that had already become known as the Vietnam Road.

# 85

Jenny clung to the swaying sides of the tray. Dead animals lay stiff-legged and bloated in frozen ditches. A truck had lost its wheel and was skewed by the side of the road; a piano had tumbled off the back and now lay on its back. An old man was standing beside it, weeping, as if it were the body of a loved one. A woman was trying to drag him away.

A death's head image swam in front of Jenny's vision in the darkness, underneath a single hand-painted word stark against the black forest: *Minen!*

The cart jolted over a hole in the road. Webb cried out in pain.

She reached for his hand. 'It's going to be okay,' she whispered.

'What am I doing here, for God's sake?' he murmured.

She looked back. Behind them Jajce was in flames, the orange glow of the fires the only light. She heard the steady crump-crump of artillery in front of them. They were shelling the convoy. Having chased them from their homes, the Serbs would even now torment them to their final destination.

A grey dawn, greasy, dirty yellow. The column stretched in both directions as far as the eye could see, a silent army of misery. In front of them was an old Volkswagen with a baby carriage tied to the roof; behind them an ancient carthorse pulled a family of seven who were crammed into the cart alongside some chickens and a few pieces of rickety furniture. The horse's heavy hooves glopped through the mud.

Irfan and his family were silent, even the children. They were fairly conservative Moslems for this part of Bosnia. Irfan wore a traditional waistcoat and a loose white linen shirt under his winter coat; his father had on a yarmulke-like cap of white loose-knit cotton. They sat together on the kickboard, while Irfan's wife and four children clustered together in the tray. The youngest of the children, a girl, was clutching a large doll. The eldest, a boy aged about eight, held a water-filled plastic bag with a pet goldfish inside. Jenny smiled at him but elicited no response. All the children's faces were fixed with the same haunted stares. Even now they seemed unable fully to comprehend the enormity of what had happened in their lives.

Jenny thought of another exodus, a long time ago, in a leaking boat putting out to sea from Vung Tau in Vietnam. This was how she must have looked. She wanted to explain to these people that she knew perhaps a little of how they were feeling. Yet how would it help them?

In fact, she wondered if she really did know how they felt. It had been so long ago. She was one of the lucky ones now. If she survived, she had somewhere to go.

They passed an old farmhouse, four blackened walls, the roof gone. Jenny, exhausted and half asleep, detected the stench of decomposing bodies, the acrid smell of smoke.

They had been travelling all night and all day.

Webb winced at every jolt. The doctors had had no morphine to give him. He and Jenny had brought a few ampoules into Jajce with them as part of their kit but they had given them to the doctors at the hospital the very first morning. Now he was paying the price for his act of charity.

Darkness fell soon after five in the afternoon. The air was frigid. The road hugged the shadows of the pines. Webb was groaning almost constantly now as the cart creaked and bounced over the potholed road.

Ryan took the last pack of cigarettes from his pocket, offered them to Irfan and his father. They both accepted one gratefully but did not light them. Instead they put them in their coats. Irfan explained that they did not want to attract the attention of any sniper watching in the hills. Perhaps in the morning.

'How is it, Spider?'

'Never felt better,' Webb grunted.

'Grzic thinks the bullet may have splintered your hip,' Ryan said. 'That's the bad news. The good news is it will give you something to talk about with David Letterman.'

Webb grimaced. 'That really . . . irks you . . . doesn't it?'

'I never wanted to be famous, Spider. I'll settle for being a legend.'

The cart trundled on through the night. There were occasional shouts in the darkness, sounds of explosions ahead. The speed of the column slowed. Still there was no end in sight.

The shell landed less than fifty metres away, without warning. A hot sliver of shrapnel struck their horse just behind the shoulder and it reared in pain and panic, then staggered sideways, losing its footing on the broken edge of the road. It went down, pulling the cart with it.

Webb screamed with pain as he was thrown into the mud.

The rolling motion of the cart had lulled Ryan to a tormented half-sleep. He was jarred violently awake and found himself rolling down the embankment beside the road. He woke in a shallow pool of muddy and freezing water. He scrambled to his feet, groggy from exhaustion, was searching for his dressing gown on the bathroom door of his room in the Intercontinental when he remembered where he was.

'Jesus. Jesus H.' He staggered, hearing shouts in the darkness, yelling, confusion. He fumbled in his jacket for his pencil light and flicked it on. He would have to risk snipers. The thin beam illuminated Irfan's face. He was kneeling beside his horse, crying, his hands dark with blood from the animal's shoulder wound.

'Fuck,' Ryan said.

Webb was screaming. He lay a few yards away, his body twisted. Jenny knelt beside him, trying to roll him on to his uninjured side. He went to help her, slipped in the mud, dropped the torch.

More shouts. Someone was collecting the family's bags from the road and transferring them to their own cart. Irfan howled in rage and launched himself into the shadows. Another shell burst close to the road, a hundred metres away.

If I ever get out of this, Ryan promised himself, I'm never getting near a front line again.

But then he always promised himself that.

They painstakingly collected what the looters had left. Irfan's son had cut his head on a rock and Ryan helped dress the wound with the supply of dressings he kept in one of the pockets of the fishing vest. Miraculously, the boy was still holding the plastic bag with the goldfish. It was intact.

The remains of the family's possessions were gathered in a sorry pile by the side of the road: a few plastic bags of clothes, a pram, some blankets, a suitcase with broken locks held together with string.

The horse, still whimpering, lay beside the road, dying. There was nothing they could do for her.

Ryan knelt beside Webb. 'Spider.' He shone the torch on his face.

'Just leave me,' Webb murmured. 'I'm tired. I hurt. I want to go to sleep.'

'If we leave you here, you're going to die,' Ryan said. 'The only way to get you out is for us to carry you on the stretcher the rest of the way. But my shoulder's buggered so I can't.'

'What are you telling me?'

'I'm telling you you're going to die.'

Webb closed his eyes.

'Spider?'

'Go away, Ryan.'

'I wouldn't really leave you, mate. I just don't know how we're going to bloody shift you.'

'Just go away.'

Jenny knelt down beside them. 'Sean,' she whispered.

He turned around and shone the torch. Irfan was standing beside them with the pram. He gave a sheepish smile, as if his own generosity humbled him.

'Perhaps if it will help your friend,' he said.

Webb lay sprawled in the pram, arms and legs dangling over the sides, head lolling backwards. The fall had reopened the bullet wound, and the bottom of the pram was saturated with fresh blood. They had rejoined the column on foot, Irfan and his father leading the way, his wife waddling behind with the children and the bags. Ryan and Jenny took the rear, taking turns to push the pram.

'Like taking baby for a walk,' Ryan said. 'Bloody ugly baby, but.'

Shell bursts flashed around the horizon like sheet lightning. A blood moon rose over the hills; torn pieces of human meat on the road appeared to be lit by phosphorous. Rockets arced across the sky. There was fresh blood on the asphalt, sticky underfoot.

The column ground to a halt. People were screaming in panic. Cars and trucks tried to turn on the road; people rushed past them, heading back towards Jajce.

'What's going on?' Ryan shouted to Irfan.

'Serb, boom-boom,' he said, trying to explain with his few words of English. 'No can, no can.'

But Ryan understood immediately. The Serb artillery had trapped them in a deadly bottleneck. They could not go forward; they could scarcely go back.

He saw an old man dragging his horse and cart off the road, up a mud track through the pine forest. Impossible for cars or trucks to follow, but on foot . . .

He pointed the way.

Irfan helped them drag Webb and the ancient pram down the embankment and up the muddy slope. Ryan threw the helmets and the flak jackets into the bushes. Too heavy to carry now. Even the spare cameras were ditched by the side of the road. He was too exhausted now to care about how much they cost, too tired even to think of the dangers ahead. I've got out of worse messes than this, he told himself. I can do it again.

A dirty light tried to pierce a dense mist. Their breath formed thick clouds on the still morning air. They stopped to rest, stamping their feet against the cold. They were alone on the muddy track, the forest around them still dark.

'How far are we from Travnik?' Jenny asked.

'I don't know.'

'We must be close.'

Four soldiers appeared out of the mist on the path ahead of them.

They all wore brimless olive wool Chetnik caps, and their hair and beards were long and unkempt in trademark fashion. They were well armed. Even at this distance Ryan could see they were all carrying Kalashnikovs and had Bowie knives in their belts. One of them had an RPG strapped to his back.

He heard them release the safeties on their weapons.

Irfan and his family were far ahead of them, at the crest of the rise. Irfan was now carrying his youngest daughter in his arms;

his old father, still in his carpet slippers, was being supported by Irfan's wife. They had abandoned many of their possessions by the road during the night. Now the woman carried just one black plastic bag of clothes, all that was left of their former life.

The three small boys trotted bravely behind.

When he saw the soldiers, Irfan lowered his daughter to the ground, scrambled around in the black plastic bag, took out a white shirt and waved it above his head.

Ryan stopped, breathing hard.

He did not like the look of this. The Chetniks were silhouetted against a lightening sky. They swaggered across the path in the attitude of bullies in a ghetto street. Ryan felt a chill in his stomach as he watched Irfan and his family trudge towards them. The sixth sense that had served him well all through his life was like a fire alarm in his head.

'Jump ship,' he said, and pushed the pram towards the edge of the road. Then he was running down the slope, through the forest of oak and chestnut trees. He could hear Jenny crashing through the undergrowth behind him.

We must look ridiculous, he thought.

He was running too fast, the hill was too steep. The pram tipped. Ryan felt it wrench his wrist and then he was falling too, rolling down the slope. The breath was hammered out of him. He heard Webb scream, a short high-pitched sound like a wounded animal.

Then silence.

He lay on his back. Through a break in the mist he saw a handful of stars overhead, cold and white, through the skeletal fingers of the trees. He felt the adrenalin pumping through his body. A long time since he had panicked. Perhaps the soldiers would have let them past after all.

He heard the Chetniks calling to each other on the track, less than fifty metres away.

Close.

Closer.

Too close . . .

Then another shout, from further up the road, and he heard the heavy fall of boots in the mud as the soldier nearest them ran to rejoin his companions. Ryan could imagine the conversation:

*They must have run into the woods.*

*I can't see them.*

*Leave them. It doesn't matter.*

And then a short burst of gunfire. A shrill scream, a terrible sound suddenly cut off by another burst from a Kalashnikov.

You mongrel bastards, Ryan thought. May you all rot in hell.

They were coming back down the road.

They were searching the forest. They'll see that old perambulator sticking out of the undergrowth, Ryan thought. Unless. The sun had not yet risen over the mountains and the gloom was deeper beneath the canopy of the trees. The mist had cut visibility down to a few yards. With the casual violence of rogue soldiers, they might just get tired of the search and move on, forget them as easily as they would soon forget the bodies they had left behind them on the road.

Ryan heard Webb moan.

Shit, shit, shit. He crawled towards the sound, found Webb sprawled on his side, unconscious. He moaned again. Ryan put his hand over his mouth.

Shut up, you useless bastard, he thought. I'll choke you if I have to.

He heard another hurried exchange between the soldiers, very close. They were making up their minds.

Please, Spider, not a sound.

He felt a warm wetness against his thigh, Webb's blood leaking through his fatigue trousers. Webb twitched, and for a moment Ryan thought he was going to spasm. He held him. Fuck you, Spider, you always make trouble for me.

Then he heard the soldiers moving away, heard the crunch of their boots on the frozen mud of the track.

Slowly he released his grip. Christ, it wasn't blood; the ground frost had melted on his clothes, soaked him right through. He started to shiver. If the sun did not break through soon they would be in real trouble.

What the hell were they going to do?

Almost at once his instinct for survival kicked in. We must stay where we are, he thought. Sit out the day, wait until dusk. We can't risk blundering into any more of these bastards in the daylight.

He wondered about Jenny, heard her moving through the undergrowth nearby. He hoped she had not hurt herself. He guessed it was still a long walk to Travnik.

# 86

An hour later Ryan picked his way carefully back up the slope to the road. He did not imagine that any of Irfan's family had been left alive, but he had to be sure.

By now the sun had risen over the mountains, but a heavy mist still clung to the trees. He reached the edge of the track and waited. No sign of the Chetniks. In the distance he could hear the distant crump of artillery. Travnik.

The bodies lay a hundred yards away, in the tangled and unnatural attitude of the dead. He steeled himself. It was always easier to look at corpses when they were anonymous.

He walked slowly up the road.

Oh yes, they were dead.

You didn't have to be a marksman when you had an automatic weapon and your victim was standing a few yards away. Pieces of unidentifiable flesh lay in the mud. He felt the bitter taste of his own bile in the back of his throat. Oh, for God's sake. He counted the bodies. Irfan, his wife, his father, looking a little surprised to have died in his carpet slippers. The three boys.

The goldfish was dead, too. The plastic bag had burst on the road where the boy had dropped it, and the fish lay on its side, partly frozen.

And where was the girl?

He looked further up the road. There she was. They had let her run for a while.

He routinely checked the bodies for signs of life. Irfan and his father were too badly mauled by the bullets to warrant more than a cursory inspection. So obscene, so . . . humiliating. He made up his mind that he didn't want to die like this, guts spilled all over the road.

It was the little girl that really upset him. He noticed the scars in the frozen ground where she had pawed a hole with her fingers, like a small puppy. He wondered how long she had been alive after they left her.

Some of those Chetnik bastards might have daughters of their own at home. People.

He picked up the old plastic bag Irfan's wife had been carrying and lugged it back up the track. He found Jenny and Webb among the trees.

'If we stay on the road we could get picked off by snipers, or run into more Chetnik patrols. If we don't, we could get lost, or stumble into a minefield.'

Jenny's face had half a dozen deep scratches inflicted by tree branches during their flight into the forest that morning. She sat with her back against a chestnut tree, cradling Webb's head in her lap. He was conscious again, but his face was grey.

They had found the old perambulator. The axle had broken in the wild ride down the hill after it had struck the trunk of the old horse chestnut under which they were now sitting. It was no longer any use to them. If they were going to get Webb to Travnik, Ryan would have to carry him on his shoulders. It would not be easy, he decided. The shrapnel wounds in his arm were aching with the cold, and there was fresh blood on the dressings.

'So what should we do?' Jenny asked. 'You're the expert.'

'This is why I don't like taking partners along. If I was on my own I'd manage all right, no worries.' He looked down at Webb. 'Perhaps we'd better leave him behind.'

'You're not serious?'

Webb turned his head slightly to look at him. 'You leave me here . . . you bastard . . . and I'll come back . . . and haunt you.'

He laughed. 'That's not what they say in the films. Where's your sense of self-sacrifice, Spider?'

'We can't leave him,' Jenny said.

'Well then, it looks like we'll have to take our chances on the track. I can't walk through this shit. My vote, we wait for tonight. There's a stream down there, so we've got fresh water. I also rescued some dry clothes. They belong to Irfan and his wife. If we stay in this wet gear all day we'll get hypothermia. Besides, this way we'll pass for refugees.'

'Poor Irfan,' Jenny said. 'Poor kids.'

'I don't think they're any kinder to war correspondents. Okay, let's keep our heads down until dusk and pray we don't freeze to death. Maybe even get some sleep. If I'm going to carry that great long streak to Travnik I need a rest.'

They woke soon after dusk, stiff and cold from the damp ground. They had heard intermittent bursts of small-arms fire and mortar duels from Travnik right through the day. They had slept; staccato spells when they surfed the black waves of exhaustion, sometimes dipping below the surface, fear constantly bringing them back to gritty wakefulness once more. Once Ryan had ventured down to the stream at the bottom of the valley to refill their canteens.

Now that it was time to make their way back up to the road he felt too cold, too hungry, too tired to move. He recognised this as the beginnings of hypothermia. It would be so easy just to curl up and sleep. The night and the ground frost would do the rest.

He looked over at the others. Webb looked shrunken and haggard, his jaw slack, either asleep or unconscious. Jenny's head was lolling against the trunk of the tree, her eyes glassy with fatigue. But she was awake. At his urging she painfully pushed herself to her feet, staggered, almost fell, supported herself against the tree. She wasn't going to take the easy way out, he thought. Not this one. A real survivor.

Like me.

He looked down at Webb. Despite how he had ridden him about selling out, he wondered now why his friend had chosen to put himself in danger again. He had always admired him for getting out when he'd had enough, for building a normal life for himself, and most of all for doing what he did for Jenny. He still sometimes flirted with the notion of doing the same. When Webb had showed up in Jajce he had realised that this was no longer an option. If a normal life wasn't enough for Spider, it wouldn't be enough for him.

Besides, he'd tried that road once before and it hadn't worked.

'He mustn't die,' Jenny said.

'Spider won't die. Not while I'm still around. He's too bloody-minded.' He watched her kneel over him, check his pulse and breathing yet again. 'You really care about him, don't you?'

'He's my father. He's been my father.'

Ryan thought about that. 'Yeah, I suppose he is. He was there for you. I guess that's what being a father is.' Their eyes met.

He shrugged. 'I can do one thing for you. I can get you out of this.'

She took a deep breath, seemed to be gathering herself for this one final effort. 'I wonder if it was worth it.'

'What?'

'Jajce. Us being there. Is anything I write, your photographs, is any of it going to make any difference?'

My photographs, Ryan thought.

'Ryan? Ryan, what is it?'

He breathed in the cold mountain air. It had hit him first when they had discarded the camera gear, at the start of the trek. The realisation of what he had done, or what he had not done, had gnawed at him ever since. Christ. There goes the legend. There goes a career.

Perhaps he could lie, say he lost the film.

But he would know. It was explaining this to himself that would not be easy. What did he feel? It was not guilt, even though he had failed to do the job they paid him to do. It was something else. Despair perhaps. There was one thing he had lived his life to do and now he was bored even with that. He wanted to get out of the mountain and back to Travnik for Webb, and for Jenny. But if he had been on his own . . . if he had been on his own perhaps the Chetniks that morning would not have been such a bad choice.

'Ryan? What's the matter?'

'I never took any photographs.'

He climbed to his feet. His knees were aching, his shoulder just about numb, his arm hanging useless by his side. They had to start now, he told himself. The mountain cold had descended with sharp and breathtaking ferocity. They had to start moving soon, if only to stay alive.

'You didn't take any photographs?'

He shook his head.

'None at all?' When he didn't answer, she went on: 'But we were the only Western journalists in Jajce. Everyone is going to want our photographs.'

'Your photographs.'

'It's an exclusive. They're going to be worth a fortune.'

'Who gives a damn about the money?'

She stared at him, unable to comprehend. Of course she could not understand. She was young. This was her first war. 'But that's why you were there. Why else would you be there?'

Yes, why else? Because it was the toughest place to be, yet while he was there he had found no image that inspired him, none he had not captured in some other form before. It had been a personal experience, one he found he could no longer share. He wondered what there was left in life for Sean Ryan now.

'Sean?'

'I don't know. I just got so caught up in it . . . I never realised until we were leaving. Five days there and I never got one frame. Jesus.' He crouched down beside Webb. 'Help me sit him up and let's hope to Christ he doesn't wake up. This is going to hurt him like hell.'

He didn't want to think about it any more. He had to get these two back to Travnik. Then perhaps he could sit down and try to think this one through. Perhaps there was an answer for Sean Ryan on the other side of this.

But somehow he doubted it.

Shells whistled overhead, tracers lit the mountainside. A heavy machine gun boomed very close by. They had to be almost to the front lines.

It had taken them less than three hours; three hours stumbling through the darkness, stopping to rest for a few minutes, cold and fear forcing them on again. Ryan could feel Webb's blood seeping through his shirt and down his neck. Webb slipped in and out of consciousness, babbling incoherently.

He must be in terrible pain, Ryan thought. That's about the only consolation.

The journey was constructed of small landmarks: stagger towards the looming silhouette of a large tree, promise yourself you will stop there and rest, then perhaps make yourself go a little further. Or else count a hundred paces, stop again; next time force yourself to go a hundred and ten.

Waiting for the sniper's bullet to come out of the darkness.

Keep going. Shoulder a burning agony, his neck muscles cramping, Webb seeming to get heavier and heavier the further they went.

'We can do it,' Jenny whispered, somewhere behind him. He felt her stumble against him.

He was too exhausted to answer her. Stagger on, force another effort from his body. A young man's game this, he told himself. I should be in a bar somewhere, regaling some rookies with tales of my derring-do while I sip my Bushmills. Go on talk shows like Spider. Why the Christ I'm still doing this, I don't know.

The tracers were behind them now, arcing through the night sky, a poisonous green. He stumbled on the edge of the track. Jenny rushed forward to take Webb's weight, but this time he could not wait for her to help him and he toppled sideways with his load. Webb cried out in sharp pain as they crashed to the ground.

Ryan lay on his stomach, gasping for breath. Everything a screaming agony: his back, his legs, the wound in the shoulder on fire.

'Need something white,' he said.

Jenny crouched beside him. He heard her unscrew the cap of her water bottle, roll him over, hold it to his lips. 'Need something white,' he repeated.

'What?'

'So they can see us.'

She helped him sit up. After a few moments he got his breath back, recovered a little. He knew he could not allow himself to rest for too long or his muscles would cramp and stiffen and he would not be able to go on. He forced himself to his knees, steadied his weight against her and got to his feet.

'This is the tough part,' he said, his voice hoarse. 'We're walking towards the defenders now. They'll be jumpy. Nothing friendly about friendly fire.'

'I don't have anything white. Wait a minute. My underwear.'

'Now is no time to be modest,' he grunted. 'Besides, we're all family here.'

They were Gortex thermals, waist to ankle. Jenny tied the legs of the underwear to a tree branch.

'There I was thinking they'd be flimsy, lacy things,' Ryan said. 'Spider's been a bad influence on you.'

'Now I'm really cold.'

What a sight we must look, he thought, in our ragtag of Western and Moslem clothes. We might not look like Bosnians but at least we sure as hell don't look like Chetniks. He handed her his pencil light. 'Shine it on your little flag there, Jenny, and walk in front.'

'Are we going to make it?'

'Of course we will. I've always been lucky. Trust me. I owe you this, at least.'

The end, when it came, was an anticlimax. Ryan was concentrating on the next one hundred steps, his mind focused only on the load on his back. Suddenly a young man in a vintage combat helmet, the fleur-de-lys emblem of Bosnia on his shoulder flash, came towards them out of the darkness, waving a torch, his Kalashnikov on a strap over his left shoulder.

He greeted them in his own language and was astonished to hear them reply in English.

'*Presna?*' he said.

'BBC, Lonn-donn!' Ryan said.

The *armija* was impressed. He gave them cigarettes and offered them a drink from his hip flask. Lorza brandy. Ryan felt it burn all the way down and smiled.

'Christ,' he murmured. 'We did it.'

The soldier told them, in halting English, that they had not been expecting any refugees to reach them along this particular track. They had heard it was crawling with Chetniks. He was sorry but he could not help them more. He and the rest of his squad were on patrol. But he would radio back to the next guardpost and warn the HVO sentries not to shoot at them. It was not much further. About two miles.

'Two miles,' Ryan repeated.

Two miles . . .

Just over that hill and you'll be in the town, the soldier said. You're safe now.

*Welcome to Travnik!*

# 87

They stopped to rest, refilled their canteens from a cattle trough. Ryan lowered Webb gently to the ground. Somehow, knowing they were so close, that they were back in friendly territory, the weight seemed suddenly lighter.

Jenny raised Webb's head, helped him drink some of the water from her canteen. 'Almost there,' she whispered.

Webb's eyes blinked open but he was too exhausted and in too much pain to answer her.

Ryan felt his shoulder. His shirt was soaked, from Webb's blood and his own. 'Blood brothers now, Spider,' he said.

Jenny looked down into the valley. 'Almost there,' she repeated. By the sudden flare of an exploding artillery shell she could see a narrow winding road ahead of them, farmland either side. There was a stone farmhouse and a low walled courtyard in the foreground, a few low buildings, the minarets and domes of Travnik in the distance.

'It's beautiful in a strange kind of way, isn't it?' Ryan said.

'Yes, I suppose it is.'

'You can see why people love wars. Everything else is kind of dull by comparison.'

'Tell me that tomorrow. Right now I just want to get out of this.'

'Don't worry. We're okay now. I told you I was lucky, didn't I?'

She reached up and touched his face. Over the last few months, she had grown to know Sean Ryan very well and she thought she knew now why her mother had loved him so much. He did have a certain charm. Easy to be flattered by it and think it was meant for you, when the truth was he directed it at everyone.

And he was right. He was lucky. And now he had been lucky for her, too.

'Let's get going,' he said.

They were a hundred yards from the farmhouse when Jenny heard the crack of sniper fire and automatically threw herself face down on the road.

'*Americanski*!' she screamed, in shock and outrage. They were through the lines. They were supposed to be *safe*! '*Americanski*!'

For a few moments there was silence, but then she heard the heavy boots of soldiers running down the road towards them. One of them shone a torch in her face. Croat militia.

'*Presna?*' he asked.

'*Presna, presna*,' she repeated.

'We think you are Chetnik.'

'They said they'd warned you on the radio!' Her fear evaporated and now she was just angry. She turned around to look for Ryan and Webb.

Ryan lay on his side ten metres behind her. In the harsh light of the torch she saw the neat holes in the front of his fisherman's warmer.

Webb was still alive. There was fresh blood on his left arm. He was crying with pain.

She couldn't believe it, just couldn't believe it.

'I am sorry,' the Croat soldier said. 'It was a mistake. It happens. I will get an ambulance.'

# Epilogue

## McSorley's Old Alehouse, New York

Webb looked at his watch. Almost midnight. The others had drifted home in taxis, and now there was only himself and Wendy Doyle.

'Look at the time,' he said.

'Oh my God,' she said. 'My flight leaves JFK at eight in the morning, for Christ's sake. I'd better find a cab. I haven't even packed.'

'It's been nice meeting you, Miss Doyle.'

'The pleasure was mine. I've read all of your books.' She held out her hand. 'It's been a hell of an evening.' She finished her drink. 'I suppose it's the last time your old gang will be together. Do you think they'll have a fifty-year reunion?'

'I don't plan to come back for that one.'

She hesitated, appeared almost embarrassed. 'Is it true – about Ryan?'

He nodded. 'Wheelchair for the last two years. Had some movement in his arms, but not much. It sentenced him to the thing he dreaded most – boredom. I guess that's why he took the pills.'

'Where's that bottle?'

Webb reached into his case, unsnapped the lock and took out the empty bottle of Bushmills. She squinted, focusing with difficulty on the faded ink lines that had been pasted on to the back of the bottle.

*I courted the dark angel,*
*her faithful devotee,*
*saw her lay her hand on others;*
*yet she always held her touch from me.*

*I courted the dark angel*
*and followed her, as lovers will,*
*she was my fascination;*
*and yet she ever spurned me still.*

*Each day she wore some new disguise*
*yet with the same pale skin and staring eyes,*
*so I knew her all the same,*
*through every move of her deadly game.*
*I courted the dark angel*
*in the casual ways of youth,*
*a furtive smile, a wink of eye,*
*and yet she always passed me by.*

*But she won't turn from me for ever*
*for I have a certain charm,*
*even for one as cold as she;*
*one day she will come back for me.*
*I do not fear her cold, cold lips*
*or the icy touch of her fingertips,*
*for I found her secret in the chase.*
*As we lie together in the dark, in the consummate embrace*
*of our earthy, bridal bed —*
*she whispers: fear the living, not the dead.*

'When did he give you this?'

'The last time he was in New York. When he came out to the house with Mickey. He knew he was going to Yugoslavia. He told me to drink a toast to him with it if he didn't come back.'

She shook her head and handed him back the bottle 'Did he write that?'

'He probably stole it from somewhere. Knowing Ryan.' He called for the bar tab. 'I'll get it. I got a big advance for the book.'

As they walked out into the street, Doyle noticed his limp for the first time. She wondered if it was the wound, or something else, that had finally driven him back to Long Island. But that was not her business. She said: 'What do you think he meant by the last line?'

'Well, if he wrote it, and that's a big if, he could have meant that there's no need to be afraid of dying when this world's such a shit of a place. And like us, he's seen the world at its very worst. Or perhaps it was more personal.'

'Personal?'

'Well, he didn't like people.'

'Ryan was the most gregarious man I've ever met. He hated being alone.'

'I didn't say he didn't like drinking and big parties and getting laid. I said he didn't like people. Getting close one on one. You don't have to do that in a crowd.'

'You're pretty hard on the fellow.'

Webb took a letter from his jacket pocket. 'You're going back to Sarajevo?'

'It's where the big stories are at the moment.'

'Will you give this to Jenny when you see her?'

She took the envelope. 'Don't worry about her. She's a good journalist. It's in her blood.'

'I'll always worry about her. But we all have to find our own way. I guess she'll find hers.'

A chill wind snaked through the streets. Doyle flagged down a passing cab. 'Want to share a ride?'

Webb shook his head. 'I'm heading in the other direction. Have a good flight.'

She jumped in, wound down the window. 'By the way, you never finished the story. What happened to Mickey?'

'She's doing okay.'

'Do you ever see her?'

'Every morning at breakfast,' he said. 'We got married last fall.'